THE MATRY

Also by Kay Williams and Eileen Wyman

BUTCHER OF DREAMS,
a suspense novel about the theater

By Kay Williams
(co-authored with Mardo Williams and Jerri Williams Lawrence)

FICTION

ONE LAST DANCE

IT'S NEVER TOO LATE TO FALL IN LOVE

THE MATRYOSHKA MURDERS

A Thriller

by Kay Williams
and Eileen Wyman

Calliope Press

New York

This is a work of fiction. All of the characters, organizations, and events portrayed in this novel are either products of the author's imagination or are used fictitiously, and any resemblance to actual persons living or dead, business establishments, organizations, or events is entirely coincidental.

Copyright © 2015 by Kay Williams.

All rights reserved. No part of this book may be used or reproduced in any manner without written permission except in the case of brief quotations embodied in critical articles or reviews.

Published by Calliope Press. For information, contact Calliope Press, Post Office Box 2408, New York, NY 10108-2408; phone (212) 564-5068; information@CalliopePress.com.

Library of Congress Cataloging-in-Publication Data

Williams, Kay, 1933-
    The Matryoshka murders : a thriller / by Kay Williams and Eileen Wyman.
        pages ; cm
    ISBN 978-0-9847799-7-0 (acid-free paper) -- ISBN 0-9847799-7-3 (acid-free paper)
    I. Wyman, Eileen. II. Title.

PS3623.I55827M38 2015
813'.6--dc23

2014037875

www.CalliopePress.com
Printed in the United States on acid free paper
9 8 7 6 5 4 3 2 1
First Edition

Interior Design by C Linda Dingler

Acknowledgments

Many, many thanks to Olga Catalena, a translator for the Second Leningrad International Documentary Festival, who patiently answered our questions as we struggled to organize this book—Eileen and I couldn't have done it without her; the writers' group, Albert Ashforth, P. M. Carlson, Shahrzad Elghanayan, and Theasa Tuohy, who made invaluable suggestions as we read our pages to them; Lina Zeldovich for advice on early sections in Leningrad; and E. W. Count, a published author of books about late twentieth century NYPD detectives, for her insights on NYC detectives and their work.

Emily R. Johnson gave us important, detailed comments and advice on the first draft. Jerri Lawrence did a superb, insightful job of editing, twice—once after the manuscript was hot off the press, and again after several revisions.

More thanks to Jerri Lawrence for creating the superb Topics to Consider for book discussion groups.

Author's Note

This work of fiction was inspired by real events. I was in Leningrad with independent filmmaker Jack O'Connell, who had been invited to bring his film to the International Documentary Festival.

The time was late January, 1991, a little over a year after the fall of the Berlin Wall. Mikhail Gorbachev, then President of the USSR, had been awarded the Nobel Peace Prize for trying to reform the stagnating Communist Party and the state economy by introducing *glasnost* ("openness"), *perestroika* ("restructuring"), *demokratizatsiya* ("democratization"), and *uskoreniye* ("acceleration" of economic development).

His reforms were not working. Boris Yeltsin and Anatol Sobchak, the Mayor of Leningrad, among others, had resigned from the Communist Party; Foreign Minister Edward Shevardnadze left his post, warning of an impending dictatorship. Vladimir Putin, formerly with the KGB in East Germany, was Deputy Mayor of Leningrad.

Money had been devalued. Old Soviets were resisting changes, hoping to keep their perks. The Soviet Union was in severe economic and political crisis.

Political *matryoshkas,* nesting dolls, also known as Gorby dolls, were sold at the hard currency market in Pushkin Square. Each doll was opened to reveal another Russian leader inside and seemed to be a metaphor for "the more things change, the more they stay the same." Few artists signed these dolls for fear of retribution.

I took photographs, made notes, and asked questions of my new Russian friends. Still events were puzzling. Winston Churchill once compared Russia itself to a *matryoshka* doll, "a riddle wrapped in a mystery inside an enigma."

My eight days in the turmoil of Leningrad began to make sense a few months later after the attempt by the conservative establishment of the Soviet military and the Communist Party to oust Gorbachev and re-establish an authoritarian central regime. This led to Gorbachev's resignation and the dissolution of the Soviet Union. Boris Yeltsin became the first President of the Russian Federation.

Kay Williams
January 2015

PART I
Leningrad, Russia

*Sunday, January 27, 1991 through
AM Friday, February 1, 1991*

Chapter One

5:15 PM, Sunday, January 27

Kate shivered despite her bulky sweater and gabardine vest. The threadbare rug and the thin brown drapes fluttering at the window provided little insulation for Masha's living room. She picked up her audiotape recorder from the table beside the couch, her eyes shifting toward the women gathering up their belongings, about to leave. How the camera would love them. They wore no makeup—Masha had told her it was hard to come by these days—but each had striking features and glowing skin. Her lover Gilly would love them too, Kate thought. She pictured Gilly beside her (not thousands of miles away), charcoal in hand, sketching with bold, quick strokes the fleeting expressions of each. She felt happy thinking of Gilly, then sad. Don't dwell on What's Done, she told herself. Come back to the Now, Masha's flat, the brave souls she'd just met.

Masha had been a gracious hostess, her green eyes sparkling as she made introductions. "Meet my new friend Kate from America, here for the international documentary festival, where I am translator." Some smiled. Others, secretive or shy, looked away. Two young women, one blonde, the other dark-haired, sat side by side on the couch. With their nervous beauty and haunted eyes, they were the most interesting women in the room to Kate,

"*Prevyet*. I Nadya," the blonde one said softly, taking a cigarette Kate had offered. She looked about sixteen, with doe-like eyes, a fragile face. Her hair was elegantly done up. "Nadya mean hope," she said, looking sadder than anyone Kate had ever seen. Beside her, the thin woman with short, dark hair murmured with a tiny smile, "Svetlana. Sveta. My name mean light." Her skin was white, almost translucent. She opened her lips to speak. Kate thought she was going to say something provocative or shocking. But Masha broke the spell by calling out, "The cognac and the peanut butter are gifts from Kate," as her mother set a tray of refreshments on the oilcloth-covered table. A buzz of pleasure erupted from the women. The afternoon's activities—*glasnost*, sharing—began.

Kate ejected the cassette from her recorder. The sixty-minute audiotape had run through to the end. She turned to Masha, grateful for this get-together that she'd so generously arranged. "I was honored to meet your friends and I was moved that many agreed to talk for my recorder." Except for Sveta and Nadya, all had described the harshness of their lives as the tape recorder ran and, as the level of the cognac lowered in the bottle, found the courage to criticize their political leaders.

Masha brushed a strand of blonde hair from her forehead. "I think we have talked too much," she said, frowning uneasily at the tape machine as Kate slid it into the back pouch of her photographer's vest.

The women filed out, and each shook Kate's hand, murmuring "*Spaceba*," or "Nize to meet you." Nadya, the blonde waif with the soft brown eyes, said, "I like visit America one day." Her voice was flute-like, clear as her skin. She threw a backward, hopeful glance at Sveta before she followed the others out the door.

Sveta lingered. Kate's eyes expectantly met hers. Earlier, as they had stood in line for the bathroom she'd whispered to Kate, "We are afraid, Nadya and I. Will you help us? Here not good. The KGB have spies." Kate had whispered back, "Let's talk at my hotel."

Kate wanted to set up that meeting. Just as she stepped toward Sveta to arrange it, the young woman shook her head imperceptibly, glancing toward Irina who was slouching out from the kitchen. Kate thought Irina had left with the others, but she was still here, hovering. Irina's face seemed more lived-in than the faces of the other women. She had bold features and deep-set, mocking eyes under which were hollows, reddish-blue. Long greasy-looking bangs hung over her heavy brows.

Masha said, "I will take you now to your hotel, Kate."

"No, I will take her, on my way home," Irina insisted. "You stay warm inside and help your mother with the dirty dishes." Irina struggled into her coat, which looked expensive to Kate, brown suede with an extravagant white fur collar and fur trimmed sleeves. Quite a contrast to the faded blue sweater she wore underneath.

"My mom says you need to bundle up, Kate," Masha said. "The temperature has dropped to twenty below." Masha's mother smiled, her gold tooth gleaming, as she handed Kate a white knit scarf that looked new, never worn.

"*Spaceba.*" Kate hugged Masha's mother. She put on her coat and looped the scarf around her neck.

Masha led the way to the elevator. The hall was dark, the walls barren, the uncarpeted floors were rough cement. *Worse than a New York City project,* Kate thought. And Masha's mom, a pediatrician who owned her co-op apartment, was considered one of the richer Soviets.

Masha punched the button. The mechanism groaned. "These are uncertain times. There was a rape in the elevator here not long ago. Unsolved. We can't trust police these days. In fact," Masha said, "we were surprised you came to the film festival. You must have a lot of courage."

"We weren't sure—with your situation in the Baltics, our Gulf War." Kate laughed ruefully. "I even made a will."

Irina looped her arm through Kate's. "I will protect you." Kate was surprised by her sudden friendliness. Irina had been abrasive throughout most of the afternoon. Did she want to continue their debate, communism versus capitalism?

The elevator door creakily opened. The inside was lit only by a dim bulb. As Kate and Irina stepped in, Sveta suddenly appeared, her dark eyes burning in her face, which was as white as the scarf around her head.

The elevator door closed in slow motion, with Masha waving good-bye. Kate, Sveta, and Irina descended to the ground floor lobby.

Outside, Kate pulled up her coat collar. Piles of snow lined the walks. Kate followed Irina, who hurried ahead. In the middle of the walkway, Kate turned around, looking for Sveta. She stood under the lone bulb that burned at the front of the building, a tall, slim statue, pale as marble except for her light gray coat. Had she changed her mind about talking with her? Kate wondered. Was she that afraid?

Several feet away, Irina stood at the edge of the road, waving her arms as the dark cars whisked by. "We are in luck," she shouted moments later. She was talking to someone in a mud-spattered sedan. A woman emerged from the passenger side of that same car and slammed the door hard. She clicked up the walkway in stiletto heels. She was provocatively dressed, unusual for a Russian woman. Her white fur coat gaped open showing a red silk blouse, cut low. Her face was delicate, pretty, with high cheekbones, a small pointed chin.

As Kate passed this woman, she noticed that she seemed older, her features more sharp than delicate. Her dark eyes were weighted down by black eye shadow. She was crying, mascara running down her cheeks. Make-up was scarce in Leningrad these days, but obviously not for her. Kate watched her stumble toward the apartment complex. Worried, she was about to offer to help her, but Irina called, "We have a cab," signaling Kate her way.

Irina spoke in Russian to the driver, heavy-jawed, Slavic-looking. He growled something in return. Irina said, "*Spaceba*. He will do it for five American dollars." About five times more than it cost Masha to bring her in a cab here to her apartment complex a few miles from the heart of Leningrad. Kate nodded, noticing once more the deep circles under Irina's eyes, gouged out as if her face was made of clay. Was she ill? Kate wondered.

Sveta came racing up. She spoke quickly. "Excuse, please, Miss Kate. I live not far from your hotel on Petrogradskaya. I come too."

Irina stiffened for a moment. A funny look crossed her face. Dismay? Relief?

"Yes," Kate said, exultant. "We need to talk—"

Sveta frowned, her eyes darting toward Irina.

The driver, a barrel-shaped man with bushy, black hair, scrambled out and opened the back door.

Irina threw a sidelong glance, a hint of a smile at the dark-jawed man. Kate had a feeling that Irina knew him. "Your friend?" She shook her head. Her eyes were mocking. Or were they crafty? Hard to tell, Kate decided. They were hidden so deeply within her broad cheekbones.

Irina spoke to the man. He laughed, she giggled. Sveta was smiling too. Kate realized Irina and the man were flirting.

Kate motioned for Irina to get in the car first. "Oh, no, you have company. I live in another building close by. I just want to make sure you be safe." Irina quickly walked away. The driver narrowed his eyes as he watched her leave. "*Blyad,*" he yelled angrily.

A startled Kate looked at Sveta, whose eyebrows rose, then she shrugged, making a face. "It is the times," she said to Kate. "Everyone is—how you say?—on the edge."

The driver stood at attention beside the open door of his beige sedan. With a small bow, he indicated the car. "One of *perestroika's* latest model of Volga," he said in accented English.

Kate caught his measured, almost menacing glance as she slid into the back seat. Sveta, eyes downcast, sat next to Kate. The man slammed the back door shut. Sveta grabbed Kate's hand. "You will help?" she whispered. "Yes," Kate murmured with more confidence than she felt.

"Good evening, ladies," the driver said, once he was settled behind the wheel.

Not yet five-thirty, Kate thought, but already black as midnight. Beyond them, on the dark roadway, cars streaked by, flinging up brown slush that spun in the headlights of the car behind. "Hotel Leningrad, Vyborgskaya," said Kate, and handed the man a five-dollar bill, grateful to be out of the brutal cold.

Inside the car, the air was stale and smelled of sweat. Irina had called the vehicle a cab. But Kate saw no name or license number displayed. She didn't like this way of traveling, getting into a stranger's car. But according to her new Russian friends, it was done all the time.

They drove for several minutes in silence. Sveta unwrapped her scarf and ran her hand through her short, dark hair. "I learn English," she apologized, "so I come to America."

The driver rummaged around with one hand, hunting for something on the floor. The car sashayed from one side of the road to the other as he worked at twisting off the cap of a vodka bottle. He took a hearty swig.

Kate threw Sveta a worried look. She spoke to the man in Russian. Their voices rose. Sveta shrugged and whispered to Kate, "Everyone drinks. It is the only way to bear things."

The driver increased speed, passing crumbling buildings with smoking chimneys, factories perhaps. Headlights boomeranged off the white snow piled at the sides of the road.

"Kate?" Sveta said. "Is okay I call you Kate?"

"Of course."

"My friend Nadya and I . . . we are afraid," Sveta whispered, her eyes like molten lava. "They want to kill us. Or send us away."

"Who? Why?" Kate asked.

Sveta bit her lip. "They call us *rozovaya*."

"*Rozo-vaya?* What does that mean?"

Sveta shook her head and put a finger to her lips.

Kate mouthed, "Come to my hotel. We can talk there."

She shook her head. "Tonight no passport. They not let me in without."

"Come tomorrow." Kate asked for Sveta's phone number. Head bent, the woman searched through her purse. She scribbled on a scrap of paper and handed it to Kate.

The landscape grew more desolate, the buildings few and far between. Trees gradually came into focus. "Is he going the right way?" Kate asked. Sveta looked around, surprised. "Hotel Leningrad," she said shrilly to the driver.

Kate ducked to peer through the muddy windshield. Ahead, beyond a clump of trees. she spotted a long, low building, the windows lighted. People were inside. A sign hung on the building. Before Kate could decipher the name, they were past it.

Sveta spoke at length to the driver in Russian. He took a long pull of vodka, wiped his fleshy lips with the back of one hand, and muttered something in return. He lit a harsh-smelling cigarette, and silently drove on. Was he going to rob them?

Kate nudged Sveta, motioned that they must jump out of the car. Kate would go left, Sveta right. Kate groped for the door handle. Where was it? She searched frantically for a hidden latch, realizing, to her horror, that the back seat doors had no handles. She shrugged out of her coat and vest. With shaking hands, she fumbled in the vest's inside back pocket, switched on her tape recorder, and slipped into her vest again. Whatever happened, she'd leave a record. Thank god, she'd put in a fresh tape before she left Masha's flat.

"Take us to the hotel," Kate pleaded, flailing into her coat. "I will give you American dollars if you take us now." She dipped her hand in her coat pocket, held out three bills.

The driver laughed, said something in Russian, then snapped up the money.

"What did he say?" Kate asked.

Sveta shook her head, her hands to her face, moaning, "So sorry. Is my fault."

The car swung off the main thoroughfare and lurched down a narrow rutted road. Sveta spoke to the driver again in Russian, and he said something in return.

Kate could make out what looked like headstones on either side. They drove beyond the cemetery into a woods and stopped. Sveta spoke sharply to the man and he gave a harsh laugh.

"Do you want more money?" Kate asked him. She had more in her vest pocket but wouldn't tell him that. "Take us back. I have two hundred dollars in my room."

The man leaned over the front seat, slid his hand over Kate's cheek, roughly pushing back her hair, pulling at her earring.

She put up her hand to stop him. "Tell him my ears are pierced. I'll take the earrings out. He can have them." Quickly she removed them, dropped them into his palm. Gilly would understand—if she ever saw Gilly again. "Please let us go. *Pazhalsta!*"

Snow danced in the headlights which were focused on a frozen pond, its surface riddled with dark patches where the ice had broken through to the cold water beneath. Off to one side was a ramshackle shed.

Sveta spoke angrily to the man. She pleaded. He pointed at her, moving his finger in a chopping motion. Suddenly, he was quiet. He reached down, feeling around on the floor, then lifted a brown paper sack with something in it. More vodka?

Sveta screamed. He bellowed back. She grew quiet, sat still as a stone. The driver staggered out of the car, taking the package with him.

Kate's heart was thudding. What had she gotten herself into? She should never have gone to Masha's and stirred up trouble.

The man opened the back door, stuck his face into Kate's. His eyebrows, thick and black, like hairy caterpillars, almost met in the middle of his forehead. With a malevolent grin, he motioned for her to get out. Losing his balance, he steadied himself on the doorjamb and shook his head, doglike. Kate realized he was very drunk. She spotted the keys in the ignition. With a shout, she tumbled into the front seat and scrambled behind the wheel. She tried to shut the car door with one hand while pumping the accelerator and twisting the key to start the car. The motor turned over, then died. She'd flooded it.

The man grabbed Kate's arm before the door could close, and spat out a string of what must have been Russian curses. In the midst of it she heard in English, "You get what you deserve, you stupid *pizda*." Kate wedged herself under the steering wheel, resisting as he tugged. Now was the time to act. Oh god, was she ready for this? She'd just earned her green belt. Three more to go before she'd be ready to test for the black belt. She'd practiced in her *dobok* and bare feet, in street clothes and running shoes, but she'd never done the moves in slippery snow.

Suddenly she stopped struggling, wrenched the keys from the ignition, and propelled herself out of the car with all her strength, arms and legs moving in a frenzy, kicking and punching, the keys clenched in her fist, using them as brass knuckles. *Attack a vital point, an eye, an ear.* The man thrashed his arms about, trying to protect himself. "Hye," she yelled from the bottom of her abdomen where the *chi* was, the power. At the same time, she raked him with the keys, tore his cheek. He fell on one knee, cursing, holding his face.

What next? She rummaged through her brain. A crescent kick! When her leg reached its highest point, she brought it down sharply, hitting the top of his head with her heel. He collapsed.

Sveta was still huddled in the car. Kate screamed at her, "Go!"

She crawled out, looking dazed.

The man tried to get up, fell again on his side. He looked like a giant black bug thrashing in the snow.

"Sveta, come," Kate yelled, as she headed to the right.

"I come."

The man was on his feet now, and had something in his hand. A gun? He threw it, and she heard it land behind her with a soft plop. It must have been a rock.

Kate lifted her legs high to navigate the deep, soft snow. Thank god, she'd worn her running shoes, not her heavy boots. "All we have to do," she yelled to Sveta over her shoulder, "is go back through the cemetery, hit the main road, then find the lighted building." Probably less than a mile away. Kate heard grunting and thrashing behind them. The man was coming after them. "You need my big Russian *khui!*" he roared in

English. He was drunk and fat, but how fit was he? She and Sveta were ten to fifteen years younger than he was.

Kate darted into the black thicket of birch trees, fighting her way through, bumping into tree trunks. Car headlights flickered dimly through the trees like giant fireflies.

Get to the road, she told herself. Find help. Sveta was right behind her, wasn't she?

"Sveta?" she shouted. "Are you okay?" She heard a loud crack. Was he shooting? Where was Sveta?

"I okay." Sveta's hollow voice echoed back.

It was like the nightmares she often had—of running, lost and terrified. Her breath came in sharp rasps. She threw a quick look behind her, hoping to see Sveta. But if she was there, her colors, white scarf and gray coat, had blended into the trees and the snow. Don't lose your head, Kate. Get to the road. Flag down a car. Would one of them stop? The cars seemed to be whizzing by. "Sveta!" Kate called again. No answer. *She must have split off,* Kate thought, *when I headed into the trees.*

Snowflakes were falling fast. Coat flapping, scarf flying, Kate ran, trying not to fall in the ruts and slippery patches. Her hands were icy. She reached in her pocket for her gloves. It was only then that she realized she still held the keys to the car. She would have laughed if she weren't afraid her face would crack from the cold. Her coat was open. She zipped it up and tied her scarf around her neck, grateful she hadn't lost it during her acrobatics in the car. It just might save her life. She was thankful, too, that she'd taken the advice of the festival organizer to wear tights under her corduroy pants for extra warmth.

Minutes later, she burst out of the trees onto the cemetery road. Easier to run here, with the snow packed down. The road branched. She took a left, praying it was the correct choice. Her feet were numb. Her lungs ached from the icy air.

In the distance, a car whined to a start. Soon headlights surged up behind her. Was it him? He must have hot-wired the car or had a spare set of keys. She scampered off the road and hid behind a clump of trees. It looked like his car, but the windows were too dirty to see inside. Was he going to stop and search for her? The car kept going, lurching and bumping, tires squealing for purchase on the ice.

She had to find the lighted building, contact the police, tell them that Sveta might be hurt or worse. She didn't know Sveta's last name. Or Masha's. Even though Masha worked as translator for the film festival and Kate had known her, how long? Two days. It seemed they'd been friends for a long time.

Kate jogged along the pitted, slippery cemetery road, trying to hold to a steady pace while she struggled to keep her balance. She was panting, gasping for air. It hurt to breathe. She slowed to a walk. There were no sounds except her breath and the crisp crunch of her feet on the white snow. Time was a white ribbon that stretched to infinity. She had an impulse to lie down, make a snow angel as she did when she was a child. It would be like sinking into a featherbed, a giant, downy featherbed.

She shook her head violently, imagining her brain cells frozen into tiny gray bits rattling inside. She struggled to stay alert. What had actually happened at Masha's flat? She needed to go over it carefully. It might explain why she was here, in this predicament. She had told the women gathered that it was a privilege to be at their meeting at this critical time, 1991—a very exciting year in human terms. The women threw stricken looks at Masha, who spoke quickly. "Do not call it a meeting. Please. A meeting like this is not allowed." "We're an unregistered group," explained another. "We must obtain permission from the authorities to have a meeting, but we are afraid to bring attention to ourselves."

Kate said that she hoped to return after Leningrad became St. Petersburg, to make a documentary to let the world know what life was like after *glasnost* and *perestroika*. She'd pulled the tape recorder from her vest pocket. She'd asked, in case circumstances prevented her from coming back, if they'd be willing to send their messages to America to be part of her video work-in-progress, contrasting women's issues in the U.S. with those in the Soviet Union. Smiles disappeared; the women spoke Russian to Masha. Kate heard a word in English, "dangerous."

She told the women the tape would be next to her always until she left the country, that their stories would be heard by members of her New York City guerrilla film class and her teacher, a star in the film world.

A plump woman said at last, "We do not want to be identified, use only our first names."

Kate stumbled on through the cemetery. The landscape shimmered with a muted radiance, benign, eerily beautiful. The trees, branches heavy with snow, drooped—hoary old men, bowing and nodding. The gravestones, covered in white fur, hulked in the starlight like slumbering bears. She imagined a sleigh filled with people, a scene like the etchings on lacquered Russian pins, happy people, scarves flying, waving from an earlier time—before the Revolution. She leaned against a gravestone, just to rest for a moment.

As she slid slowly toward the soft, furry snow she heard in her mind Sveta's worried whisper, "The KGB have spies," saw Irina's mocking eyes.

Chapter Two

6:55 PM, Sunday, January 27

A red-haired soldier waited just inside the front door of the Hotel Leningrad, peering through the glass, anxious to hear how the operation with the American woman had ended. The Volga jerkily entered the parking lot, slid at an angle into a space marked "Taxis." The barrel-shaped man fell out and staggered toward him.

He is drunk, Andre thought, as he ushered Kolya into the

hotel. More disreputable-looking than usual. His shaggy hair was snarled, sticking up in clumps. His cheek was cut, his pocket torn, and his black coat was matted, as if he had fallen in the slush. Falling down drunk. Andre gritted his teeth, his stomach churning, impatient to ask him what happened and half-dreading Kolya's answer. Instead he blurted out, "Where is Tanya? She was with you in the car when you left." The soldier worried about his sister when Kolya was drunk.

Kolya smirked. "We parted ways. She was hysterical—squeamish at the idea of murder."

Andre shushed him. He glanced around to see who might have heard. No one close by. "I told you not to involve Tanya in this business. She is not used to it."

Kolya snorted. "Tanya has learned to do a lot of things."

"Not so loud," the soldier said, grabbing Kolya's arm, jerking him along past the red-carpeted stairs and into the bar, which was empty save for a few diehards sitting at the front, drinking and jawing with the bartender.

"What happened with the American?" Andre asked in a low voice after they were seated at a table in a far corner.

Kolya thrust his chest out boastfully. "I left her out past the Olgino Motel. In the trees by the cemetery. At the pond."

"You did it?" Andre took a closer look at the angry gash on Kolya's cheek and saw that it was seeping blood. "She must have put up a fight."

Kolya scowled. "I did not know there would be two. Two costs more money."

"Two?"

"Both with white scarves. Hard to tell one from the other in the dark when they are running away."

"She is dead? Both dead?"

The man scratched his chin. "What I did not do, the cold will finish. Do not look so gloomy, Andre."

"I am not gloomy," said Andre, "just thinking." He had received the order yesterday from Captain Iurkov to keep an eye on her comings and goings. Andre had been following her for only one day, but he felt drawn to the dark-haired woman. She was lively, fresh-looking. Different from Russian women. Even her name, Kate—it sounded like freedom, happiness.

"What is the matter, did you fall in love with her?" Kolya snorted. "You would not stand a chance."

"Do not be stupid," the soldier said. He must not show softness. He must be realistic. He needed money. He had just come back from East Germany, where he had been stationed for over a year, his salary paid in hard currency. Now he was paid in rubles, a painful cut in pay. "Who is the other one? You said there were two."

"Someone at the women's meeting. Russian. Doing something she should not. Who will care?" Kolya licked his lips. "I want my money, Andrushka."

"The Captain will want proof."

"The bodies will not be found until the spring thaw."

"I told you to make it look like an accident," Andre burst out. It was a stupid move on his part to involve Kolya in this deal. He did it to help out his sister Tanya, who had made a bad mistake marrying this *doorock*. "Why would this American woman be walking in the cemetery?"

"Plans changed. Things got out of hand." Kolya ran his tongue over his teeth. Andre could see that he was coming to some sort of decision. "I cannot wait until spring," he said. "I want my money now." Kolya reached in his coat pocket. "The proof." He dropped a pair of earrings into the soldier's hand.

Andre recognized them. Blue enamel, with little white doves of peace. She wore them always, half hidden in her hair, the blue reflected in her eyes. He felt his shoulders slump, forced himself to be business-like. "I will take these to the Captain. I will try to get your money for you."

"Try? You better. Or he will have me to deal with."

Exactly what Andre didn't need—this buffoon blustering his way to the Captain. Captain Victor Iurkov had been a member of *Spetsnaz* special forces in Afghanistan. He would chew up Kolya and swallow him whole.

"I want the earrings back," Kolya hissed. "They will be worth something. And tell him I got two. Serves the bitches right. *Pizdi.*" He lit a Belomorkanal cigarette. The strong, chemical smell—like burning rubber—stung Andre's eyes. *He will kill himself,* Andre thought, *with those cheap, unfiltered cigarettes.*

※

KATE HEARD A LOUD crack and gave a start. Where was she? What was that sound? A tree limb breaking, heavy with ice and snow? Or an animal? Ferocious and gray, with a wolf face, eyes like hot coals, and teeth sharp as knives.

Kate realized she'd stopped moving. She was sitting in the snow, leaning against something—what? A gravestone.

She'd meant to stop to catch her breath. She must have closed her eyes and fallen asleep.

Panic seized her. She was always rushing in, asking questions, demanding answers, promising help, while everyone else quietly held back, taking stock. This pell mell dash to find out had always put her in hot water. She wished she *were* in hot water. She was freezing to death. She'd be found here stiff and hard as a log if she didn't force herself to go on.

She pulled herself to her knees and struggled to her feet, stamping up and down until her legs came to life, stinging. She pumped her arms, flexing numb fingers, then rubbed her cheeks and nose. She awkwardly rearranged her scarf over her face, leaving a slit for her eyes, and trudged on, half walking, half running.

At last, ahead of her loomed two tall stone pillars, marking the end of the cemetery road, where it abutted onto the highway. She felt a spurt of energy.

She took a right, running clumsily on the left side of the road. Hang on, she told herself. Occasional cars sped by. If the drivers saw her, no one slowed. Just as well. She wouldn't get in with another stranger. That's what Sveta must have done, hitched a ride with a stranger. She spoke the language. She'd be okay.

In the black distance, pinpoints of light glimmered.

The tiny specks of light grew larger, became warm bright beacons beckoning Kate forward. Finally, she reached the long, low building, its windows blazing. Cars were parked around it. She couldn't decipher the sign, but she recognized the Intourist logo. Must be an inn or a hotel. People, warmth, safety would be inside.

Kate hobbled up the short driveway and fell against the door. She fumbled with the knob, her hands stiff as blocks of wood, and somehow managed to turn it, bumping against the door with her shoulder until it opened. She stumbled into the room, past a startled man. "*Pazhalsta*," she murmured, her lips thick with cold. "Please . . . I'm worried. My friend . . ." She unwound the scarf covering her face, gingerly took off her gloves, held her hands, blowing on them, softly rubbing, trying to bring them back to life.

"*Ahnglisky*," the man said. His long mustache twitched. He went behind a counter, and vanished through a doorway.

Kate sank onto a wooden chair beside a low table covered with magazines. When her hands began to tingle, she bent down to untie the laces of her shoes. Pain stabbed through her fingers.

The man returned with a young woman, about nineteen or twenty, blonde braids pulled over the top of her head. "*Ahnglisky?*" she asked.

"American." Kate struggled to get her shoes off.

"*Americanski*," the girl said to the man. They exchanged worried looks.

"I'm sorry. This isn't very polite." Kate stripped off her socks. Her toes were white. She wrapped her scarf around her bare feet and gently massaged them.

The girl said something to the man before she disappeared through the door behind the counter. The man stared at Kate and pulled at the ends of his bushy brown mustache.

The girl returned with a pair of long, thick gray socks. "You must wear these to warm your feet."

"*Spaceba.*" Kate smiled at the man who nodded back. She

pulled the stockings on and continued to rub her toes with her hands. "I was outside for a long time," she said to the girl.

"You are lucky there is very little wind tonight."

"My friend. Sveta—"

"You have—trouble?" The girl looked concerned, but slightly guarded.

Kate took a deep breath. "I'm a guest at the film festival in the Hotel Leningrad. Kate Hennessey, Titan Films." She showed them her festival badge. "I took a cab—with Sveta. We were supposed to go to Vyborgskaya, my hotel. But the man took us to the cemetery up the road from here. To rob us."

"Did he hurt you?" the girl asked. Her round eyes were sympathetic now.

Kate shook her head. "I ran away. I thought my friend was right behind me. But I lost her. I'm very worried." Kate cupped a hand over her nose, warming it with her breath.

The girl translated for the man. He answered, frowning, and shook his head.

"My father apologizes for our people. It's *bezpredel,* beyond the limit. We are living on the edge. It is like the time in America," she searched for words, "when it was Wild West. Come. You must be warm. I mean, we must warm you up." The girl led her behind the counter. "The cemetery is a bad place. It is well known for murders. A man was found there, hanging from a tree. Last spring, after the ice melted, a body was found in the pond."

Kate had a spasm of shivering. "I don't know what to do. I want to know Sveta is okay."

Olga conferred with her father. He frowned and nodded.

The girl said to Kate, "We must call the *militsia,* local police. Ask them to go to the cemetery and look for her."

She led Kate through the door into a small entryway. Beyond that was a doorway hung with multi-colored beads. "My room," the girl said shyly. Kate followed her through the beads. Red and orange striped curtains were at the windows. A thin, dark rug lay on the floor. Bright red knitted antimacassars covered the backs and arms of two frayed stuffed chairs. Between the chairs was a coffee table. On it sat a black rotary phone. Colorful travel posters decorated the walls. "My name is Olga," she said, color coming to her round cheeks. "Our motel, the Olgino, is named after a village, in honor of the Czar's daughter, Olga." She smiled proudly, then added, "Although I do not know why the name was not changed after the Revolution."

"Olga is a lovely name." Kate offered her hand. "Kate Hennessey. From New York City."

"New York City." Olga's eyes sparkled. "I have a poster." On the wall was the Statue of Liberty.

Olga dialed. After several minutes, she shook her head. "It is ringing but no one answers. That sometimes happens with our phones. They are very old. We hear the ring, but the other party does not." She looked thoughtful. "Or maybe the police are not answering. They are"—she looked apologetic—"in these times not dependable."

"Oh, dear," Kate said. She felt hamstrung, ready to explode with worry. "Wait a minute. I just remembered. Sveta gave me a telephone number while we were in the cab." She handed the slip of paper to the girl. "If the police don't answer, maybe Sveta's family will. We can alert them to what has happened. Ask them to come and look for her."

The girl nodded slowly, and, referring to Kate's paper, dialed again. After a time, she shook her head. "No answer. They might not be at home." She wrinkled her nose. "As I say, our phone system is old, over sixty years."

"We must keep trying. Or go out to look for her ourselves."

"We will have to use the sleigh. But we will try calling again first."

Kate tried to smile. "Where am I? I don't know where I am."

"We are located on the Primorskoye Highway, near the Gulf of Finland."

"Finland! Did he bring us to Finland?"

The girl laughed. "No. Finland is thirty minutes from here."

"How far am I from my hotel, the Leningrad?"

"Thirty minutes by *electrichka*—train—to the station. From there, only a ten-minute walk to the hotel."

"Maybe I should go back now, get help at the hotel." She had to do something. But what? She felt frustrated, powerless.

Olga looked very stern. "First, you must take a bath to warm yourself. We see many bad cases of frostbite here. You must be careful of your toes and fingers, the tips of your nose and your ears." She opened the door of the bathroom. An old-fashioned tub squatted on four legs, a shower attachment fastened to the spigot. "You must be careful, gradually warm the water. Do not start too hot."

"*Spaceba*. Will you try both numbers once more?" Kate burst out.

Olga dialed. She waited, and then began nodding. Kate heard her say, "Olga . . . Olgino Hotel." She held her hand over the receiver. "The police." She talked at length, looking very serious. She must be describing the ordeal, Kate decided.

"Do you know Sveta's last name?" she asked. Kate shook her head.

Olga spoke on. Kate heard her say her name, Kate Hennesey. At last, Olga, with a worried look, put down the phone. "They said they will check the cemetery. They wrote a protocol. I had to give your name, tell them you are American, a guest of the film festival. That you and a Russian friend were abducted to the cemetery and robbed. That you arrived here but not your friend. And that you are concerned about her safety." Olga pointed to the tub. "Now, please, you must take care of yourself."

Kate shrugged off her coat and vest.

"Here is some ointment for your lips." Olga handed her a small jar.

Kate smeared the white salve over her dry, cracked lips. "Will the police call you if they know anything?"

She sighed. "Our system is more successful for political crimes." She smiled. "I will come back when you are finished."

"Will you try Sveta's home once more?" Kate asked.

"I will try many times."

Kate put the rubber stopper in the tub, sat on the edge, and ran the water—tepid at first—over her bare feet and hands. Her toes were still white. They felt as if they were on fire. She had gone to Masha's to get material for her video work-in-progress, and she almost lost her toes and fingers. Face it, she almost lost her life.

Masha had told her, "Despite *glasnost* and *perestroika,* it is still the Dark Ages here for women. Men have all the power. They want a slave—someone to clean and cook. And hold down a regular job too. Come tonight to my flat and hear their stories." Kate had arrived with Marlboros and cognac. And peanut butter, which was the hit of the party since no one had ever tasted it. And her audiotape recorder.

By the time the cognac was gone, it had been a free-for-all—the women interrupting one another, telling secrets, laughing, cursing, criticizing. They'd forgotten about the tape recorder, sitting on a table, quietly running.

When the tub was filled, Kate stripped, felt the goose bumps rise. She locked the bathroom door. These days, in this place, one couldn't be too careful. She stepped into the tub, immersing her long body in the warmth.

She thought back again to Irina, who had argued politics with her, then pretended she was going to accompany Kate in the cab, but pulled out at the last minute. Kate had bad vibes about her, but if she were a friend of Masha's . . . At first, Irina had been flattering, calling her pretty, asking if she were an actor. No, she'd replied, "Script person, gopher. Our company, Titan Films, has brought a documentary to the festival." Kate slid down in the tub until the hot water almost covered her shoulders. She'd been surprised when Irina called her pretty. She never thought of herself as pretty. She was awkward. Her dark hair was straight, her nose had a bump; she was thin and gangly.

But Gilly didn't seem to think so. Gilly had said she had the look of a model. "With the right clothes," Gilly told her, "you'd be smashing. I'd like to pick something out for you." It was just talk in bed, Kate figured, after they made love. They'd been in Gilly's apartment in the West Village. It was summer. They'd been together almost a year. To Kate's surprise, Gilly did pick something out—a classy black dress and silver shoes from Saks and had them sent to Kate. Kate protested, but had to admit she did look smashing in the dress. Then Gilly invited her to a back yard barbecue to meet the parents.

Kate covered her face with a hot wet washcloth. She didn't want to lose the tip of her nose. Or parts of her ears. She moved the cloth to cover first one ear and then the other. That made her think of the lost earrings. And Gilly. Gilly would love the bizarre humor of it—Kate being here on the Gulf of Finland, in a stranger's bathtub. Gilly would lie in bed with her and they'd shiver and laugh, the danger over.

Nice fantasy, Kate told herself. Don't count on it. Stubbornly, her mind persisted in that vein as she bobbed in the hot water. The warmth permeated her bones. The shakes had stopped. She was glowing like a hot coal. She could almost fall asleep.

A knock sounded at the door. Olga's voice called, "Are you okay?"

"Be right out." Kate reluctantly left the tub, dried and dressed. When she put on her photographer's vest with its many pockets, she felt its heaviness, remembered the paraphernalia she carried—the audiotapes, a video with important early festival shots, her tape recorder, as well as candy bars, cigarettes, even a lacy brassiere, ways to start conversations and make friends in this fascinating country.

Kate examined the cassette player. The abduction had taped through, to the end. She pushed rewind. The machine worked. The cold hadn't damaged it. The sound, though muffled by her vest and coat, was audible. Good thing she'd left her coat open. She'd have a replay—most of it in Russian.

She unlocked the door and opened it. Olga was waiting with a tray from the kitchen.

"Did anyone answer at Sveta's?" Kate asked.

Olga shook her head. "I am sorry."

She must get back to the hotel, find the festival director, get Masha's phone number and call her about Sveta. "*Spaceba.* You're very kind . . ." Kate waved helplessly at the array of food. "Things are so scarce. I feel terrible taking your food."

"You are our guest." Olga set the tray on the coffee table. It was a sumptuous feast—kolhbasa, cheese, a small apple, bread, coffee, soft ice cream, a glass of cognac—even a half-filled jar of red caviar, something Kate was sure Olga and her father had been saving for themselves for a special occasion.

It would be impolite to refuse. "You and your father must share these with me."

The girl shook her head, smiling. "You have had a shock. Your body needs food."

Kate sat in the overstuffed chair. Olga demurely sat opposite, the tray resting on the low table between them. Kate made a sandwich of the sausage and cheese. After much encouragement, Olga smeared caviar on a chunk of bread. "Did the man rob you of a large amount of money?" she asked.

"Only twenty dollars." And a pair of earrings. Special earrings. "It could have been worse." She could be dead. Sveta could be dead.

"They stole twenty dollars," Olga said in hushed tones, her eyes wide.

Kate realized twenty dollars would be 100 rubles, half a month's pay, at the regular exchange rate; worth six times that on the streets. She drank some coffee. "What do you think—about the police? Will they investigate and call back? Should I also report the crime to the authorities when I return to my hotel?"

"They will promise to find out something, which does not mean they will do anything." Olga looked embarrassed.

Kate nodded gloomily. She ate with gusto, polishing off the sandwich in record time, gobbling down a hunk of bread and caviar, then spooning up the melting ice cream. It was very rich. She drank the rest of the strong, thick coffee. Finally, she downed the cognac. She yawned.

"If you wish," Olga smiled, "now you may sleep."

"*Spaceba.*" Kate stood. "I have to get back. It's after eight o'clock. Will you try Sveta's home once more?"

Olga dialed. Soon her face brightened. She said, "*Zdrasvuitya.*" Kate heard her ask for Sveta, then heard her say "*Americanski* . . . Kate . . . Olgino . . ." in the middle of a lengthy explanation.

Olga listened, nodding slowly at first, then suddenly faster and faster. She broke into a smile. "She is there," she whispered to Kate.

Kate could scarcely believe it. Everything had turned out all right. "May I please speak with her?"

But Olga was saying, "*Spaceba,*" and hanging up the phone. "I am sorry," she apologized. "The man was in a hurry. He said she was busy."

"Maybe thawing out in a hot tub?"

"How did he put it?" Olga frowned in concentration. "'Yes, she is taken care of.'"

"Did he say he'd tell her I called, was concerned?"

Olga shook her head. "I am sorry." She held out her hands. "He was so quick to hang up."

"No, no, you did fine." Kate would like to have heard Sveta's voice. Asked her how she got away. Arranged for a meeting with her at the hotel. Find out why she was afraid.

"I will take you to the *electrichka,* the train," Olga said. "It is very close." She gave Kate a second pair of stockings to protect her feet from the still wet shoes. Then she rummaged in her closet, pulled something down from the top shelf, held it out. "Rabbit fur. Very warm." Olga slid it on Kate's head, tied the strings under her chin. She stepped back, nodding, her mouth quivering toward a smile. "Now you are very Russian."

Kate took a quick peek at herself in the mirror and laughed. It looked like two huge squirrels were fighting on her head.

When Olga ducked into the closet again for her own coat, Kate hid fifty dollars on the tray, sure Olga and her father would refuse the money if she offered it.

On the way out, raucous laughter erupted from a hallway.

Olga made a face. "Finns. Most of our guests are Finns, men who come here to drink cheaply. Quite often we find drunken Finns lying in the hallway. We also have the French who come to ski in winter."

"No Americans?" Kate asked.

"Sometimes in summer."

At the *electrichka,* Olga bought Kate's ticket for her, found a young couple going Kate's way who promised to show her the route to her hotel from the station.

Before the train pulled away, Kate started to take off the huge fur hat. "*Spaceba.*"

"No, no," Olga insisted. "You must keep it. It will make you smile. Be a happy reminder of your stay in Russia. At the Olgino."

"You'll have to buy another one." How much would one cost in rubles? She'd seen them on sale for five dollars American at one of the hard currency markets.

"We will be hurt if you will not accept our gift."

Kate was glad she'd left the fifty dollars.

Olga, her red cheeks glowing, pressed a piece of paper into Kate's hand. "Will you write me all about your life in New York City, Kate?"

"I will," Kate said, hugging her.

Chapter Three

8:45 PM, Sunday, January 27

He must be expecting someone important, Andre thought, as the Captain opened the door of his hotel room. He wore his full dress uniform, the jacket heavy with his medals. His black hair, slicked down, sat on his head like a tight-fitting cap. He smelled of cologne.

Andre held out the blue earrings with the white doves.

"Hers?" Captain Iurkov asked. Andre nodded.

The Captain frowned, deepening the scar that zigzagged through his right eyebrow to the middle of his forehead. Another scar, thinner, was almost hidden in the fold of his cheek along his nose to his mouth. A third semi-circular red line traveled from the corner of his left eye, over the eyebrow, and down the bridge of the nose. Wounds from the Afghan War, where the Captain had served for many years. They were not the purple color of shrapnel scars. Andre had heard that the Captain never spoke about that time unless he was drunk.

"Pretty." The Captain plucked the earrings out of Andre's hand and put them in his pocket.

"What about the money?" Andre asked.

"When we have the body." The Captain smiled.

"That might not be until spring." Andre improvised, adding quickly, "Kolya—he threw her in the pond. At the cemetery."

The Captain frowned. "We agreed it should look like an accident."

"The girl fought back. Kolya's temper got the better of him." Should he mention the possibility of a second body? Better not. "It will seem to be a random crime, part of the uncertainty of the times."

The Captain rocked on his heels, his eyes never leaving Andre. He held out his hand. "The video?"

Andre felt the blood rush to his face. *We do the dirty work. He holds out on us.* Glowering, he shook his head.

The Captain's face tightened.

Be calm, Andre told himself. Ever since last December when the Chairman of the KGB made a "call for order" over Central television in Moscow, no one knew from day to day what was going to happen, who would be in charge, the KGB or President Gorbachev and the policies of *glasnost* and *perestroika*. "I have been busy in the lobby. An argument among the men. She will not be back. I will get the video later from her room."

"Do that." With a cold smile, the Captain ushered Andre out the door and closed it in his face.

Andre stood for a moment, shaking with rage. It had taken all his discipline to hold his anger in. He had been promised American dollars for setting everything up. He had been expecting at least $100, two and one-half months' pay, worth six times that on the black market. But he got nothing, even with the proof of the earrings. Kolya would be wild, out of control.

The Captain's door was opening again. Andre hurried to the stairwell, waited a few moments, peeping through the crack in the door. The Captain looked up and down the hall, then headed toward the stairwell. Andre scrambled up one flight. *Good guess,* he told himself, as he watched the Captain descend the steps. Andre followed. The Captain exited at the fourth floor. Andre stayed hidden, surprised to see the Captain stop at the room next to Kate's.

The Captain knocked. The door opened. The Captain murmured, "I hope I am not disturbing you, Gregor." Andre couldn't see the face. "Make it quick," the man snapped, "I am on the phone." The two spoke in whispers. Andre strained to hear.

The Captain handed the earrings through the doorway. "Do you recognize these?"

Andre heard a laugh from inside the room.

The Captain waited, smiling unctuously, hand outstretched. A thick envelope was placed in it. Clearly, Andre thought, filled with money.

"Half now," the voice from the room said. "Half when I get the videotape."

Andre smiled. He now knew a name—*Gregor*—and the source of the money. *Gregor.* Andre's heart pounded faster with excitement. He would be discharged from the army in a few months. What kind of work could he get? There were no jobs.

He would have a look at the video first thing, after he took it from Kate's room so he would know how valuable it might be to the mysterious Gregor—the man with the money, the man in charge of this operation. Andre had noted that he spoke Russian with an accent. Visitors were here for the festival from many countries. *Gregor.* Hungarian? German? Polish? He hurried down the stairs to the bar. He would talk it over with Kolya. They would have to find a VCR that played tapes in the American VHS format.

※

WITH MANY SMILES AND gestures, the young couple guided Kate through the train station. Outside, they pointed her in the direction of the hotel. They'd been so sweet. She'd been scattered, distant, her mind replaying events in the cemetery, her terror, her escape. She didn't even have a pack of Marlboros to offer them because she'd given them all to the women gathered at Masha's. Kate dug into her jeans pocket and pulled out two dollar bills. The couple shook their heads, beaming, waving.

After half a block, a thin boy, not more than ten, approached her. He was hatless, with a runny nose. "So good, my pins, Miss." He grinned. "Lenin pins. Only one dollar."

Despite the bushy Russian hat, she'd been spotted as an American. The boy looked so cold and vulnerable, Kate gave him the crumpled bills still in her hand. To her surprise he gave her his whole card of pins before he darted toward the metro entrance.

Fifteen or twenty metal pins were attached to the cardboard. He'd been in such a hurry to get rid of them. Leningrad was soon to be renamed St. Petersburg, the Lenin statues and pictures destroyed. A controversial decision. Maybe the boy would later regret selling his Lenins so cheaply. An item in a Film Festival press-release described the current ambivalence: "In twenty days the Lenin's Mausoleum will be closed. If it is to reopen, it will re-open in the spring."

※

KATE SHOWED HER HOTEL pass to the dour soldiers, stiff with cold, stationed at the front doors. Savoring the warmth, the safety, she hurried through the dim and cavernous lobby. The brown uniforms of the military were everywhere, as they had been each day of the festival, their movements stiff and unnatural in their studied attempts to appear casual.

Dark-jacketed men and women, lit by small pools of light, manned their stations—Information, Taxi Service, Passports, Registration. To her right was a wide marble staircase, covered by a plum red carpet. Great shot. A study in opposites. She'd return tomorrow with her video camera, shoot from the center of the lobby, zooming in on the carpeted marble stairs, dramatic, sensuous—redolent of grand entrances by czars and czarinas. At the top, she'd get a close-up of the festival posters, typically cryptic, plastered over the glass doors of the Competition Hall: a cartoon face of a man—thuggish looking—with one eye half open, the other closed, a mail slot cracking his head in two, an airmail letter sticking out of it. Message to Man, the theme of the festival, was scrawled in the left corner of the poster. Kate gave a short, shaky laugh. Now that she thought of it, the face on the poster looked a little like the face of the drunk who'd abducted her and Sveta.

On her way to the elevator her eyes scoured the bar. She spotted Dom, her boss, her friend, having a beer, and hurried over to his table.

"Hi, darlin'." Dom, his flecked green eyes warm and gentle, said, "You missed dinner."

If she focused only on his face, he'd look like an aristocrat with his brown Van Dyke, streaked with gray, immaculately trimmed. "I was at Masha's, our translator's place, to meet her friends."

He gave her a second look, eyes wide. "What happened to you?" He took her by the arm and sat her down.

She was staring, she realized. Spacey. Still on adrenalin overdrive. She covered her face with her hands. "What happened?" Dom gently pulled her hands away.

"We left Masha's, Sveta and I. We took a car, an unlicensed cab, I guess. The driver drove us to a cemetery at the edge of town. To rob us or something." She tried to keep her voice light, but it grew hoarse and unsteady as she told him about the man trying to pull her out of the car. Dom looked so worried and angry. Tears welled in her eyes. "I surprised him," she said with a burst of laughter. "I flew at him like a maniac, punching, kicking. Thank god, for my Taekwondo . . . It was scary, not like being in class. He was drunk and slipped on an icy patch."

Dom seemed stunned, at a loss for words. "You—and Sveta, was it? Neither of you were hurt?"

"I lost track of Sveta. I was terrified he'd grabbed her. When I reached the Olgino Hotel, Olga called the police, who said they'd check out the area, look for Sveta. We called her family. I'd taken Sveta's phone number." Kate was breathless. "A man answered who said she was home. I was surprised she arrived so quickly. But relieved. She must have flagged down a car and hitched a ride."

Dom gave her shoulder a rough squeeze. "You kept a cool head, kid."

"Hard not to," she said wanly. "It was twenty degrees below zero." She still wore her coat, she realized, but she was shaking. "I gave him money and my earrings. He wanted something else. My passport? To rape us, maybe. Surely not to kill us."

Dom shrugged helplessly. He stared at her hard. "How long were you out in that cold?"

"About an hour." She told him then about the kindness of Olga and her father. Kate lowered her voice so Dom had to lean in as she recounted her stay at the Olgino. She didn't want to get the lovely, kind Olga and her father into trouble for helping her, a Westerner.

Her thoughts weren't logical. That was the way things were . . . here . . . now. Illogical. Irrational.

"Let me check your hands for frostbite." He examined Kate's fingers one by one. He gave a quick nod. "You need a drink."

Still in a fog, Kate watched him amble over to the bar. He was taller than her 5'8", casual to the brink of sloppy, wearing a faded black T-shirt under a frayed light blue sports jacket, baggy jeans.

While he was gone, a woman with short blonde hair at the next table turned to stare at Kate, her icy countenance melting into a smile. Not a friendly smile. Kate wondered how much English the woman understood.

Dom handed Kate a cognac. She took a gulp, went into a coughing fit, tears streaming down her face. She wiped her eyes with Dom's handkerchief, drew in a deep breath, shuddering. "The women at Masha's . . ." she began, but before she could finish, Dom shot a glance toward the blonde woman, her back to them now, head slightly tilted, as if she were listening. "Amazing isn't it, how quickly one becomes Russianized?" Dom murmured, signaling Kate to follow him to a corner table with no one on either side. Still, Kate kept her voice barely above a whisper as she told Dom about the women who gathered at Masha's. "They were scared, hesitant to talk with my tape recorder running. When they did, most gave only their first names. Can you believe it? It's still illegal for women to meet in this country. They have to register first as a group. But they're afraid to bring attention to themselves. Masha went first, talking about her ex-husband, how he now has custody of her twelve-year-old son, how he beats and kicks her when she tries to visit him."

"Poor Masha," Dom murmured.

"Another woman," Kate continued, agitated, "her husband is an engineer who lost his job. He's sending her out to work as a prostitute. Heroin use and AIDS are growing problems."

He patted her hand. "Hey, kid, calm down. Have another slug of cognac."

She swallowed more of her drink, made a face. "I have audiotapes of everything, to use as voice overs. I can make a great video contrasting the lives of women in the U.S. with those in the U.S.S.R. I invited the women—any who want to speak in private—to come to my room here at the hotel so I can videotape them—those courageous enough to show their faces on camera."

"Now, Kate," Dom said gently, taking her hands.

Kate lowered her voice to a whisper. "Sveta agreed to tell

her story for my video. Seeing her terrified face on tape would be a real 'message to man.'"

"What *is* her story?" Dom asked.

"I don't know—yet. I said I'd help her."

"Here you are!!" Steve leaned over the table, impatience oozing from every pore, his bright yellow necktie swinging. "Schmoozing with the boss."

Kate withdrew her hands from Dom's.

"I've been looking for you for hours, Katie, dear." Steve punctuated each word with a jerk of his head, his longish black hair bouncing at the edges of his broad, flushed face. "Where in the hell have you been?"

He'd curled his hair, Kate noticed. He must have brought a hot comb with him. She didn't trust Steve, even though he was part of their Titan Films team. He was always trying to touch her, trying to show her his skin flicks whenever Dom wasn't around. Here at the hotel, luck of the draw, his room was next door to hers and he was constantly inviting her in for a drink. "What did you need me for?" Kate asked coolly.

"To get five hundred flyers done at the copy center. Hype for our film."

"What kind of hype?" Dom stared him down.

"To get us into Competition Hall as the final film of the festival!"

"We weren't invited," Kate said. Their film was part of the American Program, the anti-totalitarianism program, scheduled to play in a cinema in the central part of Leningrad, accessible to the people, to anyone who wanted—or dared?—to stop by to see a documentary film called *Revolution*.

"This is the first I've heard of this." Dom's normally smooth baritone turned choppy.

"Well, I thought—" Steve stammered, "if we want to make any sales, we have to get into the main hall with the film. No buyer's gonna trudge into town to see us."

"To try to worm our way into competition now would be rude and arrogant," Kate said.

Dom took several swallows of his beer, his eyes drilling into Steve. "You want to stay partners you don't do things behind my back."

Steve's eyes glittered with hostility. He tried to cover it by turning his head away. Then he flashed an oily grin. "Hey, it's just—hey, I think ours is the best movie here. It's in color, has great music, lots of pace. It's alive. It makes people feel good. A natural culmination to the festival." He shuddered. "These Russian films get me down. They're all in black and white. Political tracts disguised as films. Talky, heavy, morbid. Slow and BORING. I thought they'd never stop shoveling dirt on that guy's coffin last night."

"Listen to me, pal—" Dom interrupted. He slid out of his chair, eyes ablaze. "We stick together while we're here and look out for each other." When he related Kate's ordeal, Steve was impassive, so Dom pressed him. "You said you'd been looking all over for Kate. Well, that's what she's been doing, running for her life."

A flicker of impatience flashed across Steve's face. "Sorry, Kate," he said curtly, without looking at her. "Next time be more careful. It's bedlam here, every man for himself." He ran a hand through his thick hair, changing tack. "It doesn't matter about the flyers anyway—" He gave Dom a sheepish grin. "I mean, even if you agreed with my point of view about handing them out . . ." He paused for dramatic effect. ". . . they can't find our print."

"Can't find our print?" Kate and Dom spoke at once. Kate continued, "Masha told me that she'd overheard festival people talking about our film. It was shown yesterday at 4:00 PM, she said, at the Leningrad Cinema in the central part of town." Dom closed his eyes and sighed. "Well," Steve said, "they can't find it today."

"What's all this crap about PR when we don't have a print?" Dom exploded.

"I wasn't going to mention it." Steve shrugged. "Sergei thought they'd locate it in time for tomorrow's screening. 'No PROB-lem,' he said."

Sergei from Moscow, in charge of non-competition films, refused to schedule any unless they were brought to his room and remained there. Booking was easier, he said, when he knew exactly what he had on hand: many countries had canceled because of the Soviet special troops in Latvia and Lithuania. Made sense, sort of, but Dom had been reluctant to let the two cans of film out of his sight.

"Damn it!" Dom snapped. "We'll never get a new print shipped here in time." He blew air through his lips. "Just when we finally have some prospects lined up for the screening at the Molnia Cinema tomorrow." He turned away, mumbling under his breath, then spun around and scowled at Steve. "We couldn't get a schedule for two days. Now we find out the film was shown at the Leningrad Cinema, without us—or potential buyers—there."

"If there's any way these Russians can screw up something they will," Steve said.

"I think someone may be making pirated videos to sell on the black market," Dom muttered. "Other festival invitees have told me their films have mysteriously disappeared, then reappeared."

Steve narrowed his eyes.

"Right now it could be in someone's studio transferring to a video master." Dom made a derisive sound. "Pirated videos of a film called *Revolution* suddenly appearing all over Russia. Will they be surprised when they see it's about the 1960's hippies in the U.S.A." He grimaced. "If the Germans know they can get a pirated copy for cheap, they ain't gonna buy from us." He slapped Steve on the back in what was probably intended to be a gesture of reconciliation.

Steve winced, shot him a surprised look.

"I don't know about you, buddy," Dom said, "but I'm going to be banging on Sergei's door bright and early tomorrow morning. If he doesn't have answers, we're going to hotel security about our missing print."

"I'll be there," Steve replied feebly. Kate knew he loved

the night life, hated getting up early. "Now I'm going to get a *sluha*," he grinned. A *valutnaya sluha*.

Dom looked thoughtfully after his departing figure.

"What's that?" Kate asked.

"Hard currency hooker."

"That's why his hair was curled." Steve was a huckster. Dom was a real pro, with two prize-winning films under his belt. He was a sweetheart too. Two months ago he'd handed her the video camera. "Play with it," he'd said with a grin. He knew she was taking classes at Downtown TV, that she planned to apply to NYU's MFA program in filmmaking. Video was cheap. She could experiment, take chances, practice camera angles, close-ups and zooms, learn to edit as she shot. "Bring it," he'd said, "when we go to Russia. Who knows? You might get something really good."

Dom sighed heavily. "I'm beginning to regret Steve's part of the team."

"You think he might be making deals for our print with the pirates?" She wouldn't put it past him.

Dom grunted. "Maybe the film really is lost. Everything is so damn disorganized." He turned his attention back to Kate. "So all that hoodlum got was what you gave him, the twenty dollars and the earrings?"

Kate nodded.

He took her hand in his. "You upset about losing Gilly's earrings?"

"Yeah." Kate felt tears well in her eyes.

"What did this bum look like?"

Kate rubbed her forehead, speaking in fits and starts. "Shaped like a barrel, with a big stomach. Polite, as we entered the cab, saying in English, 'Good evening, ladies.' Once we started moving, he guzzled from an open bottle of vodka and spoke mostly Russian. His hair was black and bushy; his eyebrows thick." She gave a long sigh, shivering. She took a drink of cognac. "He smoked cigarettes that smelled like burning rubber tires."

Dom clenched and unclenched his fists. "I'd like to get my

hands on him." His voice was ragged. "He left you in the awful cold in that desolate place."

"I have a tape." Kate wriggled out of her coat and indicated the recorder in the inside back pocket of her vest. "I turned it on when I realized he was taking us somewhere to rob us." Tears rolled down her cheeks. Impatiently, she wiped them away. "Whatever happened, I wanted to leave a record."

Dom nodded grimly.

"Let's ask Masha to listen to the tape and translate. Then we can decide. Report the crime to hotel security or the police."

Dom's eyes were steely. "We could have lost you. The print *is* lost. We're going to lose money from this trip. Maybe we should have cancelled, after all."

They'd considered it when the wars in the Gulf and the Baltic had heated up. Instead, they'd changed carriers from Pan Am to Finn Air—in case someone had an urge to blow Americans out of the sky. Kate had even made a will leaving everything to Gilly. Not that she had much to leave anyone right now. But in nine months—when she turned twenty-six—that would change. The trust fund her parents left her would transfer to her.

"Hey, kid, don't look so glum." Dom stood suddenly. "I didn't eat much of that awful dinner. And we have to fatten you up."

"What was dinner?" Kate arranged her face in a smile.

"Potatoes, some kind of meat." He raised his brows. "Covered with sauce, chewy, like beef, absolutely tasteless."

"Same as last night."

Kate, on rubbery legs, her arm linked through Dom's, stepped on the elevator beside him. They exited at the tenth floor, entering a charming, wood-paneled room, the Russian Tea Room, where they bought delicious cream-filled pastries, thick, strong coffee in tiny cups. They paid with rubles. Coffee cost forty kopecks, less than ten cents. Pastries and sandwiches were a ruble, less than a quarter.

As Kate drank her second cup of coffee, she began to feel

less fuzzy and noticed for the first time Dom's tired eyes, the deep lines around his mouth. "You have enough to worry about—with Steve. Now me."

"You're my right hand. I worry about you even when there's nothing to worry about." He shook his head. "Steve's too reckless, impulsive. It makes me edgy." He blew out his breath hard as if he'd been running. "Steve really likes the film. If it hadn't been for him, we wouldn't have had the money to finish it."

Kate nodded. She was tempted to add her own misgivings, for instance, the way Steve treated her—yelling at her or pawing her when Dom wasn't around. But that would have to wait until she saw if Steve could come through with what he promised. He bragged about his connections to big bucks, powerful men who might be interested in investing with Dom's company, Titan Films. "I've been wondering," she asked, "where he gets his money. It can't all come from his three twenty-minute hard core movies."

Dom was thoughtful, as if considering what to say. Then he blurted out, "He also buys up negatives of bankrupt films for $10,000, $20,000, inserts hard core footage, sells the prints in South America. Makes them into videos for the hotel circuit."

Kate was floored. "What a slime ball. And he's working with us?"

Dom shrugged, but looked slightly sickened too. "He knows all the tricks. And we have to learn them, Kate, to survive in this business as an independent. Now with the Iron Curtain countries opening up—but that will be murky business for awhile."

"He gave us $80,000 to finish *Revolution,* he throws $20,000 here and there for negatives of bankrupt films—that's a lot of ready cash." She had been put off by Steve from the first, his selfishness, his arrogance, and now she disliked him even more.

"Wall Street connections. You've heard his stories."

"Over and over."

Dom finished his pastry. He was silent for a moment, as if he were deciding whether or not to confide in Kate. "I just found out," he lowered his voice, "he smuggled pornography into the country."

"You mean when we went through customs, he had his XXX videos with him?"

Dom nodded soberly.

Kate was stunned by Steve's stupidity. "We could end up in Siberia." She grew angry as she remembered it was she who'd carried the briefcase full of videos. The men had been weighted down by the film cans. They'd all marched single file behind a soldier wearing a brown uniform into a brown room. Flat suspicious eyes watched, as one by one, the soldiers stamped their visas, checked their customs declarations. Steve and Dom had unlatched the heavy, metal cans of film so the soldiers could see it was really film, five reels. She'd opened the suitcase of videos, watching as the soldier pawed through them, half expecting by the sour look on his face to be handed a pile of prison clothes.

"He hid the porn tapes in *Revolution* jackets," Dom said, "brought plain Sony jackets flattened out in his luggage. He came to my room this morning to collect the porn flicks. They were still in the brief case, mixed in with the videos of our film. He'd marked the covers of his three tapes with a red dot on the spine."

All the videos were formatted for Russian VCRs, in SECAM 6.25. If the soldiers had decided to spot check the tapes, the pornography could have been discovered by a random screening, right then and there in Customs. "What if we'd been caught?" She felt a chill.

"We'd have had a chance to test out the *blat* system," Dom grinned.

"A bribe? Do soldiers take bribes?" Those soldiers had seemed hard as nails, pitiless about the rules. She couldn't imagine them relenting.

"Everyone here takes bribes, I'm told."

"Steve is such a jackass!" Kate exclaimed.

"He thinks the newly liberated countries are sex-starved."

Dom's big hands played with the tiny demitasse cup. "No Russians have the money now to buy—except for the black market gangs that deal in illegal currency. Steve might have found some buyers for the porn—it might have been worth the risk—if the government hadn't taken fifty and one hundred ruble notes from circulation." He made a face. "We all might have found buyers."

The rubles had been withdrawn a day before the festival, part of the government's plan to curb the black market manipulation of the ruble. The country was in chaos. The festival was nearly bankrupt.

So was Dom's small company, Titan Films. If he went under, she'd be out of a job, and her "career" in the movie business would be cut short. She'd gone through tight times before with Dom. He'd take her off the payroll, she'd go back to office temps until foreign residuals rolled in and the company was flush again. "Okay, the Russians aren't buying," Kate said. "But we have West Germans and some Japanese, right? If the print doesn't turn up for tomorrow's screening, we'll show them the video."

"Yeah," he said dispiritedly.

Kate squeezed his hand. Dom hated video—the smallness of it. He wanted prospective buyers to experience the film on the big screen, to be invaded by the big sound of the sixties music, to be swept away by its psychedelic vision.

Dom returned her squeeze. "The porn makes all of us vulnerable. Not only Steve. I hope no one goes snooping in his room. Sometimes I think I'd like to be able to pay him off and get rid of him—except—a tiny part of me believes him when he says he can get the Wall Street types to come through for *The Flying Eagles.*"

This was Dom's pet project because his father had been in the famous 101st Airborne, the Flying Eagles, the parachute division. Their jump behind the German lines into Holland to win World War II was to be the subject of his next film, a feature, a tribute to his dad.

"The movie business makes us all crazy," Dom said with a sigh. "People are desperate to get in the door. They'll do anything for the glamour, potential money, access to pretty women, prestige. Some commit murder. Some," he said grimly, "kill themselves from the awful pressure of trying to raise the huge sums of money required even for a low budget film. We'll need at least twenty million for *The Flying Eagles*. That's without stars. Some, like me," he gave her a quirky grin, "get divorced." He offered her a Rolaid.

She shook her head. Poor Dom. His stomach had been a wreck since his divorce. Then the money problems had kicked in. He'd lost a big investor who said he was tired of putting money on a dead horse. In fact, Dom had been so discouraged that he'd come to her for comfort. She might have gone to bed with him out of sympathy, but by then she'd met Gilly. And so had Dom.

Chapter Four

10:45 PM, Sunday, January 27

Weary, longing for sleep, and the safety of her room, Kate stepped off the elevator at the fourth floor. There was that soldier again, with the piercing blue eyes, the white face, pale eyebrows, and dark red hair under his military cap. He was talking with the *dejurnaya,* the woman behind the glass desk who monitored the floor.

Kate had been running into him for the past two days—ever since she'd shot the video footage. She'd been aiming her camera at the man with the monkey, not seeing the scar-faced officer with his many medals sitting at a table in the bar behind him. According to her guidebook, taking pictures of the military was not allowed. Or maybe it was not allowed before *perestroika.* Anyway, the officer with the medals, the black hair plastered to his skull like a cap, and the scar through his eyebrow had stared at her fiercely. Dom said that was because she was pretty, young, and American. Steve—typical Steve—said it meant he wanted to sleep with her. But it wasn't a come on. It was a cold look, almost vicious.

Since then, the red-haired soldier seemed to be every place she was, in front of her or behind her. Maybe he wanted to requisition the footage because the man with the scar was a big-wig in the military. But the soldier wouldn't have to ask her for the video. He could wait until she went out, then search her room, getting the key from the *dejurnaya.* Maybe it was true, the rumor that these women, one in charge of every floor, worked for the KGB.

Kate passed the soldier as she went over to retrieve her room key. When he saw her, his eyes blinked rapidly and he turned paler than usual. He quickly did an about face and hurried down the hall, exiting through the stairwell door. He held his arm against his side as if he were concealing something under his jacket. He'd been in her room. She knew it. He'd taken the video. The joke would be on him since the video was blank. And the video with the scar-faced officer was in one of her vest pockets. Thank god for her vest with its many pockets! It had belonged to her mom, one of the few concrete things she had from her.

The *dejurnaya,* impassive behind her glass-topped desk, handed Kate her key. Each flicker of her cool grey eyes was like the click of a camera lens.

In her room, Kate was almost disappointed to find that everything seemed to be in order. The video camera was still hidden in the bag of dirty clothes. Were the socks on top of the camera arranged differently? *Absurd,* she told herself. She was on hyper-alert. But even before tonight's mayhem—from the moment the three of them had stepped off the airplane and were herded, exhausted, through Customs by grim-faced soldiers, she'd felt as if she were being spied on.

She'd caught the red-haired soldier watching yesterday when Steve had grabbed her by her vest outside Competition Hall, pulled her to him, and tried to kiss her. As she struggled to get away, the soldier had taken a step as if he'd wanted to help. When she'd stomped on Steve's foot, the soldier had flashed her a grin.

Maybe he was trying to work up courage to speak to her, curious about her life in America.

As she shucked off her coat, something fell out of her pocket onto the floor—the "cab" driver's car keys, a grim souvenir. She put them on her dresser.

Better take off her shoes. The cold and wetness had seeped through two pairs of socks. She stripped them off and put on dry ones. She fidgeted, too wired to think about sleeping. She opened the blue silk drapes and looked out the window. The street was lined with dingy piles of snow. Beyond, the Neva River lay like a thick black snake coiled around chunks of ice. A great shot—if the camera was good enough to catch the river's silver highlights reflected off the streetlamps, and the light from the windows of the Hermitage on the far bank.

She retrieved her video camera from the dirty clothes and aimed through the glass. What was wrong? The camera wasn't working. The tape wouldn't move. She pushed the eject button and the video cassette holder opened. There was no tape inside. She felt goosebumps all over.

Before she'd left for Masha's flat to meet with the "unregistered group" of women, she'd put the blank tape in her camera, half as a game, in keeping with the "cloak and dagger" stuff in her Russian guidebook that warned about photographing or videotaping *forbidden* subjects. She felt light-headed realizing her test produced results: proof that the red-haired soldier *had* been in her room. He'd taken her blank tape, thinking he was getting the one she'd hidden in the lower right pocket of her vest.

Did he want the footage of the scowling officer with the ribbons and the scar? Or something else?

She slid the videotape out of her vest pocket, playing it through the camera VCR to see if she could get a clue. First was stuff she'd shot in the States. Scenes with Gilly, horsing around. Her heart did a flip when she saw Gilly, grinning and waving and looking fantastic. Kate froze the frame, felt a flush of warmth. She pushed Play, saw herself walk into the scene, saw Gilly grab her, kiss her, and pretend to swoon. Kate forced her mind away from Gilly.

Quickly, she looked at the rest of the footage. Dom and Steve at the New York office, all dressed up in tuxes. The limo that had come to pick them up. Jump to the opening ceremonies of the film festival, inside the Competition Hall. The lush red curtains lifted. A twenty-member choir dressed in black and white sang a stirring, solemn song. Archival newsreel footage of Stalin, scenes of World War II flashed across a screen. After the moving intro, tinged with the orderly past (the opposite of the present chaos in the streets), the president of the festival press-centre spoke about the Soviet troops in Latvia, the order to eliminate cameras, the deliberate shooting of the cameramen in Riga. "Once again," he'd said in accented English, "people appreciate brave reporting from dangerous places. Once again, artists take risks and once again, everyone has to rethink what it means to create."

That message went straight to Kate's heart.

Next on the tape was the man with the monkey, and beyond him, the beribboned officer at a table in the bar talking deferentially to a civilian with a soft, round face—a baby face, and brown hair that fell limply over his broad forehead. Kate stopped the tape, then edged it forward, frame by frame. The picture was too small to see much detail. She remembered that the man's light-colored business suit had seemed out of place among the casual, dark clothing sported by others in the bar. Perhaps he was an important official here to attend the festival. He'd gazed briefly at her—something in his eyes, shock? anger?—before he turned away. She watched carefully. He was scooping something from the table, and putting it inside his jacket. Then he stood abruptly and disappeared into the depths of the bar.

She fast forwarded, stopping and starting, through the Russian Orthodox Church service at the Leningrad Religious Academy, then the Ceremony of the Flowers in Piskaryovskoye Cemetery to honor the 650,000 victims who'd starved to death during the Siege of Leningrad. Quite impressive, Kate remembered, with the soldiers in formation, stirring music—Tchaikowsky or Shostokovich—piped from a dirty blue van. She hadn't dared tape the soldiers. She'd had to settle for a furtive shot of Dom, as the two of them marched up the path in the midst of the mourners, seven or eight abreast, carrying red carnations. A small battalion of soldiers stood at attention as the people filed by, some weeping, and placed their flowers on the wreaths.

Kate had been very moved to be walking on Russian soil with Russian people, paying respect to their dead, thinking of the time, forty-six years ago, when they'd all been united against a common enemy. Now the country was divided, uncertain. At the end of the ceremony, the battalion goose-stepped out, broke ranks. Outside the cemetery, she and Dom tried to cross the street through a group of soldiers who strolled along, aimlessly chatting. The men, arrogant and gratuitously rude, ordered them to halt, as if they were lowlifes in an occupied country. They waited respectfully until the soldiers passed, then crossed to the museum. In a small glassed-in cubicle was a tiny chunk of brown bread, the daily food ration (five grams) during the Siege. Kate felt respect and admiration for the Russian people—and a great sadness.

She ejected the tape from the camera, slipping it once more into her right lower pocket. When she ran out of vest pockets, she'd have to secure the tapes to her belly.

How she missed Gilly. The night before Kate left for Leningrad they'd had a terrible fight about commitment, their future together. Gilly had arrived with champagne. It started as a festive going away party, but turned sour. Kate made accusations hard to take back. She hoped to patch things up when she returned to the States. She still had a key to Gilly's place. She could stop by on the pretext of returning it.

Before Gilly, she hadn't had someone to love in a long time—not since college. That had been a real disaster, a scandal, according to Aunt Maureen and Uncle Burt. She'd been afraid to try again. Oh, sure, she'd had a man here and there, but the affairs were short-lived. Not that Gilly and she went to bed right away. The night they met, at a Comedy Club in the Village, Kate felt an electric connection. They went out for coffee and dessert. At the table, Gilly popped out contact lenses, pushed on wire-rimmed glasses. "You look very intellectual. Are you a teacher?" Kate asked. Gilly said no. "I work in films. I hope to direct my own one day," Kate said. "Sounds exciting," Gilly smiled. The two talked until the place closed, found they both were fans of the movies of Fellini, Bergman and Kubrick. When the evening ended, she still didn't know what Gilly did for a living.

Kate felt again the thrill and the terror of that time. For two weeks, they saw each other constantly. When it happened, it was fantastic. Kate shivered, remembering the two of them in bed. Gilly's hands. Gilly's mouth. Gilly's beautiful body when she rose up over Kate, then bent to whisper in her ear, "I think I was always searching for my other half."

▼.▲.▼

ANDRE ENTERED THE SHABBY building. Inside, one naked, low-watt bulb burned. The elevator was broken, as usual. He climbed the cement stairs to the third floor. Food smells, stale and sour, surrounded him. He walked down the dim hallway and banged on the metal door.

His sister Tanya opened it. She was dressed in stiletto heels, a tight short skirt and a low-cut red blouse. She looked cheap and hard. Her girlish softness had disappeared. It made him sad. Her dark eyes were heavily made up, her cheeks bright with spots of rouge.

Andre peered into the apartment. "Where is Kolya?" he asked gruffly.

Kolya lumbered out of the bedroom, yawning and scratching. His shirt was open, his white belly hung over the belt of his pants.

Andre stamped his feet, knocking the snow from his boots. He stepped into the living room and closed the door before he spoke. "She is still alive!" he hissed.

"Who is still alive? My lovely wife Tanya? I doubt it," Kolya grunted. "She is like a stick in bed."

"The American, you idiot. The one you said you killed. She lives. She almost caught me as I was coming out of her room with the videotape."

"I cannot believe it," Kolya said.

"She did not even look the worse for wear." Andre wanted to bust his nose, wipe that silly look from his stupid face.

"I left her out there, in the cemetery. I swear it."

Tanya said wearily, "I am glad she is alive. I did not agree to be mixed up in murder. Neither did my friend Irina when we set this up for you."

"And what a stinking setup!" Kolya said angrily. "Your friend left me holding the bag, with two women to get rid of."

"You told me you wanted to scare her, not kill her," Tanya said disgustedly.

"You want to be liberated—like that American *pizda?*" Kolya yelled.

"Yes, I want to be liberated. From the two-hour wait for potatoes, the four-hour wait for vodka, the standing in line for brassieres and for cosmetics that smell like fish oil. Liberated from my job, eight hours a day standing on my feet, another four hours at night on my back. Liberated from washing your dirty underwear, liberated from my stinking life with you."

Kolya was open-mouthed through her speech, as if he could not believe what he heard. Half-heartedly, he slapped her. "Shut up, you slut."

"Who made me a slut?" Tanya cried.

"Cut it!" Andre yelled. "We have to figure this out. You told me you dumped her body in the pond. And finished off the other one too."

"I said I thought the cold would do the job," Kolya growled.

"Stupid fool. If the Captain has to give the money back, he will kill us all—"

Kolya's eyes were slits. "What money? You said there would not be money until the body was found."

"None for us," Andre stammered.

Kolya stuck his face in Andre's. "You have been holding out on me."

Andre pulled out the pockets of his pants to show Kolya they were empty. "Believe me, comrade, I am just as broke as you."

"How do you know there is money, if you did not get any?" Kolya glared at him suspiciously.

He would have to explain. "When the Captain refused to pay me, I followed him to the fourth floor. He knocked at a door, handed a man the earrings and told him the girl was dead. The Captain took an envelope, a fat one, filled with money. The man said he would give him the other half when he had the videotape."

"What man?"

"I did not see his face. I heard his name. Gregor. He is in the room next door to Kate."

Kolya blinked. "Gregor, eh? A Russian?"

"He spoke Russian with an accent. Maybe from East Germany."

Kolya's lips turned up in a crafty smile.

Andre was sorry now he'd spilled his guts. It was always better if he knew more than Kolya.

"That stinking Captain," Kolya muttered. "Holding out on us when we did the shit work."

"But you did not do it right."

"Next time." Kolya grinned like a shark as he rubbed his thumb over the gash on his cheek.

Andre held up the videotape he had taken from Kate's room. "Did you get it? The American VCR?"

Kolya nodded. "I have to have it back by morning. It took me hours—I had to give the guy a chicken. You owe me."

Andre clapped him on the back. Kolya might be a drunk but he was good at wheeling and dealing. He was a *biznesmany*. He would be called an entrepreneur in America.

Tanya put on her white rabbit fur jacket.

"Where are you going?" Andre asked. "You do not want to watch?"

She laughed mirthlessly. "To work." She slammed out the door. Andre heard her heels tapping on the cement floor of the hall. Poor Tanya. He had looked up to her when he was a little boy. He struggled in his mind to find the image of the old Tanya, pretty, full of life. He had loved to watch her practice, pirouetting around the room. Like a hummingbird, quick and graceful. Onstage, in costume, she was magic.

Andre made a face as Kolya lit a Belomorkanal cigarette. Soon the room was filled with the smell of burning rubber. The two men sat in the dark, each with a glass of vodka, in front of the flickering screen of the small television set. Andre felt a flutter in his chest, anticipating what might be on this video that seemed so valuable. He pushed Play. After a long two minutes, "Snow," Andre muttered. He fast forwarded the tape. Still snow. Just to be sure nothing was embedded in the middle, he started and stopped, growing more and more angry, all the way to the end. "I cannot believe it." He sat for a moment, seething, then he threw the remote on the floor.

Kolya smirked. He lit another Belomorkanal.

"Those are unfiltered," Andre said sharply. "Do you want to die? The smell is repulsive, gives me a headache."

Kolya continued to puff away with an insolent grin on his face. "Now who is the stupid fool?"

Andre was stunned that the tape was blank. Somehow he must have given away that he was after it. That woman Kate was not only hardier than he thought, she was smarter. He had checked every inch of her room. That was the only tape without the plastic wrap. It was in the video camera hidden in the bag of clothes.

He finished his vodka and splashed more into his glass. They were right back where they started. Kate was alive. And she—or one of her associates—still had the videotape they wanted. Now that the vodka had relaxed him, he admitted to himself he was glad she was alive. Maybe if he could get the right video, Captain Iurkov and Gregor, the money man, would let her live. He stood, polished off his vodka in one gulp. "Drive me back to the hotel," he said.

As soon as Kolya pulled into the Taxi stand outside the Hotel Leningrad, Andre leaped out. "Back in a few minutes," he yelled as he hurled the door shut.

Andre ran up the back stairwell to the fourth floor, checked to see the coast was clear, and woke up the *dejurnaya* behind her desk, relieved to hear that the man with the black curls was not in his room. Andre slipped inside, flipped on the lights and found what he was looking for in the dresser drawer. His heart leaped up.

He hurried back to Kolya. Once he'd scrambled into the car, Andre held up videotapes. "Not one but three. All in plain Sony boxes—without the plastic wraps. I found them in the room of the American woman's friend." The stocky man with the black curly hair who acted like he was her husband, yelling at her, touching her. "She must have given him the tape we want. He was out, and he left his key with the *dejurnaya*."

Grinning, Kolya rubbed his hands together.

Back at the apartment, Andre pushed a tape into the VCR and tried to play it. The sound was unintelligible—ghostly moans, bestial howls as if they came from the devil's workshop. The picture was a mass of jumping lines.

"What is this? A kind of code?" Kolya spluttered.

Through trial and error and after another glass of vodka, they discovered that none of the three tapes worked on the American VCR. With much cursing and fumbling, Kolya, a cigarette hanging from his mouth, unhooked it from the TV and plugged in his Russian machine. He slid in a tape. This time a picture appeared, with proper sound.

Kolya cheered and clapped his hands. Andre jumped up from the couch. "At last, things are starting to go our way." He yanked Kolya up beside him. The two did a kind of jig around the room, like two dancing bears. Andre grinned.

Breathing hard, Kolya poured them each more vodka. They clinked glasses. Andre was eager to see what the tapes contained. The man with the envelope of money seemed to want only one tape. Andre hoped he would know the right one when he saw it. His next decision would be whether to take it to the Captain or directly to Gregor, the money source.

The opening credits rolled, in English. Andre was surprised. The tape was a SECAM format for Russian video. Why no credits in Russian?

He gawked at the television, not believing what he saw. A man walked into a room. A woman sat on the bed. The man, still wearing his hat, unzipped his fly. The film went on in that fashion for twenty minutes. Andre could hear Kolya breathing through his mouth. Even Kolya is shocked, Andre thought. "Decadent," Andre murmured. "Disgusting," Kolya said.

They drank and watched all three tapes; they were much the same with slight differences. "These cannot be what they are looking for," Andre said thickly. The room was spinning. It smelled like a chemical plant. The ashtray was full of butts. His eyes stung, his throat hurt. He put his head in his hands. "Pornography. Smuggled in to sell on the black market." He swallowed the remainder of his glass in one long gulp and sank down on the couch, his brain too befuddled to think. He tried to keep his eyes open. Dimly, he saw Kolya eject the tape. Andre felt his head jerk, then he passed out.

※※※

IN THE MIDDLE OF the night, Kate woke up, sweating. Was that a noise? She rolled out of bed and listened at the door. Quiet. Spookily quiet.

Compulsively, she checked her vest, patting the lower right

pocket. All her tapes—the video and the two audiotapes—were still there.

She lay back in bed, her eyes wide open as if she'd just had three cups of coffee, her heart thumping as if she'd run a mile—or two or three in twenty-degree-below-zero weather. She was back in the cemetery, with the dead souls clamoring for her to stay. She drew in long, slow breaths, trying to stave off the panic. Soon she'd start thinking about all the bad things— the grief, the wrong decisions, the shame. Yep, here they were, flashing through her mind like a film loop, her parent's sudden death—dimly remembered—she was only five, going to live with Aunt Maureen and Uncle Dave. Not really her aunt and uncle but that's what she called them. It turned out Aunt Maureen was unable to have children, so she was happy to be a "mother" to Kate. They had become a real family. Dave died when Kate was fifteen, a painful death from cancer. It was awful, unfair. Aunt Maureen fell apart. She married Burt a year later, a huge mistake. Kate had many special memories of Dave. He taught her to catch a football. He took her ice skating. He helped her with math. Kate's eyes stung.

Fast forward through the college fiasco and humiliation, dropping out of school to live in New Jersey with Aunt Maureen and Dave's successor, Uncle Burt, Burt sniping at her all the time. She commuted daily to a local college, getting a B.A. in cinema studies, *cum laude*. She fled across the Hudson to Manhattan, lived in a women's residence, a sixth floor walk-up, did the temps for a year. The next June she answered Dom's ad in the *Village Voice* for production assistant with Titan Films, moved into Dom's building and her own apartment four weeks later, and into a new life. The deal was great—free rent on her office/apartment and a small salary—enough to give her some eats and pay for video classes at Downtown Community TV and Taekwondo lessons, which she decided she needed as a single woman living in New York City. In August she was in San Francisco, part of Dom's Titan Films crew for his six-week shoot to update *Summer of Love*, which became *Revolution*. In mid-October he'd run out of money, and she was out of work while he picked up royalties overseas. A few weeks later, she was back on Dom's payroll, and by then she'd met Gilly. A very good year. *Freeze there.*

As she felt herself relaxing, the loop came round again—with the force of a whip lash. The people she'd let down. She'd disappointed Aunt Maureen and Uncle Burt, her guardians, by being who she was. She'd pressed Gilly too hard to do things she wasn't ready to do, like march in the Gay Pride Parade. Kate had been just as scared, but she'd thought marching together would bind them as irrevocably as a blood oath.

And Sveta? *Don't go there,* Kate told herself. *Sveta made it home okay.* Tomorrow she'd ask Masha to call. She'd arrange to meet with Sveta and learn what she was so afraid of.

As she was about to doze off (finally!), her mind jumped back to the group of women at Masha's, talking about Stalin. "Some people now are beginning to feel that by their silence they were accomplices to the violence against the people." It would be the perfect lead comment into the U.S. part of her guerrilla film, if she decided to have a U.S. part.

She'd come on camera, say something like: "By my silence, I too have had occasion to be an accomplice to the violence against my people." She'd tell how she'd tried to be straight, and when she realized she wasn't, had tried to pass for straight. She was still doing it. She'd wanted to ask Masha about gays in Leningrad, but she'd chickened out. She was such a fraud. A coward.

What the heck, she told herself. What do you care what Masha thinks? You're a documentary filmmaker.

▼▲▼

TANYA KNEW BY HIS clothes he was an American. She liked Americans. They dressed well and they smelled good. They were generous with their money. But they were plastic, without the Russian soul. Kolya, when he had not been so desperate, before he became such a drunk, once had it. So had she. It made her want to cry. Instead, she smiled and raised her glass, toasting the man opposite. He was not bad looking, with his curly dark hair.

"What is your name?" she asked.

"Steve," he said, smiling.

The music was joyful, the champagne and sandwiches excellent. Almost like a vacation. For six months, she had been working out of the back seat of Kolya's car for about twenty-five rubles for every Russian, most of them so drunk they could sleep with a goat and think it was Venus. Foreigners brought much more money. And much more class. She had met him—Steve, now he had a name—two days ago in the hotel bar. They had some drinks. She went to his room.

"This is Dixieland," Steve said in amazement, touching his champagne glass to hers. "American jazz."

The trumpet player lowered his instrument and sang in English, "When the Saints Go Marchin' In." The crowd in the Jazz Bar clapped their hands and stamped their feet. Some danced.

When the song was over, Steve laughed. "He sounds just like Louis Armstrong! Fantastic!"

The band played a slower number, "In the Mood." Tanya hoped he would ask her to dance. But he drank and gave her a lecture about the movie business. The noise was loud. He talked between the songs. He told her she had good bones that would show up well in films. He took her phone number, said he could make her another Greta Garbo.

After the champagne and sandwiches, he asked what else she wanted. "Chocolates." Chocolate was scarce. She hadn't had any in months. He bought her a box. She gorged herself. It was almost a romantic evening.

She hoped he would invite her back to his hotel room—even though she would be taking the chance of running into that American girl. The hotel was like a palace, with the red-carpeted stairs, the marble staircase. Instead, he hailed a taxi, jumped on her in the back seat. Just like old times, she thought sourly. Except he gave her thirty dollars—ten dollars more than the other night, worth over nine hundred rubles on the black market, and he said he might have a job for her. "I will call you," he said, "about an audition for my next film. I plan to shoot it here in Leningrad."

Climbing the stairs to her flat, she allowed herself a little hope. Maybe her new friend Steve would help her get out of this dismal life. Her beginnings had been promising. At twelve, she was a star pupil at the ballet school. At sixteen she had danced professionally at the Kirov. At twenty, she landed hard on a jump, popped a knee. The ligament was badly torn. She needed surgery. That ended her career. She still limped when the weather changed.

She met Kolya at the university. He was thinner then, aggressive but not so domineering. He was in radio engineering. Not much money there. After they married, she took a job in an art store, did modeling on the side. Modeling became escort and escort became . . . hell. Kolya said it would be temporary—a year ago. But the shortages, the rationing, the queues seemed to get worse. Soon a loaf of bread would cost a month's pay—if you could find any bread to buy. She was almost thirty, she looked forty when her knee was hurting. How much longer could she live this way?

She unlocked the door. At least they did not have to share a *kommunalka* with fifteen other people. Lucky for them, the flat came to her after her parents died.

Inside, Andre was asleep sitting up on the couch. Kolya was gathering up a package, on his way out the door. He held out his hand. She passed him twenty dollars, sneaking out ten dollars for herself. He held the package tenderly as if it were a baby. "Here is what we have been waiting for." He motioned for her to come with him.

Chapter Five

2:30 AM, Monday, January 28

Ten minutes later, Tanya sat in the car, slumped next to Kolya. Snow was falling, her knee was killing her, and she was oh so tired. Kolya prodded her with his elbow. "Put on lipstick."

"No more work tonight. It's 2:00 AM," Tanya said. "I already gave you money."

When Kolya pulled up at the Hotel Leningrad, she sat up with a start. "Are you stupid? We could run into that American girl. She will recognize you."

"She will be in bed." Kolya took out a videotape in a Sony box from the package on the seat beside him. He grinned. "We will play this Gregor, this money guy, like a fish."

The soldiers at the front door knew Tanya, so they let her and Kolya through the barricade.

"Andre said he was on the fourth floor—next to the girl." Kolya took her arm and marched her, limping, to the elevator.

Tanya racked her brain. Fourth floor? Steve's floor! She did not like this one bit.

The elevator opened. Tanya stepped out, looked both ways. All clear—so far. The *dejurnaya*, a blanket pulled up to her neck, slept on two chairs behind her desk. From her station, three corridors branched out like spokes in a wheel.

"Ask where the girl is," Kolya whispered. "Tell her she is expecting us."

"Excuse me," Tanya said. The woman yawned and rubbed her eyes. Tanya held out two rubles. "The tall, dark-haired American girl? She is waiting for a delivery." Tanya nodded toward the tape Kolya held. The *dejurnaya* lethargically reached for the money. "Second door on the right." She pointed down a hallway.

Tanya had been drinking quite a bit the night she came here with Steve but she was almost sure that his was the first room in this corridor, the one closest to the *dejurnaya*. The

American girl's would be next to his. Tanya pointed, whispering, her nerves screaming. "This is hers."

"Gregor. The man with the money is in which room?" Kolya frowned. "Right or left of her?"

"This one," Tanya said quickly, indicating the room on the left, hoping she was correct. She did not want to wake up the film producer at this hour, especially with Kolya here.

Kolya told her what to say and tapped at the door. Silence.

"Probably in bed." Tanya turned to leave. Kolya roughly pulled her back. He knocked again more loudly. A man's voice, thick with sleep, asked through the door, "*Da?*"

"Gregor, I am a friend of the Captain. I have important information," Tanya said, her voice wavering.

After a pause, the door opened. A man in a bulky white bathrobe appeared, one hand in his pocket, his eyes puffy with sleep.

Kolya thrust Tanya forward, grinning.

The man was tall, his shoulders broad, but he had a softness about him, like rotten fruit. Tanya gave him her business smile, perfunctorily coquettish. With an insolent stare, he looked her up and down. She quickly pointed to the tape Kolya held. "We are here for the rest of the money."

Gregor ran a hand, the one that wasn't in his pocket, through his limp brown hair.

Kolya held out the videotape, still grinning.

Gregor took it as if it were something dirty. His eyes were light blue, clear but hard like glass. His face was broad and chubby.

She felt perspiration on her upper lip. She wanted to turn and run. Kolya nudged her. She said, "Well, Gregor, we know all about you and the American girl." She pointed to the right, toward her room.

His jaw tightened. Then he smiled, a dimple showing in his plump cheek. He motioned for them to come in. Tanya didn't like his sudden shift of mood, but as soon as he opened the door wider, Kolya barged through. Tanya followed uneasily.

The man sat on his rumpled bed and gestured for the two to sit opposite. Maybe he knew the girl was still alive. His room was next to hers. But Tanya told him, "The American woman is not dead."

His face flushed, the veins in his forehead popped out. "Who are you? What is your game?"

Tanya, her heart pounding in her ears, spoke in a rush. "We are here to help you. I am Tanya, the sister of Andre, the soldier who works for the Captain. This is my husband, Kolya."

Gregor lurched to his feet, strode over to the dresser.

Tanya held her breath as Kolya jabbered, blaming Andre in the bungling of her death, saying he was spineless, that he'd wanted it to look like an accident. Kolya drew himself up, pacing the room, rubbing his cheek where the American woman had cut him. "I will take my time," he muttered, "then kill her." He took out a knife strapped to his ankle, ran a finger along its edge, drew blood.

Tanya's eyes flicked to Gregor. His hand left the pocket of his robe and he reached for something on the dresser. When he brought it up, she saw, with relief, that it was his wallet, not a weapon. He handed Kolya two fifty dollar bills, American.

Tanya felt faint, thinking about the groceries that would buy. If Kolya did not drink it up. Or buy more goods to sell on the black market. If food miraculously appeared again on the shelves.

Kolya seemed stunned too, mumbling, "You will see. I will get that *pizda*."

Gregor scooped up the videotape in the Sony box from the unkempt bed. His eyes drilled through Tanya, ground into her very bones. She felt as if she might float to the ceiling, leaving a pile of white dust on the floor. "I am not sure if it is what you want," she said breathlessly. "But it was taken from the American woman's room."

Gregor nodded brusquely, his hand back in his pocket. "I will watch it with interest."

He didn't roll the r's like the Russians, Tanya decided, but he didn't pronounce the letter like an English r either. He didn't sing his sentences like a native, but went up at the end. His speech was hard and flat, he was unable to say soft vowels correctly. Maybe an Eastern European accent, with a trace of something else. Arrogance, perhaps.

Gregor opened his door and motioned they should leave.

As soon as the two were gone, Gregor viewed the video, quickly saw it was not what he wanted. He felt a flash of anger, followed by a barrage of doubts. None of this was working out the way he had hoped. He should be in Nizhnevartovsk now, and from there to Moscow for the last step in this intricate dance. He had given the pair two fifties, as much to get rid of them as anything else. The machinery was delicate, the structure like a house of cards. He was disturbed that they now knew what he looked like and how to find him. He played a bit more of the tape, distracted by the crudeness of it. He rewound it and slid it into its package.

Gregor drew the gun from the pocket of his robe, savoring the feel of its slim handle, its easy balance. The Sig-Sauer, a semi-automatic, was the Rolex of the nines. He had purchased it knowing he would be foolish not to come protected, but he preferred to pay other people to do his dirty work.

He was not sure about Captain Iurkov, who, on the surface, sucked up to him. Gregor felt his underlying contempt. The man was unpredictable. As a member of *Spetsnaz,* he had committed unspeakable acts. Nor was Gregor sure about the tricky *apparatchiks,* now involved. They were greedy, but not too precise about getting the job done. He would pay a visit to the Captain. Perhaps he could shed some light on the unexpected visitors, the fat drunk Kolya and his pale, limping wife Tanya. Gregor debated about taking the gun with him, but decided not to. He opened the briefcase on his dresser, placed the weapon inside, next to the silencer, a magazine with nine shots, and a black balaclava. Beneath his artillery was a thick envelope filled with papers important to his future. He locked the briefcase and put it in the dresser drawer.

The next decision: what to wear for Captain Victor Iurkov. He had with him several costumes in preparation for what might develop. He removed his bathrobe, put on a white shirt and light gray tie, donned his gray designer suit, his power suit. This, plus the hour—it was almost three o'clock in the morning—would give him a distinct advantage.

He walked up the back stairs to the seventh floor, carrying the tape. He knocked on the door. "Captain Iurkov." When the door opened, he felt, as always, repulsed, fascinated, and a little frightened by the man's disfigured face. With each change of expression, the Captain's scars writhed like worms.

Gregor pushed his way inside with a bravado he did not feel. "I hope I did not wake you," he said. The loud beating of his heart subsided when he saw that he had roused Captain Victor Iurkov from his bed, caught him in his underwear. Out of uniform, without his ribbons and his tall boots, in his briefs and old fashioned *mika* (sleeveless undershirt), he looked almost like a bank clerk or a streetcar conductor—from the neck down. "Two idiots, stinking of alcohol, came to my room just now with this." He held the video in the Captain's face. "They said you had sent them. They wanted money. What is going on? Are you trying to trick me?"

Victor Iurkov blinked several times, apparently trying to wake up. "Say that again."

Gregor did, more forcefully. "Supposedly, this video was taken from the American woman's room. *Dermo.* Pornography."

"Someone brought you a pornographic video and asked for money?"

"Not even good pornography." He was amused by the perplexity on the Captain's face.

At last the light seemed to dawn. Suspicion replaced confusion. "What did he look like?" the Captain asked. "Was he a soldier?"

"Civilian. With a fat gut. He had a woman with him. Pretty, with a limp. Hard looking."

"I did not send them." Captain Iurkov frowned. "I think I

know, from your description, who they are. They were helping my soldier Andre do the job you wanted done."

"Everything was to be discreet."

"Believe me, it is not in my best interest either." After a moment, Captain Iurkov spoke softly, almost to himself. "Andre must have followed me when I brought you the earrings. And he passed on his information to your visitors."

"You should have been more careful."

The Captain's face flushed. The zigzag scar through his eyebrow glowed in *bas relief*.

"You have gotten soft, sloppy without a war."

The Captain's mouth tightened. His eyes flashed with anger.

Gregor felt a flutter of fear. He forced himself to stare the Captain down. "Did you know the girl is still alive?" He was mollified to see the Captain look flabbergasted.

"Andre said— He had her earrings. As proof."

"Andre is a *dolboeb*."

The Captain marched over to the night table. In spite of his underwear riding up his leg, he achieved a pathetic dignity. He fumbled a cigarette, black with a gold foil tip, from a pack of Sobranies, lit it, inhaled deeply. Made from the best tobaccos, Gregor knew. A strong but pleasant smell filled the room.

"I was told by my contacts in Moscow that the job could be done cheaply and easily. You seem to have taken my money under false pretenses." Gregor paused, relishing the panic on the Captain's face. He had probably spent it. He smoked expensive cigarettes. A nearly empty champagne bottle stood on the nightstand, alongside two fluted glasses. Gregor was curious about the sort of woman who might be attracted to the scar-faced Captain. His hair was styled, Gregor suspected, to intimidate, shaved close to the skull up the sides and in the back, longer on the top but flattened to look like a cap.

"We will try again, with your permission." Captain Iurkov made a slight, formal bow, his eyes like black ice. "If we fail, I will return your money. I am a man of honor."

On the way out the door, Gregor tossed the video to the Captain. "You have four days to kill the girl, requisition her video." He exited. The door closed softly.

Gregor heaved a sigh, relieved to be out of that room, away from that disturbing presence, but pleased with his own performance. Captain Victor Iurkov had been put on notice to take his job more seriously. Then, too, that fat slob Kolya he had just paid handsomely might accomplish something on his own. Kolya looked as if he had a debt to settle. It always paid to hedge your bets. In a few days, the festival would end and the American *pizda* would leave. Gregor walked to the stairs at the end of the hall. In addition to his Moscow contact and the ugly Captain, three more people knew about him. He might have to cut his losses, try a different tack.

When he returned to his room, his clothes were soaked with sweat. He stripped off the gray jacket, the pants, his shirt and tie, leaving them in a sodden heap on the floor. He rinsed off in the tub, then hung up his clothes in the bathroom to dry. He would have to send his suit jacket out to be cleaned. He could not go to Nizhnevartovsk stinking.

What had seemed so brilliantly simple now seemed filled with pitfalls. He must call Moscow to say he was delayed. He hoped he could get through. The phone system was crap.

He must call his boss too and cover his tracks. "Do what you have to do," his boss had said, but he did not want to know the particulars, the unpleasant, gritty reality of what must be done to achieve the desired results. His boss was weak. His weakness was his love for her.

••*•*

ANDRE WOKE UP. HE ached all over. What time was it? 3:00 AM. He had better hustle. "Kolya? Tanya?" He staggered toward the bedroom. The door gaped open. The unmade bed was empty. They were gone. He lurched back into the living room. The porno tapes were missing. Where could Kolya sell them at this hour?

Andre sat down, his head in his hands. He should never try to drink as much as Kolya. What should he do? He had to level with the Captain, tell him she was still alive, that he could not find the video. He felt his knee jump up and down. He was trembling like a girl. He went into the bathroom and poured cold water over his head, shaking it fiercely. He stared at himself in the mirror. He was unshaven, with dark circles under his eyes. If he did not go to the Captain, the Captain would come to him.

❧

AT THE SOUND OF the alarm, Kate's eyes flew open, her heart pounding loudly in her ears. She was surprised she'd slept at all. She'd survived the night. Should she report the abduction to the authorities? Tell hotel security the red-haired soldier had been snooping in her room? Run to the Embassy? Go home?

She sprang out of bed, felt the lower right pocket of her vest. The videotape and two audiotapes were safe. This was the trip of a lifetime, she decided, a crucial moment in Soviet history. She'd regret it the rest of her life if she wimped out now. Things here just weren't the same as in the U.S.

She pushed back the drapes. The Neva River sparkled in the sunshine, not nearly as sinister-looking as last night. On the far bank was the cruiser Aurora, whose guns had fired the blank round that signaled the beginning of the October Revolution in 1917. Behind it was the Hermitage Museum, baroquely ornate, the Winter Palace of Czar Nicholas II until it was stormed by the Bolsheviks.

She opened a new tape and slid it in her video camera. She started wide, capturing the Hermitage, zoomed in on the Aurora, gleaming in the sunshine—silent for the moment.

She dressed. This was the morning she and Dom planned to storm Sergei's room, demanding to know the whereabouts of *Revolution*.

Even though she planned to carry her camera with her, she

layered her socks carefully at the top of her bag of dirty clothes. First, a sock with a blue trim, then a red trim, a plain white one, two reds, a blue, another red. If the soldier came snooping while she was out, she wanted to know. She wrote down the sock order on the back of one of her business cards, sliding it in her jeans pocket.

She knocked at Steve's door. "Who's there?" he asked in a low voice. He sounded so suspicious she couldn't resist teasing him. She put her face close to the crack in the door and whispered, with an accent, "It is Anastasia. Please. You not remember me?"

He opened the door and faked a laugh. He knotted his necktie, the same yellow one he'd worn last night. His dark hair hung limply almost to his collar. Not a curl left. His eyes were bloodshot. "Late night." He tried to grin. "Too much champagne." He glanced down at the video camera she held. "Hey, can I borrow that tonight?"

"Sure. If I'm not using it," Kate said cautiously, curious about his plans for the camera. "Dom's expecting us to pick him up."

They walked silently past the *dejurnaya* to the other hall, and knocked on Dominick's door. "I'll be a minute." He motioned them inside, sat on the bed, putting on his shoes, looking up at Steve. "Have fun last night?"

"I went to the Jazz Club. Really something. The guy there, he sang like Louis Armstrong." Steve paused, then blurted out in a whisper, "My triple-X videos are gone. All three were missing from my dresser drawer when I came back last night."

"Are you kidding?" Dom asked, his face ashen.

"Did anyone besides us know about them?" Kate asked. "Did you try to sell them?"

Steve shook his head. "No one else knew." He looked helplessly at Dom, who threw a quick, worried glance at Kate.

"Somebody's been in my room too," Kate said. "A videotape was stolen from my camera."

"They think we all have pornography. Good work, Steve," Dom said sarcastically. Shoelaces flapping, he rushed over to the *Revolution* tapes stacked on the dresser and shuffled through them, making sure a video was inside every box. "All accounted for."

"That girl outside behind the glass desk—always watching. I bet she knows something." Steve turned, as if to confront her.

Dom grabbed his arm, biting his words off. "Don't fly off half-cocked."

Steve yanked his arm away. The two men glared at each other. Steve's jaw was thrust out aggressively. If only once he'd admit he was wrong. "I think I know who it was," Kate said quietly. "That soldier who's been following me, the one with the pale face and the red hair."

The men looked at her in surprise.

"You saw him, Steve, yesterday, near the entrance to Competition Hall, watching us."

"I don't remember," Steve mumbled.

"You didn't tell me about the red-haired soldier." The concern in Dom's eyes changed to hurt.

Kate smiled. If he couldn't be her lover, he'd be her father. And that was okay. She scarcely remembered her father. He'd died so long ago. "The soldier's been tailing me—ever since I took the video footage. You know, the man with the monkey and the military officer behind him in the bar . . ."

"I remember," Dom, frowning, pulled at his beard, "the ugly scar. The Tatar face, the weird haircut—like a black skull cap."

"I think they want that tape."

Steve broke in. "Because you took his picture with a monkey?" He forced a laugh. "Great imagination, Katie."

"Let me finish, please." Kate took a deep breath, turned back to Dom. "Last night, when I returned to my room, the soldier came out of my corridor, almost bumping into me. He seemed guilty and afraid." She ignored Steve's snort. "I knew in my gut he'd been in my room. He was holding something under his jacket. I was sure it was the blank video I'd deliberately put in my camera."

"Why would he want a blank video?" Steve asked scornfully.

"He didn't know it was blank." Kate was ready to slug him.

"I took out the tape they wanted and put in a substitute. As a test, to see if I was being overly paranoid." She looked at Dom for backup. "Last night, after I left you, I opened my camera. My test video was gone." Dom nodded. Steve squinted, pretending to think.

"I have the tape they were after—or I think they were after." She patted her lower right vest pocket.

Dominick frowned, then groaned. "Maybe the soldiers at the airport were suspicious and alerted the soldiers here to keep an eye on us, search our rooms."

"Why don't they confront us face to face, instead of pussyfooting around?" Kate fumed. "What do they really want? Steve's porn? My videotape of the officer with the scarred face and the chest full of medals?" Tapes, Kate reminded herself. She had three now, counting the audio-taped criticisms from the women at Masha's meeting and the secret audiotape she'd made of the abduction. "Are they going to threaten to arrest us and demand a bribe to let us go?" Kate realized they were all whispering, as if the room were bugged. "One thing we know for sure," she said, loudly and defiantly. "We're under scrutiny." She had a sudden thought. Had the fat drunk with his fake cab followed her and Masha last night to Masha's apartment? Had he waited specifically for Kate—or for just anyone who might be leaving that illegal meeting?

Dom bent to tie his shoelaces.

Kate swallowed hard. "We all may get a long vacation in Siberia. Hope you brought enough underwear, Steve."

His face turned a dull red. "Come off it, Catherine the Great. Those tapes are better than a sex manual. They'll be begging me for more."

"Okay, guys," Dom said, "our next challenge awaits—to find the print." They walked down to the second floor to confront Sergei, the *apparatchik* from Moscow who was here to schedule the non-competition films.

Angry voices floated out through the open door to his room. The three of them peeked in. The floor was strewn with film cans. Getting from the bed to the bathroom in the dark without stubbing a toe would be a feat, Kate thought. In the middle of the mess, Sergei stood, slightly bewildered, looking somewhat like a dumpling with his sloping shoulders and broad derriere. Shirttail out, his feet bare, he listened to the complaints of a tall man and a thin-faced woman.

Scattered over what remained of the floor space were socks and underwear. Papers were stacked wildly on the dresser and nightstand. The room was recklessly picturesque, seeming symbolic of the confusion of the festival—and the country. Should she ask him if it was okay for her to shoot? It might spoil the freshness of the moment. Kate hefted her video camera to her shoulder, panning the room. A pair of trousers and a wrinkled short-sleeved shirt were draped over two canisters of film. Part of a title peeped out from beneath the crotch of the pants. . . . *Tunnels.* She zoomed in on it. Quickly, surreptitiously, she widened the frame to include Sergei and the irate couple, then she lowered the camera to her side.

Dom threw her a look, eyebrow raised. "It's professional to ask, less likely to cause problems." He grinned wryly. "We've already got the Russian army after us. We don't need anyone else."

She nodded sheepishly.

His hands clasped in front of him, as if he were praying, Sergei smiled at the tall man and the frowning thin-faced woman, "The schedule will be posted tomorrow morning on Information Board, level B." He lit a cigarette, ran a hand tiredly through his straggly dark blond hair.

"That leaves only two more days," said the man with a plummy British accent, glowering. "What was the purpose of coming if my film is not to be screened?"

Sergei yawned widely. Several teeth were missing. He seemed less sinister. If he were a fat Party cat from Moscow, Kate decided, surely they'd have sprung for his dental bills.

"We can schedule only films we have in hand," Sergei chided. "Many people have cancelled because of the uncertain situation in the Baltic Republics. . . ."

"I sent pictures and a synopsis," the woman grumbled. Her badge said she was from Denmark. "As of today, we have no catalogue—"

"The catalogue is being printed now," Sergei smiled smoothly, "in Helsinki."

"But will we see it before we leave?" the Danish woman growled.

Sergei shrugged with passive resignation.

The two filmmakers, muttering, left. Sergei cast a wary eye at Dom, Steve, and Kate. "Did you find it?" Steve asked abruptly.

"*Revolution*," Kate said. Sergei seemed startled. He must have thought she was recommending it. "Our film," she explained, smiling. "About the hippies in San Francisco."

"Shown by mistake Saturday at the Leningrad Cinema," Dom said. "Without us there to answer questions."

"How did that happen?" Sergei asked, looking surprised.

"You tell us," Dom said politely.

Sergei frowned. "It wasn't scheduled for the Leningrad."

"But it *is* scheduled for the Molnia Cinema at 6:00 PM tonight." Steve planted his stocky figure in front of Sergei, taking a fighter's stance. "If you can find the print. Yesterday you told me it was lost."

Sergei, the cigarette that hung from his mouth dripping ashes, rummaged through a pile of papers on the dresser. He stopped for a moment, his hand hovering over another stack, dug out his wire-rimmed glasses from his pocket, and pushed them onto his face. "I will check the list." The fate of over 100 non-competition films rested on those slumping shoulders. At last he found the sheet he was looking for. He scanned it very slowly.

Kate edged over beside him, peering over his shoulder. The page was in Russian.

"No, the Leningrad is not on the list. It must have been shipped there by mistake. And since it was there," he shrugged, "they showed it."

Intrigued no doubt by its title. "Maybe it's still there," Kate said.

"Playing by mistake," Dom added with a dry smile.

"I will telephone," Sergei said at last, glancing up. "Come back after breakfast."

"I hope you'll have some good news for us by then," Dom said quietly.

"Yeah," Steve broke in, "We'll be back after breakfast. That should give you time to call Transport, get them to pick up the film from the video studio, and hustle it over to the Molnia."

Dom took Steve's arm, pulling him toward the door.

Steve continued. "You know, the studio where they're making illegal copies of all the festival films."

Sergei blinked and smiled tiredly.

Kate was embarrassed by Steve's outburst. But Sergei didn't seem to mind. The angry words rolled off him as if he were made of Teflon. "I will telephone the Molnia to see if the film arrived. If not, I will telephone Transport." Sergei spread his hands, shrugged. "We have many festival volunteers."

"I'll bet you do," Steve said, breaking free of Dom's grip. "Sounds like a cushy job. Over a hundred films to steal. What's your cut?"

Sergei's face was blank.

Dom almost carried Steve from the room. "Look, pal," he said when they were out of earshot. "We're guests here. We don't make accusations like that, not without proof."

As the three of them walked down the stairs to the Mezzanine, Steve made a stab at apologizing. "Sorry. But Dominick, old buddy, you're just too damn polite."

On their way to the Festival Center mailboxes to pick up the morning's press release, Dom nudged Kate, "There's Masha." Kate waved. She noticed Dom following Masha with his eyes as she made her way gracefully toward them, dodging the festival guests milling about. "Did you know," Kate asked, "she was a professional figure skater and won many ribbons? But when she married, her husband made her give up her skates."

"Selfish," Dom murmured, a dark look on his face, perhaps remembering his ex-wife who'd demanded he give up his life in films or she would leave him.

"Masha's divorced now," Kate whispered in his ear, as Masha approached smiling, her blonde hair pulled back in an elegant upsweep. Once again, Kate marveled at her clear skin, her slightly slanted green eyes. "Kate, my friends were so happy to meet you." Masha took Kate's hands. "My mother says you are lovely. And so nice." Masha's eyes narrowed in concern. "Something is wrong?"

"After we left your apartment last night—" Kate blurted out, about to spill details of the terrifying cab ride.

Dom shot Kate a frown, interjecting smoothly, "We need something translated. From Russian to English."

Dom was right. Too many people were drifting around, listening. "Can you come to my hotel room after lunch?" Kate asked.

"We'll pay you for your time," Dom smiled gently down at her.

"Please, no. That is why I am here. To translate."

"Masha." From a few feet away, a harried-looking gentleman, probably a festival official beckoned, calling out, "We need you. You do speak Italian?"

"I do."

How many languages did Masha know? Kate wondered.

"Kate, I will come to your room at one-thirty today." Before Masha hurried away, she said shyly to Dom. "I hope you will be there too."

Dom grinned all the way to the Festival Center. "What a beautiful woman," he exclaimed. "Smart too. You say she's divorced?"

Kate nodded. "With a twelve-year old son. But her ex-husband, who's mentally unstable, has custody of the child. She told her story on my tape last night."

"How on earth did he get custody?"

"When he became sick, the son helped him for a weekend.

Then her ex told her, 'He's not coming back.' He told the son terrible things about her, all untrue. The son's behavior became bad, his grades fell. Her ex even wrote to a Communist Party leader where she worked, saying she was influenced by the West. Luckily, the leader didn't fire her. At that time, no personal contact was allowed with foreigners. Masha didn't want to traumatize her son so she gave custody rights to his father."

"Terrible."

"Now when she visits her son, her ex kicks and beats her."

Dom said, "What a dismal life for poor Masha. And her boy."

Dodging a man's elbow, Kate reached into her mailbox, plucked out several pages copied onto shiny paper, stapled together. These film festival press-releases, delivered in both English and Russian, generated daily by the hotel's press center, were filled with vignettes of festival life, articles about filmmakers, and the philosophy of documentary filmmaking. The days were so full that Kate had trouble finding time to read them—until she discovered that hidden among the informational pieces were political tidbits, guarded but critical of current events in the Baltic countries of Latvia, Lithuania, and Estonia, and in Leningrad. These gems were written in a kind of code, it seemed to her, designed to be deciphered by festival attendees.

Next to the mailboxes, a typewritten list of films (for both Competition Hall and cinemas in the city) had been posted. Despite some countries boycotting the festival, over one hundred fifty films were to be screened. So a start had been made in scheduling! Yay! The titles went on and on, sheet after sheet, wall after wall. From what Kate could see, competition films were mainly from West Germany, USSR, Czechoslovakia, probably heavy, political works. There were "lighter weight" contenders too (not more than two each) from Great Britain, Norway, Japan, USA, France and Switzerland. So far no sign of *Revolution* on the schedule.

By the time she, Dom, and Steve arrived in the dining room, it was filled with filmmakers. *The whole two hundred fifty of them must be here,* Kate thought. The vast hall had an almost cozy feel, with the din of voices, the clatter of plates and silverware, the hot, humid smell of the steam table. No soldiers were present, and, despite the stern-faced uniformed waitresses stationed throughout, an atmosphere of freedom prevailed.

Masha on last night's audiotape had spoken cryptically, as most Russians did, afraid of reprisals. But she'd become almost lyrical as she talked about the soul of the Russian people, their expansiveness, easily expressed feelings, the opposite of what the old regime rewarded—discipline, orderliness, strict observance of the rules.

For her video project, Kate decided she'd dub Masha's speech under footage of the dark-jacketed waitresses here in the dining room, who stood stone-faced, at attention, eyes deep in their heads. It would show how remnants of the old still clung as the country struggled with change.

In a sneaky wide shot, Kate caught the waitresses, then closed in on the array of food behind the metal counter. As she zoomed in for a close-up, she caught the edge of a tall man in a stained white apron that stretched across his huge belly. Under his high chef's hat, his jowly face scowled. She pointed to her camera. He broke into a smile and nodded, stood proudly at attention behind the beets and shredded carrots, hands folded across his stomach.

"*Spaceba,*" she said. "*Pazhalsta,*" he answered, beaming at the white-aproned woman next to him. The woman frowned, shook her head no, and waddled away. Kate focused on the cold appetizers, *zakuski*. Breakfast (and every other meal) started with *zakuski*—beets, shredded carrots, shredded cabbage, cheese, salami, sardines, herrings—everything pickled that could be pickled. She traveled down the length of the steam table, the lens hovering over the potato cakes, the mountain of hard boiled eggs, the puddingy looking *kasha*, hot cereal.

She stowed her camera at the table with Steve and Dom and went again through the cafeteria line. Most Russians would have been delighted by the abundance of food, but Kate longed for scrambled eggs, bacon, hot cakes. The pickled and salty appetizers were hard to take at 8:00 AM. She chose beets and sardines, two hard boiled eggs and a large roll, hoping it was filled with jam, from the stack of breads—always fresh and delicious. From the metal samovar she drew a cup of tea, more satisfying than the weak coffee.

When Kate arrived at the table, three men, Russian-looking and wearing cowboy shirts, were seated across from Steve and Dom. "*Zdrasvuitya,*" Kate said. The men smiled briefly, their eyes hard.

Kate noticed that Dom was having only bread and tea. Steve's plate, on the other hand, was piled high with something of everything. Being such a jerk had made him hungry. "What's that?" she asked, reaching for a large metal pitcher beaded with water.

"Juice," Dom said. "I think."

She poured a pale reddish stream into a glass and tasted it with the tip of her tongue. Cherry juice. Very watered down. Better not drink it, in case it had been diluted with tap water instead of bottled water. She'd been warned that Leningrad tap water carried giardia, a very unpleasant intestinal parasite.

She bit into her roll. No jam, but warm and yeasty. She scanned the pages of that day's press release, her attention caught by: *Forgetting to be prudent, believing only in the importance of information, citizens (during the Peking student uprising of 1989) talked quite freely. Millions watched TV with sympathy. The Secret Police watched and worked, searching for those people who told the foreigners what they thought about the events. Nowadays a situation can change around, plus becomes minus and a hero becomes a supporter of the regime.*

The piece left the reader to fill in the blanks: For China in 1989, one might substitute the USSR in 1991.

Further down, she saw the phrase, *documentary film is evidence.*

Evidence is what she carried in her vest's zippered pocket. One audiotape was critical of Stalin, of the "so-called" democrats, Gorbachev and Yeltsin, of the treatment of women as second-class citizens. If confiscated, it could be used against the women at Masha's—if the rules changed, if plus became minus. The audiotape of the abduction was evidence to give the police if she decided to press charges against the drunken driver who'd left her in the cemetery to freeze to death. The videotape of the scar-faced officer talking with the civilian in the bar—evidence too? Something to consider.

Kate leafed through the pages to find her favorite column, *Through the Window Glass,* that dealt with "the winds of change" in Leningrad. She read:*Leningrad supermarkets are starting to throw out unsold rotten eggs, this, at a time when eggs are rationed. Sexual minorities are protesting.* She wondered if food shortages were so bad that people ate rotten eggs. Or could they not afford the eggs, so they rotted on the shelves? "Sexual minorities" gave her pause. Was it an actual printed reference to gays?

The recent money reform is considered a success. The mafia has lost millions.

In 1989 in the Soviet Union, 276 people were shot. Shot as what? Political dissidents? *The data for 1990 is more accurate.* Did that mean more protesters were killed in 1990 than in 1989?

Kate looked up from her press release. An American filmmaker had joined the table and was chatting with Dom, discussing the price of fame in the U.S—unusual in the documentary world. He'd just come from Sundance. His film was about unions so he'd worn a bulletproof vest when he appeared on the Donohue Show. The men in the cowboy shirts feigned indifference, but one, his eyes tiny and piercing, stopped eating, his fork frozen in mid-air.

Dom, Steve and Kate left the dining room. Kate dawdled outside the main screening hall, scanning the day's list of films in competition. As she rounded the corner, rushing to catch up with Dom, she collided with the red-haired soldier and nearly dropped her video camera. She felt his hands at her waist, steadying her. They were almost dancing. Then, without a sound, he turned and marched back the way he'd come.

Kate watched the soldier until he disappeared beyond the elevator bank. He'd run his hands along her waist. She brushed her palms over the same area, felt the outline of the videotape in her lower right hand pocket.

Thank god for zippers. He could have snatched out the tape in an instant.

She smiled grimly to herself. She'd stay one step ahead of him.

⋮⋰⋮

THE CAPTAIN'S DOOR OPENED. Andre stood at attention, and, bracing himself for a tirade, told him the girl was still alive. The Captain simply stared, his slanted eyes hypnotic.

Andre was tired, hung over, his guard was down. He said more than he intended. That the girl was clever and strong, but he knew now where the tape was. He had confirmed it by bumping into her, had felt something rectangular and hard, the size of a videotape in the lower right pocket of her vest.

"Tonight," Andre said, "when she is asleep I will go into her room, take it from her vest." Then he was sorry he had said it. He did not want the Captain to order him to murder her as she slept.

The Captain nodded. "You have four days until the festival ends. She returns to America."

Andre's throat was dry. He had touched her warm body for an instant. He did not want to kill her. But if he did not complete his assignment as the Captain ordered, it could mean prison for him or worse on some manufactured reason.

"Higher-ups in Moscow have their eyes on us. Get me the tape. Do not screw it up," the Captain said harshly. "I will take care of the rest."

"Killing her, you mean?" Andre's voice cracked.

The Captain nodded.

Andre rubbed his eyes, pretending they were sore, so the Captain would not see the relief—and sadness—in them. "How will you do it?"

"It must look like *avarya,* accident." The Captain glared. "I understand Cultural Programs have been scheduled by festival officials for the rest of the week." His eyes gleamed, his mouth twisted in a smile that quickly disappeared as he held up a videotape. "What do you know about this?"

Andre's heart sank. He recognized the Sony box. So this was where Kolya was last night—not selling the pornographic tapes on the street but bringing them to Captain Iurkov. Did he ask for money? That would have been a terrible mistake. Or was Kolya trying to ingratiate himself with the Captain, edge Andre out?

"Did Kolya bring them?" Andre glanced surreptitiously around the room for the other two pornographic tapes but did not see them.

The Captain wore a thin cold smile. "Not to me."

So that *doorock* Kolya had gone to Gregor with the tapes. Greedy Kolya, always on the prowl for money, alcohol numbing his sense of self-preservation. Not good for Kolya. Not good for Andre either because how else would Kolya know about Gregor, if not for Andre.

The Captain's eyes bored through him. Andre's knees felt weak, but he thrust his chest out, trying to bluff. "I found the tapes. Three of them. From the room of the man with the curls and the bright-colored clothes. Next door to the American girl. The man is her friend. I thought the tape you wanted might be hidden in his room." His face felt hot. "Pornography. We watched, Kolya and I. Filthy Western decadence."

The Captain glanced down at the Sony box in his hand. He was silent for so long that Andre began to sweat. He wanted to unbutton his coat but did not dare move. At last, the Captain raised his eyes. "Three tapes, you said?"

"Kolya must have kept the other two." At the door, Andre stammered, "I am sorry. Kolya overstepped his bounds. I will talk to him."

The Captain's lips curved up. "I will take care of Kolya. You get that *pizda's* videotape." His eyes were merciless.

The door closed in Andre's face. He murmured, "*Mne kreshka.* I am a dead man." He would be if he did not get the tape. He should have stayed in Germany, paid a German woman to marry him. He would be free from this torment.

Kolya, the stupid pig, did not know enough to be afraid.

Chapter Six

1:30 PM, Monday, January 28

Kate, boots off, leaned against the headboard. Dom lounged on the twin bed opposite. Masha sat in the room's one comfortable chair. On the surface, Kate thought, a casual scene, three people relaxing in a small hotel room, a cozy space but austere, decorated in military brown, a length of decadent blue silk draping the window. If you looked closely, her hand that held the audiotape machine was trembling. Dom's face was very stern, his black felt pen poised above the yellow tablet. Masha was frowning, her slim body tense.

"I hope the tape will tell us if it was a random crime, or if it was me," Kate sucked in her breath, "the man was after."

"The times are very bad," Masha murmured with a troubled frown. "He may have wanted your passport. There is an international trade in fake passports stolen from tourists and sold to criminals."

"Ready when you are, K.H.," Dom said.

Kate pushed the play button, feeling half-sick, dreading to re-live this, worried the recorder in her vest under her coat might not have caught it all intelligibly. She'd kept her coat unzipped—to get the best sound quality.

Masha leaned forward, her sleek blonde head bent attentively as Kate's muffled voice filtered through the speaker. *Take us to the hotel. I will give you American dollars.* "I gave him twenty dollars," Kate said. They heard the driver laugh, then say something in Russian. Kate paused the tape.

"He says something like, 'We get more money than that.'" Masha's eyebrows raised. "Taxi drivers sometimes work for and report to KGB."

Kate pushed Play. Next came Sveta, moaning, *So sorry. I think is my fault.* Kate pushed Pause. "Why her fault?"

Masha shook her head. "We shall see."

Kate started the tape again, her finger poised to push the Pause button as soon as Masha was ready to translate. It was tough to sit and listen.

Masha narrowed her eyes in concentration. "Now Sveta says, 'Don't hurt her. Take us to the Olgino.' The man answers, 'We will stay here where we will not be bothered. Scare her, get her money. Get anything we want.' Sveta says, 'Do not try anything funny.' 'Why not?' he asks."

Was he going to rape them? A ramshackle shed stood at the edge of the pond. *Take me to the hotel,* Kate heard herself say. Then, *Tell him my ears are pierced,* her voice husky with fear. She saw the scene through the dirty windows of the car, the falling snow, the pond with dark holes in the ice. She could be buried there. "We're at the cemetery now," she said, sweat trickling down her armpits. She saw Dom's troubled glance.

Sveta's shrill voice cut through Kate. "She tells him," Masha struggled to be heard over Sveta, "'Let her go. This is mistake.' Something about—it is difficult to hear—please play again." Kate did. Masha shook her head.

Then came a clear shout, in Russian.

"What's that?" Dom asked.

"A curse word." Masha blushed. A spate of Russian followed, punctuated by Sveta's high-pitched pleas. Kate stopped the tape, waited for Masha.

"She is angry, says, 'Why are you doing this?' She begs, 'Do not hurt her. Take her money, let her go.' Would you play again, please?" Kate did. "The man says something about Andre—a person called Andre."

Kate shook her head. Who was Andre? "Was the driver talking about himself?"

Masha shrugged, but didn't look convinced.

Silence. The crackle of paper. The scene replayed in Kate's mind: the man picking up the brown paper sack from the floor. The car door opening. An ear-splitting scream.

"Sveta says, 'What are you going to do?' He says, 'Teach her a lesson. And if you don't shut up—'" Masha looked at Kate, alarm in her green eyes.

Kate paused the tape. "Why just me? Scare *me*? Teach *me* a lesson?" She pushed Play, heard herself grunt. "I'm climbing over the front seat, grabbing his keys. He's yanking my arm." *You get what you deserve . . .* He spat out the words as if he wanted to kill her. Kate gave Masha a questioning look.

"You are American," Masha said, "a woman, wearing pants, independent—different from Russian women."

They heard the man roar in pain. "I caught him on the cheek. I cut him." Kate stood, scooped up the keys to the fat man's car from her dresser top, and slashed at the air with them.

"Now I'm running." Kate heard the man behind her, his growls and grunts a macabre accompaniment to her sighs and groans. His blaring voice, *You need my big Russian . . .*

Kate fast forwarded the tape. It shrieked. Then she slowed it to normal, heard herself yell, *Sveta, are you okay?* A loud crack, like a shot. Sveta's disembodied voice, *I'm okay.* Another loud crack. The snapping of twigs, muffled sounds of her feet pounding the ground, panting and wheezing. The tape stopped. It had played through to the end.

Kate closed her eyes, exhausted.

"Did he have a gun?" Masha asked.

Kate shook her head uncertainly. "He had a brown paper bag in his hand when he left the car. I thought it was more vodka. As I was running, he threw something. It plopped in the snow—like it was heavy. Maybe a rock was in that bag. Or he might have had a gun. Sveta went one way and I went another. I remember only one loud crack. It sounded before Sveta called out she was okay. But I heard two in the tape just now. You think he'd have killed me—us—just for the hell of it?" Hearing now that second shot—if that's what it was—gave Kate pause. Did Sveta get home after all? Or did a bullet bring her down?

"They kill people for the hell of it in New York City," Dom said.

Masha winced.

"Olga called Sveta's home. She was there, according to the man who answered." Kate groaned. "I wish I'd heard her voice. Oh, boy, oh, boy." Kate paced the room in a panic. She stopped in front of Masha. "In the cab, Sveta agreed to meet me today, but we didn't set a time. Will you help me reach her?"

Masha nodded, her eyes worried.

Kate resumed her pacing. "The question is, what would the driver have done if I hadn't fought back? Would he have taken what he wanted—my passport, for instance, and then returned both Sveta and me to civilization? Maybe he didn't intend to leave us there to freeze to death. He was drunk, disorganized. I must have changed his game plan."

Dom waved the yellow tablet he'd been scrawling on. "We now have a transcript, of sorts. Good work, kids! We have a name. Andre. But what does it all mean?" he asked softly, scratching his beard.

"We have Sveta saying to Kate, *So sorry. Is my fault.* Then she begs the man, *Let her go. This is mistake,*" Masha said.

Dom held up a cardboard box of Danish water sitting on the sill. "Water, anyone?"

Masha's eyes lit up. "Such water is a luxury."

Dom gallantly opened the container and handed it to Masha. He pitched one underhand to Kate and opened a carton for himself.

"I can help you with police report, if you like." Masha hesitated. "I personally do not believe it will help. So seldom would they find anybody. In addition, you are foreigners. It will bring you into the spotlight, as far as they are concerned."

"It may bring you into the spotlight too," Kate said slowly.

"Why was I there, at your apartment, they'd ask, so far from my hotel?" She grimaced. "It's not exactly on the list of cultural programs sponsored by Intourist and provided by festival management."

Masha dropped her eyes.

Then there was the matter of the pornographic tapes stolen from Steve's room. Kate took a chug of her bottled water. "No reason for any of us to get involved with the police. Right, Dom?"

Dom, with a strained smile, nodded yes. He asked, "Did Sveta get the car for you?"

"Irina did. Masha was going to bring me back to the hotel. But Irina insisted she would. She flagged down the car. Then suddenly she wasn't going with me after Sveta arrived on the scene." Maybe Irina never intended to go. A strange look had briefly crossed her face. Irina and the driver seemed to know each other. Or were they simply flirting? Sveta didn't seem to notice anything wrong. Maybe she was in on it. With Irina. Was it meant to be a robbery of a "rich American"? Things got out of hand? Was *So sorry. My fault. It is mistake* Sveta's apology to Kate? But she'd seemed so terrified.

Kate's head was reeling. "Do you think we were followed to your apartment?" she asked Masha. "Or maybe the car you flagged outside the hotel to take us to your building—maybe the driver reported us—you a Russian with a foreigner."

"Anything is possible," Masha murmured, continuing in her official voice, "I will let the festival administrators know about your trouble, Kate, so word can spread that getting in unlicensed taxis is now a danger."

The room was hot. Kate flung back the thin silk curtain, cracked the window.

Masha murmured, "I am sorry. I should have accompanied you back to your hotel, as planned."

"You would have been in danger too. The scarf your mom gave me helped save my life. I'm sure of that." Kate managed a smile. "Who's hungry?" She lifted up the jar of peanut butter sitting on her dresser, and a package of crackers.

"More peanut butter?" Masha clapped her hands.

Kate spread some on a cracker, and handed it to Masha. "Dom?" Dom patted his stomach. "Just a cracker, plain." He turned to Masha with a short laugh. "We read about the shortages. Kate came prepared."

"I was surprised," Kate said, "by the tons of food at the opening night banquet." The tables had groaned under the weight of cheeses, salamis, rolls, pastries, fancy hors d'oeuvres, champagne, vodka, cognac, Pepsi, and bottled water.

Masha nodded. "All brought in from Helsinki."

That night Kate and Dom had been the first to arrive in the huge lower room. They were starving. Soldiers from above had spotted them, quickly bounded down the stairs, and ordered them to leave, saying the party would not start for thirty minutes. She and Dom weren't eating, just admiring. The soldiers, as usual, had been intimidating.

Kate asked Masha, "Why are all the soldiers here?"

"Many have been taken from East Germany. Work must be created for them, apartments found." She looked away. "And they may be here . . . Moscow considers Leningrad an upstart city. Maybe they worry that Leningrad is too close in distance and in sympathy to Latvia."

Kate bit into a peanut butter covered cracker. "Something weird. Funny, I didn't think of it earlier . . . The back doors of that so-called cab had no handles on the inside. I had to vault over the seat to get to the front door."

Masha sighed, "KGB car. I am thinking," she said reluctantly, "that our unregistered group may have KGB informer."

"An informer among your friends?"

"We are more acquaintances than friends."

Of all those she'd met at Masha's last evening, the wise women who'd spoken for her tape recorder, afraid to give their names, one stood out. Irina, with the dark smudges under her eyes, pushy, smarmy, and critical of the U.S all evening. She was the KGB informer, Kate was sure. "You Americans think you've won a victory by making us believe your experts," she'd baited Kate. Then she'd suddenly turned lovey dovey.

Masha brushed a strand of blonde hair from her forehead. "Word has spread in the apartment complex and through work," she said uneasily, "that we are hoping to bring about some changes, not only for women."

"Your group is like the U.S. consciousness raising groups in the sixties and seventies," Kate said. "I read about them in my Women's Studies classes. They did make life better."

Masha pressed her lips together.

"Even with *perestroika,* the KGB is still collecting information?" Dom asked.

Masha stiffened. "They say Gorbachev's policy of restructuring assures public control of security so that nothing unfortunate will be repeated, as happened before." Her mouth twisted. "You cannot trust Gorbachev. You ask him question. His answer: *lit vodu,* pour water. You pour water and it spreads and you cannot find water."

"He went up and up when they saw how acceptable he was to the people, to the West," Masha continued. "He secretly sticks to the agenda of the Party, pretending he is trying to bring about change. Boris Yeltsin is no better."

Dom asked, "So you don't trust the democrats?"

Masha considered carefully before she spoke. "It is very easy now," she said, her eyes apologetic, "to steal money from the government, go abroad and teach in U.S. about Russia. These people don't care about Russia."

"What do you think of the Mayor of Leningrad—Sobchak?"

Masha made a face. "He made a big show of resigning from the Communist Party. If something happens, he just becomes a professor at a university in America. Many believe Putin—his Deputy—was placed here by KGB to keep an eye on things."

Kate clumsily patted Masha's arm. "Have you had personal experience with the KGB?" she asked softly.

"No one wants to be called to their office." Masha rose from her chair.

Kate watched Dom as his gaze lingered on Masha. Her movements were fluid, elegant, as if she were skimming over ice. Too bad she'd had to give up skating in competitions. She'd hoped to travel abroad. Now she was a producer of medical films. She also swam in the Neva in the winter and avoided colds. An amazing woman, Kate thought. She'd go far in the U.S.

Masha faced the window, her voice floating back into the room, low and melodious. "When I was student at University, I invited English students from exchange program and some Russians to visit my apartment. I was called to the Department for Foreign Students and told the KGB did not allow it. There was no explanation why. I had a fit of hysteria. It was forbidden to me to tell the foreigners why I changed my mind. I made up some story of my mom being ill."

"Someone must have snitched," Dom said. "One of the Russians you'd invited?"

Masha gave a weary shrug.

"How terrible to have someone always waiting for you to make a mistake," Kate said.

"They have made us into a country of snoops and informers," Masha said bitterly. "Before 1988, all people going abroad had to have their documents approved by the KGB."

Just three years ago, Kate thought.

Masha's voice was flat. "I was refused once a visit to Poland, because of the 'solidarity' movement there. Later I was going to visit U.S.A. as guide of a Soviet group. All my documents were approved in many places—quite a long procedure. One week before departure they informed me the KGB did not approve."

"You must have been scared."

"Very." Masha nodded. "I found out afterward they thought we had relatives in U.S. because in the sixties we had correspondence with my father's aunt there. Later she died, leaving no relatives. So the KGB had us on a 'black list' but even they did not know the woman died long ago and had no relative." Her face was flushed. She hesitated. "Some people say the KGB is waiting until the reforms fail. Then they'll be back, in full force."

"What do you think?"

She looked frightened. "KGB has control now of what is printed and copied."

Dom asked, "Does that mean KGB censors have to approve what is printed by the newspapers?"

Masha nodded.

Kate said thoughtfully, "That's why the festival catalogue is being printed in Helsinki." The festival press releases perhaps were printed in Finland too so they could be critical—if only in a puzzling way—of current events.

Masha nodded. "I used to be proud to live here," she sighed. "Even with Stalin's Gulags, we had order, and artists were supported by the government. Gorbachev and the so-called Democrats have messed it up. Now it's such a confusion. There is a joke that expresses it exactly. A man wanted to buy a new car. His name was put on the list. He would get it in five years, in 1996. 'What month?' he asked. 'October.' 'What date?' 'Oh, for God's sake, October 1.' 'Morning or afternoon?' 'For God's sake, okay, afternoon!' 'Good. They are coming to fix my toilet in the morning.'" Masha laughed weakly. "Nothing works in this country. There is no fairness here. I hope some day someone will be able to do something about it." She stared dejectedly into space, tears running down her cheeks.

Dom hurried into the bathroom, returned with tissues, and stood by her side as she blotted her eyes.

A series of loud knocks sounded on the door.

Masha jumped. Dom grabbed his notes strewn across the bed, stuffing them in his pocket.

Kate hid the tape recorder in her bag of dirty clothes, then sprang to the door. "Who is it?"

"Dom, you there?" Steve sang out.

When Kate opened the door, Steve barged through, grinning like a maniac. He carried two heavy canisters of film. "Our film was hidden in plain sight," he crowed, "in the festival office."

"And Sergei, the scheduler, didn't know?" Kate asked dubiously.

"The projectionist in Competition Hall knew. He directed me there."

"Good work." Dom held up two sets of crossed fingers. "The screening will take place at 6:00 PM tonight, as scheduled. And we'll be there to answer questions. Wonder of wonders."

"The squeaky wheel gets the grease, pal." Steve's broad face was flushed with triumph. "Picture this. There was a room within the room. A glass door opened and a man popped out. 'We have the film here,' he said, pointing to a corner where it was stashed with other films." Steve's brows lifted meaningfully. "He was in a big fur hat and his coat hung open. He wore a cowboy shirt." Smirking, Steve added, "I guess he's in love with America, like everyone else here. He handed over the film without a quibble. After he left, I asked a woman in the office, 'Who was that very nice gentleman in the cowboy shirt who had my movie?' 'Vladimir Putin,' she answered."

Dom made a sound between a sigh and a groan. "You didn't make any reference to pirating?" he asked Steve carefully.

Steve waved his hand impatiently.

Kate caught a look from Dom, knew they both were thinking that Steve wasn't stupid but he had a short fuse and was impulsive.

"Remember," Kate asked Steve excitedly, "the three men in cowboy shirts at our breakfast table? Was one of them Putin?"

"Now that you mention it . . ." Steve nodded slowly. "Yeah, I think he was."

Why did the men come to their table—out of all the tables in the dining room? Steve's porn? Her tapes? Or just chance? Kate tried to remember what had been said at their table.

"In all hotels where foreigners stay," Masha said, "there are KGB. They call in extras for festival this large. KGB can't hide. They look at you suspicious-like, eyes wide, staring."

Like the eyes of the three men at their breakfast table.

"Why wear cowboy shirts? To blend in, seem one of the gang?" Had one or more of these KGB played a hand in her abduction?

Suddenly, Dom was galvanized. "Kate, get reminders about the screening into the mailboxes of the Japanese and West Germans. Steve, you and I will check the film for tears."

On his way out, Dom doubled back to Masha, looking deep into her eyes. He took her hand. "I'd love it if you could come tonight to see our film."

"I will try. I have made arrangements to see my son. If my ex-husband allows it."

"Kate told me he has custody. That he tried to get you fired from your job. That he beats and kicks you when you visit your son. A vicious man."

"He is sick, but that does not change the fact that I am scared for my life each time I go," Masha smiled bravely. "I hope to see your film before you leave."

Dom, still holding Masha's hand, said softly, "Me too." He blushed. "I mean, I want you to see it—to see my work." He's so driven, Kate thought, anyone who can distract him—even briefly—is quite a force.

Steve called impatiently, "Hey, Dom, it's almost two o'clock."

Dom and Steve left, each carrying a canister of film. Kate stayed behind as Masha tried to call Sveta. "No answer," Masha said, putting down the phone. "If you wish, I will keep trying."

"Please do." Kate trusted Masha. Right from the first, she'd made herself valuable. Today with her helpful, honest answers, she'd made herself indispensable. "Do you know Sveta well? Her situation?"

Masha said uncertainly, "She is eighteen. She lives at home. Has a father and a brother with whom she does not get along. She has a man who wants to marry her."

Kate hesitated, should she tell her? "She told me she's afraid . . ."

"Afraid?"

"That she may be killed or sent away."

Masha's eyes grew wide. "Did she give a reason?"

"She said, 'They call us *rozo . . . rozovaya.*'"

Masha looked stunned.

"What does that mean?"

She shook her head slowly. "Pink. She is a moonlight person. She is in love with a female friend."

"Nadya," Kate said softly. She remembered the two of them, side by side, on Masha's couch. So young. Nadya, blonde, with doe-like eyes, and dark haired Sveta, her skin glowing, lighting Nadya's cigarette. The tender look that passed between them. She should have guessed.

Masha shrugged and gave a half nod. "Not wise to make that sort of thing public."

Kate knew that was true. Her eyes fell on her stack of business cards on her dresser top. She handed one to Masha. "I want to give you my address and phone in the States."

"And I will give you mine." Masha printed the information on the back of another of Kate's cards. "Now," she smiled, "if it is okay, I will have more peanut butter."

"Help yourself. And take what's left to your son."

"He will love it." Masha picked up the phone. "We will try Sveta again. If we cannot reach her, we will call Nadya." She pursed her lips, and put the phone back in its cradle. "But perhaps I should make those calls from my home."

Chapter Seven

4:10 PM, Monday January 28

Bundled up in her coat and two scarves, a perspiring Kate stood beside Dom and Steve in the hotel lobby. The company video camera was at her feet. "Festival Transport is ten minutes late," Dom fumed, understandably jumpy, Kate thought, hopeful that his prospective buyers would show up at the Molnia Cinema, would love *Revolution,* and snap up the rights. Worried about the size of the audience and how the beleaguered Russian people would react to this film about spoiled kids, hippies in the sixties, rebelling because they had too much, instead of too little.

"Anyone surprised they're late?" Steve grunted.

"Prepared." Kate drew a slip of paper from her coat pocket. "The cinema address, in cyrillic." They stuck around five more minutes before ordering a cab from Taxi Service. Kate showed the driver the address, half expecting him to say he couldn't read it and shake his head. But he nodded, drove them to the cinema without a hitch, pulling up in front at 5:00 PM, a full hour before the scheduled screening. It went so smoothly Kate was stunned, then wary. Nothing in Russia was ever that easy.

Dom was fretting, chewing on his antacids. "Let's find the projectionist," he murmured to Steve as they clambered out of the cab, each lugging a heavy canister of the five-reel print.

"Relax, old buddy." Steve bent down to the driver, rummaging in his pocket, pulling out a five dollar bill, which the driver seized with the speed of a chameleon. "Come back for us at 8:15. We need to get to the Tbilisi Restaurant."

Steve had sniffed out a party organized by American filmmakers—dinner with unlimited champagne at a Georgian restaurant.

"You know where that is?" Steve demanded of the driver.

"Tbilisi?" he asked with an uncertain grin. He nodded his head emphatically. Then he beamed, pointed at the cinema, and at his watch. "8:15."

The walks were clear, enormous piles of snow stacked alongside. It must snow almost every day, all winter long, Kate thought. The wind was raw. She zipped up her coat, thankful she'd again worn tights under her jeans.

"Are we at the right place?" Steve asked after the cab left. "I don't see any announcements of our film."

The theater had no marquee. Glassed-in posters, which seemed handmade, framed the door. On one, a man's face was sketched, his expression too menacing to be a character from their film. "We're at the Molnia." Kate aimed her video camera at the sign above the theater, Молния Киноin in large red letters. "But are we where we need to be?"

"The expensive still photos we mailed never made it to the Molnia," Dom muttered.

At the side of the walkway was a large white billboard which appeared to be a list of titles in bold black, handwritten in Cyrillic. "Here we are," Kate said excitedly, taking the shot. "The title has США after it. That means USA. It's ninety minutes. Like ours. Uh-oh." She slid her finger over to the left, where 2000 was printed in red. "We're scheduled for eight o'clock, not six."

"I don't believe it," Dom groaned.

The purpose of Information Screenings was to allow the director to watch with the Russian audience and afterwards answer questions. A true exchange of information. *Glasnost.*

"The Japanese and the West Germans—if they do show up—won't wait around for two more hours," Dom said. He strode up to the ticket-seller seated in the kiosk. "*Americanski.* Film festival. We're here with our film." The woman looked blank, opened the door behind her, conferred with a woman in a blue sweater, who shook her head uneasily.

"*Americanski* feelm." Kate showed her Festival badge. The ticket-seller broke into a relieved grin, signaled them inside, handing them over to the blue-sweatered woman who pointed up a carpeted flight of stairs, which they climbed.

Dom opened a door. A movie was playing, it wasn't theirs. Audience members turned and glared. Dom quickly shut the door. "This place seems to have more than one cinema," he mumbled, scrutinizing the other closed doors from which sounds emanated. "I feel like a rat in a maze." They went back downstairs.

The blue-sweatered woman, smiling patiently, guided them up the steps once more, leading them into another corridor past a tiny bar where people sat before small cups of coffee, small glasses of cognac, smoked harsh smelling cigarettes and talked in low voices. The woman pointed to the room opposite the bar.

Success. The woman had understood, had brought them to where they wanted to go.

The door opened, the audience filed out, five people with long, serious faces, who were bundled up in hats, scarves, and coats, looking as if they'd just trudged across Siberia.

Who are these people? Kate wondered. Three women, rather fat, looked like housewives. The young couple—students perhaps. She hoped their film would attract a larger audience.

Just then a breathless young man arrived, "I've been looking all over for you," he wailed.

Kate saw the festival badge on his lapel. "You're Transport?"

"Yes." His broad cheeks were flushed. "Why didn't you wait?"

"We did, until 4:15."

"I was there at 4:20," he pouted, sorrowful and indignant at the same time.

"I'm sorry," Kate said. "But we didn't think you were coming."

The young man's hurt look was replaced with a broad smile. "I'm Vasily."

"I'm Kate." She shook his hand. "This is Dom and Steve. We may have a problem. The film was to be shown at six. Outside on the marquee—we think it says eight o'clock."

Steve's mouth was tight. "If it's eight, we lose what might be our only chance to sell it."

Dom explained. "We've invited potential buyers."

Vasily's face lost some of its shine. Behind him, a plump, worried-looking woman in a long skirt and high boots was advancing, followed by the Blue Sweater. "Ah," Vasily said. He pulled the plump woman to one side, where they conferred for several minutes before he brought her forward. "This is the manageress. She tells me the film is scheduled for six *and* eight. So," he said with a wide grin, "everything is fine."

Smiling, the manageress shook hands with everyone, and bustled back down the corridor, Vasily scurrying behind.

Mumbling under his breath, Steve headed for the projection booth with the cans of film. Dom hurried downstairs to wait at the front door for the Japanese and West Germans. Kate wandered into the narrow auditorium. Old-fashioned Siamese lamps, spaced at intervals, glowed dimly on the paneled walls. The screen was small, about the size of a home projection monitor. She panned the room with her camera. Against the back wall was a small desk that held a microphone and a goose-necked lamp. Behind the desk was a wooden chair, where the narrator would sit, reading the transcript of *Revolution* in Russian.

Kate felt a thrill of anticipation. She sat in the second row, periodically twisting around to check the door, relieved to see her colleagues enter with a Japanese woman and two European-looking men. They sat two rows behind her, the potential buyers sandwiched between Dom and Steve. They couldn't escape if they wanted.

The audience trickled in slowly, then arrived in a flood. By six, the room was nearly full. Kate counted eighty-nine people, all wrapped like mummies in coats, scarves, gloves. The room was cold as a freezer. Kate slid her camera inside her coat, hoping the heat would be turned on soon.

The cinema manager reappeared, wearing a black fur hat, a black cloth coat. She delivered a short welcome to the audience as a proudly smiling Vasily translated. She then introduced the three American film artists—Dominick, Steve, and Kate—beckoning each to the front to receive a red carnation. The audience applauded. Kate felt like a star. Dom and Steve were grinning broadly. The Japanese woman and the German men looked impressed.

The manager then apologized for the lack of heat. The heating system couldn't cope with the temperature, she said, now thirty-five degrees below zero. Oh, no, Kate thought, could conditions be any worse for their film, with its depiction of the "Summer of Love"?

Kate and Steve took their seats, while Dom remained at the front of the house. He pushed the stem of his red carnation through the buttonhole of his coat, which hung open. He was dressed in her favorite outfit: beige jacket, a deep blue turtleneck sweater underneath. The blue picked up his eyes, already vibrant with excitement. He stood tall, proud. All his hard work was paying off. He had a crowd, the potential buyers had come. She prayed everyone would fall in love with the film.

Coffee cup in hand, a slim blonde woman, pale and business-like, took her place in the translator's box against the back wall. She wore a cloche hat and flowing gray coat, which gave her a dated elegance, a forties look. Dom, his immaculately trimmed beard adding a touch of aristocracy, held his hand up. "I just want to say a few words." The narrator nodded, translating as he read from a sheet of paper.

> In 1967, we went to San Francisco because we realized something important was going on out there—and in other cities around the world.
>
> We shot thousands of feet of film which took us many months to put together in a form that captured the vitality, color, naivete, and optimism of groups of kids who wanted to change the old established order. Our major character is a young, beautiful, free spirit living in a commune in the Haight. She calls herself TODAY.
>
> There were bad aspects as well as good—drugs, sexual promiscuity. But the moment did free many people's minds, resulting in vibrant, earthy music and art, as well as social changes. A preference for the spiritual over the material. And I believe the hippie movement was partially responsible for ending the Vietnam War.
>
> Then came the backlash against the freedoms these kids had won—which brought us all the yuppies.
>
> I revisited many of the same characters 24 years later. Today, then a flower child, is now a warm and caring mother of two teenage children.
>
> We made *Revolution* partly as a social commentary about the sixties, partly to show today's uptight, money grabbing world what it's missing. I look forward to your comments after the film.

Dom nodded at the manageress and headed for his seat. The cinema went dark, except for the small circle of light from the narrator's lamp.

Although Kate had seen the film many times in many versions, she was drawn in again by the narrator's charm and skill, delighted to hear the speeches in Russian. The woman deftly handled the many transitions with sensitivity—the quick jumps between then and now, footage from the sixties intercut with scenes filmed twenty-four years later—as a gifted actress might read a script "cold." She spoke the words of the songs—not too loudly, so the wonderful, funky music of Steve Miller, Mother Earth, Country Joe and The Fish, and Quicksilver could be appreciated.

Motionless, propped up by thick coats and heavy scarves, the audience watched in absolute silence. Were they appalled by the rebellion of the pampered youth of the sixties? The vibrant colors, the festive music didn't seem to stir them. They were frozen, Kate thought. So was she, her hands and feet lumps of ice. At any rate, the print was bright and clean, seemingly unscathed by its inadvertent screening at the Leningrad Cinema. Just then, in the middle of the acid trip, the film jumped to the next scene. Behind her, Kate heard Dom's sharp intake of breath. The narrator didn't seem to lose her place. What had been cut, besides the last part of the LSD trip? Kate took a few moments to figure it out. The nude beach scene with members of the Sexual Freedom League. Had they been chewed up by an ancient projector at the Leningrad Cinema? Or had someone deliberately snipped them out, altering the transcript to match the film?

When the lights came up, hordes of people crowded around Dom, excited, eager for information about the hippies, about America. Kate asked for permission to videotape. No one minded. So she lifted her camera, captured a glowing Dom in the frame, as he congratulated the narrator for her beautiful handling of the script.

A female art student, sheik-like in a white hood, praised the movie for its bright colors and joyful music. The narrator graciously translated. A bearded young man, his pale, thin face intense, announced, "Our war in Afghanistan was like your Vietnam War." He argued heatedly with an older man about the layers of meaning in the film. Others were smiling like children let into a candy store. How wonderful, they seemed to be thinking, that these kids had been able to run away to San Francisco, have fun, do what they wanted—without government permission.

Steve, the collar of his lilac shirt and the purple knot of his necktie peeking out from his coat, sat with the buyers who seemed engrossed, despite the cold.

Uh, oh. At the edge of the crowd, a soldier leaned again the wall, arms crossed, studiedly bored. Not Red Hair, but perhaps he'd been replaced. His eyes caught hers. He looked alert. Kate dropped the camera to her side. Maybe he wasn't her new "tail" but had simply drifted into the movie on his own. Or perhaps he'd been ordered to check it out because of the provocative title. She'd love to ask him what he thought of the drugs, the nude girls laughing, breasts bouncing as they ran through fields, and swung high in swings. If someone had snipped out the Sexual Freedom League on the nude beach, why did he leave the naked girls in the swings? And the Ann Halprin nude dancers? Maybe the nudity didn't bother the censor, but the philosophy of the Sexual Freedom League did. The group advocated anything sexual in any combination, including orgies.

Kate had been an infant during Dom's first shoot in sixties San Francisco, the THEN part of the film. But she'd been with Dom and the San Francisco crew last year for the updates, proud to be associated with the NOW segments.

Near the back of the hall, lurking in the shadows, was a man in a dark coat, a scarf around his neck. He sidestepped so that light from the overhead lamp bathed his face. Round dark glasses rested on high cheekbones. The hollows of his face were pitted with old acne scars. He stood silently, watching and listening, his full lips curled in a sneer. Had he deliberately stepped into the light so she could see him? He looked more menacing than the soldier. Kate's stomach knotted. *Cut it out,* she told herself. *No, he's not following you. He's just an audience member turned off by the nudity.* She edged her camera up, to take his picture. He stepped back into the shadows.

"My brother was a heepie," Vasily confided to Kate. "He lived on a farm with other heepies. I always wondered what his life was like."

"He was?" How could there be Russian hippies?

"I loved the film." Vasily's eyes were sparkling.

"What's its title in Russian?" she asked.

"*Heepie Music,*" he said.

Kate gave a short laugh. No one was inflamed by the title, *Revolution.* Eighty-nine people came to hear hippie music.

The crowd thinned. Why, there was Masha, standing against the wall, looking elegant in her brown coat edged with white fur. Kate expected her to be visiting her son. Her ex-husband must not have allowed it. Beside Masha was a woman in a dark grey coat, and a rose knitted hood with long scarf-like flaps that wound around her neck. She held one end of her scarf over the right side of her face. Sveta? Oh, god, Kate hoped so. She drew closer. Blonde hair poked out. Nadya, the urchin with the burning eyes. Now only one burned, for the scarf almost covered her right eye.

"Nadya hasn't seen Sveta since yesterday," Masha murmured, "when we all were at my apartment."

"I worry," Nadya said, her voice barely a whisper.

"Wait for me. We'll go to my hotel and talk," Kate said softly as Dom headed their way with the Japanese woman and the two men. "Why, hello," Dom said to Masha, his eyes glowing.

"I am sorry," Masha apologized. "I saw only the last part of your movie. It is wonderful."

With a wide grin, Dom introduced Masha and Kate to the prospective rights buyers, blushing, calling Masha, "a beautiful translator and friend," and Kate "my right hand, my administrator."

"And this is?" he glanced toward Nadya. "A new Russian friend," Kate said.

"Will you join us for a party at the Tbilisi?" Dom asked the buyers. They declined. "We'll be in touch," said one of the men, shaking Dom's hand. As they walked away, Steve whispered, "I think we made a sale."

"Hope so," Dom said. "No more screenings scheduled after tonight."

They'd been promised two screenings; they'd had two, one at the Leningrad without them present and one tonight. A third, an unexpected bonus, would be at eight, but Dom wouldn't be in the audience to answer questions and there'd be no potential buyers. *Okay, we had one grand time just now,* Kate decided, *with a theater full of people who didn't walk out despite the freezing cold, who were excited by the film and stayed to talk about it.*

"Let's make sure the print gets delivered to us, not to the Festival office," Dom said.

Steve, Dom, and Kate, Vasily in tow, approached the manageress who still hovered, smiling, in the auditorium. The request for the print was quickly answered.

"It is so cold they are shutting down the theater," Vasily said sadly. "There will be no eight o'clock showing."

There goes our bonus screening, Kate thought.

"We'll take the print with us," Steve announced.

"To the restaurant?" Kate asked.

"I'm not letting it out of my sight."

Vasily spoke again with the manageress before turning to Steve and Dom. "Tomorrow," Vasily translated. "It will be delivered tomorrow. It must be rewound. All five reels will take over an hour."

"Antiquated equipment," Kate reminded Steve, whose chest puffed out as if he were gearing up for a fight. "Remember? We were told to bring our senses of humor." As she left the cinema, Kate wore her red carnation in the buttonhole of her coat, still feeling like a star.

At curbside, their cab waited, the driver standing by the car's fender, grinning proudly. Also, their official "transport"

Vasily, waited, smiling. "A car for each of us," Kate said to Dom. "But aren't you coming to the Tbilisi?" he asked.

Kate shook her head, indicating Masha and Nadya. "Stop by my room when you get back."

⁂

MASHA, AS A BADGE-WEARING translator for the festival, chatted with the soldiers at the front door of the Hotel Leningrad, diverting them, while Kate, flashing her festival badge, maneuvered Nadya into the hotel and past the front desk, holding her breath all the way to the elevator, waiting for a tap on the shoulder, and an order that her guest must show her passport and sign the register opposite Kate's name. If caught, Kate would simply say she didn't know that rule. That people in the U.S. could enter hotels without signing in, even if they weren't paying guests. The KGB, Masha had said, sometimes examine the hotel registration book to see who has visited certain people.

As the three women rode up to the fourth floor, Nadya murmured something, her voice muffled behind her scarf. "She says she has never seen such beauty, the lobby with its marble staircase, the bright red carpet," Masha translated. She sighed, "It is an elegance denied most Russian citizens."

Kate collected her key from the *dejurnaya*, feeling the woman's eyes drilling into her as she unlocked her door. Everywhere everybody was watching. At some point, just to breathe, you had to say to yourself, the hell with it, and do what you had to do.

As Masha and Nadya followed her into the room, the *dejurnaya* called out something. "What did she say?" Kate asked when the door was closed. Masha replied, "Your guests must leave by eleven o'clock." Kate rolled her eyes.

Masha said softly to Kate, "I have told Nadya about the abduction of Sveta and you to the cemetery, and that someone at Sveta's home said she had made it home safely."

Speaking rapidly, Nadya took away the scarf she held over the right side of her face, revealing a cut on her reddened cheek, a bruise in the corner of her eye. "What happened?" Kate asked. Masha translated.

"I call Sveta. Her brother answers. He laughs. So I go to police to report her missing. They laugh." Nadya tore off her coat and threw it on the floor. "Everyone laugh and do not listen and do not care about Sveta at all." Her face collapsed. "A policeman took me to back room for questions. He raped me." She was shaking all over, tears in her eyes. "He say we need to learn a lesson. Sveta's brother reported us to police . . . as *rozovaya*."

Kate turned to Masha. "We must tell someone in authority about this rape."

"Who?" Masha asked, with a sigh.

Not the police, of course. "Nadya's parents?"

Nadya shook her head violently. "My mother has ordered me to leave Sveta alone. She would be happy to know I had been with a man."

What kind of mother was that? Kate, angry, her brain in a turmoil, poured glasses of cognac for all.

Nadya sat in the chair, looking nervous and ashamed. She raised her head, took a deep breath, and spoke, as Masha translated, "When you were with us at Masha's, Kate, you told us you had video camera. And those who were brave could speak for camera, and you would carry our stories to America. I want to talk for your video."

Kate threw Masha a worried look. "You mustn't put yourselves in danger. For all I know, you may be at risk now. Just by being here with me." Kate explained, "I seem to have a soldier after me—maybe more than one—who wants my tapes. We still don't know why Sveta and I were taken to that desolate place by that so-called cab driver."

Nadya looked a little fragile but spoke determinedly, "*Me ne boemsya*. We are not afraid."

"If we are silent," Masha said heatedly, "the criminals will win."

A part of Kate felt reckless. She didn't care. She wanted that footage. "I can put you in the shadows."

"I want my face be seen." Nadya sat up straighter.

Kate handed her the red carnation. Nadya jabbed it through the buttonhole of her faded blue blouse, waiting while Kate positioned the camera and adjusted the focus. "We're set," Kate told her. Masha, off-camera, her voice smooth and soft in contrast to what was being said, repeated Nadya's words in English. "I am Nadya. I am seventeen." Nadya held her chin up. Her voice was clear. She looked almost impish, heartbreakingly young. The cut on her cheek still oozed a little blood. Her eye was growing blacker by the minute. "In Soviet Union, they call us hooligans or pinks. We are raped and beaten or sent away if we are *rozavaya* and do not follow orders. It is not fair. I have a good friend, Sveta. It was miracle we find each other. She has made my life so happy this past year. Sveta's parents have a man chosen for her to marry. They want to separate us. We do not want to be a man's slave. We love each other. We do not want to be with anyone else."

Nadya asked Kate hopefully, "Is it better in America?"

Kate hesitated. These women trusted her. She must trust them. She must show her own courage by answering "on the record," on videotape. "In America, they call us dykes, queers, lesbians, gays," she blurted out, her heart thudding. "I'd rather be called pink or a hooligan."

As Masha repeated Kate's words to Nadya, comprehension dawned in her eyes. She gave Kate a grateful smile. "You? *Rozovaya?*"

Kate looked away from the camera's viewfinder to nod. She glanced at Masha. Was she shocked? Dismayed?

"Why they have to call us something?" Nadya asked Kate "It is no one's business."

"I understand your feelings." Masha, biting her lip, looked from one to the other. She pushed a tense breath through pursed lips, then marched over to the still seated Nadya and stood beside her. Kate widened the shot to include both in the frame. Masha faced the camera, speaking softly, first in English, then in Russian. "I am Masha, age thirty-nine, part Jewish. Luckily, I married a man with a Russian name, which I have kept. Otherwise, I would not have my job where I work now with a Jewish name." She took Nadya's hand. "If it is not known, you are not bothered."

Nadya smiled a broken smile. "But you are free, Kate, to be with your female friend?"

"Even in America, families, jobs get in the way . . ." Kate's voice trailed away. "Nadya, you must tell me, what do you think has happened to Sveta?"

"She is not in any of our usual places. I am afraid they have sent her to a psychiatric clinic for the Cure. She told me they have said if this is the way she behaves she must become a man. We saw an interview on TV—Sveta and I—of a transsexual, a woman who had become a man. If this is what one of has to be—" She put her face in her hands. "The woman on TV had Sveta's gestures. Sveta thought she was looking at herself. We could not talk to each other, see each other for a week. Then Sveta told me, 'I do not care what happens, I will not change my sex.' When she said that, we both felt like we had our lives back again." Nadya's eyes brimmed with tears. "We want to be together—as women. She does not want to be a man. Or marry one."

Masha put her arms around her. Kate, hiding behind the camera, was silent, her insides in a knot. She wished she could help Nadya and all these women. But how? She was being tailed. For god's sake, she'd been left in a cemetery to die for reasons still unknown to her.

"I hope she is in a clinic. If not," Nadya sobbed, "I am afraid she may be dead. Her brother is very wild." Masha handed her a tissue. She wiped her eyes. "Also my mother said . . ." she gave a shuddering sigh. Kate zoomed in on her face and held the close-up. ". . . if I did not stop she would find a way to end it. Meaning, she would kill Sveta." Her eyes were pleading. "Or send me to a mental institution."

An idea was forming in Kate's brain. "Sveta's brother? Is he fat? Drinks a lot? The man who abducted us—maybe Sveta was his target. Not me. Sveta had said, *It is my fault.*"

Nadya shook her head. "*Nyet.* Not fat."

"Is her brother's name Andre?" Masha asked. Again, Nadya shook her head.

"On the phone, I didn't really talk to Sveta." Kate felt sick. "Olga, who called from the Olgino, spoke to a man. Who said all is okay or something like that . . . she's taken care of."

"Her brother," Nadya whispered with dread.

Still hefting the video camera on her shoulder, Kate sidestepped to the dresser, lifted her glass of cognac and sipped. She was sorry now she hadn't taken the phone from Olga, demanding to speak to Sveta. "One other thing. Olga reported Sveta missing to the *militsia,* who wrote a protocol and said they would search the cemetery. I wonder if they did, if they are as corrupt and inefficient as you say."

"Did Olga contact the *militsia* again to inform them that Sveta arrived home safely?" Masha asked with a frown.

"Not unless she called after she took me to the *electrichka.*" Now Kate worried that Olga's report to the police about Sveta would somehow boomerang. "Nadya, there must be other women like you and Sveta? That we can go to for advice?"

"We do not know any others like ourselves. For awhile, we almost thought we were the only two in the world like this."

Kate, surprised, threw a quick glance at Masha, who nodded. "Sexual things are kept very private here in Russia."

"It was a secret," Nadya murmured, "until our families found out. I have heard of a place," she said haltingly, "a social club where these women meet, a café. They may know how to help us find Sveta."

"You have the address?"

"Yes. Sveta and I were trying to get up our courage to go."

"Let's do it. Tomorrow. Are you both game?" Kate asked.

The two women slowly nodded.

"What time? Do you have school?" Kate asked Nadya.

She shook her head, looked away. "I have dropped out of school; I sell items in a kiosk on the street—food, souvenirs."

They agreed to meet at the hotel the next day at five.

The camera was growing heavy. As Kate was about to turn it off, Nadya asked, "Kate, tell me how it is in America for you, as *rozovaya*?" Her eyes were hopeful in her bruised face.

"Not as bad as here. Not easy either." Kate wanted to leave it at that, but she decided she had a duty to tell Nadya something true about herself, to show her that things, though different in America, were in some ways the same. "When I was about your age, eighteen, I had a special friend—like you. Her name was Amy." Kate held the shot on Nadya whose lips pushed toward a smile as Masha translated.

Kate's stomach clenched. "We were in college in a small Midwestern town. Like living in a fish bowl. Someone sent a letter about us to her parents." Kate lifted her glass from the dresser, taking a swallow of cognac; it burned her throat. "They came charging down to campus. Amy's mom and dad. My guardians, Aunt Maureen and Uncle Burt. We had a free-for-all in the Dean's Office. Aunt Maureen was upset. Uncle Burt obnoxious."

"Free-for-all?" Masha asked.

"A terrible fight."

Masha, with a stern face, relayed Kate's word to Nadya, whose eyes filled . "Poor Kate."

"Families are hard." Kate felt tears on her cheeks, rubbed them away with the palm of her hand, holding the camera as steadily as she could. "It was just a fight. No one threatened to kill me."

"What happened to you and your special friend?"

"Amy and I had sworn to be together forever. But she couldn't take the pressure." Kate still remembered Amy's eyes, begging Kate to understand when she broke down, sobbing to her parents, the Dean, Kate's guardians that Kate had seemed so lonely—"such a loner" was what she said—that she felt sorry for her. "She said she never meant for anything perverted to happen, that she would undo it if she could and it would never take place again."

As Masha translated, Nadya's face grew darker and darker. She let loose a heated barrage of Russian, and Masha said in English, "She betrayed you."

"She was scared. I was too. Look, it's nothing compared to what you must go through. No one tried to put me in a mental institution." She finished her cognac. "Times are better now, six years later. We're fighting for rights—at least, for domestic partnerships." She gave a smile, meant to be reassuring, then burst out, "It's scary too. Things can always go back to the way they were thirty years ago when psychiatrists called it a mental illness."

Nadya nodded solemnly.

Kate heard a click. The tape had gone through to the end. She turned off the video camera and set it on the dresser, relieved to have the weight off her shoulder.

Nadya sighed. "You can't be left in peace?"

Kate shook her head grimly. "You have to fight." She made an apologetic face. "I'm not very good at it myself."

"And now," Nadya asked gently, "do you have anyone special?"

"Gilly." Kate hoped she would still have Gilly. "So they call you hooligans? In the U.S. that is an old-fashioned, gang-type word."

Masha explained, "The term covers a wide variety of crimes against the government."

Crimes against the government. Kate felt a chill. She took Nadya's hand. "Let me know through Masha if you find out anything before we meet tomorrow."

"By the way," Masha turned to Kate, "I reported to festival officials about your cab ride. They have received complaints from others."

"What kind?"

"In one case, the driver carried a gun and demanded more dollars; in the other, the driver refused a three-dollar offer, usually standard, and asked for five dollars. When the customer refused, the cab driver drove him out of town to rob him. Both men paid up and were taken to their destinations unharmed. This is not usual behavior," she apologized. "It seems everyone is angry, grabbing what they can."

Kate brightened. "Maybe it's not a conspiracy to get me. Or Sveta. Just that we were in the wrong place at the wrong time. I gave the man more money, but I fought back, which changed everything. What do you think?" she asked, wanting reassurance.

Masha raised her eyebrows, slowly shaking her head.

As the two women were about to leave, Kate asked Masha, "I take it you weren't able to see your son tonight?"

"I will try again tomorrow." Masha's eyes were filled with pain. "But today is his birthday. He is thirteen. I had taken the peanut butter and a small camera as gifts. My ex stomped on the camera. He threw the jar of peanut butter against the wall. My son watched everything, as terrified as I was."

"Poor, dear Masha." Kate hugged her. Nadya embraced them both. Kind of like a football huddle, Kate thought. And she was beginning to feel like the quarterback.

Chapter Eight

After 11:00 PM, Monday, January 28

After the two women left, Kate rewound the videotape, set the camera to VCR and played back the footage. She peeked through the viewfinder, revolted once again by Nadya's chilling story, stirred by her bravery. She was moved by Masha's courage, too, and elated that she'd entered the scene with Nadya. The picture was tiny, but on the close-ups she could see that the camera loved both: Masha's slim face, wide cheekbones, and slanted green eyes; Nadya, pale and small, her elfin face cut and bruised, her back ramrod straight, her eyes flashing. Dynamite! This was the most important scene she had so far. Kate ejected the tape and slipped it into a *Revolution* jacket that she'd filched from Dom. On the front, below *For Preview Only, 3rd generation,* was a photo of a smiling, young, blonde TODAY, the lead character in *Revolution*. And under her picture:

> Back in the STONED age we all went to San
> Francisco to escape our parents and the Vietnam War.
> To laugh and dance and love each other.
> Sex, drugs and rock 'n' roll were all so easy then.
> We had good trips and bad trips. And a few of us
> flipped out forever. But . . . It was one helluva summer.

Kate put a tiny black dot on the spine and slid the videotape into the roomy inside back pouch of her vest, next to her other valuable (though she didn't know why) video—the scar-faced officer with the enigmatic civilian in the gray suit—camouflaged in an identical *Revolution* box. Oh, yes, in case the red-haired soldier who felt her up this morning got frisky again . . . she pushed a Russian-formatted tape of their movie *Revolution* into a plain Sony box. She thumbed through her pocket Russian dictionary, found *Message,* and marked the word in Cyrillic, *Poslanie,* on the box with a black felt pen. She stashed it in her lower right vest pocket, the very pocket the soldier had patted this morning.

As she was about to take a shower, a rat-a-tat-tat sounded at her door. Dom called out, "Good news."

"Just a minute." She quickly climbed back into jeans, wrestled into her sweater, dashed out of the bathroom, and threw open her door.

"Katie, you missed a great party at the Tbilisi," Steve announced. "Unlimited champagne. Luscious food—chicken salad, shishkebob."

Kate's mouth watered. She'd give anything for decent food.

"Only four dollars American each for everything," Steve said.

"Four dollars is one hundred rubles." Dom gave his head a mournful shake. "Half a month's pay at the black market exchange rate."

"Delicious bread with melted cheese in it." Steve licked his lips. "Real tomatoes."

"*Hachapura*," Dom said.

Beyond the two men, Kate saw the *dejurnaya* rise up from her sleeping couch—two chairs pushed together—behind her desk. She frowned at Kate, yelped out something in Russian, her pale lips mobile, kaleidoscopic in her otherwise rigid face. Kate wanted a close-up of those lips. She motioned for the two men to come in, then she shut the door. "We woke up the *dejurnaya*."

"We may have a Dutch backer!" Dom was jubilant. "He was at the party." He held up a business card. "We gave him the pitch about *The Flying Eagles*. He loves the idea of a movie about the 101st Airborne, who jumped behind German lines to win World War II. Since we plan to shoot part of it in Holland, he thinks he can raise maybe half the budget, if . . ." he crossed his fingers, "we can raise the other half."

Steve nodded enthusiastically.

"Good work, guys!" Kate said. "What a piece of luck!" Hope fluttered in her chest. Dom's tribute to his dad, who had been a Flying Eagle, might be made. She would be a part of the team.

"We're meeting him again tomorrow, with his partners. We'll need to get him a full treatment and a revised budget."

Kate nodded. Dom looked beat. His eyes were bloodshot, his face pasty.

"Everything okay with Masha," he asked worriedly, adding with a curious look, "and her friend?"

Kate shot a quick glance at Steve, who was looking covertly at his watch, then at the door.

She shook her head imperceptibly at Dom, who understood she didn't want to talk in front of Steve. He nodded slowly. "See you at breakfast. I'm a zombie." He opened the door, stifling a yawn. With a half wave he stepped into the hall.

Trying to appear casual, Steve leaned against the doorjamb. "You should have been there, Kate. This Russian woman, stunning, a hooker—she was dancing to rock music, Jerry Lee Lewis, on the table tops. In high heels."

"She was invited to the party?"

"She was with the American who provided the champagne. The joint was rocking. Her husband, a civil engineer who lost his job, sends her out as a hard currency hooker," he said matter-of-factly. "She has a heroin habit and plans to check into a detox place next week."

The story sounded painfully familiar. Was she the same woman, anxious and afraid, who'd spoken into Kate's tape recorder at Masha's? "Women don't have it easy here." Yawning, Kate opened her door further, hoping to see the frowning *dejurnaya* suddenly rise up, swoop over and shoo Steve next door to his room.

"I need the company video camera," he blurted out.

"Now?"

He shrugged, mumbling, "For early tomorrow."

He never gets up early, she thought. He's up to something tonight.

"Okay." He grinned at her. "I'll come clean." He adjusted his purple tie and made his face look very businesslike. "I decided to collect brief auditions, just to remind me when we get back to the States. Lots of beautiful girls here. We may want to refer to the footage when we cast *The Flying Eagles*."

Kate had an idea what the auditions would consist of. Surely even Steve wouldn't be that crass.

He blathered on, smiling, "I have a good feeling about this guy from Holland. He may be able to help us raise the seed money, as well as fifty per cent of the entire budget."

She handed the camera over to him, saying coolly, "You'll have to put in a tape. I need it back tomorrow for the tour to Pavlovsk." She added mechanically, "You coming?"

"Maybe." He left.

She closed her door and locked it. As she took her shower, she thought about Dom—he so deserved this Dutch deal. His directorial debut, *Summer of Love* about the hippies in San Franciso, had been invited to the Cannes Festival in 1968, the year the French students went on strike. The film was pulled as too inciting. The distributor stole all the rights to his second film, award-winning and shot cheaply in New York, and put the film on the shelf after six months. Dom was now living on proceeds from his third movie, made in Denmark; he'd learned his lesson. He'd traveled around the world, singlehandedly selling international rights, country by country. She loved that about him—his tenacity, as well as his artistry. He lived an original life. She hoped someday she'd be able to say the same about herself.

She changed into her sleep gear, running pants and T-shirt, then sat up in bed re-reading three days' worth of past press releases, searching for clues she might have missed about the unrest in the country. In a release dated January 25—the first day of the festival, the day Dom, Steve and she arrived—were remarks made by the festival director at that morning's hotel press conference, ". . . an appeal to all people of the Earth to protest against the turn to dictatorship in this country, against the tendency of the current political situation to the cold war." There it was in black and white—stated plainly, not hinted at.

Another release, about the festival's sumptuous Opening Ceremony, where tables were filled with caviar, champagne, cheeses, sausages and vodka, ended with: *One of Pushkin's little tragedies: I hope we won't be guests at a feast during the plague.*

Through the Window Glass, as usual, gave her more items to ponder. Below the cryptic comment, *The critic Murzenko believes that the idea of the doom of Russia is becoming a reality,* was an outrageous sentence, *At a tattooed buttocks exhibition in England, the most popular exhibitions were not only of Margaret Thatcher.* Included for laughs? To demonstrate the shallowness of Westerners? Maybe an imperfect translation.

Kate couldn't keep her eyes open. She turned off the bedside lamp and sank down into the pillow. As she fell asleep, she heard giggles from the hall, a door opening, Steve's voice, then a woman with a Russian accent murmuring, "I am here for screen test."

※※※

AN HOUR LATER, ANDRE tapped the arm of the sleeping *dejurnaya*. She twitched, then sat up so quickly she almost fell off her chairs. Her eyes blinked rapidly before they focused. She looked at her watch. "It is after one o'clock."

Andre whispered, "The American woman—is she in?" She nodded warily. "Alone?" With a half-shrug, she nodded again. Andre asked for the master key. She hesitated. Andre shook her arm roughly, "Captain Iurkov's orders. We are looking for contraband."

The woman's eyes grew wide. She accompanied him to Kate's door. As the *dejurnaya* very quietly unlocked it, Andre stood behind her, peering over her shoulder. The girl was asleep in the bed closest to the door. The other bed was empty, with a suitcase sitting on it. The drape was closed, only a crack of light shining through from the outside streetlamps. The *dejurnaya* motioned for him to enter and retreated to her station.

He slipped into the darkness and eased the door shut.

He was in her room, standing over her as she slept. He could see a wedge of her face, the rest was crammed into her pillow. His eyes traveled down the blanket that covered her. He made out the lines of her body, dim and shifting, as if drawn in sand. He wished he had never become involved in this plot. Why must she die? His country was falling apart. He cursed Gorbachev for letting it happen. He took a deep breath and, as tears welled, rubbed his eyes with his knuckle. The room smelled of oranges.

Get down to business, he told himself. He shined his light on the floor and found the dresser. His pencil thin beam hovered over a stack of unopened videotapes and audiotapes, two oranges, a carton of water.

What was this? A stack of business cards. He rifled through them. The name Kate Hennessey was printed on one, below it an address in New York City. He put it in his pocket. Why, he didn't know. If the Captain had his way, she would soon be dead.

He very slowly opened each dresser drawer, shining his light inside, and finding each one empty, shut it—except for the bottom drawer, which, as he pushed, went crooked on him, making a cracking noise that echoed in the silent room. He froze.

She stirred. What would he do if she woke up? Put his hands around her throat? A pillow over her face? If he killed her, he would be in the Captain's good graces again. She turned on her side.

He waited, his heartbeat settling down, until she was motionless and breathing deeply. He very slowly coaxed out the bottom drawer, straightened it on the runners, and slid it closed. Sweat trickled through his eyebrow into his eye. He wiped it off with his sleeve. Shielding the beam with a hand and checking from time to time that she still slept, he shined his light over a chair, the table and the floor, searching for her camera, her vest, or a videotape without its cellophane wrap. He looked in the closet. He crept into the bathroom waving the narrow line of light over the walls, the tub, the towel racks, the shower curtain rod, the back of the door. Her video camera was nowhere to be found. Neither was the vest. He felt ready to jump out of his skin.

If he could not find the tape—no, that could not happen. If he could not find it, he would wake her up, demand to know its hiding place. Sweat poured in rivulets down his back. If he woke her, he would have to kill her.

He left the bathroom. He focused his light on the valise sitting on the other bed.

There was the vest, in a jumble, half in and half out of the suitcase, almost hidden among some bedclothes. A wild surge of hope made him dizzy.

A knock sounded. He turned off the flashlight, ran his shaking hand over the right side of the vest, felt the rectangular square in the lower pocket—exactly where it was this morning when he had patted her down. He remembered the look on her face when he touched it. He unzipped the pocket, and pulled out the video.

Kate, her voice heavy with sleep, asked, "Who's there?"

"Steve," a voice said from the hall.

Clutching the tape, Andre dropped to his hands and knees, and slid under the empty bed. Was it the man next door? Coming for a late night rendezvous? Andre hoped not. He could be stuck here for a long, dismal time.

"Hey, it's Steve." The man knocked again.

Kate threw off the bedclothes. "Yes?" she asked tersely through the door. She wouldn't open it, she decided.

"Hey, Katie," Steve crooned. "Come on over. Join the party."

"Go back to your room."

"Maybe you'd like to learn some techniques." He laughed. "Film techniques."

Kate heard the *dejurnaya* hiss, "Be quiet," as if she were standing outside the door. Good. The woman had left her perch to sort him out. It seemed she did know some English though she pretended not to.

Steve muttered something in return.

"Leave," the *dejurnaya* ordered.

"The girl works for me, for Titan Films," Steve spluttered, "my company."

Kate wanted to yell, "I'm not a girl and Titan Films is not your company."

"Go," the woman insisted. "I call security."

Kate waited. She heard Steve open the door to his room, heard him say, "Snooping busybody. My assistant is being temperamental."

"Your assistant! In your dreams," she muttered. She fell back into bed, edgy, but oh, so tired. Not enough sleep the four days she'd been here.

❦

TANYA, SHOES OFF, LAY on the bed, feeling pampered, slightly drunk. She held out her glass for more champagne. Steve, the film producer, poured. "Now, let's shoot a few frames," he said, smiling. "See how you look on camera, how you take direction."

She stumbled a bit as she stood up, did a few self-conscious poses. Then she pirouetted across the room in her stocking feet, praying her bad leg would hold up. It did. She laughed and clapped her hands.

"Beautiful."

"At sixteen I danced professionally at the Kirov," she said proudly.

He continued in soothing tones, "Now if you don't mind, please take off your blouse. The camera puts on a few pounds. Terrific," he said. "Please turn around slowly. Take off your skirt . . . and stockings . . . Please sit on the bed."

She did as she was told, a cold feeling in the bottom of her stomach.

"I'm putting the camera on the table," he said, "and will let it roll by itself. We'll do the scene together. I'll be actor as well as director."

"You want me to read from script?" she asked hopefully. "My English okay, not great."

Steve cleared his throat and pulled on his tie. "This technique is what we call MOS, Motor Only Shot, without sound. The director, if we go to America for the final screen test, will tell you what to do while the camera rolls. It's one continuous take. If you interrupt," he said sternly, "he'll have to stop the camera and start over from the beginning. That costs money. He'll want to be sure, before he hires you, that you can follow orders, as well as act." He removed his trousers and sat next to her on the bed "You understand?"

She nodded.

She did not like what he commanded her to do, but she did it. She gave her best performance, using all her skill, fearful he'd think she wasn't talented enough to be a film actress in America.

When the audition was over, she felt angry and ashamed.

He looked at the scene through the camera VCR, murmuring, "You're an artist, my dear." He asked her as she dressed, "Can you round up other good-looking women who might be interested in a film career? Even a few young men with hard bodies?"

"What about my screen test in America?" she asked sharply.

He took some bills from his pants which hung on a chair. "First we'll set up a co-op venture here. You help supply the talent. We give you a commission." He pressed the money into her hand.

"I want to go to America." Tears came to her eyes.

"Trust me. When we make money, I'll invite you to America. You'll have your choice of scripts." He brushed his hand across her face. "You've got the cheekbones of a Garbo."

You already told me that, she thought angrily.

He continued smoothly, "With the right lighting . . ."

She would not allow herself to be used. But she would take a chance with this Steve, see what she would be required to do. She would get out of this dismal life in this dismal country one way or another.

"Do you have a girlfriend you can call?" Steve asked as he dressed.

"Now?"

He nodded. "I leave the country soon. I'd like to take back several screen tests. I'll give her twenty dollars American. You'll get another twenty for bringing her in." He gave her a meaningful smile. "The two of you can do a scene together."

Twenty dollars was not to be ignored. Tanya dialed Irina. "She will be here," Tanya said, lowering the phone to its cradle.

"I have a gift for you to wear tonight." From a dresser drawer, Steve pulled out a black lacy brassiere and panties. Never in her life had she seen such things. "Remember," he warned, "this co-op film venture is very hush-hush. We don't want the wrong people barging in."

ANDRE WAITED UNDER THE bedsprings, claustrophobic, hoping he wouldn't sneeze. He heard Kate tossing and turning in the opposite bed. When would she go back to sleep? He had had a long day, trying to keep order among the bored, restless soldiers. Everyone was on edge, waiting for the word from Moscow.

Then, too, there was his unpleasant meeting with Kolya. *Watch yourself,* Andre had warned him. *Major players from Moscow are keeping their eyes on us. The Captain is angry about your disrespect. You shouldn't have gone to the money man behind his back. And stay away from Kate. The Captain will find other means to kill her.* Kolya especially had not liked it when Andre demanded the return of the two porno tapes Kolya planned to sell. Better that Kolya give the tapes to Andre, for him to pass on to the Captain, than have the Captain seek out Kolya.

When Andre handed the *pornografia* over to Captain Iurkov, he had smiled like a cat who ate the cream.

Andre felt his eyes close. He pictured Kolya at their meeting, drunk, furious and posturing, but giving in with a grin when Andre told him he would split with him, fifty-fifty, any money he received.

Andre jerked awake. He must not be found here. He pinched his face to keep alert.

How would the Captain manage her death? An accident, he had said, during one of the Cultural Program Excursions. So American authorities would not be nosing in.

That is what Andre had told Kolya from the first, "Make it look like an accident." That fat oaf had messed up big-time. But maybe, Andre thought, that is why I gave him the job.

At last, Andre could tell by her breathing that Kate was asleep. He crawled from under the bed, tiptoed across the room, and gave her one last look. "What a pity," he said softly before he let himself out the door.

In the light of the hall, he glanced quickly at the tape. It was in a plain Sony wrapper, and marked in black ink, *Poslanie*

(*Message*). He held it up for the *dejurnaya*, waving it like a gladiator, but she was sound asleep behind her desk.

⁂

KATE SAT UP IN bed. What had wakened her? A squeak from a door? Voices? Yes. Steve and female voices, talking in the hall. When she heard Steve's door close, she scurried to her own door and cracked it. Two women were talking to the *dejurnaya*, who seemed to know them both. One woman, her back to Kate, wore spike heels and a long white fur coat. The other was—well, what do you know—Irina. Kate recognized the expensive-looking brown suede coat, fur-trimmed, the reddish-blue circles under her deep-set eyes. She'd been at Masha's "social" gathering, had taunted Kate about the greedy West; had gone out of her way to procure the special "cab" for Kate and Sveta outside Masha's apartment building. Was Irina one of the "beautiful" women Steve wanted to audition? Or his hard currency hooker? She seemed too unattractive to be either.

⁂

ANDRE TRUDGED FOUR FLIGHTS down the back stairs. It was 4:00 AM, a very long day. He needed a drink. As he stumbled through the bar, he noticed a familiar barrel-shaped hulk, hunched at the counter, smoking, surrounded by the smell of burning rubber tires. Andre slid onto a stool beside him. "Kolya, how did you get into the hotel?" Andre whispered. What was going on? They had made no plans to meet.

"With a little *blat*," Kolya grinned. "Some of the soldiers know me as your relative," he said mockingly, giving Andre a punch on the arm. "Good to have friends in high places."

Andre frowned. What did he mean by that?

"Friends like you, Comrade." Kolya signaled the bartender. "Vodka for each of us." He stubbed out his Belomorkanal into an ashtray overflowing with butts.

When the drinks arrived, the two took them to a back table. Andre laid the videotape between them. "I took it from the American woman's room while she slept." He told Kolya about hiding there after the woman Kate was awakened by a member of her film company. "I was trapped under her bed for hours." Yawning, Andre rubbed his eyes, his face. "We need to watch it on your machine before I bring it to the Captain."

Kolya grunted.

Why was Kolya not excited that he had found the tape? "Why are you here?" Andre asked suspiciously.

"Checking up on you!" Kolya laughed. "A joke, Comrade. I wanted to mix with the big shots." He patted Andre's arm, condescendingly, like he would pat a dog.

Kolya's behavior was unnatural, falsely enthusiastic. Flippant even. Maybe he was mixing something else with the alcohol. Andre clinked his glass against Kolya's. "To a fifty-fifty split of American dollars," he said, pointedly reminding him of his generosity even though the Captain had officially removed Kolya from the job.

With a wide smile, Kolya pulled the videotape from its Sony box. His eyes blinked. He did a double take.

Andre's face fell as he saw the tape's wide white core. A Russian-formatted tape. He ripped it from Kolya's hand. "It is the movie they came to sell." His fingers traced the title pasted on the side, with the picture of a smiling girl underneath. "Revolution," he spat out. His anger made him dizzy. This woman—she was cunning, a tease and a cheat. If he had her now in front of him he would take her by the neck and squeeze, watch her face turn red, her lips blue. Pound her head against a wall.

Andre threw the tape on the floor; the plastic covering broke apart, spilling out the ribbon. The bartender smirked at him. *He probably was one of the* stukachi, Andre thought, *secret informers hired by the KGB to watch the watchers.* Andre gave him the finger before he sank down into his chair, battered, bewildered, exhausted. He had been sleeping badly ever since he took this Special Assignment. Something important was developing in Moscow. Tonight was a setback, but he could still prove himself to be a valuable player, be asked to take a role in the coming events, which could mean a raise in pay.

Kolya's lips curled. "Who is the screw-up now? You should have pulled the tape out of its box to check it." Andre held his head with both hands. He had a raging headache. "It was dark. People were pounding on her door."

Kolya leaned his face close to Andre's. Andre smelled his foul breath. Kolya growled, "You should have slapped her awake, beaten her until she told you the hiding place." He slammed his fist on the table. "You should have killed her," he said savagely. "This would be finished."

"Finished is right, stupid" Andre hissed, "The American authorities would be on my tail. The captain would pretend he didn't know me. The *dejurnaya* would say I threatened her, that is why she let me into the American's room."

Kolya looked sorrowful. "You know better than me what it means to fail." He shrugged. "You could be posted to the Baltics."

Or to a distant post in Siberia. Could his term of service be extended? Or he could be brought up before a tribunal for insubordination and sentenced to hard labor. Or worse.

Dimly, through his fatigue, Andre noticed Kolya's mouth twitch toward a grin, which he quickly stifled. But he could not quite hide the triumph in his eyes as he said, "I may be the one now with friends in high places."

He is glad I failed, Andre's sluggish brain registered. "If by friends in high places, you plan to deal directly with Gregor, the money man, better not. The Captain was *Spetsnaz*, special force of the KGB in Afghanistan. Their motto is, *We know no mercy and do not ask for any*. I know we once talked about double crossing the Captain." He shook his head. "Not if you want to stay alive."

Kolya flipped his hand in a casual manner. "Calm down, Comrade." He fetched them each another drink.

Andre slugged the vodka down as Kolya puffed away on yet

another cigarette, blowing smoke rings, saying smoothly, "Not having the *pornografia* to sell on the black market has left me broke."

"You had money to bribe the soldiers at the front door," Andre snapped. Kolya scowled, his eyes fierce under his bushy, black brows. *At least,* Andre thought, *he was not accusing him of a betrayal, for instance, of splitting profits with the Captain on the porn, leaving Kolya in the cold.* He would placate Kolya for his sister's sake. "And too bad, now this—the wrong tape yet again." Andre felt his eyes closing. "No fifty-fifty for you and me, Comrade, tonight," he mumbled, sprawling over the table top, his head on his arms, one eye open.

Kolya leaned in close and blew smoke in his face. Andre coughed. He saw Kolya's expression, a familiar one of desperation and slyness, as the man patted him on the shoulder, crooning, "No matter that you are a slimy weasel and stupid bungler. Get some sleep."

Andre woke up at dawn, still slumped over the table. No one, not even the bartender, was in the bar. Despite his throbbing head, he reminded himself to be watchful that sneaky Kolya did not pull a fast one. After all, he had gone once directly to the money man, Gregor. Who knew what they discussed?

Chapter Nine

9:00 AM, Tuesday, January 29

The next morning as Kate slipped into her photographer's vest, she felt an empty pocket—and it hit her. Where was the tape? Last night, she'd put it in her lower right pocket, hadn't she? Could she possibly have added it to her back pouch with the others? She was losing it, moving tapes from one spot to another, scurrying to keep one step ahead of Red Hair.

She searched the large inside back pocket of the vest and was relieved to find her two important videotapes were there, looking innocuous in their *Revolution* jackets, resting beside the two cassette audiotapes. The third, the Russian-formatted video of their movie, was the missing one.

When she stepped out her door, the *dejurnaya* was staring at her as if she'd risen from the dead. Kate pointedly asked, "Did you come into my room last night as I slept? Are you working for the red-haired soldier?" The woman, her sullen eyes showing a hint of fear, pretended she didn't understand English.

Kate banged on Steve's door, delighted to see when he opened it, that she'd roused him out of bed. His hair was a tangle, his eyes puffy. "What?" he asked grouchily.

"Who were the women visiting you last night?" she asked.

He blushed, his upper lip curling in a smile. "Festival hangers-on."

Did he even know Irina's name? she wondered. So Irina and the other woman were satellites, charming their way past the soldiers at the front doors, desperate to earn hard currency.

"I guess you're here for this," Steve mumbled, handing her the camera, then quickly snatching it back and ejecting the tape. Kate gave him a knowing smile, but he didn't drop his eyes.

In her room, heart in her throat, she removed from the inside back pouch of her vest both videos—the one with the scar-faced officer talking with the gray-suited civilian and the interview with brave Nadya, checking them through the camera VCR, hoping the intruder hadn't swapped tapes. No, he—or she—hadn't made a switch. Kate quickly stowed her treasures again in her back pouch, feeling a little like a genetically modified kangaroo and put a fresh tape in the video camera.

As she drank early morning tea, strong and sweet, in the hotel dining room, Kate perused the morning's press release she'd just picked up from her Festival mailbox, lingering over an article entitled *We'll Go Further: Dancing to the Music of Firing from the Other Side*.

"The press conference, 'The Baltic Republics: January of

1991,' was held yesterday in the Hotel Leningrad. Its theme: 'the military-communist conspiracy against democracy.' And too much attention is paid to a petty KGB agent. Well, it is easier to fight the 'demon-speaker' than the dark third force, the quite real 'Third group' of Omon (disguised as soldiers).

"Why do people of Latvia and Lithuania seem so optimistic, saying, 'We are united. They are afraid of bloodshed.' And why are Leningrad deputies so pessimistic? 'General Gromov is going to kill many people.' 'Don't count on hundreds of thousands to defend Leningrad or Moscow City Councils.'"

Defending Leningrad City Council from whom? she wondered. Latvians or General Gromov? When Dom joined her, she slid the release to him. "This seems to be a warning." Dom read it, swallowed hard, and murmured with a bleak smile, "Military-communist conspiracy against democracy, eh? Enough troops in this place now to commandeer the hotel."

"What's this dark third force, Omon?" Kate asked.

"Experts in small arms and hand-to-hand combat, taught to follow orders at any cost." He raised his brows. "Specially trained for urban combat and the entering and clearing of buildings."

"Like here," Kate said, with a shiver.

Dom nodded. "Some say Gorbachev is losing control of Omon."

"And General Gromov, who's he? They say he is going to kill many people."

"He was the Commander in Afghanistan, I believe, and received the highest military award for his bravery there."

The two of them were alone at the table, no stern-faced waitress stood nearby. Kate slid her chair close to Dom's. The clatter of plates and silverware echoed throughout the huge room, providing white sound. She spoke in low tones, telling him about her nighttime visitor and the missing tape.

Dom groaned. "It's time we leave this country."

"No, listen to me, it's part of their game plan of intimidation. I'll barricade my door for the next three nights," she said, trying to sound tougher than she felt. "Anyway, you're still negotiating film deals." Every day the circles under Dom's eyes seemed darker, the lines in his face deeper.

"I'm sleeping with you—in your room, in the other bed—until we leave," he said intensely. "Don't argue."

"Okay, deal." Kate twisted around to look at the people eating, talking and laughing, seemingly unconcerned about the third dark force taking over Leningrad. She described to Dom the shell game she'd been playing, ever since Red Hair had bumped into her and run his hand over the videotape in her pocket. "If the zipper hadn't been closed, the tape he wants might be in his hands now." Kate looked sideways at Dom, managing a smile.

"So you did a switch and put the Russian-formatted version of our movie in that rght pocket?"

"He'll love the hippie music, the beautiful women, the freedom . . ."

Dom broke in. "He may be livid to find you've fooled him again." Shaking his head in a school-teacherish way, he glanced at the press release still in front of him. "What's so important about that tape?" he mused, half to himself.

"The man in his expensive-looking gray suit seemed out of place in the bar." She replayed the scene in her mind. "When he saw me pointing the camera his way, he scooped something off the table and walked out of frame, leaving behind the officer who glared at me as if I'd interrupted a transaction. What if the civilian is the petty KGB agent—the 'demon-speaker' the release refers to—who's part of the military-communist conspiracy? Maybe someone doesn't want that kind of proof, the taped footage linking the two of them if there's a coup and it goes bad."

They finished breakfast in silence and threaded their way out of the still crowded dining room. "Shall we do the tour to Pavlovsk this morning?" Dom's mouth twisted into a smile. "Or stay inside and barricade our doors?"

Festival management had scheduled daily "Cultural Excursions." On the first day they'd visited the legendary Aurora, the ship that fired a blank round to signal the storming of the Winter Palace. From the ship across the Neva, their hotel had loomed, dark and grand, partly institution, partly palace. Despite economic chaos and crumbling infrastructures, the excursions doggedly continued. "We'll be in a group," Kate decided. "We may find out what's really going on, instead of getting vague hints and rumors."

At five minutes of eleven, Kate, video camera in hand, waved at Dom, who stood just inside the hotel's front doors. "Great hat," he said half-heartedly. She wore the black, bushy fur hat that Olga, from the Olgino, had given her. "You think it makes me look like Rasputin?" Kate asked.

"Harpo Marx." Dom gave her a crooked grin. "Our print was delivered to me after breakfast, as promised. What do you think of that?"

"I'm stunned . . . and impressed," Kate said.

"The metal reels are missing. I pray they haven't been sold as scrap. The projectionist took the film off the reels for yesterday's show." He sighed. "Russia has a different system. Oh, well, it's back in our hands. The Americans who organized the Tbilisi party told me their film about the underground tunnels in North Vietnam has disappeared. An expensive print, and they won't get a single screening."

"It was in Sergei's room," Kate said, "when we stopped by looking for *our* missing movie. I panned the room, and I taped the film cans with the title, *Tunnels,* peeping out from underneath a pile of clothes."

Dom said nothing, his mouth a grim line.

The two stepped outside. A stiff wind blew in from the Neva River, found them where they stood under the overhang. Dom put on his earmuffs. Kate tucked in her scarf more tightly around her neck. The river had frozen over again and was covered with a thin layer of snow. "Footprints in the snow, across the river to the Aurora." Kate raised her camera, zeroed in on the footprints, widened the shot to include the ship and the Hermitage. She slid the camera inside her coat to keep it warm.

"You don't suppose," she asked, half-joking, "that a revolutionary sneaked over the ice to the ship to sound the call to arms?"

Dom grunted out a laugh. He said, still gazing at the river, "One of the Czarinas had an ice palace built on the Neva as a marriage present for her son. It was furnished with ornate furniture, all carved out of ice. She made the couple spend their wedding night there. She was quite a practical joker."

The tour bus appeared at 11:30 AM. People poured out from the lobby. "Looks like the coup is off. For now," Dom said in a low voice as they took their seats. The bus filled up, the doors closed. Pavlovsk, with its Palace of Catherine the Great, was sixteen miles south of the city. The bus lunged out of the hotel parking lot.

Alexei, from Sovintour, their guide for all festival excursions, had a gallant demeanor. Kate loved the way he said—slightly rolling his r's—"*verra* beautiful," as he delivered his commentary from the aisle, behind the driver. "May I videotape you?" Kate asked. He hesitated briefly, then nodded yes. "Our first stop is Pushkin Square where shopping is done in hard currency; they sell *matryoshka* (nesting) dolls, lacquered pins, military watches. Don't buy the caviar in glass jars," Alexei warned. "It's fake, made from fish paste."

Through the bus windows, to Kate's eyes, the city had the genteel decrepitude described by her tour book. Pigeons huddled in the crevices of decaying buildings, trying to dodge the cold wind. Pedestrians hurried along the street in dark coats, heads down.

When the bus stopped at Pushkin Square, Dom and Kate disgorged with the rest of the tourists. Gentility disappeared. Kate shot the chaotic scene. As soon as money appeared, the hawkers left their kiosks, circling their prey. "Real rabbit fur on this hat, real military watch, caviar in tins." The mob looked cold and hungry, a little like sharks, as they jostled potential buyers. Dom had her back so the video camera wouldn't be stolen from her hands.

"Please you Madame, look you here, so good painted." Cigarette hanging out of his mouth, hands red and trembling, a young man unscrewed a *matryoshka* doll, piece by piece. Even the tiniest doll had the intricate detail of the largest: the flowered dress, the cap, a miniature face with tiny eyes, nose and mouth. "Only ten dollars American," he grinned. In the hotel gift shop, Kate had seen identical *matryoshkas* for ninety dollars.

Huddled between two kiosks, another youngish man loitered, hatless, his thin face pinched with cold. His eyes darted nervously toward dark cars covered with brown mud, parked curbside, then flicked back to the tourists. He hissed, "Change, change," offering thirty-five rubles for a dollar. Kate had been offered twenty-five rubles outside the hotel yesterday. It was illegal to deal in black market money, but daily the rate seemed to be going up.

The mud-spattered cars, bumper-to-bumper, sat silent, anonymous through all the whispered offers.

Back on the bus, Alexei said the brown cars that enclosed the Square on every side were KGB. Kate felt a chill, remembering the man who'd abducted her. His car—without handles on the inside back doors—was KGB. Had he watched her just now as she videotaped the sellers and their wares?

Alexei continued, "The KGB mafia are encouraging the black market, hoping to throw a monkey wrench in the country's attempts to move from communism to capitalism."

Kate turned to Dom, astonished. Why were Masha and others reluctant to speak out on tape and Alexei seemingly fearless? Anyone could be on this bus disguised as a tourist.

A middle-aged gentleman across the aisle whispered, "The KGB fear their time is almost over and they want to make all the money they can." He had an accent. Obviously, he considered himself an expert in Soviet affairs.

Two people up the aisle had bought Gorby *matryoshka* dolls from a kiosk Kate had missed. As the couple took the dolls apart, Kate stood for a closer look. Inside Gorbachev was Andropov, next was Brezhnev, followed by Kruschev, then Stalin (with blood on his hands), a small Lenin, the Czar Nicholas, and finally Peter the Great. The Gorby dolls seemed to say perfectly what the Russian people felt about *glasnost,* Gorbachev: The more things change the more they stay the same.

Kate asked Alexei, "How can Gorby dolls be sold so openly in front of KGB cars?"

He shrugged. "Political *matryoshka*s didn't exist before *glasnost.* You could have gone to jail. But," he added, with a weary smile, "the dolls sold here are unsigned by the artists who paint them."

The bus jerked forward, on its way again. Kate decided to return later to the Square to buy Gorby dolls for her video project. "On your right," Alexei said in his soft, tenor voice, "is St. Isaac's, once the most important church in Leningrad, decorated with semi-precious stones and paintings. *Verra* beautiful," he said softly. The murmurings of a man in love. "But," he added mournfully, "the cathedral is now closed for renovations."

Alexei answered questions put to him by the busload of tourists. He spoke of the Russian people's disenchantment with Gorbachev and Yeltsin. As for *perestroika,* he said, things hadn't changed much. Tax money was mostly going to the military, to the powerful Party leaders in Moscow, not to the people. Leningrad was falling apart, its roads, buildings, and homes. Kate focused tightly on his pleasant face. He didn't seem worried that the rules might change and he'd find himself on the wrong side.

The "Expert" across the aisle called out to Alexei. "What about the food shortages, the chaotic money situation—what do you think will happen?" Alexei smiled grimly. "The recent money scheme, the withdrawing of fifty- and one hundred-ruble notes, was really an attack on small businesses, free enterprise, not the black market. The real crooks deal in hard currency."

Kate did a slow zoom into Alexei's face. His sad smile filled up the frame. "Nostradamus predicted a great upheaval for the USSR—to take place this year, in six months and 24 days." Not this week, as the press release she'd read at breakfast hinted. She tightened the shot to focus on Alexei's eyes, full of anguish.

"It's too late to put the genie back in the bottle," proclaimed the Expert. "*Glasnost* and *perestroika* have given the Russian people a taste of freedom."

Through the bus window were long queues. "There is a very high rate of alcoholism in the USSR," Alexei said, "which Gorbachev is trying to reduce by making alcohol hard to get."

Soon they were moving along snowy country roads. Finally, the bus pulled through a stone entrance. "We are driving through the Theater Gate," Alexei said, "past the Common Grave of the Heroes of the October Revolution." The tour bus rolled into a parking lot, its tires crunching on the snow.

"How many acres here?" a voice asked.

"Over a thousand," Alexei answered. He raised his arms in an expansive gesture. "All this, with the marble and bronze sculptures, the beautiful shrubs and trees, makes the park grounds verra poetical and perfect." His chest rose like Romeo's must have risen when he first saw Juliet. Now Kate understood what was meant by the Russian soul.

The group disembarked and sauntered down the snowy tree-lined road to the Great Palace. Kate felt transported back to the Eighteenth Century, "We're actually walking where Catherine the Great once walked," she said to Dom, focusing her camera on the palace with its curved connecting buildings, the exterior a creamy yellow trimmed in white.

In the courtyard, she looked back from where they'd come. People on the road were dwarfed by the giant, thickly branched trees, their barren look softened by a thick coating of powdery snow. At the palace entrance, the tour group crowded around Alexei. His soft voice was like a breath of spring in the clear, cold air. "Pavlovsk took fifty years to build. In 1917 after the Great October Socialist Revolution, the palace and park became property of the people and was made into a State Museum."

Inside, everyone wore cloth slippers over their shoes to preserve the lovely hardwood floors. An old man with a long beard, in charge of the slippers, spotted Kate's video camera. "*Nelzya!* Not allowed to take pictures," he announced loudly, just as she was about to ask if she could tape him. He had a perfect Russian face, right out of Chekhov. "Why not?" she asked. "It will damage the art works," he said. "I don't use a lamp," she replied. "No matter," he shrugged, then added severely, "It is the rule. And we don't break rules here." When the others followed Alexei to begin the palace tour, Kate stayed behind. She asked the old man what he thought the future of Russia would be.

"Lenin won't fall out of favor," he answered gruffly. "Even if his statues are destroyed. He had a dream that everyone was equal. A good dream. Why do we have to follow your path in the West—greed, homelessness, billionaires whose only skill is in making a deal."

Kate nodded. "True. All some people do is make money out of money. They offer no skills or services to society."

"I'm told everyone in America who wants a BMW or a gold credit card can have one. Is the price worth it?" He glared.

"I don't have either," she said defensively. He spoke English very well. Maybe he'd been a teacher in another life. His question, *is the price worth it?*, made her think of polyester clothes, mattresses with toxic emissions, vegetables and fruits tainted with pesticides—all the short cuts entrepreneurs devised to earn bigger profits. Capitalism gone wild.

The old man's voice took a high-pitched, reedy turn. "You people in the West think you've won the Cold War, that you've convinced us of the superiority of your views. You haven't convinced everyone." He walked away.

Did he hate all Americans? All American women wearing pants? Kate was shaken, but she called after him, "Thank you." A sliver of ice in her heart told her that would have been dynamite on tape.

She caught up with Dom and the others, marveling at the paintings, crystal chandeliers, tapestries, decorative vases, Italian marble sculptures, the carved gilded furniture. Forty-five opulent rooms. Alexei seemed as proud of the furnishings as if he lived here. Well, in a way, it was his. It was property of the People.

At the end of his spiel, Alexei added, shaking his head sadly, "During the Great War, the palace was reduced to ruins by the Nazis, who slashed the paintings, kept their horses inside in the lovely palace rooms. They cut down thousands of trees and bushes. When they retreated, they set the palace on fire. Restoration work was begun in 1944 and still continues to this day."

Still continues, Kate thought, in the midst of the terrible poverty of the Russian people. She decided to risk the old man's wrath and ask him his opinion of that. He was gone when they returned their slippers to the bin.

Outside, snow was falling lazily. In the distance, the trees had a silvery sheen. Dom and Kate walked desultorily back to the bus. Away from the city's turmoil and spying eyes, Kate felt relaxed, refreshed by the peace and beauty. "Look out!" Dom suddenly shouted, pushing Kate to the side of the road into a snow drift. He fell on top of her. Kate looked up to see a truck roar by. In the back in the open bed sat a group of laughing soldiers.

Dom scrambled to his feet, brushing off his clothes. "They must have been going fifty miles an hour," he spat out. He gave Kate a hand, his face chalky white. "I turned around to take one last look at the palace. They seemed to be headed directly for us. Are you hurt?"

"I'm okay." She turned on her camera, relieved to see it still worked, and fumbled with the zoom, capturing a close-up of the soldiers in the back of the truck.

Just then another truckload of shouting soldiers rocketed by, weaving all over the road. Ahead of them pedestrians jumped out of their way. "It seems to be a game," Kate said. "Scare the tourists." She quickly dropped the camera to her side and flicked the off switch. The truck squealed off onto another road. "What are soldiers doing in this enchanting place?" she asked shakily.

"Maybe they're based here, like the Nazis in World War II,

waiting for orders about the coup." Dom gave a sick grin. "The palace has rooms—off to the side that we didn't see—" He opened a flyer with a map of the area, showing a maze of roads, various outbuildings. "Over a thousand acres. They could be staying in buildings all over the grounds. Part of the demobilization Masha talked about."

"They seemed revved up, so arrogant—" A shadow passed over her. "You don't think the driver deliberately aimed for me? You just happened to be in the way?"

"Probably bored and hitting the bottle," Dom said slowly.

"Yeah." She'd been in this country four days. Her brain was hardening into a knot of fear and suspicion.

In the bus, on the way back to the hotel, Dom asked, "What was that all about last night? With Masha and her friend?"

"Masha's friend was Nadya, close with Sveta," Kate said carefully. Dom looked expectant. "Can you come to my room after we arrive at the hotel?" He nodded.

In Kate's room, Dom watched the footage of Nadya and Masha through the camera VCR. "I pity the women in this country," he murmured, adding worriedly, "So Sveta is missing. She didn't get away."

Kate sighed. "Maybe she did and is a prisoner in her own home. Or in the Psychiatric Clinic. You heard Nadya describe Sveta's brother as a devil. He reported both Sveta and Nadya to the police as hooligans. Gay lovers."

"You're really going—the three of you—to this supposed *gay* hangout, this café?"

"We have to find Sveta, know for sure what's happened. These women at the café may be able to help, if they're willing to speak up."

"Wait a minute," Dom frowned. "You're an American, barging into this 'underground' café, leading a search for a disenfranchised young woman that you just met. You're already in the spotlight, as Masha would say. Be careful, be smart."

"I made a promise to Sveta to help her if I could," she said stubbornly.

Dom stole a sidelong look at his watch. "Steve and I have a five-thirty meeting with the Dutch investor and his partners." He massaged his forehead. "And we have to collect the metal film reels from the Molnia." He groaned. "I should come with you."

"We'll do better, as women, checking out the café," Kate said. "Masha's very sensible and knows the protocol."

"Kate, you're unique. If I ever have a daughter, I want her to be just like you."

Tears sprang to her eyes. Nobody had ever said that to her before. Dom held her face with both hands. "If you run into trouble," he said, "get to the American Embassy as fast as you can."

Chapter Ten

4:00 PM, Tuesday, January 29

As the electric tram bounced along its tracks, Kate's eyes swept over the car. No soldiers skulking, no acne-scarred creeps staring at them. A babushka, fast asleep, her head resting on the palm of her hand, jiggled in her seat. Another woman cuddled a black dog, whispering in its ear. A man folded his newspaper in quarters and read.

Were Masha and Nadya, seated on either side of her, as nervous as she? A muscle twitched in the corner of Masha's mouth. Nadya held the flap of her scarf over her eye, which had grown very ugly in the past twenty-four hours, the bruised discoloration in the corner blooming into a circle of purple, blue and green that covered the eyelid and the socket. Her knuckles were white. The piece of paper crushed in her hand held the address of the café.

Neither Nadya nor Sveta had known there was a word for what they felt. They'd only heard rumors about this secret meeting place for women who loved other women. Did it exist? If so, would anyone talk to them? Would they learn anything to help Nadya find Sveta? Two days had passed since Sveta went missing. Kate's chest tightened every time she thought about that call Olga made to Sveta's home. The man who answered was most likely Sveta's brother, a hothead, according to Nadya. He rang off so quickly, before Olga could get more information.

Nadya peered through the tram window, nodding her head excitedly. "We get off here." The three women disembarked at the next stop. "Petrogradskaya Storona, the oldest part of the city," Masha said to Kate as Nadya led the way. The trio stepped over icy mounds of hard packed snow, lost their footing on slippery patches as they turned one corner, then another. Easy to fall or break an ankle, Kate thought, cradling her video camera in her arms.

Masha chattered nervously, "It is mainly residential. See the little yards with wooden houses, almost like Paris. Small parks are nearby. Cafés are hidden away on side streets." The late afternoon sun hung at the horizon line. The three made a sharp right into a dead-end. Halfway down the block, Nadya referred to the wrinkled paper in her hand and pointed excitedly. "There it is. The sign. In the window. Kafé Dushá." Masha translated, "Café Soul."

The women drew in an almost simultaneous deep breath. We should have made a plan, Kate thought, panicked. She couldn't see in the windows. The blue door was wooden, no panes of glass to peek through. Masha and Nadya seemed to be looking to her for guidance. Was the door locked? The place closed by order of the police? Should she knock three times, or give some kind of secret signal to admit them? Suddenly Nadya was turning the knob. Lo and behold, the door yawned open. Nadya crept in, beckoning Kate and Masha to follow.

At the windows were faded blue drapes and tattered, dingy white sheers. Scarred wooden tables and wooden chairs filled the edges of the room, empty except for four women, near the front, drinking coffee and eating ice cream and pastries. Only four? Were women scared to come here? Kate looked at her watch. 4:30 PM. Early.

Kate's eyes raked over the table of four. In a blur, she saw two blondes. Two with short, shaggy, dark hair. One of the blondes wore a maroon dress. The three others wore pants.

One in a dress, three in pants, Kate thought. Were they into role playing? Was the maroon dress the only *femme*? Wait a minute, she told herself, we don't know these women are gay. The New York City bars had taught her that looks could be deceiving.

"*Zdrasvuitya*," Nadya stammered with a half wave. The women glanced up. When Nadya removed her scarf, revealing her discolored eye, they uneasily turned away. A man with short brown hair, wearing a butcher's apron over a deep blue T-shirt, quickly stepped out from behind a back counter, as if to protect his clientele. No one smiled.

From the table nearest the four women, Nadya pulled out a chair—it moaned as it slid over the floor. She plunked herself down. Kate and Masha joined her. Kate pushed her video camera under the table, keeping track of it between her feet.

Nadya whispered, "Do you see? It is as Sveta and I were told."

Just as Kate was wondering if they would be ignored until they slunk away none the wiser, the aproned man approached. "What you want?" he asked gruffly. He was broad-chested, his arms smooth and muscled. Masha, ignoring his scowl, answered in Russian, then in English, "My friends and I will have *morozhenoe*, vanilla ice cream and coffee." She smiled serenely, as if she were sitting in an elegant Paris bistro. When the man turned to leave, she tinkled out a laugh, "Russian vanilla ice cream is the best vanilla ice cream in the world."

Kate shed her coat, conscious of her precious cargo in the inside back pouch of her vest. To camouflage her videos and audiotapes she'd padded them with socks so their outlines were not obvious. Did the bump on her back make her look deformed?

After what seemed a long wait, their order was delivered, coffee and for each a mound of ice cream with jam on top.

Kate ate nervously, oblivious to the taste. No one said a word.

Over coffee, Kate offered cigarettes. Nadya lit up. Her blonde hair was tightly pulled back, her face white, except for the cut on her cheek and her multicolored eye. She blew smoke rings and nervously tapped her fingers.

Kate leaned over to the adjacent table. The women looked very young, like teenagers. "*Prevyet.* Marlboro?" She held out the pack.

Each solemnly took a cigarette, murmuring "*Spaceba.*" As they smoked, their eyes skimmed over Masha and Kate, resting on Nadya for several seconds before they flicked away.

Nadya's shrill voice broke the silence. Masha whispered into Kate's ear, "She says, *I hope you will help me.*" The young women stared at Nadya with frozen faces.

"My friend Sveta and I heard about you," Nadya continued, "that you are *tusovka*, a social club who meet here." Masha translated *sotto voce.*

The young women buzzed among themselves. One with dark hair, close-cropped like a man's, evidently the spokesperson of the group, asked, "Who are you?" She wore black trousers, a white shirt with a black string tie, and over that a dark jacket. "Did someone send you?"

At the same time Nadya rose and approached their table. "No one sent us. My friend is in trouble." She showed them a photo of Sveta "Would you have advice? Where I can turn?"

The women seem intrigued by Nadya, Kate thought, probably curious about her black eye, the reddened cheek. They listened respectfully, even sympathetically. One murmured, "Bella," when Sveta's photo was shown.

"*Americanski?*" A punk-looking young woman with short, white-blonde hair, a dark streak at the part, pointed at Kate. She sat next to Black String Tie. Were they a couple? Kate wondered.

"Kate is my friend from New York City," Nadya said.

"Kate was invited here by the film festival," Masha explained. "She wishes to help Nadya find Sveta."

Kate broke in, "I was with Sveta the night we were attacked and she disappeared. We don't understand why this happened, but Nadya has been bullied by her family and even beaten and raped by police. Because of her love for Sveta."

With animated gestures, Masha relayed Kate's words in Russian. The women nodded, their eyes wary.

"I am desperate to find my friend," Nadya pleaded. "She is missing for two days now. I do not know if she is alive or dead. I hear rumors that others like us meet here at the Café Soul. Can you help me?"

Still the women were silent. They're probably afraid, Kate thought, because I'm American. A Westerner.

A dark-haired young woman—this one in gray suspenders—stubbed out her cigarette. Kate offered her another. "We like American films," Gray Suspenders said cautiously, looking at the video camera sitting by Kate's feet.

A big mistake, bringing that camera. "What are your favorites?" Kate asked.

"Charlie Chaplin," she said in English, grinning, wagging her head, snapping her suspenders with her thumbs. She did a Charlie Chaplin wiggle. "*Some Like it Hot.*" She turned to the woman in the maroon dress, who laughed. "Arnold Schwarzenegger in *Commandos.*" She held her arms up, pretending to flex her muscles.

The young woman in the maroon dress was beautiful, fine-featured, Kate thought, her golden hair falling softly to her shoulders. The dress, old-fashioned, was draped at the waist. She looked like a World War II heroine from one of those old B&W movies.

"*Rozovaya?*" the punk blonde with the dark streak nodded toward Kate, then Masha.

Kate pointed to herself. "I am gay. *Rozovaya.*"

Masha shook her head. "I am here as translator. We women must stick together. We must all speak up and fight for our rights."

Gray Suspenders twisted in her chair. "The problems for us only start when we fight for our rights."

"This is a social club," her golden-haired friend announced, "not political. We need a place to meet. Not hide."

The Black String Tie introduced herself as Anya and nodded toward the punk-looking bleached blonde. "This is Martina." Anya crossed to the window, parted the drape, and looked outside, turning her head from right to left. She seemed satisfied.

She signaled Masha, Nadya, and Kate to follow her and Martina to a small alcove at the back of the room. The waiter, who'd silently watched the careful introductions, glowered.

After the five women were settled at the table, Masha asked for permission to translate. Dark haired Anya and white-blonde Martina nodded. Anya, pointing, at Kate's camera, confided, "We thought you were sent by someone. But curiosity has overcome my fear. I would like to talk to you. But not on camera. I could not be sure if the video was leaving for Moscow or America."

Nadya, her eyes intense, reached across the table, grabbing Anya's hand. Her small body trembled, her sentences went up and down in pitch and volume, as if she were singing an aria. To Kate's ears, Masha's interpretation of her words kept every nuance. "Sveta's family has said, if she does not marry, she must go to the Psychiatric Clinic. That is what I think has happened. I hope it has happened. I do not want her to be dead." Tears ran down Nadya's cheeks. Impatiently, she rubbed them away. "Why can't Sveta and I remain friends as we are?"

Anya sighed. "Because the experts have decided this is wrong." Her voice was dry and flat. "For the men, the *goluboi*, the light blues, there is Article 121 and jail. For the women, not jail, but just as cruel. The *psikushka*s, the psychiatric hospitals, and the Cure—"

"Ask her, *What is the Cure?*" Kate broke in.

Masha did and repeated Anya's answer in English. "Shock treatments, insulin and other drugs." She shook her head, dismayed. "Barbaric."

Kate was appalled.

"What will happen to Sveta after this Cure? Will I see her

again?" Nadya cried out, her words echoing in the nearly empty room.

The waiter, now seated at the front table with Anya's and Martina's friends, frowned and half rose from his chair. Shaking her head, Anya waved him off.

Anya fumbled with her black string tie. "I can only speak from my experience. After the Cure you must register with the KGB. And report to them regularly." She pressed her lips together, nodding, watching Kate's face as Masha translated. "If you do not cooperate, they will tell others at your job or in your neighborhood. You will be looked at as freak and avoided."

This young woman, Anya, was she Nadya's age? Kate wondered. Perhaps a year older. Still a teenager. Her deep-set eyes had been unflinching as she spoke. No self-pity. Look at all she's gone through—first the Cure, her brain scrambled by electro-shock therapy, treatment with insulin and who knows what other drugs. Surviving that, she now must report to the KGB as if she's a criminal. "Oh, Anya . . ." Kate could only shake her head in sympathy.

Anya nodded grimly. "It makes you crazy. You must prove every day that you're normal. Marry a man and have a family." She made a face, then suddenly grinned. "If you like adventure, you can always have a double life. Do what the authorities demand and have your true love elsewhere. It takes some nerve," she admitted. "Or you can be married, just for day. Any means to get their gaze off you."

Nadya cringed. "What if I have no wish for a double life?"

Anya shrugged. "If the Cure does not cure you, you become like me, transsexual."

"Transsexual? You?" Nadya asked, her eyes wide.

"The doctor told me, 'There is no need to suffer when we can treat such things with an operation.' He did x-rays, blood and urine tests. If they show I am a man, he could send me to Moscow for an operation." Her tough façade collapsed. "I like my body as it is."

Kate was horrified. She turned to Nadya, who sat still and

stiff, as if she were asleep with her eyes open. Kate squeezed her hand and received in return a wild, frightened look. "Surgery would mean . . ." Kate said numbly . . . "removal of the breasts." Masha repeated this to Anya, who swallowed hard and nodded.

In America, Kate thought, transsexuals—people who believed their bodies were the wrong sex—were counseled, and absolutely had to be sure they wanted this transformation. They weren't browbeaten into doing it.

Anya frowned. "Some who have had the surgery have advised me not to." She darted a glance at the waiter who'd gravitated from the front and hovered nearby. She continued in a softer voice, Masha leaning in to hear her better.

"What did she say?" Kate asked.

Masha's green eyes were icy with anger. "Women are more easily intimidated. There are many more women than men who take the option of the surgery."

Kate had never met a man who'd once been a woman, but she'd talked with a woman at a New York City bar who'd once been a man. She had an Adam's apple and large hands, was very tall, looked neither male nor female. She had problems with the hormones, she'd said, but changing her sex was the best thing she ever did. She frequented lesbian bars, so she was a man who'd become a woman and liked sex with women. Why hadn't she remained a man who liked women? Kate wondered.

Masha murmured to Kate, "How can these things happen?" She repeated the question to Anya who barked out a laugh, then released a steady stream of Russian, which Masha passed on to Kate in fits and starts, visibly struggling to keep up. "Someone in the KGB is in charge of homosexual affairs. The phone rings; someone may say, 'This is the KGB.' In my case, he showed me lists, asking me to inform on others. Threatened to tell my friends, my family, my job. If I get fired because of whatever they call it—criminal hooliganism or a mental illness, 'sluggishly manifesting schizophrenia'—I cannot move to another city and get another job." Anya jabbed her hand toward the floor. "I am registered here. Without *propiska* (residency permit*)*, we cannot find steady job or apartment. Everyone I meet I think, do they work for the Captain?" Her deep-set eyes were tormented.

The waiter was edging closer to the table.

Anya scooted her chair around, her back to him, speaking directly to Kate as Masha translated. "Here many generations live in one apartment. Impossible to have private moments. The way we are now—even if I do not have the surgery—we are accepted as a couple. We can register for a place to live together."

"How can that be?" Nadya asked.

"After psychological tests, the computer made a decision and an official issued a *spravka* which I took to a passport office. They changed my sex from female to male." Anya grinned, half proud, half still amazed.

She didn't look male, or have male gestures. She looked young and vulnerable with a haircut short as a man's. "This is just too bizarre," Kate burst out angrily. "That any woman who wants to be with another woman is forced through this hell. And it's all decided by a computer! If your behavior isn't what the authorities want, they will force you to change your sex."

Masha, with a warning glance at Kate, repeated her words softly in Russian. Kate reminded herself to be quieter. She didn't trust that nosy waiter.

Anya whispered, "Documents are everything: workbooks, residency permits, passports. Whatever the passport says is the truth." She winked.

Kate was amazed that Anya still had a sense of humor. She'd endured the Cure. Then was put on the KGB list, forced to be "normal." She couldn't hack it and so became a "man" after being humiliated by a psychiatrist who pretended to be understanding but offered her a chilling solution so authorities wouldn't bug her: *Take our tests, if they show you're a man, we will issue proper papers documenting this. You will be liberated into the life you want.* Oh my word, Kate thought, my problems are paltry in comparison. "Martina, what about you?" she asked the punk-looking blonde.

Martina sat up proudly, "I am *naturalka*. This"—she pointed to the dark-haired Anya beside her—"is my man."

Kate's mind was whirling, processing all the pieces of the system these women were trapped in. She turned in dismay to Masha, whose eyes were stunned in disbelief. Nadya's face was drained of color, except for the angry multi-colored eye, the livid red slit on her cheek. "This is a mockery," Kate spluttered. "You must organize, stop these barbaric practices, cruel laws."

"America is better?" Martina asked in English with a skeptical smile.

"We can live together as two women," Kate said, hearing Masha, behind her, repeat her words in Russian. "In my state, New York, we have dances, bars, places to meet. And our own newspapers. No harsh cures, no threats of surgery." She sagged. "Family, friends, and your job can be problems. But we are free to move to another city, take another job." She asked Anya. "Do you mind being called transsexual?"

"It is less shameful than to be called *lesbianka*."

Now Kate saw clearly. To be a lesbian was against the law. And so it was shameful. But if the bureaucrats declared one of the couple, in this case Anya, still in her woman's body, a man, the other woman is not a lesbian but normal. The two are a legal couple in the eyes of the psychiatrists and the KGB.

"Do you have jobs?" Kate asked. She kept her eyes steady on Anya and Martina, hearing Masha's musical voice in the background. Like watching a foreign film, dubbed into English.

"Yes. We have dropped out of school. I work in a factory," said Anya.

"And your co-workers accept you as a man?"

Anya's mouth twisted. "Whatever they think is not my business. My papers prove it." She hesitated, adding, "Some women like me fear they will lose their jobs if it is discovered they are women."

Anya seemed too feminine to Kate to pass as a man. When

she moved and talked, she seemed to put on gruffness and bold movements. But now, speaking earnestly with Kate, she looked scared, a slender reed who might break. "Do you feel you might be forced to have the operation?" Kate supposed for any excuse the bureaucrats might threaten her with it. Or the KGB Captain, if he was a sadist.

"You may be persuaded," her eyes grew sardonic, "to ask for permission for the surgery and the sexologist will put in the order. I try not to attract attention." Anya bit her lower lip, and then turned to her punk blonde friend. "Martina works as a kiosk attendant."

"I too work in a kiosk," Nadya said, coming out of her fog. Coming to terms, Kate supposed, with what might be required of her. "I hope Sveta and I can manage a life together, as you have." Such a wave of longing passed over her waif's face. It changed to despair. "But first I must find her. Can you help me?"

Anya, with a sympathetic look, gave Nadya her phone number. "We are hoping for an international rights conference in Leningrad and Moscow in the summer."

"Summer is too late," cried Nadya.

Anya shook her head sadly.

"I have an idea," Martina said. "Go to the Psychiatric Clinic, find out if she is there. They allow visits." She jotted an address on a paper napkin. "Be careful. They may put you on a list."

Kate also took Anya's contact information. "I want to come back with a film crew this summer. If there's a rights conference, would you speak to me on camera?"

Anya frowned. "If the film would be shown here, I would not let my face be seen."

Kate nodded, wondering about herself, about Gilly. Would they have the courage to come out on camera—even in America? How would her guardians, Aunt Maureen and narrow-minded Uncle Burt, react? Burt would probably die of apoplexy. What about Gilly's dad, who thought money could buy anything?

"*Spaceba*." Kate stood. She shook Anya's hand, and then Martina's, moved and inspired by their strength. Impulsively, Kate threw her arms around Martina, and pulled Anya over to join them. They hugged back. "*Das Vedanya*," Kate whispered, blinking away tears, wishing she knew Russian for "Good luck," "God be with you," "I wish I could help."

As Masha, Kate and Nadya were leaving, other women were drifting in. The waiter roughly grabbed Kate's arm, growled out a warning in Russian, his eyes pinpoints of anger.

Kate, frozen for a moment, twisted free. The waiter followed the three women to the door, haranguing all the way until they burst out of the café. "What did he say" Kate asked, rubbing her arm.

"He says—America has two hundred years of culture. Russia has a thousand years." Masha scrunched her eyes, remembering. "How dare you come here to teach them to organize? You leave and they stay. Who knows who will be in power? Anything can happen. These people have to live here—with the consequences."

"He's right," Kate sighed. She gave Masha a questioning look. "The waiter—probably he's the proprietor? I had the feeling he's a transsexual who's had the surgery." It was sinking in—the danger these women might have placed themselves in by speaking frankly with her, an American. "Maybe he's an informer for the KGB?"

A shadow passed over Masha's face. "He may be forced to report all contact with foreigners. Westerners."

Kate was losing her edge, her heart for fighting the System. Her hope for these new friends was fading. And as far as finding Sveta was concerned, they were right back at the same brick wall. She took Nadya and Masha by the hand. "I hope the authorities won't come after you because of me."

Masha lifted her head in defiance. "If we do not stand up now and talk to others, try to change lives, we may never have another chance." Nadya slowly nodded, her face pinched.

It was dark, the street lights sparkled on the snow. As the

three headed toward the tram stop, they were caught for an instant in the headlights of a car. It followed them around the corner, tires crunching on the frozen slush.

Kate turned up her coat collar against the wind.

Masha took Nadya's arm. "Tomorrow we will call the Clinic to find out if Sveta is admitted there."

※※※

CAPTAIN VICTOR IURKOV WATCHED as the three women exited the Kafé Dushá. He took a last puff of his Sobranie Black Russian, stubbing it out in the ashtray, then disengaged the brake. The proprietor had phoned his office to report snoops—one American and two Russians—asking questions, stirring up trouble. His car coasted forward.

The glow of the streetlight briefly caught the women's faces before they turned toward the corner. Interesting, he thought, with a rush. The tall one was the American filmmaker. Kate Hennessey. She did get around.

She carried her video camera. Always nosing in where she should not, recording things that should not be recorded. Was she also *rozovaya*? And the two Russian women—what were their roles?

He hated the *rozovaya* and the *goluboi*. They were perverse and unnatural. All should be sent to Siberia.

He resisted the urge to accelerate, climb the curb and crush them against the building. He must not be impatient. An idea was forming. He had never been told why Gregor had put a price on the American woman's head. He had received the order from Moscow four days ago to meet with Gregor and give him what he wanted. No one questioned an order from the right office in Moscow.

This American woman was cunning. She had escaped the blundering cab driver. Survived a long exposure in below zero weather. Dodged the speeding convoy truck at Pavlovsk. He had to terminate her and do it soon to fulfill his obligation.

He could arrest her now, as a spy, an activist. Remove the women with her. Again he told himself, patience. Three days ago President Gorbachev had issued directives to be implemented by the KGB if a state of emergency was declared: army and police would patrol the streets of Soviet cities as a preparation for KGB administrative control.

Crime was rising rapidly. He had a feeling the President would at any moment be persuaded to "restore order." Once that happened, the KGB would be back in full power. He could proceed without fear of consequences.

That would also be the time for him to pay a visit to the Kafé Dushá, to teach the women there to keep their mouths shut.

As he drove back to the hotel, he entertained himself with thoughts of how to punish them. He would storm into the cafe with his officers. Fill the room with a blinding bright light. Line everyone up against the wall. Frisk them and, he smiled, take extra time to fondle them. Then, person by person, they would begin videotaping, forcibly lifting the chins of those who hung their heads. They would ask for names and IDs. Many would fear the loss of their jobs—if the footage were released to television. And they could threaten them with that. Any woman who dared argue about her rights would be told, "You are *rozovaya*. You have no rights," and dragged outside and beaten.

When he arrived back at the hotel, he asked the *dejurnaya* on his floor to deliver a note to a room on the fourth floor. Thirty minutes later, he heard a knock at his door and opened it.

The man with the curls looked shocked. The Captain was used to that when people first saw his face. The thick white scar that zigzagged through his right eyebrow into his forehead was the most dramatic. The red line from the corner of his left eye over the eyebrow was lyrical, almost like a backward question mark. A few women were excited by the cruelty of his scars, the harshness of his partially shaved head. His full dress uniform, the Captain thought, added to the spectacle.

The man stammered, "There must be some mistake. You wanted to see me?"

The Captain signaled him in and shut his door. He clicked his heels together. "I am Captain Iurkov. Your full name, please."

"Steve Valvano." The short, square man with the flowered yellow tie looked as if he wanted to dash out of the room.

The Captain held up three videotapes in plain Sony boxes. "Contraband, contraband," he sang out with a gleeful smile. He stepped in close to Steve, peeling off each tape, one by one, "Darla Does Dobrovsk," "Flygirls," "Behind the Red Door." He sneered. "Filthy Western decadence."

Steve, his eyes wide, blustered. "I don't know what you're talking about."

"You are in violation of Article 228, the manufacture and sale of *pornografia*," the Captain barked out.

"What do you mean? What right do you have to accuse me?"

The officer smiled an oily smile. "What have you done, Mr. Steve? You have committed a crime against the Soviet people."

"I'm an American, a visitor. I have my rights."

"These videos were confiscated from your room. By my soldier."

"He had no right to be there." Steve caught himself. "What proof do you have they were taken from my room?"

"You could go to jail for a long time." The Captain carefully stacked the tapes on his dresser.

"You can't scare me."

"Not so nice, our jails. You would be held in a basement cell, with spiders and rats, sleeping on an iron bed, no mattress, living on a diet of kasha and bread. You could be a slave in a chalk mine." Good, the Captain thought, beads of sweat were forming on the man's forehead. Eyeing him stonily, the Captain lowered himself into a chair, sitting upright, at attention.

Steve offered the officer a cigarette. The Captain was gratified to see some bills peeping out of the open pack. "Keep the pack," Steve told him. The Captain pocketed the money—three fifty dollar bills—and pulled out a cigarette.

Steve lit it for him.

The Captain poured two drinks from a bottle of cognac on his nightstand. He handed a glass to Steve. The two sipped their drinks. Steve seemed to be waiting for a cue from him. He would let him squirm a little longer, the Captain thought. He finished his cognac before he spoke. He fingered the medals on his chest. "My only reward from my country for my years fighting the Afghan War."

Steve nodded several times. "I know what it is," he said, "to be under-appreciated." He bit his lip. "I have a proposition, General."

"Captain." He stifled a laugh. This man was licking his boots.

"Captain. We both know the film industry here—which was supported by the government—has collapsed. We can revive it, you and I."

"Tell me more," the Captain replied.

"I'm talking quick money. Hard currency. A joint venture in capitalism." Steve gave him a crafty look. "Much more money than you're getting now, copying festival films into videos for the black market."

The Captain stared at him, unblinking.

"We guessed," Steve said, staring back. His lips twitched into a half smile. "Films are lost for a day or two and magically re-appear. Filmmakers who arrive late from other festivals—sometimes their movies are lost for good."

The Captain shrugged. He raised an eyebrow. "A pity."

"Peanuts," Steve said. "I'm talking hundreds of thousands in profits. I've got good distribution channels. Connoisseurs of pornography in the U.S. and elsewhere. I can dub in what little dialogue is needed. But the films will be basically silent. Made MOS, 'mitout sound.' The action will say it all. Shot in eight millimeter. Inexpensive to make."

The Captain gave him an imperceptible nod.

"People here are desperate, will work for five, ten bucks

American. We'll have cheap talent. Male and female. And you smooth the way for distribution across the Soviet Union. We split the profits in your territories."

This American was a dealer. The Captain was used to dealers. They were always expendable. He ground out the cigarette Steve had given him and lit one of his own Sobranie Black Russians, inhaling deeply. Now this was a good smoke, strong and rich. He poured more cognac and raised his glass to Steve. "To a fifty-fifty split of *worldwide* profits."

Steve's smile faded. He finished his drink in a gulp. Then he managed a quick, nervous grin. "Worldwide profits," he nodded. "I'll have video footage to pass on to you before I leave the country. A sample of the work my team can produce."

"If we like what we see, we will prepare a contract that benefits us both." The Captain gave him a hard stare. "If we do not like it . . ."

Steve took out a handkerchief and wiped his brow. "I promise you I'll deliver a variety of scripts to please your most discriminating viewers."

The two men shook hands.

After Steve left, the Captain treated himself to another cognac. Everyone these days needed *na levo,* a job on the left. He had this man under his thumb and he was squirming.

❧

BACK AT THE HOTEL, Kate tried to read, but couldn't. The room was closing in on her. The women at the Café Soul . . . Nadya and Sveta . . . Masha . . . . all the lovely people she'd met, so oppressed, pinched off at the bud before they could flower.

Maybe their strength would give Gilly the nerve to do what Kate had asked, *Stand up to your father, don't be so dependent on his approval.*

"My father doesn't want me to be an artist," Gilly had told her last fall as they lay in her bed in the Village. "He calls it an unstructured life."

"How can he be so judgmental when what he does is gamble?" Kate asked, tight-lipped, remembering his drunken proposition to her in his library after the backyard barbecue. She'd kept it from Gilly, knowing how it would hurt her. "Your dad makes money from money, does not provide a service or a product. With so much suffering in the world, it seems obscene for people like him to have millions of dollars while others are homeless and begging on the streets."

While Dom, a prize winner at film festivals, tried to scrape up cash from any source he could for his masterpiece about World War II.

Gilly had looked upset. "Money is all my father talks about. He's devoted his life to making money. I hate what it's turned him and my mother into. When I was little, I remember his laugh—warm, infectious. I haven't heard it in years."

Before Kate left for Leningrad, she'd feared her plane might be shot out of the skies because of the Gulf War. As an act of good faith, she'd made her will, leaving all her money to Gilly. So she could get out from under her father's thumb if something happened to Kate. Kate didn't have much now but in nine months when she turned twenty-six she'd collect her trust.

Kate sat on the bed, and pulled from her wallet a photograph—"Lake of Fire," a spectacular sunset, her favorite of all Gilly's artworks. Seeing the photo now was almost like being there for The Magic Hour, watching Gilly paint the sun as it exploded in all the hues of the rainbow before it dipped into the lake.

A montage of scenes ran through her mind. Gilly and her speeding out to Montauk in Dom's ramshackle car borrowed for the week-end, windows down—Gilly driving, as always, the two of them singing loudly and off-key, the other drivers frowning, as if they were crazy. She and Gilly walking on the beach, sniffing the sea air; making a wish one enchanted night on a shooting star.

Gilly knew all the cool places to go; she'd been driving since she was a teenager, exploring Long Island to Sheepshead

Bay in Brooklyn, venturing down the Jersey coast, searching out landscapes and people to paint.

Kate slid the photo back into her wallet, feeling refreshed and limitless. She dressed for dinner.

Chapter Eleven

9:30 PM, Tuesday, January 29

Sipping cognac, Kate sat across from Dom in the Dom Kino Bar of the House of Cinema, lulled by the low buzz of conversation. Her eyes traveled over faces at nearby tables: mostly couples, intense-looking men with dark-rimmed glasses arguing or flirting with serious-faced women. Comfortingly ordinary, after the Café Soul.

"I was relieved to see you at dinner," Dom said with an apologetic smile

Dear, dear Dom, embarrassed for worrying about her. "Masha took care of us." She wouldn't tell him about the angry Café Soul proprietor, warning her to mind her own business.

"Did you get answers about Sveta?"

"Ideas about next steps." She was still wrapping her head around everything she learned, in awe of the women's spunk. "How was your meeting with the Dutch investors?"

"They seemed impressed with my credits." He warmed his brandy glass between his hands.

"Award-winning credits." He smiled, looking pleased to be reminded. In this business, thought Kate, you're only as good as your last work. Dom's last fiction film was eight years old. Ancient.

"We'll know more tomorrow," he said stoically. "Steve made points too with the Dutch with his silver tongue. He tossed about names of millionaires and Wall Street firms. The Channel Islands." He crossed his fingers.

Kate nodded, ambivalent about Steve and his grandiose claims. On the other hand, he'd rounded up the money for Dom when Titan Films was on the rocks.

Dom looked off in the distance. "Steve hinted at something he has in his back pocket that will create income for us. Millions." Dom made a face. "With Steve, it's always millions. Hey, cheer up." He clinked his glass to hers. "Good news, we retrieved the metal reels from the Molnia."

A heavy-set, bearded man in a rumpled suit stopped by their table. "Are you here in the House of Cinema for the midnight style show?" Kate said yes. "Ah, *Americanski*," he smiled. "You may be shocked and charmed by the show's irreverence. It's a combination vaudeville and strip show, with performers in outrageous costumes. May I?" he asked as he sat down. "My name is Alexander." Dom shook his hand, and introduced Kate and himself.

Alexander took off his spectacles and polished them on a handkerchief. Puffy bags hung under his mournful eyes. After a few minutes of chit-chat, he said, "Did you know, it was in this bar, the Dom Kino, that the filmmaker from Riga described the death of the Latvian cameraman, Andreas Slapinsh?"

Kate shook her head, remembering he was shot a few days before the festival began. "I understand Bulgaria and a few other countries withdrew their films from competition in protest."

"Slapinsh passed his camera over to his assistant, yelling 'the bastards got me. They killed me. I'm dying. What a pity.'" Alexander locked Kate and Dom in his puffy-eyed gaze. "Omon, a Soviet Special Military Detachment, fired at unarmed people. Slapinsh was one of six civilians killed. Another cameraman was shot in the spine." He pulled at his beard. "Latvia had declared independence from the Soviet Union less than a year ago." He leaned across the table and spoke so softly that Kate had to strain to hear. "Riga was a rehearsal, a way of preparing the public for a justification of possible bloodshed here."

What this morning's press release hinted at, Kate thought. But why is Alexander speaking so boldly to us, perfect strangers? Kate read his festival ID, "Alexander, Russian cameraman."

Of course, he feels vulnerable himself. His eyes—watery, naked, intense—demanded a response.

Kate burst out, "Everyone does seem to be waiting for even more dreadful news. We wish we could help. We feel powerless."

Alexander pushed his spectacles on his face, glanced right, then left. He hesitated, decided, whispered urgently, "There is a rumor that on February 1 Leningrad and Moscow will be taken over by troops. They'll come in the night when there are fewer photographers. They'll have nerve gas and water cannons to disperse the crowd, then KGB troops will storm the Russian Parliament in Moscow. I understand Arrest Forms have been printed. But they expect most protestors to flee the tanks and slink away."

"How do you know this?" Dom asked.

His bushy eyebrows lifted. "I am a member of the Jury, judging the films in competition. We were warned by someone who has an 'in' with the State Department. By Friday, the country could be under martial law."

"The day we're scheduled to fly home." Kate threw a panicked look at Dom. She couldn't wait to get out of this place, where everyone lived, boiling, with the lid clamped down tightly.

"The KGB will most likely close the airports. You may have to flee to your Embassies."

Dom said slowly, "There are over 200 filmmakers here from 23 different countries."

What a nightmare, Kate thought. Most important, what would happen to her new friends, Masha, Masha's son and mother, Nadya and Sveta, the women of the Café Soul, the rapturous Sovintour guide Andrei, critical of his country on the bus tour to Pavlovsk, and so in love with it.

Alexander, his mouth a bitter line, said, "I will quote you a verse that is going around, a parody of a Pushkin poem:

Comrade, you must believe, the star
Of our glasnost will set
And the Committee for State Security
Will take down our names . . .

Kate asked, "If this is the sentiment, why aren't more people afraid to speak out?"

Alexander gave a wry smile. "To a sociological survey that asked, 'What do people around you feel,' 42% of those polled replied, 'exhaustion and indifference,' 36% feel 'anger and aggressiveness'; only 22% said 'fear.'"

Interesting that the question was, What do those around you feel? Not, What do you feel? Kate thought.

Two young men, slim and taut, in dark blue suits, stopped by their table, introducing themselves as Voice of America, Moscow. "Here by special invitation to see the midnight show," one grinned. He had a tough, narrow face.

The VOA men lingered chatting, standing, until Dom offered them a seat.

The Moscow contingent has arrived, Kate thought, *to take charge of feisty, upstart Leningrad.* No more confidences spilled from Alexander, only small talk and pleasantries dribbled from the mouths of the Moscow men. Kate hardly listened, until a loud "Boolshit" erupted from the tough-faced one, jarring her awake just as she was drifting off. To stay alert for the show, she drank two cups of coffee with lots of sugar.

The bar was filling up, the noise level increasing. Images from the Café Soul jumped into her mind. Worries about Sveta ate at her. What would Nadya do if Sveta were lost to her? How would they both survive if, miraculously, Sveta were found intact and they both had the courage to continue their relationship?

Steve at last arrived, his hair freshly curled, wearing a blue jacket, black shirt, and bright red tie. He seemed flustered, she thought, as he'd been earlier when he came to her room once again to borrow the video camera.

GREGOR SET HIS COGNAC on the nightstand and stretched out on his bed with his shoes on, trying to concentrate on reading the newspaper. This waiting was driving him crazy. His suitcase was ready for the trip to Nizhnevartovsk, the gray designer suit, back from the cleaner's, packed neatly inside. The papers in his briefcase were ready to be signed by officials.

He was startled by a pounding on his door. He leaped from the bed. "Who is it?"

"Kolya."

Kolya and his wife had barged into this room less than twenty-four hours before. Trolling for money. Gregor had handed over $100 hard currency on the slim chance Kolya might succeed where others had failed.

The pounding continued.

He could not leave him in the hall, attracting attention. Gregor cracked the door and signaled him inside.

Nervously smoothing back his bushy hair, Kolya closed the door behind him. His fleshy lips curled in a smile.

Gregor had to let this fat punk know who was boss. "You tricked me last time, you and your wife Tanya. With *pornografia*. Pretending it was the videotape I want." He had only himself to blame for getting in the bitch's camera range. Who would have thought he would be in Kate's viewfinder just as he was showing her photograph to Captain Victor Iurkov?

"My wife's mistake. She had been drinking. These stressful times . . ." Kolya made a little bow. "I am sorry."

Gregor barked out a laugh. "*Dermo*. You used the pornographic video as a ruse to get into my room that night. Have you done what you promised? Settled your debt with the American woman? Or was that more hot air?"

"I gave Andre another chance. After all, he is my brother-in-law." Kolya's mouth turned down, his eyes grew sorrowful. "I do not want him sent to Siberia for not completing his assignment." His thick black eyebrows lifted as he sneered. "Andre was in the American woman's room as she slept." He shrugged. "He did not kill her. He did not collect the video."

"I do not need reports on failures; I need action." Kolya was all but holding out his hand. for another payment, Gregor thought.

"I understand the importance of this venture," Kolya licked his lips, "to those in Moscow."

"What do you know about Moscow?" Gregor snapped.

"Only that important people watch. If I do well, they will offer me more jobs."

"That is true," Gregor smiled. "If you succeed, Moscow will be pleased that I am pleased. Now, here's another fifty dollars. This is all you get, no more. It must be done quickly. She leaves the country in three days."

"You will see." Kolya shook his fist in the air. "Kolya, my name, means victorious warrior."

Gregor ushered him toward the door, warning him, "If you have something to say to me, do not stop by this room. Arrange to meet me in the bar."

⁂

TANYA SCANNED HER FACE in the mirror from all angles. She had been doing much thinking since her screen test. Should she take the job with Steve or give Kolya another chance? On good days her delicate features and high cheekbones made her photogenic. Tonight, dark bags under her eyes made her face long and dismal. Her knee hurt badly. She filled a hot water bottle, lay back in bed, the warmth soothing her pain. She turned on the radio beside her. Tchaikovsky's "Romeo and Juliet" was playing. She closed her eyes, let herself be swept away by the beautiful music.

Someone had her by the arms, was pulling her. Tanya twisted away, burying her face in her pillow. She did not want to leave her dream of being in America with a chauffeur to drive her everywhere. Eating chocolates—all she wanted, drinking champagne.

"Why are you not working?" Kolya snapped off the radio. "Your brother is a loser." He roughly pulled her out of bed.

"Be careful," she moaned. "My knee." She leaned against the mattress, massaging her leg. Kolya towered over her, his face unshaven, eyes bloodshot. Steve was polite, his hair clean and curled, always nicely dressed in a shirt and tie.

Kolya patted her cheek. "Put in a couple of hours, sweetheart. We are low on money."

"What happened to the money Gregor gave us?" One hundred dollars American would buy many groceries, and time off for her.

He gave a guilty start. "What money?" he asked suspiciously. "Oh, you mean the other night? I used it to purchase goods. Military uniforms, military watches are hot now. Soon we will spread out into guns, other military weapons." Kolya licked his lips.

To think I once loved him, she thought. He is and always will be a *Farzofchik*, a dealer in currency. He first bought clothes in rubles, then sold them at a higher rate of rubles; then moved on to hard currency. Now he has made friends with the girls in *Beryozka* shops who themselves deal in hard currency. Money we could use to make life nicer is put into his ever-growing supply of black market goods.

Kolya opened a dresser drawer, rifling through her underwear. "Where is your cash from last night?"

She pulled bills out from under her pillow—one-third of the dollars she had received from Steve—handing it over. It had been an easy night last night, fucking Steve. Doing it for the camera was not bad once she forgot it was there. With the extra bonus, for Irina's participation, she got three times as much as on ordinary nights when she did seven or eight stinking strangers. She sank back on the bed, hanging her head. "I am sick of this life. The dirty men, the diseases I could pick up—and give to you! Have you thought of that?" Her heart was pounding so loudly she thought it might jump out of her chest. "I have met an American, a filmmaker who has auditioned me for his movie. I am going to America to be in his films."

Kolya left the bedroom. Limping, she followed him to the kitchen. He acted as if he had not heard her say she was leaving him.

As he headed toward the refrigerator, she suddenly became alert. Her secret stash of money, her savings account earmarked for her new life, was in the refrigerator—inside a sock, wrapped in plastic and stuck in a jar of cooking fat. The most secure place to hide it since he never cooked, but still—he was more and more unpredictable.

"This is all? I hope you are not holding out." With one hand, he clutched the bills she had given him. With the other, he rummaged in the refrigerator and pulled the vodka out. He drank from the bottle. "Just a little longer," he wheedled, "you must work. Until I am in a situation to get extra dollars, maybe many." His chest swelled with pride. "Soon I might be in the big time."

"You better shave then." He had always been an exaggerator of his own importance.

He glared, so long and hard that she began to feel afraid. Then he shrugged it off. "I do not need you and the money you bring in. Not with what I have working on the burner."

"Besides the *Chermyiryimok,* the black market?" She was skeptical. But if he had something better to offer her, she might stick around.

He rubbed his cheek, still red from where the girl had cut him with her keys.

"You mean, the American girl?" she asked.

He gave her a sly smile. "Gregor—who gave us the dollars—I met with him just now."

She felt a chill under her heart. "Why?" She remembered their late night visit to Gregor's hotel room. His hand was in his bathrobe pocket the whole time. She had feared at any moment he was going to shoot them both. "I do not trust him." He did not rant and rage like Kolya. He pretended to be easy. His hard eyes gave him away, and he smiled like a crocodile. "He makes me afraid."

"He needs to get a job done and stay in the shadows. He is a target for more money. Even blackmail." He took a long drink of vodka before sliding the bottle back in the refrigerator.

"What happened at your meeting?"

"I told him Andre is a pussy and to give the job to me."

Kolya flicked his nail against a kitchen match, lighting the Belomorkanal he took from his shirt pocket,

"My brother is a better man than you," she muttered. It had been for her sake that Andre had included Kolya in his Special Assignment from his Captain. Andre had wanted to make life easier for his little sister.

"He will never survive the way things are going to be, in the New Russia." Kolya went on, "He had a chance to kill the girl as she slept. He did not. He managed to smuggle a videotape out but it was the wrong one, yet again." He puffed himself up. "Gregor is giving me double the money to do both—kill the girl and get the tape. Plus a bonus."

So that is why he had looked guilty. The man had given Kolya more hard currency at their meeting tonight. "I heard Andre warn you," she said sternly. "His Captain ordered you to stay away from the girl."

"If I get to her first, she is mine," Kolya spat, his face red.

The American girl, Tanya thought, her mind racing, is part of the film company, Steve's assistant. Better not do anything to make Steve mad, spoil my own chances. On the other hand, Steve did not seem to like the girl that much, called her temperamental. Maybe he would not be sad if the girl died. Soon, Tanya thought, her own body would not be that good for the camera. She could be Steve's assistant, instead of taking off her clothes.

"If Gregor likes the job I do . . . He has big contacts in Moscow." Kolya strutted around the room. "He told me I will be rewarded. Trips to foreign countries," he said expansively, "for you and me. A summer *dacha*."

These were made up stories to keep her under Kolya's thumb. That and a beating thrown in here and there. She told herself to stick to her plan of getting out.

"Now get dressed and get to work." Kolya was pushing her out into the cold—with her bad leg hurting like hell—saying they needed the cash. She had almost fallen for it. He had cash in his pocket from Gregor, fresh from a half hour ago. "I told you, the American film director has promised me hard currency, a trip to America." Her voice quivered with rage. Steve hadn't exactly set a date; a lot of paperwork would be required. She should not burn her bridges before things were set in motion. But Kolya's smugness made her so damn angry.

"Who is this American film director," he sneered, "you keep blabbering about?"

"He has brought me to his hotel room many times and given me champagne. He treats me like a lady," she taunted. "Unlike you!"

"Liar! There is no such person."

"His room is next to the American girl," she said harshly. "She is part of his film company. He will make me a star."

He snorted. "You are a cripple."

"You are a loser. A drunk. You talk big, but nothing big ever happens."

"Keep your mouth shut." Kolya, cigarette hanging between his lips, shoved her. She shoved back. He threw his cigarette on the kitchen floor, stamped it out, and charged at her, pushing hard with both hands. She fell, her bad leg crumpling under her.

She moaned, "I will leave you."

"And I will find you, *pizda*," he growled, bending over her, his hand raised.

She turned her face away. "I warn the Americans. I will tell Andre what you are up to."

Kolya jerked her by the hair. He held so tightly that her eyes watered. She was afraid her hair would come out in a clump. He twisted her around and stuck his face in hers. "Do that and I will kill you." He took out his knife and pricked her neck with the point. Then he suddenly released her. She slumped on the floor, sobbing. The front door slammed.

Where was he going? It was almost midnight. The girl would likely be in her locked hotel room. Or would he drive around for awhile and come whimpering back to apologize? Another time when he left in a rage, he slept in his car, which he parked at Pushkin Square. He stayed on through the next day, making deals with the vendors there, he bragged, for his black market goods.

Slowly, she crawled into the living room to a chair and painfully pulled herself up from the floor. She would beg Steve for a ticket to America. She once had a respectable life, one in the arts as a ballerina. She could have that life again. With good scripts, *pornografia* could one day become respectable films.

No more would she sleep with strangers to get money for Kolya. She felt free, as she did when she was dancing, leaping into the air, surrounded by the music and the applause.

She could not be in the apartment when Kolya came back. She called her friend Irina and asked to stay the night.

※※※

LEANING ACROSS DOM SO Steve could hear, Kate read aloud from a festival press release: "This performance of LEM (Laboratory of Experimental Modeling), a satirical fashion show will start at midnight at the House of Cinema. The lucky people invited will have a possibility to relax in an unusual way, not well known to society in the Soviet Union."

"Tantalizing," Dom said. Steve grinned and wiggled his eyebrows.

The House of Cinema auditorium filled up. Midnight came and went. Thirty minutes passed, the crowd grew restless. Kate wondered if the show had been canceled and the audience forgotten. Maybe tanks with nerve gas had rolled into the city.

Just then (1:00 AM), a woman in punk makeup, a short black dress, black opera hose, and very high heels, marched in from the wings. A professorial-looking, gray-haired man with a goatee slid onstage beside her. "This show is a critical view of Soviet policy. People are suffering from economic havoc," he announced in English, his green-sweatered shoulders slumping, concluding lamely, "especially the poor and the handicapped."

The economic havoc, Kate knew, was the result of the government's recent withdrawal of fifty and one hundred ruble notes—supposedly to undermine the black market, but according to tour guide Alexei, it was really an attack on free enterprise. The economic chaos affected more than the poor and the handicapped. The professor had waffled at the end of his speech, it seemed.

The punk woman in black, sleek and sinuous, was now curled on top of the piano, smiling like the Cheshire Cat. Rock music blared from the sound system. In a high nasal voice the Cheshire Cat screeched out what sounded like insults in Russian. "We and Eggs," the woman on Kate's right whispered in accented English, explaining, "Each skit will have a title." Kate gave her a grateful glance before turning her attention to the stage.

The first performer appeared, a beautiful, dark-haired young woman in a floor-length black dress whose voluminous skirt gently bobbed up and down. She faced front, smiling demurely. A hand in a pink glove suddenly pushed through the folds of the skirt. Someone was hiding between her legs. The Cheshire Cat screamed from the piano top, her voice like fingernails on chalkboard. "Hello from East. The Iron Curtain is Broken," the woman next to Kate translated. The audience laughed nervously.

"Red Ku Klux Klan" the Cheshire Cat yelped in English as the pink-gloved man who'd been hiding under the woman's skirt suddenly rose up behind her. He wore a pink hood and languorously slipped off her dress. She was swathed from chest to knees in a wide pink flag covered with words, written large in cursive. As the Cheshire Cat on the piano shrilled, the interpreter beside Kate spoke softly near Kate's ear, "The most popular material in Soviet Union is slogans—so we give you dress with slogans. Slogans say: 'Any nightingale can accept the slogan' and 'With an iron hand we can lead mankind to happiness.'"

Most certainly an iron hand still led, Kate thought, thinking of the tragic events in Latvia, and the brow-beaten *rozovaya* who gathered at the Café Soul. But what guts to say it so bluntly. Kate was shocked, although Alexander had alerted Dom and her to expect extreme costumes, striptease and disrespectful messages. The slogans were more than disrespectful; they were caustic.

The banner-covered woman strutted across the stage in time to the beat of the music. She twirled and posed like a fashion model, slowly unwinding the wide pink streamer from her body, revealing a black leather bra and garter belt. She slung the banner over a shoulder, and dragged it behind her as if it were a feather boa, swinging her hips. With a sudden move, she looped it around the neck of the pink-hooded man and pulled him offstage.

The pink banner, did it mean the reds (communists) had been diluted to pink? Or maybe it simply stood for the sugary blandness of the slogans that, stripped away, revealed black leather underwear or gritty reality. Kate was confused but fascinated. "I wish I had my camera," she murmured to Dom, who pointed out the man below the apron of the stage, obviously taping it all.

They're taping this? It will be better than a list for the Committee for State Security, Kate thought, nudging Dom. "You have to hear in English what's going on. It's incredible."

The woman next to Kate agreed to sit between her and Dom to translate. The move was made as a new skit began.

A young female soldier swung onstage. She saluted smartly, pivoted to reveal a backless uniform, the face of Gorbachev painted on her skin. The Cheshire Cat atop the piano screwed up her mouth and shrieked. The Translator spoke in a low voice, first to Kate and then to Dom, "What if your friend will be imprisoned by the President's rule?"

A man with heavy blue eye shadow, mascara, his lips painted bright red, joined the female soldier. He too wore boots and a khaki outfit, but a skirt, not pants, the shirt backless, with military caps making puffed sleeves. On his head was a puffy blue beret adorned with a curling peacock feather.

"How should you be dressed if you're taken to prosecutor if friend arrested?" the Translator whispered. Kate wondered if the blue beret meant the performer was portraying a *goluboi*, a gay man, and if the pink in the first sketch was a reference to the *rozovaya?*

The man onstage turned his back and bent over, showing blue underwear. Kate leaned in to hear the Translator better. "By rule of our president we will show even our ass to him."

Who is this woman explaining the show to us? Kate wondered. *A festival official perhaps, who wants to be sure we two Americans carry out these performers'"messages." "Message to Man" is, after all, the theme of this year's film festival.*

Next what had to be the prosecutor strolled in, smirking arrogantly, covered in a huge brown cape. Atop his head sat a jester's cap outlined with small lights twinkling on and off. The two "soldiers" removed his cape to reveal a foppish-looking tunic and pants. The Translator sucked in her breath audibly before murmuring the message screamed by the Cheshire Cat. "How should we return the honor and dignity of Soviet KGB man if he never had them?"

The audience turned very still. Kate noted there was no program with the actors' names. The videotape would have their faces, but not their names. What if the KGB returned to power? Surely the performers had heard the rumors. Now that Kate thought about it, the actors sometimes seemed tentative, as if afraid. Or were they simply under-rehearsed?

Onstage, the two soldiers stripped the prosecutor down to a white sleeveless jumper, with ruffles on the bottom, a red star in the middle of his chest. The woman on the piano screeched, the Translator giggled, as she whispered, "LEM will suggest a new underwear for men, especially for Communist Party members on Central Committee."

A number of prominent leaders, according to Masha, had recently made a point of resigning from the Communist Party. But to imply the Central Committee were a bunch of eunuchs in ruffled underwear . . . No wonder this show was not meant for the eyes of the ordinary Russian. The audience sighed as one, then gave a smattering of applause as if fearful to be too enthusiastic.

A woman in a black backless gown sidled sexily onto the stage, a net veil over her face. "Lenin used to say that communism is the Soviet power (in addition to electrification of the country). Any man will respond to such." Stage lights went out. In the dark, small lights on the woman's legs, from ankle to knee, sparkled, bouncing as she danced.

The stage lights came on. "The light arrangement today is not so good but it sees the most important part, a woman's legs."

Light arrangement? Power, Kate supposed. What was the power structure these days? "Not so good," it seemed.

A man staggered onstage. He wore the bowl of a pipe as underpants, the stem sticking out in front like a giant phallus. "It is Stalin wearing his pipe," laughed the Translator.

A dancer in a white tutu pirouetted across the stage on toe shoes to the music of *Swan Lake.* Wings adorned her shoulders, large headlights were fastened to her breasts, a black thatch of fur covered her crotch. She danced with "Stalin," the pipe stem thrusting between her legs as he lifted her. She pulled him off stage by the pipe stem.

What was the meaning of the wings and headlights? Kate wished the show would pause after each skit so she could question the woman who sat between her and Dom.

Next a female wearing a man's black suit was wheeled in on a little trolley. The Translator whispered: "She wears mustaches like Lavrentzi Beriya, Georgian Jew, member of inner office of Stalin, more cruel than Stalin. Also a womanizer, he slept with many outstanding men's wives. The women were afraid if they didn't they would be executed."

The mustached woman, Beriya, lit a fuse perched on the head of another woman. An explosive? Kate wondered, as the woman exited, her head "on fire." Beriya removed her black jacket, pants, and vest, her tie and white shirt. She was now standing in black garters, holey socks, a pink frilly outline of a bra, through which her bare breasts showed, and a G string, black feathers arranged in front. She sashayed off stage covering her buttocks with her black fedora.

What was the symbolism of Beriya riding in on a trolley? That (s)he, as a member of the inner circle, was pulled along as Stalin rose to power? Why did Beriya strip and reveal him/herself as a woman? A gender-bending show. Kate was excited. She needed these shots for her video project. She could hire a translator and use English subtitles as the punk Cheshire Cat screamed out her insults. These beautiful women with their beautiful bodies would end the stereotype of the fat Russian frump, clothed in a shapeless dress.

"Long Russian evenings and talks," the Cheshire Cat curled on the piano purred. A woman in white, blonde hair in braids, strolled in playing a white and gold accordion. She looked angelic, like an "old-fashioned" woman, Kate thought. A grinning man darted in, whisked off her clothes, ready for romance: "Before you make love, look what's in front of her." A reel to reel audiotape was attached to her breasts.

Kate suddenly wondered if her hotel room was bugged. Someone had been in her room at least twice, looking for the videotape. That first press release in her mailbox had included a statement by the festival director about the current leaders' tendencies to turn to methods of the cold war, which would surely include hidden listening devices.

A blonde woman in black wriggled across the stage, a steaming stove pipe seeming to run through her middle. "Marilyn Monroe," the Translator said. "*Some Like it Hot* is very popular here."

How were the men from Moscow Voice of America reacting? Kate longed to see their faces, as the skits continued, each rawer and more critical of leaders than the last. A woman was a bed, the springs attached to her back. A man embraced her. She lay down, ready to work. Referring to the current trend of prostituting your wife to put food on the table, Kate supposed.

A kaleidoscope of images filled the stage: female performers sporting gas masks or military caps as underwear. "Erotic underwear—the dream of the man," the Cheshire Cat howled, coiled like a panther atop the piano. Next, the women wore coke cans as brassieres, red coca cola underpants. "The new generation of reds chooses Coca Cola," the Cheshire Cat screeched.

A definite swipe at communism selling out to capitalism. Just as Kate marveled once more at the courage of the actors, the woman beside her sighed, "This young, untested generation is not afraid of anything, even the KGB." "Brave enough," Kate whispered back, "to stand up to tanks in the cities?" The woman replied, her lips close to Kate's ear, "A tank under the window does not mean the end of the world."

Kate was startled by what the woman said. Another message, she decided, to ponder over later, with the others: "The genie is out of the bottle," "General Gromov is going to kill many people." "Riga is a rehearsal for bloodshed here."

The men swaggered onstage, wearing guns for penises. Doctors in white swarmed about, their gloved hands glittering with needles for fingers. Kate thought of Sveta, the psychiatric clinic where she might be imprisoned, undergoing injections to "cure" her.

The Cheshire Cat screamed suddenly in English, "We must forget everything," and scrambled down from the piano. The cast filed in beside her. All took awkward bows, throwing kisses to the audience. "Thank you. We love you," said the Cheshire Cat. Her face, hardened by outrage and contempt throughout the program, was soft and uncertain as if she were fearful that she—the show—had gone too far. The house lights came up. Kate turned to the Translator about to invite her to join them for a tete-a-tete over a drink in the upstairs bar. The woman smiled, but her eyes held a warning, as if to say *in the dark was okay to talk, but not in the light.* Kate stammered, *Spaceba,* as the tall elegant figure, her blonde hair carefully coiffed, passed in front of her.

Kate was very stirred by the performers' courage and vulnerability. Poking fun at Beriya was understandable. Stalin was out of favor for the moment. Poking fun at the KGB and military—risky—despite the Translator's optimism that kids today would fight against a takeover. Too the woman had pooh poohed the prospect of tanks in the streets. Obviously, she was one of the 42% in Alexander's sociological survey who were exhausted and indifferent. Had the show started an hour late because even more inflammatory material had to be cut? Or had performers, taking the latest rumors to heart, dropped out and others quickly rehearsed to take their places?

Dom seemed as stunned by the fury of the show as she. "If Alexander's sociological survey is correct, the performers are either very angry, or very exhausted and don't care."

"Or desperate," said Kate. It occurred to her that tonight's program, the daily Press Releases with their hidden meanings, the courageous straight talk from tour guide Alexei, the revelations from Alexander, from the women at the Café Soul—all were desperate messages by despairing people who needed to be heard now in case the Iron Curtain slammed shut once more.

Kate watched as Dom dickered for a taped copy of the show with the videographer. The man looked so grim, maybe uneasy too. Was he gathering evidence for the KGB? Or working to get these messages into foreign filmmakers' hands before they left the country?

Kate entered the dressing room to congratulate the cast and was surprised to find Steve in deep conversation with a blond young man in tights, bare-chested, his body beautifully muscled. He still wore his white-feathered swan costume, its long neck and head jiggling in front of him like an exotic penis. A harried-looking Steve scribbled on the back of his business card before handing it to the blond man. Steve's eyes lit briefly on Kate. He gave her a furtive smile, murmured something to the young man, then moved away to charm the women seated at a long table, removing their make-up. He gave each his card. He stopped working the room when Dom stepped in.

"We loved it!" Kate said to the performers, adding, "You're very brave." They either didn't understand *brave* or they refused to acknowledge what she'd said. "*Spaceba.*" Dom shook everyone's hand. He turned to Kate and Steve, "We've been invited to a party, in the room of the men from Voice of America Moscow. They're staying at our hotel." Steve declined, claiming he had a headache. He went back to chatting with the beautiful dark-haired woman who'd played Beriya. She still wore her black garters. As Kate and Dom left, Kate heard Steve say, "I'm a movie producer looking for talent."

More "screen tests"? Or was Steve making deals for film projects other than Dom's?

Chapter Twelve

2:30 AM, Wednesday, January 30

Outside the Laboratory of Experimental Modeling dressing room, the two Voice of America men from Moscow were waiting, hands in the pockets of their boxy overcoats with padded shoulders. *We can't back out,* Kate thought, feeling trapped. One wore thick glasses, the eyes behind them bulging, as if he were trying to read her mind. Gads, if she lived here, she'd never survive.

The party was a small one, in the men's hotel room on the seventh floor. Kate hoped they might reveal inside information about the rumored military take-over. But they became drunk quickly. The tough-faced VOA man with the glasses kept saying "No PROBlem" and "Boolshit." Was he pretending to be a hard-hitting, loud-mouthed Texan? she wondered sourly. He noticed her staring and sauntered over. "Come to Moscow. I can really show you around," he said from the corner of his mouth, his eyes seductive. He bragged about the exotic nightlife. She shook her head politely. The second VOA man posed from time to time, his herringbone coat hung over one shoulder like a foreign correspondent. What was it with these Russian men? She remembered the three men in cowboy shirts at their breakfast table. They seemed to love playing the caricature of the American he-man. A third VOA man, Leonid, beautiful, with a sculpted face and tight blond curls, sat on the couch, drunk as the others. He'd been in the Afghan war, Dom told her. He'd lost part of his foot. He'd been a dancer. "Did you like tonight's show?" she asked. He wrinkled his nose and called it "Decadent."

Why were these men in Leningrad? To have a holiday? To report the military take-over, if it happened? To turn in the dissenters responsible for tonight's satirical fashion show?

The party ended at 4:00 AM when the *dejurnaya* sternly ordered everyone to leave. Kate had to suppress a smile at the clout of these women who managed the floors of hotels. They just might be the most powerful women in Russia. Kate's head was splitting and her eyes stung from the smoke.

"Don't forget, I'm sleeping with you," Dom teased, as he and Kate took the elevator down to their rooms on the fourth floor.

She took his arm. "I had a paranoid thought. What if my room is bugged?"

"That skit tonight—the woman with the reel-to-reel tape under her blouse . . ." Dom's jaw was tight. "We'll use my room."

"Good." Kate said. She felt physically ill at the thought of sleeping in her own room, even with Dom in the opposite bed. "Did you get a video of the show?"

He nodded. "For fifteen dollars American. I pick it up tomorrow."

"I'm worried copies will fall into the wrong hands."

"Me too. " Dom gave a weary sigh. The elevator door opened. The *dejurnaya* was asleep. They wouldn't have to wake her. Neither had turned in their keys when they left for the House of Cinema, a small victory that made Kate ecstatic. As she gathered clothes from her room, Dom chewed his lower lip. "Where's the video camera?"

"Steve borrowed it." Dom looked surprised, a question in his eyes. Kate longed to tell him her concerns about Steve's "auditions," but she would wait. Their film company must present a united front while the two men were in negotiations with potential investors. She wanted, needed this job, the most exciting she'd ever had. Too exciting at the moment. If huckster Steve could raise the money for their next film, maybe she could ignore his lack of scruples. After all, tonight's performers were adults.

Kate half expected to hear murmurs and giggles as they passed Steve's room but all was silent. He'd had ninety minutes to tape his auditions while she and Dom were at the party. Kate tiptoed past the snoring *dejurnaya* through Dom's corridor and into his room. Once the door was locked, a heavy weight slid off her shoulders.

"Just in case," he said, jamming a chair back under the doorknob, "old Eagle Eye wasn't asleep." His mouth was a grim line. "In case the soldier is waiting for her report." He frowned. "I'll sleep in the bed closest to the door. Put your videos under your pillow. Leave your vest hanging on the chair."

"Then what?" Her brain was foggy from too much cognac and champagne.

"This," he said, putting a finger to his lips, as he took out his pocket knife, opened it, and laid it on the bedside stand. Next he packed a laundry bag with a heavy glass ashtray and his leather shoes, placing it on the floor between the beds.

❦

ANDRE RUBBED HIS DRY eyes. The floor was hard, the air was bad, the wall was hurting his back. He had been a prisoner in the fourth floor stairwell ever since the *dejurnaya* told him she had seen the American woman disappear inside the older man's room. *My sweet, slippery Kate,* he thought, *so this is your next game.* Did she suppose there was safety in numbers? Or was she sleeping with the old man?

His nerves were tight, he was ready to explode. He stood up, breathing hard. He paced within the confines of the small space; then he ran up and down several flights of stairs, occasionally cracking the stairwell door and peeping out to make sure Kate didn't have another trick up her sleeve, like sneaking away before dawn. Sweat dripped from his armpits, his face was slick. From his pocket, he drew out the razor and flicked his wrist. With a thwack, the glistening blade appeared. He had oiled and sharpened it with loving care as he prepared himself for this mission.

▼▲▼

"ARE YOU AWAKE?" KATE asked, keeping her voice low. Lying here in the dark with Dom, a thin light leaking from the bathroom, was almost cozy.

He grunted.

This was her chance. He was a captive audience. "You insisted I bring the camera. I'm thrilled I did. I've already chosen a title for my video project—*Border Crossing.*"

Dom broke in, "Because of that camera, we're barricaded in my room." He grumbled, "How naïve I was. Before we left the U.S, I thought hey, this is the sixth year of *glasnost* and *perestroika*. It must be working. We might get some fascinating footage . . ."

Kate interrupted. "Something important is happening here, Dom. Just like it was in San Francisco in the sixties when you took a chance and went out there to shoot the hippies' Summer of Love. I need to tell you what we found out at the Café Soul."

"I want to know," he said, stifling a yawn.

Kate sat on the edge of her bed. In a hushed voice, using no names, she told him about the KGB's sadistic control over the women at the Café Soul, the shady psychiatrists, the mind altering drugs and unwanted surgeries, the threats of outing the women to their jobs and neighbors. "My freedom as a gay woman in the States is infinite compared to theirs," she burst out, forgetting to whisper. If Dom's room had a hidden microphone, she'd just outed herself to the military and the KGB. She felt a wave of fear and shame. Programmed response. She told herself to remember Nadya, her elfin face resolute, saying, *We are not afraid.* "We have a lead about Sveta," she whispered close to his ear. "She may have 'disappeared' into the psychiatric clinic, where she's being burned with electroshock treatments." Silence. "Dom, are you awake?"

"I'm out of words, appalled by what you just described."

She stood beside Dom's bed, speaking softly, urgently. "I was told a human rights conference may take place this summer in Leningrad and Moscow. We have to return . . ."

"I hope by then we'll be in pre-production for our World War II film."

"We can bring a 16mm camera, raw film stock, pick up a crew here!" she insisted. "We can shoot it—just you and me—like you shot *Revolution.* Set up interviews—we'll have to advertise underground, probably meet secretly in someone's apartment. If things are still uncertain, the women, the pinks, and men, light blues, may want to speak from the shadows. Or maybe," she said wistfully, "life will have changed for the better and they'll be willing to show their faces."

"We might take a week off," he said cautiously, "if the country is stable."

She'd hooked him! "We must film not only gays but women like those at the meeting at Masha's, with drunks for husbands and custody issues, who suffer beatings and are sent out to work as prostitutes."

"I know this means a lot to you, Kate."

She tried to keep her voice soft. "The men too are ground down, with no jobs, nothing to do but drink and mistreat their wives, while the mafia rake in millions. What a sham the leaders are." Her feelings overcame her and she heard herself ranting, "People have resigned—even the Mayor of Leningrad—from the Communist Party. Now supposedly the Democrats are in power. The KGB is hungry to take control. The military is swarming around, bored and restless, obviously expecting something big to happen. No one knows what the rules are now, and most don't care. It's every man for himself." Her voice rang out angrily. She hoped it burst the eardrums of anyone listening—if anyone was.

Kate knew another way to hook Dom. "We have to come back," she murmured, "to rescue Masha and her son and her mother." He was silent. She feared she'd worn him down to an exhausted nub, ready to pass out from fatigue.

ANDRE SAT ON THE hard floor of his "cell" in the stairwell, his head in his hands. He could not turn his mind off. He was tortured by images: Kate, in her blue jeans, her lovely, long legs; Kate, his hands at her waist, as if they were dancing; Kate, asleep, her face calm and beautiful, framed by dark hair.

He exploded into the corridor. Before he knew what he was doing, he was standing outside the door that Kate and her lover were hiding behind. He felt like a wild animal enraged by Kate's betrayal, her arrogance, the softness of her life.

He would burst into the room, rush the old man, slice him open, hold Kate hostage. Do anything he wanted with her.

"DO YOU HEAR SOMETHING?" Dom asked softly. He sprang out of bed at the same time she did, almost knocking her down. He put his ear to the door.

Kate's heart pounded wildly. Dom would be no match for the soldier. She took a Taekwondo stance, feet apart, knees bent, did breathing exercises to make herself calm and ready.

"If he comes through that door, I'll beat him off," Dom whispered. "You run through the corridors yelling for security."

Kate made fists, folding her thumbs over to lock her fingers into place. She chambered her arms by her sides as she'd done many times in her classes, elbows bent at a ninety-degree angle, ready to whirl and kick, lash out with fists and feet.

They waited for what seemed an eternity to Kate. At last, Dom slid into bed, placing the open pocket knife on the nightstand, the laundry bag with the ashtray and shoes under his blanket.

Her adrenalin pumping hard, Kate, too, crawled back into bed. She forced herself to take long, deep breaths.

※

ANDRE HELD HIS BODY rigid, fearful he would break into pieces, then he turned and fled back to the stairwell where he paced for several minutes, his head pounding. He slumped to the floor. Today he would stick to her like glue, wait until she was alone, then act. He needed a bath. The stubble on his face was thick. He did a "dry" shave, using the razor in his pocket, managing a ragged trim, cutting his jaw, his neck. It would have to do, he thought with a bitter smile. He wiped away the blood. He folded his jacket into a pillow and leaned into a corner, closing his eyes to rest them.

He woke with a jerk, razor still in hand. Voices in the hallway. He stood up so suddenly he felt dizzy. His foot was asleep. He kicked it against the wall as he peered out into the hall. Kate and the older man were outside the room. They turned away from him, toward the elevator. He hurried down the stairs in time to see them head for the dining room.

He hung around until they finished breakfast, then followed Kate back to the room. The man with the beard stuck to her side like glue. Andre watched as the two, now in coats, walked through the lobby and out the exit, passing through the line of soldiers, and boarding a tour bus to the Hermitage.

Good! She would be occupied for the next two hours. It had been a long, hard night. He needed breakfast. About to turn away, he noticed at the taxi stand, a familiar car, a fat man asleep behind the wheel. Andre ran outside, slamming into a soldier, who cursed. The wind was icy. He beat his arms against his chest as he jogged over to the car. Snow drifts were piled against the doors. Kolya's eyes were closed, his mouth open. A ragged blanket covered with cigarette ash was pulled up to his chin. Andre pounded on the window. Kolya stirred and rose up like a bear from hibernation. Andre motioned him to roll down the window, snarling, "What are you doing here?"

"Have you seen your little sister Tanya?" Kolya wheedled, his face mottled, his eyes angry slits.

Andre shook his head. He guessed the two had had a fight.

"She did not come home. She is a crazy woman." Deep, dark pouches were under his eyes, his hair was wild.

"You are the crazy," Andre hissed. He would find his sister. But first he must finish this job from his Captain. "You send her out to sleep with strangers. She may be dead."

"Not yet dead," Kolya said sullenly. "I know her plan. Not so good for you or me. She is a double crossing whore."

Andre did an about face while the imbecile was still spluttering. He ran into the hotel.

※

WOOZY AND RAGGED FROM last night's vigil, Kate followed Dom and Masha into the Russian Tea Room on the hotel's tenth floor. She was almost sorry the soldier hadn't made another try to retrieve the videotape. She and Dom could have confronted him, demanded answers.

The Tea Room was elegant and rustic, with wood-paneled walls, beautiful dark blue chandeliers with deep red highlights, the bulbs shaped like flames. Along one wall, decorative plates, jugs and tureens rested on a polished wooden shelf that ran just under the ceiling. The average Russian was denied a glimpse of this. Even Masha wouldn't be here if she weren't a festival translator. The decor must be PR for the foreign guests, Kate decided, lulling them with a stock image of an "old fashioned Russia," implying that this gentility and low key richness flourished in the lives of Russian citizens. Kate remembered the co-op apartment Masha and her mother shared, the decrepit elevator, the dark hallways, uncovered cement floors.

The three chose cream-filled pastries at the counter. Dom and Masha carried the breakfast treats to a small table in the corner as Kate, her mouth watering, paid the bill, four rubles, less than one dollar American.

Dom fetched cups of tea from the nearby samovar. Kate whispered to Masha, "We heard a rumor last night, about a possible military take-over Friday . . ."

Masha waved a weary hand. "I am exhausted by the turmoil and the uncertainty. There are always rumors. Many do not happen." She sighed. "In our country even a *putsch* cannot be organized efficiently."

The three settled into their chairs. "About Sveta—" Masha shot a questioning look toward Dom.

"He knows everything," Kate said.

"I called the Psychiatric Clinic to find if Sveta is there. I was transferred from one person to the next. I learned nothing," she groaned in exasperation. She added, "I pretended I was a relative. I was careful not to give my name over the phone."

Kate said, "We'll go in person—you and I."

Masha shook her head. "The authorities might blame you, an American, for making trouble. Best Nadya and I visit on our own, as concerned Soviet citizens. We will go next week after the festival ends."

"I wish we knew for sure she made it home. I wish I'd heard her voice." Why hadn't she taken the phone from Olga, demanded from the man at the other end to speak to Sveta? Kate pushed the pastry around on her plate. "She must be in the clinic, don't you think?"

Masha nodded uncertainly. "Did you enjoy the Hermitage?" she asked.

"Unbelievable. The marble staircases, crystal chandeliers...." With an effort, Kate tried to push her fears aside.

"Oh, yes," said Masha proudly, "the interiors are as much a part of the museum as the collections themselves." She turned to Dom. "This afternoon, Kate and I are seeing *Letters to Leningrad* in Competition Hall, about the current situation. Many Jewish people have been arrested for teaching Hebrew and holding Jewish religious services. As you know, I am a 'halfer,' half-Jewish . . . Perhaps you will join us for the film?" Masha asked Dom shyly.

Dom looked apologetic. "Steve and I have meetings all afternoon, with the Dutch." He grinned at Kate. "And the West Germans and Japanese. They've asked for terms." He finished off most of his dessert in one bite.

"I wish you success." Masha took Kate's hand, then Dom's. "I will miss you when you leave."

"We may be back in summer—"

Dom warned, "Hold on, Kate. No promises."

"Why not visit us?" Kate exclaimed. "We could show you New York City."

"Brilliant." Dom sat up straighter. He looked years younger.

Masha's eyes lit up. "It is a long process. If you can sponsor me, I will tell you what papers must be filed." She gave Dom her wide, beautiful smile.

Dom smiled in return, and saluted. "Steve is waiting."

"Good luck," Kate said. "See you at dinner. After the movie, Masha is taking me to Nevsky Prospect, so I can buy my gifts. And my Gorbies."

Dom's brows knitted. He looked from one to the other. "Be careful," he said before he hurried off.

Masha took Kate's arm as they left the Tea Room, walking toward the elevator. "You will see our wonderful subways. They are very deep, used as bomb shelters during the Great Patriotic War of 1941–1945."

"That's what you call World War II?" Kate asked,

Masha nodded. "First, we must stop by Gostinyy Dvor," she

said, "our best department store, a famous landmark. Then we will go on to Pushkin Square so you can buy your Gorby dolls." She made a face. "I am shocked the authorities allow them to be sold."

❦

ANDRE, HIDDEN BEHIND A film festival billboard, sprang to attention as the two women passed. He overheard *Gostinyy Dvor, Pushkin Square.* So they were going to visit shops along the Nevsky. Many crimes happened at Pushkin Square, as the hordes of insistent hustlers and money changers swarmed like hungry flies around the buyers.

An hour later, the women exited the screening room. Andre hurried ahead to the front doors of the hotel. Soon Kate and the blonde woman, wearing coats, appeared. He hid himself among the soldiers. He would be required to take care of two. No matter, the Square was a frenzy. They would no doubt become separated from each other.

As he covertly watched, a man hurried up to Kate's blonde friend, taking her by the arm. An animated conversation followed about a translator becoming ill and the blonde being needed for the 4:00 PM discussion. "I am sorry," Andre heard her tell Kate.

He held his breath. Kate was taking a piece of paper from a large cloth bag she held. She handed it to the blonde woman. She was asking directions! She would be going off alone. His mind felt like pudding. He gathered his thoughts, stirring himself to anger. She had made a fool of him. Misled him, toyed with him even. Put him in very deep trouble with the Captain.

Andre fingered the folded razor in his pocket. He had never been in combat. Today he must be ready. If required, he would slash through her coat to her vest and slice open every pocket to find every tape she carried. Cut through to her skin, cut the tapes off her body if they were hidden there. He was not a killer. But if it meant killing her, so be it.

Chapter Thirteen

3:00 PM, Wednesday, January 30

Kate would have loved Masha's company, but she looked forward to the adventure of going to the Nevsky alone. Masha had scoffed at Alexander's dire pronouncement about the military take-over. To be safe, Kate carried the address of the American Embassy in her bra.

She stepped through the barricade of soldiers at the hotel's front door, scrutinizing every face, looking not only for the soldier's familiar red hair, the pale freckles, but also for eyes "wide, staring, suspicious-like," a dead giveaway, according to Masha, that they were KGB. She saw no threat. Had "they" given up in defeat? She'd put them through their paces.

With her map, a Russian Berlitz, and a large cloth duffel for gifts, Kate headed for the metro, *Ploschad Lenina*. "Take the Red Line two stops to a large interchange where many lines cross." Masha had said, pointing it out on Kate's map. "Change to the Green Line and go one stop to Nevsky Prospect."

It was the second sunny day in a row. Not bad, considering there were supposedly only fifty sunny days a year in Leningrad. She felt exhilarated to be out in the crisp air, mingling with the ordinary people hurrying along the streets, seeing everyday life outside the confines of the festival, the hotel, the planned cultural excursions. After a few minutes, the statue of Lenin loomed in the distance. Outside the *Ploschad Lenina*, a small brass band played "Waltz of the Flowers." People smiled. Spring was in the air though it was January. Donations were accepted, like New York City. Kate put two American dollars in the pot. Inside the metro station, much more attractive and cleaner than New York City subways, travelers were dwarfed by the cavernous waiting room, the gigantic floor-to-ceiling color portrait of a scowling Lenin. The portrait, the statue, and the Lenin's Mausoleum were scheduled to disappear in just a few months, when Leningrad became St. Petersburg.

Escalators moved rapidly—not a ride for anyone with vertigo. Kate clutched the handrail—mahogany, polished, gleaming. The ceiling above was rounded like a dome. To her right, the Up escalator was filled with people in dark hats and coats, looking pale and battle-weary, just as New Yorkers did when *they* emerged from the subway after a long day's work. Not many people were headed to the train below. It was late afternoon. To fall down these almost vertical stairs would be a long, hard drop. Why was she thinking like that? As she sped toward the bottom, she held the banister more tightly, feeling as if she were descending into a long tunnel, suffused in the rosy, subdued glow which came from the white-domed lamps placed on the wide wooden beam between the Up and Down escalators. The whole effect, a diffuse, other-worldly radiance, was sumptuous and solemn. She should have brought her camera. She'd stepped back in time. Did the lamps go back to the Great Patriotic War of 1941–1945? she wondered.

ANDRE, CLOSE BEHIND HER, smiled. She was easy to keep in sight, with the white scarf, the bushy Russian fur hat, and her American padded coat. Just two people stood between them. He could reach out, give her a little push, and she would tumble down the steep steps. Or he could wait and shove her under a moving train. She was at his mercy. But he needed the videotape intact. When Andre reached the metro platform, he scurried from pillar to pillar to stay out of sight. When the train arrived, he quickly slid into the car behind her.

KATE, ONCE IN THE train, realized the metro stops were written in Cyrillic, and panicked. She asked a young couple for help. "*Pazalstah?* Nevsky?" They smiled, and seemed excited to be talking to her, an American. Suddenly, their eyes darted away. In front of the sliding doors, two soldiers in long coats stood at attention. The couple flashed Kate an apologetic look, kept furtive eye contact. After two stops, they exited the train, gently pushing Kate off with them. This must be the interchange Masha spoke of, Kate thought, where many subway lines crossed.

Now that the soldiers were gone, the couple were freer, more animated. They led Kate up the steps and over to the correct train, saying, "Sorry. No English." Kate apologized too for knowing so little Russian. "*Spaceba*," she said, offering Marlboros. They refused, smiling.

One stop later, she was on the Nevsky Prospect outside a block-long building, its exterior dowdy, the paint chipped and peeling, the city's main department store, Gostinyy Dvor. According to Masha, she couldn't leave Leningrad without visiting it.

She stepped inside. The shelves were almost bare. In Women's Dresses, no one shopped and very few dresses hung on the racks. In Men's Suits, three women pushed through the meager supply of hanging trousers. When Kate thought of department stores back home with their quantities and varieties of clothing, she felt embarrassed by her country's plenty. Many parts of the store were closed for restoration. She bought a striped tasseled cap for five rubles (under one dollar American). She'd never wear it, but it was charming, reminding her of Borodin's music, which reminded her of Gilly. She'd have so much to tell her.

She'd keep it light, at first. Gilly loved to laugh. She'd tell her about the fiasco with the lost print of *Revolution*, the Molnia Cinema audience bundled in coats and scarves as they watched the hippie Summer of Love. She'd interject black humor: Steve, with his loud neckties, and his pornography, his hard currency hooker, his "auditions." She'd show Gilly the tape of last night's breath-taking fashion show at the House of Cinema.

Tell her the ways she fooled Red Hair. The author of her Bantam Guide to the Soviet Union had included a warning, *Don't be surprised if you discover you're being tailed.* The author had been followed, and had asked her pursuer for help in carrying her packages. He'd obliged—exactly what *glasnost* was supposed to be about. Kate made a snap decision: If she ran into Red Hair, she'd do the same, engage him on a human level. Maybe he'd be forthcoming, and tell her why he wanted the videotape.

As Kate left Gostinyy Dvor, she realized she'd exited through a different door than she'd entered. Was she even on Nevsky Prospect? She located a street sign. She couldn't read Cyrillic. People hurried past her. Would anyone know English? Where was the Square?

◆◆◆

ANDRE'S HEAD WAS THROBBING, his eyes about to pop out—from watching and waiting and trying to stay out of sight. Not many people in Gostinyy Dvor and very little merchandise to hide behind. Luckily, he had followed Kate inside instead of waiting by the entrance. He might have lost her because she left by another door, exiting onto a street where money changers loitered. They weaved among passers-by, hissing like snakes, offering rubles for dollars.

Now he had his plan, to slide in among them, march her off into a deserted side street—as if arresting her for black market activities. He was about to pounce, when Kate boldly approached two young men, begging, "*Pazhalsta,* Pushkin Square?"

◆◆◆

WHAT LUCK, KATE THOUGHT, the young men she'd stopped, Sergei and Sergei, were students. Both knew a little English, they'd studied it for a year in school. Offering to guide her to Pushkin Square, the taller blonde Sergei led the way. The dark-haired Sergei, a painter, walked beside her. "Do you paint houses or pictures?" Kate asked. "I am surrealist," he answered. He said he'd just come back from London, where he'd lived six months with a 51-year-old wealthy woman (whom he'd found "too possessive"). He was also teaching English to Russian children. The three walked for blocks, communicating haltingly, twisting and turning down side streets.

In New York City no one would go this far out of their way to help someone, Kate thought, suspicious. Just as she began to fear the two Sergeis were taking her to a deserted spot to rob her, she recognized the rows of kiosks filled with goods, and the brown cars—KGB cars, according to Alexei, their tour guide—that ringed the Square. The two boys were curious about Americans, no skulduggery intended. "*Spaceba.*" Kate waved good-bye to the young men.

A surge of sellers flooded toward her, children and young men, pushing against her. In her jeans pockets, she'd stowed rubles for Gostinyy Dvor and American dollars for Pushkin Square, so she wouldn't have to reach into her money belt hidden under her sweater. It had grown very cold, almost dark; the sharp-nosed sellers and money changers seemed desperate, as they surrounded her, aggressively pitching their goods.

She twisted and turned to escape their jostling bodies and pushing hands, stepped off the curb between two of the parked KGB cars. Was anybody inside those cars? Kate tried to see, but the windshields were dirty or maybe of darkened glass. As she stood by a front bumper, the headlights flashed. She was already rattled, but the lights clicking on and off frightened her more. The men in the brown cars became real.

She moved back on the sidewalk, glanced in the side window of the car with the flashing headlights. Was that the man who abducted her? He had the same bulbous nose, thick, dark curly hair. He turned to face her with a sinister smile. She jumped, felt the urge to run, but held her gaze. Not her kidnapper. His eyebrows were not as thick and erratic. On the seat beside him was a square-jawed, scowling driver. She shivered. These men were vultures, waiting.

"Please you, Madame, look you here. A real photo-realism," a young man standing beside his kiosk, called out. Cigarette hanging from his mouth, he lifted a grim-faced Gorby doll, complete with birth mark on his bald head, from his shelf of nested *matryoshkas* and took it apart. It had six pieces, the last being a tiny Peter the Great.

Several versions, sizes, styles of Gorby dolls sat side by side, some realistic, some caricatures. An interesting combination consisted of Gorbachev, George H.W. Bush, Raisa (Gorby's wife), a West German leader, and finally a small Saddam Hussein. Kate moved among the vendors, checking out their displays, opening many Gorbies with the hope of finding a Stalin with blood on his hands. She was disappointed.

Despite the confusion of the sellers hawking their wares and the gawkers on the sidewalk, Kate managed to buy four Gorby dolls, lacquered pins for Aunt Maureen and Gilly, and an army watch for Uncle Burt. It would suit him perfectly. He always seemed to march, not walk. He barked out orders and expected everyone to heel.

Everything fit in her duffel. Even though she didn't find the bloodied Stalin, she felt triumphant at getting the political *matryoshka*s. She'd worried that the dolls might be destroyed if/when the military took over the city.

When she took the Gorby doll apart in front of her camera, she'd use the tape recordings from the meeting at Masha's as voice-overs. First, the criticisms of current leaders, Gorbachev and Yeltsin, from the women brave enough to speak, followed by stories related by Masha and her mother: how Stalin gave candy to the children in the schools when candy was nowhere to be found. How he replaced God. Only later—when Kruschev opened the files—did the people find out about all those that Stalin had murdered.

According to Masha's mother, Brezhnev's rule, during Masha's childhood, was a very happy time, with free education, medical services, even clubs for drama and figure skating. Masha, mocking, had added, "Also in this time the Soviet Army invaded Czechoslovakia and forced repeal of Communist reforms. That was 1968. The invasion of Afghanistan followed. Our Vietnam." Kate remembered Masha's fierce green eyes as she spoke about Yuri Andropov's rule, "People were scared, as Andropov had been a chairman of the KGB." He was the one who'd established a plan for the psychiatric hospitals to protect the Soviet government from "dissidents." It would be a knockout section of her video project, and a beautiful lead-in to Nadya's story: her rape by the police, threats to her by family members of incarceration in a psychiatric clinic for the Cure.

❦

ANDRE TOOK HIS FOLDED razor from his pocket and snapped it open. She was a perfect target, dreamy-eyed, both arms clutching her bag of souvenirs. He moved up behind her, lightly touching her coat. It was thick. His razor was sharp. As he was about to slice it up one side, a wave of people flooded down the sidewalk toward her.

In front of Kate, from out of nowhere appeared several children dressed in rags and a mother carrying a baby in a sling over her back. The baby was large, its head misshapen, so still that Kate wondered if it were dead. The group looked very cold and very ill, with sores on their faces. They surrounded her, literally hung on her, moaning, making catlike sounds, begging for money. Shaken, Kate gave the mother a few of the rubles she had in her pocket. Still, the pack clung to her, a miasmic cloud of need and sickness. She couldn't breathe. She ran across the street. They followed making the same unearthly, whimpering sounds. They wanted American dollars. Kate was not going to open her money belt under her sweater to search for dollars. They would pick her clean. She took out her remaining rubles and threw them on the sidewalk, hoping to distract them. The pack scattered, one or two pausing to pick up the bills before surrounding her again.

THE MATRYOSHKA MURDERS

AS A STUNNED ANDRE watched the gypsies close ranks around Kate, from the corner of his eye, over to his left, was a solitary movement. A bear-like figure was lurching out of one of the cars surrounding the Square.

Kolya! The fat man pushed and shoved his way into the middle of the ragged pack.

That is why he was parked outside the hotel this morning, Andre thought. He was keeping an eye on Kate, just as Andre was. Andre knew Kolya's plan: He intended to kill her himself, blame it on the disreputable mob. He was going against the Captain's orders, playing the imbecile to the end. Unless he had set up his own deal with Gregor or the Captain.

Andre felt a murderous rage. He could strike this man dead.

Andre was military. He was in charge. He would storm his way into the crowd, disperse them, order Kolya to get the hell away. He would use his razor. Yes, if he had to, he would cut his brother-in-law, show him who was boss. He would lead Kate to a deserted street, as her protector, and explain what he wanted. What happened next would be up to her.

Now what? Kolya was dropping away from the gypsies. Andre saw why. A passer-by, a motherly looking *babushka* was marching up to the ruffians, wagging her finger, and speaking severely.

KATE FLED ON. THE *woman must know by my coat I'm American and out of my depth,* she thought. She glanced back. The ragged pack had halted for an instant, probably in shock that the Russian woman dared to scold them. Now they resumed the chase. Kate ducked into a small bookstore, crouching inside until she saw them pass by. Thank god, she'd lost them.

She was surprised she still wore her coat, that they hadn't

torn it off. They could have stabbed her. No one would have seen. What if they were tubercular? They'd been pressed so closely against her, their hands insistent, scrabbling all over her, searching for valuables. She was still holding her duffel. She shakily sorted through her gifts. All were intact. She took off her coat. No knife cuts. Just to make sure those skillful hands hadn't gone up under her coat and vest, under her sweater, she felt for her money belt. Still there. She took off her vest, opened the inside pouch at the back, compulsively checking that her tapes hadn't been lifted out by nimble fingers.

ANDRE, FROM HIS HIDING place in a doorway, saw Kate run into the Dom Knigi Bookstore. Where was Kolya? He must keep an eye on him. Was he hidden behind a car or in a doorway? Nowhere to be seen. Andre mixed in with passers-by, darting glances behind him, searching the street and sidewalk in front. He edged close to the large window of the bookstore and peeked in, careful not to show himself too plainly. Kate had removed her coat, her fur hat and scarf. Now she took off her vest and opened a large inside pocket in the back. Well, well, he had not known about that pocket. She pulled out what looked like a tangle of stockings. Ah, they were wrapped around two videotapes. She gave them a quick look, rewrapped them and slid the jumble back into the pouch.

KATE LOOKED UP TO see a blonde woman in a pink sweater and a long black skirt in front of her. "Everything okay?" she asked in accented English. *She must be the clerk,* Kate thought. "The gypsies," Kate said. "Just checking I still have my valuables. *Spaceba.*" The clerk nodded sympathetically and walked back behind a counter. Kate donned her vest and coat, lingering to look around. She bought a Russian wall calendar, a real art piece for

2.80 rubles (under fifty cents American). On the cover was a painting of a female figure, masked, clothed in black, head-to-toe. A wide splash of crimson bloomed like a flower in her center. The painting seemed to embody the soul of Russia, held in the black grip of authority, a pulsating red core—vitality, muscle, chutzpah—impatient to be free. Kate also purchased two posters: a loaf of bread, *Without Value* written on its label; the other, a burning ruble. Even inside this store, the black market money changers were quite blatant. Coming up behind her, whispering "change" with such force she thought at first she was being sworn at or that it was a sexual come-on.

She left the bookstore, her rolled-up calendar and posters carefully stowed in her duffel. Now it was dark, a beautiful night, crisp and clear. No sign of the gypsies. She checked her watch. Plenty of time to get back and change for the eight-thirty panel. The snow crunched underfoot. She must find the subway. It was to her right. Right? She'd been so busy talking with the two Sergeis she hadn't paid attention when they brought her to the Square. She stopped a boy for directions. He turned out to be an American who was in Leningrad to teach English to a mime troupe. That made her smile. He didn't know the way to the hotel.

"Metro? Hotel Leningrad?" Kate asked a jolly-looking, red-cheeked Russian woman hurrying along the street, most likely in a rush to get home, She looked blank. Kate showed her the subway map. "*Ploschad Lenina?*"

The woman's face was thoughtful. "*Americanski?*"

Kate nodded. The woman brightened, led Kate to a subway train, transferred with her to the Red Line at the interchange, and insisted on traveling with Kate the two stops to *Ploschad Lenina*. Kate thanked her, wondering how far out of her way she'd gone to bring her here.

She offered the woman a pack of Marlboros. The woman smiled and shook her head. She must not be a smoker, Kate thought. Wait, she still had a lacy bra in her vest. One woman filmmaker told her they were going over big here. "*Spaceba,*"

Kate said, handing it to her. The woman looked shocked, then laughingly refused, indicating her bosom. Kate wasn't sure what she meant—too small, too large, or she didn't wear a bra. Maybe she thought the lace was decadent. Kate would love to hear her describe her adventure with the *Americanski* when she got home.

Almost every Russian she'd met today, their eyes lit up when they realized she was American. They wanted to help, exchange whatever information was possible with their limited English and Kate's inadequate Russian.

Kate exited the metro station. There it was, the huge statue of Lenin, arms outstretched to greet her. Now, turn right. Yay, she was on her way to the hotel. She'd have time to grab a bite at the Café Neva and change clothes for the panel. Her adventures had been fascinating and fun, despite the creepiness of the gypsy children clinging to her as she ran.

※※※

ANDRE STUCK CLOSE TO Kate, on the alert for Kolya. Had he given up so easily? Or had he, drunk as usual, staggered back to his car at the Square to sleep it off?

Andre had felt pity, ready to come to Kate's aid as the gypsies chased her like a swarm of sharks. *Numbskull,* he said to himself. He stepped up his pace, walking in the soft snow to be as silent as possible. The street was dark, deserted, without shops or homes. From time to time, a glow from the streetlamps along the highway by the Neva washed over the snow. Now was the time to spring, before she was nearer the hotel. The distance between the two of them was short. He would sneak up beside her, say "*Prevyet,* Kate." She would be surprised to hear someone calling her by name. When she saw his face, she would know this meeting had been meant from the beginning.

As she passed a construction site, Andre could hardly believe what he was seeing. A shadowy figure lurched out from behind a storage bin, grabbing her from behind. She screamed, twisted away and ran. The man staggered after her, roaring, "*Blyad! Pizda!*" Andre recognized the voice, the rolling gait. Kolya! Andre's blood boiled. He could scarcely breathe. Kolya had driven here from the Square and waited, knowing she would return this way to the hotel.

KATE RAN, HER LEGS like pistons, holding tightly to her duffel of gifts. She slipped on a patch of ice and almost fell. He was right behind her. He could have the gifts if that's what he wanted. She whirled around and threw the bag in his face, stopping him for an instant before it dropped to the ground. The man was not interested in what was inside.

She quickened her pace. She heard him gasp and felt him snatch the back of her coat, holding fast with both hands. She strained to get away, frantically working the front zipper. Almost there. It stopped, cloth caught in its teeth. She forced the coat open with both hands, popping the zipper, struggling to release one arm from its sleeve, then the other, until finally she jerked free. "Help," she screamed, her feet pounding on the ground. Now he was so close she could feel the breeze from his flailing hands as he tried to reach her. She turned into him, kneed him in the groin. He groaned and bent down, holding himself. Yelling "Hye!" she snapped a front kick to his head, connected, kicked again, and missed. He reached out and grabbed the flap of her vest. She thrashed about, puffing and panting, finally sloughing off her vest, and staggered on. Several seconds later, a great weight slammed against her. She fell face down. It knocked her breath away. She was pinned to the ground with him on top.

He gave a bark of a laugh as he peered into her face. His stinking breath enveloped her. She realized with a sudden shock he was the man who'd abducted her in the illegal cab. He had a hand on her throat, squeezing. She squirmed and bucked, but couldn't budge his bulky body. Every time she moved, his hand gripped her throat more tightly. She was blacking out. Suddenly, he took a handful of her hair and jerked her head to the side. Grunting, shouting, spitting, he held a knife to her throat. She stiffened, preparing herself for the piercing pain.

Dimly, she heard a second man yell, "Kolya!" She heard thuds, a loud smack above her. The two were fighting. The man sitting on her back swayed and lurched, as if he were riding a bronco. Still he was dead weight, trapping her underneath him. Still he gripped the knife. With all her strength she moved an arm caught under her body, bringing up her hand to shield her throat. Just in time to feel a slicing pain. More thrashing and then the fat man—Kolya was his name, she must remember it—shrieked. He jabbered a string of words she didn't understand, except for one. "Andre." Now there are two, she thought dully, two here to kill me. Kolya and Andre.

※※※

ANDRE WAS CHOKING WITH rage. "You dirty double-crosser." Kolya stared at him as if at a ghost. Andre grabbed him with both hands, tearing at his hair, his clothes, trying to flip him off Kate's body.

"Get off!" Andre punched him in the ear, the face.

"You are a crazy man," Kolya roared.

Andre flipped his razor open.

"She is mine," Kolya screamed.

Andre slashed at him in a frenzy, hardly knowing what he was doing.

Kolya squealed, his knife falling from his hand. He held his arm, cursing, "They will send you to Siberia for this."

Andre kicked him in the shoulder, in the head, in the face. He heard a snapping sound. Kolya groaned and collapsed. Andre pushed him off Kate's body.

He stooped. "You okay, my Kate?" he asked softly. She spoke his name, "Andre," her face as close to his as if they were in bed together. Her eyes were confused, afraid. She was staring at his hand. It was bloody, he realized. He still held the razor. He wiped his hand and the razor on his coat.

Her shrieks snapped him out of his daydream. He watched her struggle to her knees, still screaming. If he wanted to survive, he must kill her. He couldn't move. What had he done? Kolya lay motionless on the ground.

Shouts mingled with Kate's cries. A man and a woman were running his way. Andre scurried toward the metro, his eyes searching the ground for her vest, a blob of darkness on the snow. And there it was. From the inside back pouch he scooped out the videotapes, wrapped in a wad of stockings. He heard a male voice yelling. He looked over his shoulder. The man was chasing him. On the ground, Kolya was unmoving, his bulk caught in the glimmer of the lights near the river.

Andre ran as fast as he could toward *Ploschad Lenina*.

Chapter Fourteen

6:30 PM, Wednesday, January 30

Kate managed to stand, her legs quivering like Jello. A man and a woman were peering into her face. "You're bleeding," the woman cried. "You have no coat!" She had a British accent.

"What happened?" the man asked.

Kate pointed at the inert Kolya. "He tried to kill me." His eyes were closed, his face was bloody, his chest was moving up and down. "There's another one," she said, turning, her eyes raking the dimly lit area, spotting a dim shape several yards away as he picked up something from the ground. Her vest! She broke away from the couple. "He's stealing my tapes." She stumbled toward him, shrieking, "Stop! I know who you are!"

The British man trotted up beside her, patting her shoulder, "Here, here. You're hurt." He jerked a thumb toward the man on the ground behind them. "Looks like he's out for awhile. I'll give chase."

"He's military. He has a razor," Kate cried. Now the woman was beside her, gently blotting Kate's bloody hand with a tissue. "I don't think the cut is deep," Kate, breathing hard, licked her lips and tasted blood. She must have bitten herself when the fat man pushed her down.

"The back of your sweater, it's covered in blood."

"It's his. The man on the ground," Kate explained, through chattering teeth, "was sitting on me, trying to slit my throat, when the soldier—who's running—attacked him."

"The soldier saved your life?" she asked uncertainly.

Kate shook her head slowly. "I think it was a contest between them, who would kill me."

"Where's your coat?" The woman put her own scarf around Kate's shoulders.

"I had to ditch it to get away." Her knee hurt. She must have twisted it. The woman held her by her waist as the two searched the ground for items Kate had shed.

"My hat!" Kate hadn't noticed when it fell off. Her ears were numb, she realized, as she slid the bushy Russian fur hat onto her head. A few feet away in a pile of snow was the vest. With a sickening feeling, Kate reached into the inside back pouch, pulling out treasures, still wrapped in a pair of tights— which she unwound. Her two audiotapes and one videotape were safe. The videos wrapped in her knee high stockings were gone. "He took two tapes." Which two? She'd put all three in *Revolution* jackets. Tears of anger pricked her eyes.

"The tapes. That's all? You have your money?"

Kate felt her money belt under her sweater. "Yes." She'd rather he'd taken her money, her passport. "My most important footage," she moaned. If one of the missing tapes was of Nadya, where she'd described the horror of being *rozovaya*— Kate put her face in her hands.

The woman patted her shoulder. "You're here for the film

festival, I see. We had a wonderful time last year, the first year, so we decided to come again—a big mistake."

"Yes," Kate nodded. She zipped up the inside pouch, brushed snow off the vest, and carried it over her arm. She didn't want to get blood on it. She was shivering uncontrollably. She turned to the woman. "I'm beginning to worry about your—"

"My husband learned to fight in the army," the woman said. But she looked anxious now that he was out of sight.

Further up the way, Kate found her coat, gratefully snuggling into it, as she handed the woman her scarf. "I'm afraid I've ruined it. I'll buy you another."

"Oh, no. I'll soak it in cold water." The woman folded it, covering up the bloodied side.

Kate spotted her duffel of gifts. Two Gorby dolls had bounced out of the bag. With trembling hands, she brushed snow off them, relieved to see they hadn't cracked. The calendar and posters were crumpled but not torn. She held the military watch to her ear. Still ticking.

"Halloo." The husband was half running, half walking their way. When he reached them, he was huffing and puffing. "The soldier disappeared in the metro."

His wife embraced him.

"I'm sorry," he said to Kate.

"Thank you. You could have been hurt. Or arrested." Kate held her coat closed with one hand—the zipper was ruined. The icy fingers of the wind found its way through the gaps.

The three made their way back toward the hotel. Kate realized she was limping. She stopped to push some cold snow up her pant leg and pack it around her knee, explaining, "I hurt it when I fell. Not serious."

When they reached the spot where the fat man, Kolya, had been lying, he was gone.

Kate felt like screaming. He could have answered important questions. He was a big man. If he remained unconscious, they would have had to drag him like a sack of potatoes. If he was awake, well, maybe the husband could have controlled him and marched him to the hotel. But then, they—Westerners—would bring attention to themselves. Not that she herself wasn't already under scrutiny.

"We must report this to hotel security," said the British man.

"Please don't," Kate said, panicked. "First, I must talk to my boss."

"She's here for the festival," the woman said to her husband.

"Awkward time," the man mumbled.

The understatement of the year, Kate thought. So British. "You saved my life. I can't thank you enough." She exchanged business cards and room numbers with the couple. "I may need you as a witness," Kate said. "But it may be best to let it go." She gave each a hug. "A lucky pleasure to meet you, Deborah and Peter Kempson."

※

AT THE FOURTH FLOOR, Kate stepped off the elevator, averting her face and trying not to limp as she passed the *dejurnaya's* desk. Her lip was ballooning up. Her knee felt swollen. The icy snow she'd packed around it had melted and was dripping into her sock. She prayed Dom was in his room. She knocked. His door opened. He stared blankly as if he didn't know her, then a look of horror crossed his face. "Oh, my god," he sighed, taking her arm as she hobbled in. She sank carefully into the chair, cuddling her bag of gifts in her arms. "What happened?"

"I know their names—Andre and Kolya," she cried. "Andre is the soldier who's been stalking me. On the tape of the abduction—remember?—we heard the fat man, Kolya, say *Andre*."

Dom eased the gifts from Kate's lap, setting them on the floor. He lifted off the vest that hung over her arm. He removed her coat and bushy fur hat. "There's blood on the back of your sweater," he said, his voice shaky. "We must get you to a doctor."

"It's Kolya's. He was sitting on me, about to slit my throat when Andre attacked him."

"My poor girl." Dom held her close, patting her like she was a baby.

She took deep breaths, telling herself, *It's over. Calm down.* She pulled away. "I'm okay, really. Just a split lip, a twisted knee. A superficial cut." She pulled off the tissue stuck in the dried blood of her hand. "See?"

He poured her a glass of cognac and opened a carton of water. She drank gingerly, alternating sips of cognac with water. "It's all connected. Kolya, who drove the illegal cab and left Sveta and me in the cemetery, and Andre, Red Hair, who's been after the tape. Someone in charge of those two wants me dead. The abduction wasn't random." She'd been clinging to that hope, she realized, not choosing to believe someone wanted to kill her. Why did Andre fight Kolya? So he could kill her himself? Or did he save her life? As he'd held the bloody razor in front of her eyes, he seemed unsure what to do next. How did Sveta fit in? Maybe she wasn't confined to the psychiatric clinic after all. Maybe Kolya had killed her by mistake that night in the cemetery. Both she and Sveta were wearing white scarves.

"Kate!" Dom leaned over her. He held her face with both hands, forcing her to look into his eyes. "Tell me again. Everything. Slowly."

By the time she finished relating the ordeal and reliving it, the glass of cognac was gone.

"Thank God for the Brits," Dom sighed. "What about Masha?" he asked anxiously. "The last I heard she was going with you—right?"

Kate shook her head. "Last-minute panel to translate." Her arms felt like lead pipes. She was stiffening up. Tomorrow she'd ache all over.

"You went to the Nevsky Prospect alone." Dom looked so perturbed, his eyes big, his mouth drooping, like a disappointed father. She almost smiled. Instead, tears rolled down her cheeks. "Andre—the soldier—took two of my videotapes." She sat up straighter, suddenly electrified. "I need the camera VCR. I have to check the one video that I have left."

"Let's get something cold on your knee." He went into the bathroom and brought back a wet washcloth. Kate draped the cold rag over her jeans on the puffy knee.

Dom looked at his watch. "Steve and I are on tonight's panel, practically a command performance, a summing up, with kernels about American documentary films. You take a warm bath, stay here . . ."

"No, no, I don't want to be alone. We agreed I'd tape the panel discussion as part of our company's archives. I want to see Masha. We have the gifts to give her." She moaned softly, "If the missing tape is of her and Nadya—" She slumped in her chair.

"Where's the video camera?"

"Steve has it."

Dom nodded. "I'll get it. Then we're clearing everything out of your room."

While Dom was gone, she checked herself out in his bathroom mirror. Her lip was split and swollen, her cheek red and rough—a snow burn. She cautiously washed her face and hands. The knife wound on her palm oozed and stung. Already it was closing. Among Dom's toiletries, she found bandaids and pasted three over the cut. Her coat and vest were damp but otherwise okay—except her coat had a busted zipper. Her jeans were soaked. She couldn't wait to get into a dry pair and take a look at her knee while she was at it. She threw away the bloody sweater and put on a shirt of Dom's.

"That was a piece of luck," Dom announced as he came through the door. "I was heading toward Steve's room when he exited the elevator, camera in hand. I took it, saying, "We need it," leaving him spluttering. "What's he using it for?" Dom asked.

Kate opened the camera, ejecting Steve's tape and inserting her own. She realized from the first frame it was her least important video, the footage of the visit to the Palace of Pavlovsk. "Oh, Dom," she wailed, "The soldier has the tape with the interview of

Nadya and Masha. It could get them both in deep trouble." She groaned softly. "He also has the tape of the scar-faced officer in the bar with the man in the gray business suit."

"Maybe now they'll leave you alone."

"I wish I believed that," Kate said.

Dom nodded slowly. "Right. They'll just have two more women, Masha and Nadya, in their crosshairs."

Kate said miserably, "You and I will leave Friday, hopefully standing up—not in a wooden box. Masha and Nadya will stay." She frowned. "Andre and Kolya are the key to everything. We have to find them."

"No more amateur detective work," Dom said gruffly. "We must report everything. First, to the organizers of the festival. We'll ask them the safest way to proceed."

Kate sat glumly, tears in her eyes. "I lost irreplaceable shots, the festival's opening ceremonies, Piskarovoye Cemetery, the Molnia cinema with the wonderful translator, the dining room, Sergei, the Scheduler, his messy room with the cans of film . . . Nadya . . . Masha . . ." By the end of the list, she was sobbing. "This country. These people. Damn that man with the monkey. If I hadn't wanted that shot, I wouldn't have taped the two men behind him in the bar. None of this would have happened."

Dom hugged her, stroking her hair.

After she was calmer, she and Dom went to her room, to gather the rest of her belongings. Kate dreaded walking past the snooping *dejurnaya,* but she was away from her post. Kate heard her scolding someone in the other wing as she hurried past the woman's desk, loaded down with her audiotape player, her bag of dirty clothes, a plastic bag of unopened tapes, and presents for Masha. Dom carted in her suitcase, stuffed with clothes and toiletries. "We have time to grab a bite before the tour bus leaves for the House of Cinema," he said.

In the bathroom, Kate undressed, climbing into the tub with care. Her knee hurt with every move. It was swollen, but wasn't black and blue. The hot water pelted her. W*hen the soldier plays the tapes,* she fretted, *he'll hear Nadya's confession about being* rozovaya. *He'll hear Masha talk about being half-Jewish, and me call myself a hooligan, a moonlight person.*

Before she dressed in clean, dry clothes, she taped to her stomach the one remaining video and the two audiotapes, using masking tape that Dom brought with him. She applied make-up to cover her reddened cheek.

She inserted a new tape into her camera and grabbed the bag of presents for Masha, important because the custom here was to exchange small gifts with special friends. Dom and she hurried out the door, stopping to pick up Steve, who was dressed extravagantly, looking the part of a film producer in a white jacket and black shirt with a pink and gold ascot tie. He wore an off-white fedora on his head. He'd recently washed his hair and used his curling iron, Kate noticed. Dark curls, soft and glossy, hung down to his shoulders. The three headed for the Russian Tea Room.

While Dom was at the counter ordering cold sandwiches for all, Steve sidled up to Kate, "I'd like my tape back."

That's right, Kate thought, in triumph, a tape remained inside when Dom brought her the camera he'd commandeered from Steve.

Steve gave her a piercing stare, menacing and scared, as if to say *If you've looked at it, better keep your mouth shut.*

Look at it she would, later tonight. If it confirmed her suspicions, she'd inform Dom. "It's in my room." She was not about to tell Steve about the mugging or that she was now staying in Dom's room. "I'll give it to you after the panel."

He refocused, really looking at her for once. "What happened to your lip?" he asked.

"I'm getting a cold sore."

Chapter Fifteen

8:15 PM, Wednesday, January 30

Kate's eyes scoured the audience seated in the House of Cinema auditorium. No Kolya, no scar-faced officer, or civilian in a gray business suit, no Andre, no soldiers of any sort. Dom was speaking with last night's videographer who was setting up his camera below the apron of the stage. The man slid a videotape from inside his jacket, passing it to Dom who handed it to Kate. She was thrilled the man kept his promise to deliver them a copy of last night's inflammatory fashion show. Before she put the tape in her vest pocket, she noted with disappointment it was in the Russian format. She'd have to wait to watch it until she was back home. She savored the word *home,* allowing it to melt in her mouth, the sweetness spreading through her body. When she arrived in the States, she'd kiss the ground. She'd do a dance. She'd be nice to everyone, even Uncle Burt.

Kate stood to one side, lifted the video camera to her shoulder, and did a slow establishing shot of the American documentary filmmakers seated onstage. Dom looked very cool in his "informal costume"—jeans and maroon sweater, a white shirt collar peeping out. His Van Dyke beard added authority. "Everyone has to wear a costume in this business," he'd told her when she first went to work for him. Steve took it too far with his flashy style, verging on pimp. Just as she was saying to herself, *Steve, take off that stupid hat,* he reached up for his fedora and, with a little flourish, placed it on his lap. At the far end of the group was Masha, sleek and blonde, naturally poised, who'd be translating for the predominantly Russian audience.

She videotaped each American director as they spoke about their work and what it meant to be at the festival. Among the films represented were an exposé of American white Supremacist groups; a portrait of a Salvadoran woman, peasant, wife, mother, and guerrilla leader; a documentary about the secret underground Cu Chi tunnels during the Vietnam War; General Motor's massive downsizing in Flint, Michigan. All were about freedom as a goal of the people depicted, which must have been inspiring to the Russian audience. Dom spoke eloquently for *Revolution* and the thrill it was for him and his colleagues to meet the gifted translator, the very appreciative Russian audience and to answer their questions. He introduced Steve, beside him on the stage, and Kate, who waved one hand as she zoomed in on Dom's face.

A Q&A followed, with fewer questions than comments, which Masha translated, wearing her official smile. A middle-aged man stood, addressing the audience around him as well the panel, insisting that democratic breakthroughs were taking place in the Soviet Union, even though reactionary forces still fought to suppress the process. Another audience member praised documentary films as an important means of fixating history, adding, "They will help in the revival of the Russian state structure and culture."

Kate was touched by the speakers' earnestness and optimism that the good guys would win. Who were the good guys? Kate flashed back to the KGB cars that, like a wall, enclosed Pushkin Square. Someone had told her that many former KGB worked as security guards, adding "There's no such thing as an ex-KGB officer." These guys wanted back on the national payroll and were willing to do anything to get there.

The one question asked of the panel was: Are most American documentary filmmakers women? It looked that way from the representation on the stage. Dom answered, "Three-fourths are. Men in America don't gravitate to documentaries because there's little money in it."

Kate's knee throbbed, the cut on her palm stung, as she grasped the heavy camera resting on her shoulder with both hands. She stood the entire time. It was worth it. The evening's discussion—caught on tape by her—was a candle of hope in the darkness of the times.

Why Steve was on the panel she didn't know. He'd sat there silently, upstaging everyone else with his flashy outfit. After concluding remarks were made, he delivered a pitch that *Revolution* be screened in the main competition hall after the festival's closing ceremonies as a celebratory finale. Kate was appalled by his bad taste. Masha didn't translate. Good for her!

Steve disappeared quickly. Dom remained onstage, whispering intently to Masha, who shot a worried glance at Kate before she signaled Dom to follow her. She spoke to a man and a woman who'd come up from the audience to congratulate the panel. *Most likely Russian festival officials,* Kate thought. Dom beckoned Kate to join them. She mounted the steps to the stage, a lump the size of a grapefruit in the pit of her stomach. "Oh, Masha, I'm so sorry," Kate cried at the same time that Masha exclaimed, "I see what they have done to you. My dear Kate, if only I had gone with you to the Nevsky Prospect."

The festival officials drew Kate off to the side, with Masha translating Kate's report of the crimes against her, starting with her abduction to the cemetery, continuing through tonight's attempted murder.

"My recommendation is to file police report," the man said, turning to the woman.

Kate winced. Dom nodded, rubbing his face nervously.

The woman said apologetically, "A detective may come to the hotel to take your statement."

He'll have to do it by tomorrow, Kate thought, for she, Dom, and Steve and would be on their way to the airport very early Friday. Kate fervently hoped the detective wouldn't be that organized. Still she had to put on a cooperative face for these officials. "*Spaceba.* I made an audiotape of the abduction. In it, Kolya, the cab driver, talks about the soldier Andre. I also have the room number of witnesses, the British couple who arrived tonight in the nick of time."

Smiling, the officials shook Kate's hand and Dom's hand before they departed the stage.

"Maybe we go to embassy tomorrow when it opens," Masha said in a low voice.

"Another tack might be to inform the media gathered for the festival," Dom suggested. "Reporters are here from the U.S. as well as other countries. A Western reporter might be very interested in Kate's story."

Masha nodded. "It could mean a public outcry against the rise in crime, which is something the authorities here hate."

Kate touched Masha's shoulder. "The soldier now has the video interview of Nadya and you."

"Dom told me," Masha said bleakly. "I must warn Nadya."

"But you didn't reveal your last names," Kate said, grabbing her hand, feeling dismal. She'd messed up Nadya's life—Masha's too. She'd lost Sveta during that terrible chase through the cemetery. She was a loser, just as her guardian Uncle Burt had predicted years ago.

❦

IN THE DOM KINO Bar, Kate scrutinized the room as Dom pulled out chairs for her and Masha. She spotted Steve at another table, alone, but not for long. A limping woman approached him. Steve looked startled as she pulled out a chair and sat across from him. She took off her white fur coat, then turned worriedly toward the entrance. Her face, heavily made up, had a hard sort of prettiness. Her red blouse was low cut. Suddenly, for Kate, things fell into place. This was the woman who'd slammed out of the fat man's—Kolya's—car, crying, just before Kate and Sveta had stepped into his car and the nightmare.

Another picture slid into Kate's mind: the woman's dark hair against the white fur coat, as she left Steve's room, arm-in-arm with Irina. It was the night Steve knocked at Kate's door, inviting her over for the party. The night someone—the soldier?—searched her room as she slept. So this woman—Irina too—must be linked with Andre and Kolya in the plan to "get" her.

Was Steve in cahoots with them? Kate felt as if the wind had been knocked out of her.

A subdued Dom, Kate and Masha drank coffee and cognac. Masha presented gifts of friendship to Kate and Dom: pins for "Peace," small souvenirs, and a beautiful book of Matisse's drawings and paintings with comments in Russian.

Kate and Dom gave Masha T-shirts, blue jeans from the *Beryozka* shop for her son, cognac, cigarettes to use for bartering, and gum, mints, candies and nuts.

"We'd like to give you American dollars. Can you accept?" Dom asked.

Masha made a face. "More than fifty dollars hard currency is illegal."

"While the bigger crooks get away with much more in bribes and on the black market," Kate said. A woman was crying behind her. Kate turned. The woman in the red blouse, the white fur. Steve seemed to think he had her in hand as he led her toward the exit. Kate heard her say, "America," through her sobs.

Dom and Masha hadn't noticed that little drama. Too busy looking soulfully into each other's eyes. Kate decided to mull it over and save it—with all the other Steve stuff—for discussion tonight in Dom's room.

Dom took Masha's hand. "How do we invite you to America?"

"It is more than a letter. I need an official invitation. You must ask for forms from the Soviet consulate in Washington. Fill out your part, have papers notarized, and send them here."

Dom said, "I'll send for the forms as soon as we get back."

What a drawn-out hassle Soviet authorities have created for Russians wanting to visit the U.S., Kate thought. Maybe because they were afraid many would defect.

"Don't send by regular mail," Masha said apologetically. "That can take six weeks, if it gets here at all. Express mail takes only a week and a half."

"What about your son? Would he like to visit?"

She shook her head sadly. "I am certain my ex-husband will not let him. Even though we are divorced, his permission is required by law."

▼▪▴▾

TANYA, HER CHEEKS WET with tears, slipped out of her coat, laying it carefully in a chair in Steve's hotel room. The coat was beginning to shed, but still looked elegant. Many people thought it was white sable, not rabbit fur. Wearing it made her feel proud and beautiful. Steve handed her a handkerchief. She blotted her eyes carefully. She did not want to smear her mascara further. "My life is in danger," she whispered. "You must help me. I must leave Leningrad as soon as possible." She put her arms around Steve's neck.

"Shhh. Shh" Impatiently, Steve pried himself out of her arms her and closed the door. She felt uncomfortable with the thoughtful look he was giving her. She must persuade him of the danger she was in. "Kolya will find me and kill me. He might be sorry afterwards but then it will be too late. More and more he is a crazy man."

"Who is Kolya?" Steve asked.

"My husband."

"You're married?" Steve looked stunned. "He knows what you do?"

She grabbed his hand. "You must understand. He is the one who sends me out. Every night, no matter the weather, no matter how I feel. I do not like this job of being with strangers. I want to be with you in films. In America." She realized she was shaking.

"That's .. uh . . . in the future. A possibility. If all goes well." He chewed his lower lip. "We agreed. You'll be my contact here and scout around for talent." He grinned nervously. "You'll get a percent, an agent's fee."

Hollywood, he had promised. A job in films. Tanya dissolved once more in tears. "I am scared of Kolya. He is in a panic I will leave him. He does not care about me. He fears only to lose the money I bring in."

Steve groaned. "How much did you tell him?"

"I am sorry." She put her face in her hands. "We had a fight. I told him I had a job in the movies with you." She looked up. "And you were taking me out of this terrible life to America."

"Jesus!" Steve grunted. She cringed when he brought his hand up. He didn't slap her but patted her perfunctorily on the shoulder. "Look, I'll talk to him. Maybe I can find work for him too in our movie business."

It would be poison to have Kolya working with them. "He is dangerous if he has been drinking," she said, her voice rising. She mustn't get hysterical. "He carries a knife."

"Calm down, calm down," Steve said, his eyes suddenly frantic.

"We had a fight last night. He left in a rage. I stayed overnight with my friend, Irina. I am frightened not just for me. But also for the girl who works—Where are you going?" She had told him too much.

Steve, his jaw set, was scrambling into his coat. "Look, I'm out of booze. I'll just go around the corner to the *Beryozka* shop. You fix yourself up. We'll relax, figure this mess out."

After he left, Tanya sat on the bed. He was changing his mind. He would leave for America without her. She had ruined her chances. No, it was Kolya, on a path of destruction. Where it would lead she was afraid to know. She limped into the bathroom and washed her face. Her leg had never been this bad. Her stomach was upset all the time. She put on fresh makeup. She rummaged through her purse and found a pain-killer. She stripped down to the black lacy underwear Steve had given her the night of her audition. She waited in his bed, half dozing. When Steve returned, she would pull him to her, tell him she had never met a man as exciting as he . . . He might even marry her some day.

She jerked awake. Someone was banging on the door, yelling her name. "Tanya! I know you are there!" She thought she was going to faint. Kolya was roaring like a maddened bull.

"Tanya. Let me in, you whore. I am hurt. Your stupid brother Andre has almost killed me."

Better that, Tanya thought bitterly, than *you* almost killed *him.*

"Tanya." His voice was wheedling. "Please come home."

Never, she said to herself. She remained still for several minutes, hoping the *dejurnaya* would come to her aid, not daring even to scratch her nose, for fear the bedclothes would rustle.

⸮⸮⸮

A FRUSTRATED GREGOR, JUST two doors down, was deciding next steps. Moscow was waiting. His boss was waiting. Kate should be disposed of. But he had heard nothing from Captain Iurkov, nothing from Kolya, who had yesterday accepted a second payment, proclaiming himself, *victorious warrior,* and promising results. Gregor stopped his pacing. What was going on in the hall? He cracked his door. Kolya was bellowing and pounding on the door of the American film director, the man with the gaudy neckties and the dark curls.

The American woman's room was between his and the film director's. The noise could bring her out for a look—if she was still alive and Gregor had heard nothing to the contrary. If she recognized this fat boob as the man who left her in the cemetery to die—Gregor wiped the perspiration from his face—and the slimy weasel ratted on him . . .

Why was he knocking at the film director's door? The numbskull was roaring, "Tanya, come home," like a wounded animal, then bleating something about Andre. Gregor saw the *dejurnaya* had left her post and was fearfully approaching. It was all turning to crap. Gregor gritted his teeth. "Kolya!" he hissed.

The fool looked his way in a daze. Was he drunk or on drugs? His face was battered, bloody. He'd been in a fight. He watched as Kolya took a step, then in slow motion turned back to stare at the closed door.

Gregor unlocked his briefcase. He took out his gun, inserted the ammunition magazine inside the grip, and attached the silencer. He placed it on his dresser under a towel. He hurried into the corridor, grabbed Kolya firmly by the shoulders, assuring the *dejurnaya,* "I'll take care of him." He marched Kolya, cursing, down the hall. "Comrade, settle down," Gregor soothed as he pushed him into his room.

Kolya's nose was crooked and swollen as if broken. Black rings were under both eyes. A large bandage covered one hand, a cut slashed across his forehead.

Gregor closed his door. "I told you to stay away from my room," he said through gritted teeth.

Kolya shook his bandaged hand in the air, grimaced, emptied pills from a small bottle in his pocket and swallowed them without water. "He tried to kill me. I lost almost a pint of blood. The doctors stitched me up like a turkey . . ." His face was shiny with sweat. He breathed through his mouth.

"Who tried to kill you?"

"Andre. That whore's brother." He jerked his head to the right, toward the room on whose door he had been beating. "Tanya is with that *mudak, derrmo,* her film director boy friend." His lips curled. "They are double crossing me."

Gregor realized he was caught in the middle of a domestic fight between this buffoon and his hooker wife. "She is in the film director's room?"

He shook his head gloomily. "She is not at home."

Gregor did not smell booze but he was certain Kolya was high, most likely on those pills he was gobbling. "Listen to me," Gregor said sharply. "I have to be out of Leningrad by tomorrow evening. What is going on?"

Kolya's heavy black brows converged in the middle of his forehead. "I had her on the ground, my knife at her throat. Andre came from nowhere. He stabbed me." Kolya waved his bandaged hand in Gregor's face, then struggled out of his coat and let it fall to the floor. He stumbled, regained his balance. "I jerked away. Or he would have gotten me in the heart." He put his hand on his chest. "He would kill me to protect the American girl."

Was this a bunch of horseshit? A way to gouge more money out of him?

"He kicked me in the face. I was done for. She got away." The fat man was breathing hard. His face was red and puffing up, his eyes like slits. "He grabbed the videotape for himself and ran."

If that tape gets in the wrong hands, my career is over, Gregor thought.

"Andre is not to be trusted." Kolya painfully arranged his face in a smile. "I know his plan—to use the tape to blackmail you."

Gregor turned away, toward the dresser top where, under the towel his Sig-Sauer lay, the silencer attached.

"Tanya, my wife," Kolya muttered, "she is mixed up with that movie director. Steve is his name." Again, he jerked his head to the right. "He has promised her a job with his film company. Now that she is cozy with the Americans, she is going to tell them," his voice dropped to a growl, "that you hired me to kill the girl."

Gregor would like nothing better than to shoot this fat blubbering slob and leave this city. But the body would be found here in his room. Not good, even though he had the protection of important officials.

He reluctantly reconsidered. *These maniacs have had a falling out. And they will take me down with them.* He did not want to give away his turmoil. He clapped a hand on Kolya's shoulder. "We must stick together, Comrade, like brothers. I will inform the Captain of Andre's betrayal." He propelled Kolya toward the door. "You find your wife and shut her up—one way or another. Then come back to me."

Gregor closed his door part way, watching through the crack. Kolya, his coat dragging behind him as he stumbled down the hall, hesitated at the American film director's door. With his good hand, he knocked twice, quickly, half-heartedly.

"Steve?" a female voice from inside asked.

Kolya grunted, tapped again. The door creaked open slowly.

Gregor heard the elevator door open. He saw the film director—Steve—step out and turn the corner into the hall, a bottle of vodka in hand, just as Kolya charged into Steve's room with a triumphant cry. Wisely, Gregor thought, the film director quickly assessed the situation, turned on his heel and fled, exiting by the back stairs. Gregor almost smiled. Now Tanya and Kolya could tear each other apart in Steve's room.

▼▲▼

TANYA COULD NOT BELIEVE her eyes. Kolya was in the room, less than four feet away. His face was swollen, covered in blood. His eyes ringed like a raccoon dog's. How did he get past the soldiers at the front door? A large bandage was pasted to his cheek, another covered an ear, his clothes were torn. He stormed her way, his fist raised. She dodged and scurried around the room, cringing in a corner near the bathroom. "Ha!!" he exclaimed. A gleeful bark, a roar, a cry to battle. A thick, white bandage was wrapped around his right hand. Suddenly, he stopped, looked her up and down. His eyes grew steely as they fastened on the black underwear she wore. "From your boyfriend?"

She stood up straight. She would not let him bully her. "Who else? Not from you, certainly," she said in a ragged voice.

He spat out, "Whore."

"Thanks to you." Tanya grabbed her blouse and put it on. "I have a job. Are you blind? I am out working as you asked."

"Where is he? Your big shot American boyfriend?"

"At the *Beryozka* shop. Getting a bottle. He will be back soon. You better leave," she said nervously. "What happened to you?"

"Andre, your stupid brother, has tried to kill me. He has thrown a monkey wrench into everything. Thanks to him, the American girl has escaped once more. Gregor is very angry.

We have lost many dollars because of Andre. And you"—he roared, sticking his face in hers—"shut your mouth about it. If you want to stay alive."

"You shut *your* mouth," she screeched. "For all we know the girl is in her room next door, listening, ready to call in the authorities."

His eyes were like black ice. "Have you already puked out everything to your film director boyfriend? Better not." She truly felt afraid. But he was bandaged on the arm, as well as the hand. She could take care of him, she hoped.

"I have told him nothing," she said quietly. She gave him a bright smile. "He said he may have work for you, also in the movie business," her lips were dry, "if your other duties give you time—"

"Do not try to put one over on me!" He slapped her face with his unbandaged hand, the left one.

Not as hard as usual. "Steve can give you a job. He will be back soon. We can all have a drink."

"I will wait," he said with a slow smile. He sat down and took the knife from its sheath on his ankle.

She made a dash, hoping to get out the door. He lumbered out of the chair, blocking her way, murder in his eyes.

☙❧

GREGOR FUMED AND FRETTED. He had never seen so many mistakes. These people were nut cases, wild dogs, ready to attack anything—even their own tails. He came to a decision. He opened his suitcase, removing a navy blue jacket, which he put on over his sweater. He detached the silencer from his gun with trembling hands and placed both pieces into his jacket pocket, then opened his door. As he crept past the film director's room, he listened. A thud. A soft cry. Then silence.

Gregor rounded the corner and briskly headed to the desk of the *dejurnaya*. "Bring me a bottle of cognac from the bar. A steak sandwich—well done, if you can manage—from the restaurant."

The *dejurnaya* frowned. "I do not know, sir . . ."

"I am waiting for an important call." He gave her a stern glance, full of meaning. "From Moscow." He gave her two one hundred dollar bills. "Keep the change for yourself."

As soon as she did the calculation in her head, she relented, took his money, and stepped out from behind her desk. "By the way, the girl," he indicated the American's room. "Is she in? I thought I might ask her to join me for a drink."

The *dejurnaya* warily shook her head. "She has not come back since she left three hours ago." She frowned in distaste. "She did not leave me her key."

"Another time," he said. He waited until the elevator arrived and the *dejurnaya* stepped in. She turned and nodded at him, smiling. "I will bring back something very tasty."

As soon as the *dejurnaya* left, Gregor saw Steve's door burst open and the woman Tanya flee into the hall. She wore a short-sleeved red blouse and nothing else. No, she wore black panties. Her arm was bleeding. She was screaming at Kolya, who had followed her. "Please, I will go home. We will talk later about our work together, Steve, and you and me." Kolya punched, kicked, and threatened her with his knife, until he forced her back inside.

Gregor watched unnoticed and quickly followed them into the room. He closed the door. The film director might return any minute. He had to make it quick. From his jacket pocket he removed his gun, attached the silencer. Now if he could only hold his shaking hand still enough to aim and fire.

❦

TANYA COWERED ON THE floor near the bed. Kolya had cut her. He had never done that before. "Be sensible," she begged. He lurched toward her, his face ugly. "I will do what you ask," she screamed.

Over Kolya's shoulder, she saw the top of another man's head. "Steve!" she cried, hoping he had come to save her. Kolya turned to look. At the same time, she saw the man's face—Gregor, his eyes blue and clear like glass—you almost felt you could see through to his soul. But what you saw was an empty space. He held a gun, strange-looking, with a very long barrel. He pointed it at Kolya. "Be careful," she shouted. She heard a dull pop. Kolya fell to the floor with a heavy thud, a hole in the middle of his forehead.

"Oh, no," she cried out, rising to her feet, rushing to him. "You have killed my husband." She felt a punch in the chest. It knocked her breath away. Something wet was bubbling out the front of her, spoiling her lacy underwear, her blouse. She looked at her hand. Covered in blood. She saw Gregor, no more than a dim shape now, touch his lighter to the drapes. With a whoosh, they flared up. Hot and bright as the summer sun, thought Tanya, who shivered and grew cold. The light vanished into darkness.

GREGOR HURRIED BACK TO his room. His heart beat so violently his whole body shook. Now he was a murderer. He had done the deed himself. Part of him felt proud, part of him was afraid it was a stupid move that would bring him down.

What he had come here to accomplish had exploded before his eyes. His contacts in Moscow promised him that killing the girl could be done cheaply and easily in these frenzied times. They had assured him Captain Victor Iurkov was a ruthless and efficient man who could be counted on. He blamed himself, his carelessness in being captured on the videotape, frozen in a time and place until the tape could be destroyed. He unlocked his briefcase, placed his gun and silencer inside, took out the black balaclava, then relocked the case. He struggled into his overcoat.

The black balaclava covering his face, suitcase in one hand, briefcase in the other, he ran down the stairs, yelling "*Pozhar*," "Fire" at every floor. "Fire, fire. The fourth floor," he called as he dashed past the bar, through the lobby, past the soldiers at the front door. Once he was outside, he ripped off the black mask, stuffing it in his coat pocket, and hurried to the taxi stand, where he found a waiting cab. He jumped in. "Pulkovo Airport."

Why had he set the fire to the drapes with his lighter? It was overkill. He had panicked. But wait, the charred bodies would be found in Steve's room, next to Kate's. The Americans would be blamed, he hoped. At any rate, to identify the bodies would take some time. Only the *dejurnaya* could connect the dead Kolya to him, since she had seen him bring Kolya into his room. But by the time that happened he would be gone.

The fat buffoon was a minor KGB informer, a member of the shadow people, *stukachi*. No one would care about his death. Or that of his hooker wife, Tanya. Because of their greed, they planned to bring him to the attention of American authorities, who would be more scrupulous in following up than the bureaucrats in lawless Leningrad. Too, these killings would be a message to others, here and in Moscow: I am a player to be respected. Do not fool with me.

If the authorities—whoever was or would be in power—tried to charge him for murder, he would simply offer a little *blat*. These bureaucrats were even greedier than before, and getting more so every day. He was sweating. He wiped his face with his handkerchief. If Captain Victor Iurkov failed to eliminate the bitch and secure the incriminating tape, it would require a change in his own plans. He almost looked forward to a face-to-face with Kate. Now that he had killed, the next time would be easier. For now, he was under pressure to close the deal in Nizhnevartovsk, Siberia.

Chapter Sixteen

12:01 AM, Thursday, January 31

Kate climbed wearily into the bus parked outside the House of Cinema, sinking into a seat beside Dom. She ached all over. Trying to shake that big hunk of blubber Kolya off her back had found muscles she never knew she had. She leaned against Dom's arm, and closed her eyes, lulled by the rhythmic movements of the bus. She jerked awake when she felt it bounce, tires crunching over packed snow. It stopped behind several other vehicles on a shoulder of the highway beside the ice-encrusted Neva River. Passengers gravitated to her side of the bus, exclaiming and pointing as they peered out the windows.

Black smoke and flames poured out of their hotel. Kate was speechless. Fire trucks—she counted four, lights flashing and sirens shrieking—battled the fire, hoses gushing full force. Buses and taxis had been cleared from the parking lot; only a single dark car remained, parked along the far edge closest to the river. "Our things," a woman passenger cried. "We have to get our things." The clamor grew with increasing urgency. Kate looked at Dom in horror. "The film," Dom groaned. *Revolution*—in its metal cans—sat in his room.

Dom and Kate, lugging her video camera, joined the line of panicked passengers who exited the bus, hurried along the snow-covered shoulder and into the hotel parking lot, where they squeezed through the hordes of people that milled about. The acrid smell of smoke made Kate cough. Hoping to find someone who had answers and spoke English, she and Dom circulated through the crowd, asking, "What happened? Did everyone get out alive?"

She rested her video camera on her shoulder, capturing a row of flaming windows; firemen ducking for cover in the midst of raining glass. A column of soldiers blocked people from running into the conflagration. She surreptitiously did a close-up of every soldier, hoping to spot the red-haired Andre. No such luck. She panned the chaotic scene in the parking lot. Some evacuees were without gloves or scarves. Others wore coats thrown over sleeping attire. She overheard an agitated female voice, "I was asleep. Someone yelled *Fire* and banged on my door. It was almost 11:30. I threw on my coat and followed him outside." Kate looked at her watch. 12:15. The fire had been burning about 45 minutes.

Firefighters shouted, trampling over dirty, crusted snow, cheeks scarlet. Someone—a paramedic probably—peeled off a fireman's gloves, revealing fingers thick and red, likely on the verge of frostbite. Rivulets of water ran along the ground, freezing into ice.

Kate's eyes watered. The smell of smoke was choking, even in this frigid air. She and Dom, shivering, watched the firemen battle the fire for another twenty minutes. At last, an occasional tongue of flame licked out and disappeared. Black smoke turned to wisps of gray. The fire appeared to be under control.

Kate counted the floors to the worst of the blaze, where windows had popped out and the building's exterior was blackened. One, two, three, four. "The fourth floor. Our floor," Kate yelled to Dom, trying to get her voice above the din. Her Gorbies and her gifts, the print of their film must be ashes. A new print would be expensive. If her Gorbies were lost, the shape of her video project would drastically change. Just then, she saw a body bag shoved into an ambulance. An icy chill slid down her backbone. She nudged Dom, pointing, "Dear god, people are dead."

CAPTAIN VICTOR IURKOV, WHO had been parked at the edge of the hotel lot for over an hour, stepped out of his car yet again, his eyes traveling over the mass of displaced guests—over two hundred, the hotel manager had reported—who huddled in groups in the icy air, gaping, gasping, and wringing their hands.

Hotel and fire officials had told him what they knew: A man, a black balaclava covering his face, had issued the fire alarm. Three rooms on the fourth floor were burnt to a crisp. They belonged to the fast talking Steve, Kate, the trouble-maker, and the tricky Gregor. The *dejurnaya* had left her post, he had been told. He must question her.

Two bodies had been found in his new friend Steve's room, charred badly. But not so badly one could see one was male and the other female.

If the male body was Steve's, that would be the end of their joint venture in pornography. A pity. Was the female Kate, or "talent" Steve was interviewing? The Captain lifted his binoculars and meticulously swept the crowd, trying to spot the snooping Kate or Steve or Gregor. His persistence paid off, for on his second scan of the crowd he caught a glimpse of a tall female figure. He adjusted his binoculars for a close-up. Yes, there she was, standing beside an older man with a small gray beard. She had survived the fire.

KATE LOCKED HER ARM into Dom's. She'd almost been killed tonight by Andre and Kolya. Now her hotel had caught fire—surely arson—the damage concentrated on their floor. "I saw Steve leave the Dom Kino bar at 10:15 PM. He could have been here—maybe in his room—when the fire started."

She and Dom frantically searched the milling crowd. Kate recognized a woman, a festival official who spoke English, and approached her. "Can anyone tell us about fatalities? A member of our company, Titan Films, may be missing." The woman led them to a yellow-helmeted man, with brilliant black eyes, wearing an army uniform. The fire marshal, Kate decided.

The woman, her jaw tight, relayed to Kate what the fireman said, "Three rooms in a wing on the fourth floor were gutted. Floors above and below those rooms were damaged. Four firemen have been overcome and taken to the hospital. They've pulled out two bodies, badly burned, one male, one female, from the room of Steve Valvano."

Kate and Dom looked at each other in horror.

"Preliminary guess," the woman said, "Steve Valvano is one of the dead. The other body is female, possibly his colleague, Kate Hennessy, from the room adjoining."

Kate was thunderstruck. Had they—whoever *they* were, thinking she was in her room, set the fire hoping to kill her? "I'm not dead," Kate exclaimed, nearly hysterical, showing her festival ID, as Dom echoed, "She's not dead."

"We must report this error," the woman said, hurrying after the departing fire marshal.

Kate fought down nausea. A horrible way to die. Steve didn't deserve to die that way. If he was in tight with Andre and Kolya, and whoever else were after her . . . maybe they turned on him. She told Dom, "Steve was with a woman in the Dom Kino. It may be her body found with his." She added, "As the two left the bar, I recognized her. She was the woman who'd stepped out of Kolya's illegal cab the evening Sveta and I got in."

"Are you sure?" Dom asked, his face collapsing. "This is a nightmare beyond belief."

Kate nodded. "Same white fur coat, low-cut red blouse. Same face."

"I don't want to believe," Dom murmured, "that Steve is involved with the thugs who are after you." His eyes were red, dark pouches underneath, blazing in his white face.

༺༻

CAPTAIN IURKOV SAID, "GOOD work," as the hotel official handed him a list of Intourist hotels. The Captain nodded. Empty rooms were plentiful. Winter was not a big tourist season. Two hundred guests, most of them film festival attendees, had to be re-situated immediately to warm, secure places. He added casually, "American filmmakers—they are the largest group—will be transported to the Hotel Pulkovskaya." He would place them in one spot for easy access. "The others will be siphoned into remaining hotels."

As the bus deposited the Americans tonight at the Hotel Pulkovskaya, he would be waiting, take Kate prisoner, throw her into detention, and charge her with spying, Anti-Soviet agitation and propaganda, conspiracy to overthrow Soviet laws. She was guilty of Article 130 (Libel), knowingly disseminating fraudulent stories. He would tell her, "I have witnesses at the Café Soul who will testify to this." The women would say whatever he asked.

He doubted that passengers—even the woman's graybearded friend—numb with fatigue, would put up too much of a fight. Captain Iurkov put a check beside another hotel on the list. "Evacuees unconnected with the festival will be placed in this establishment, on the outskirts of Leningrad."

As the official was about to leave, the Captain held up his hand. "Wait." Was that Steve standing with his hands in his pockets near the fire truck farthest from his car? He picked up his binoculars, adjusting the focus. So he had not died in the fire. "The American man with the dark curls, the tan overcoat and beige hat, standing near the far fire truck. Bring him to my car." The hotel official nodded and set off in that direction.

KATE RAISED HER CAMERA, turning in a 180 degree arc. The fire was smoldering, nearly extinguished. She panned the blackened façade of the hotel, the weary looking firemen, the uprooted guests, and finally zoomed in on a close-up of the dark car at the edge of the parking lot.

"*Vnimanie. Pahzalsta!* Attention, please." A hoarse voice boomed through a loudspeaker, hushing the crowd, who eddied around him. "Guests will go to other hotels," the man who belonged to the voice announced through a blow horn in accented English. Large earmuffs covered his ears, his dark topcoat with padded shoulders was buttoned up to his neck. His face was pinched, his nose red as he directed American festival goers to take the bus marked *Hotel Pulkovskaya* and ordered all other festival guests to get on buses to four other hotels. Non-festival evacuees were to journey to the Olgino Motel. He added that hotel guests were to remove belongings from undamaged rooms tomorrow, that it was too dangerous to attempt tonight while the fire might still be smoldering, hidden within the walls.

Several minutes later, buses left the shoulder of the highway, and moved slowly into the parking lot, forming a line. Staff with placards designating hotels stood beside each vehicle. Systematically, quickly, buses filled with displaced visitors impatient to escape the bitter cold.

The third bus in the line was for the Olgino. Kate made a snap decision, grabbing Dom's hand. "Let's take it. We'll have a friend there, Olga, who saved my life the night I almost froze to death in the cemetery." If anyone—Kolya or Andre, or whoever was in that dark car—was searching for her, she'd be where they wouldn't expect. Dom nodded grimly.

Kate and Dom stepped on board. As people entered, each gave his or her name to a young man who stood ready to take it down. "*Prevyet,*" Dom said, about to give his name. Kate interrupted, speaking with the best British accent she could muster, "Deborah and Peter Kempson from London." She drew a business card from her pocket, flashing it toward the young man. Dom gave her an astounded look.

"Not with the festival?" the young man asked.

She did a quick scan of the bus, praying the real Kempsons weren't on their way to the Olgino. They shouldn't be since they were guests of the festival. No Kempsons. Kate sighed with relief. "No, we're visiting tourists," she answered crisply.

Dom's eyes were wide with admiration as they took their seats. Kate was ecstatic to be finished with the Hotel Leningrad. Its hulking, granite, ominous presence was equal in her mind to KGB headquarters. She would be overjoyed to see the gentle Olga again and her courtly father. Two more nights to spend on Soviet soil and then she and Dom would be on their way to freedom. But not Steve, their wheeling and dealing, fast-talking huckster. She felt a pang, worried that Titan Films might not survive without Steve's silver tongue.

※※※

CAPTAIN VICTOR IURKOV WATCHED as a confused and frightened-looking Steve approached. He smelled of alcohol. "Get in the car," the Captain snapped with his most menacing look.

Steve entered on the passenger side. The Captain slid behind the wheel. "Not smart to burn down a hotel. You could have caused many deaths."

"What are you talking about?"

"It is very suspicious that the fire seems to have started in your room and the bodies found there, as well." He watched Steve closely.

"In my room? Bodies? There were bodies?" Steve made a noise as if he had been punched in the stomach. He ran his hand over his hair, flattening his curls. "I brought my date Tanya, a gifted woman . . . you saw her talents on the video . . . she was in my room."

The Captain nodded, his eyes never leaving Steve's face.

"Oh, God, I can't believe it," Steve blurted.

"There will be an investigation. Two people dead in your hotel room. The fact that you are connected with the female, your 'date' for the evening . . ."

Steve broke in, "No, no, it was her husband, Kolya. I saw him go into my room. She told me he carried a knife. Very jealous, she said. Kolya must have killed her, set the fire, and killed himself." Steve stammered and stuttered as he told his story about leaving Tanya alone while he bought a bottle at the *Beryozka* shop. "Just as I was about to step out of the elevator, her husband—he knocked at my door. She must have thought he was me. She let him in. I left by the stairs. I didn't want to get involved in their fight."

Coward, thought the Captain. *Interesting, Kolya carried a knife but the two had been shot.* He would question the *dejurnaya* early tomorrow.

"I didn't know he would kill her. Poor Tanya." Steve rubbed his eyes with the heel of his hand. "She was going to help us find talent." He sighed. "Well, we have Irina."

The Captain started the car and drove out of the lot. Steve, beside him, asked in a strangled voice, "Where are you taking me?"

The Captain was putting together all the facts he had. Steve could be telling the truth. An informer had reported to him earlier that a badly beaten Kolya had barged through the soldiers at the hotel entrance, cursing about his traitorous wife and yelling for a double crossing Andre. He had already put out the word, "Find Andre and bring him to me."

"I stayed downstairs in the bar," a rattled Steve continued feverishly, "to let the two of them duke it out. The bartender can verify my story. I had a few drinks. I must have dozed off. The next thing I know it's almost eleven-thirty, firemen are shaking me, ordering me out, there's a fire."

The Captain picked up speed, amused to see Steve quicky look out the window, his mouth slack, his eyes glassy. He was panic-stricken. "By the way," the Captain said, "the revisions you offered to make of the very entertaining short films I viewed earlier today on your camera VCR? After you've edited the sequences, send them to me by Express Mail."

"What about our contract? We don't have one," Steve fumed. "If it's in Russian, I'll need a translation."

The Captain slowed the car in front of a large building with several lighted windows. He purred, "You will have to trust me."

Looking like a rabbit about to be eaten by a wolf, Steve mumbled, "Where are we?"

The Captain resisted the urge to say, "Kresty Prison." He said briskly, "Hotel Pulkovskaya. All American festival people have been sent here. I will come by tomorrow with a contract for you to sign." He added as an afterthought, "The police will want to question you about the fire."

"I'm a suspect?"

"Perhaps I can smooth the way. For my efforts on your behalf I will change the terms of our contract from a fifty/fifty split to a seventy-five/twenty-five split. And," he added brusquely, "when you send the edited films, include Head and Shoulders Shampoo."

"Sure," Steve said, after a lengthy pause.

"Register with the front desk," he said as Steve climbed out of the car. "They are expecting other Americans from the Hotel Leningrad."

The Captain searched the deserted street. The bus should be arriving soon. Had it come, discharged its passengers, and left? Just as he was about to check the hotel register, the bus turned into the parking lot. He stepped out of his car. He unbuttoned his overcoat, his gun within easy reach, and was in place beside the door as soon as the vehicle stopped. As passengers stumbled out, he examined each face. Some he detained and asked to remove a scarf for a closer look.

No Kate. No friend with the gray beard.

He clenched his fists and took a deep breath. He must ask for the bus lists of who went to which hotel. But first he would do some damage control. It was not good publicity to print in the newspaper that the fire was arson or that the bodies found were not those of hotel guests, but a prostitute and her pimp of a husband.

The Captain stopped by the morning newspaper. He found the reporter writing his story about the fire, and gave him *deza* (disinformation) he had carefully prepared.

KATE AND DOM, ALONG with several other evacuees, staggered into the Olgino after 2:00 AM. Neither Olga nor her father was at the front counter. The nightshift clerk mumbled zombie-like to each, "Please sign register. We check passports tomorrow." Kate and Dom signed as Deborah and Peter Kempson. They were escorted to a double room, with twin beds. Like automatons, she and Dom pulled off their coats, barricaded the door, and dropped fully clothed into a bed.

⁂

ANDRE TRUDGED THROUGH THE snow. Ahead of him loomed the hotel, pale and still, caught in the wash of lights from the highway. His legs were heavy, his head spinning. He had ridden the metro for hours, his brain on overload. What had he set in motion?

Kate now knew his name was Andre. No doubt she had reported him to hotel security. The Captain could take care of that. It was almost 2:30 AM. Safe to try to find a buddy? He had hurt Kolya bad, but surely not enough to kill him.

As he drew closer he saw that every window in the hotel was dark, the air heavy with the smell of smoke. A line of soldiers wearing thick overcoats, fur-lined hats and gloves blocked the chained and padlocked entrance. They stamped their feet and flailed their arms, stepping up from time to time to warm themselves over a fire burning in a trash can. He approached the group of men, who stared at him suspiciously. Andre recognized a friend. "What happened?"

"Arson," the soldier grunted. "The hotel was vacated. Two dead on the fourth floor."

"Fourth floor?" Andre felt numb. Kate's floor.

"Rumor is two Americans."

"Have they identified the bodies?"

The soldier shrugged. He drew Andre aside and whispered, "Captain Iurkov is asking for you."

His gut wrenched. "Oh?"

"Your brother-in-law barged into the hotel, beat-up and bloody, accusing you of many things."

So Kolya was alive and kicking. Loud-mouthed and slimy as ever. "I will explain to the Captain tomorrow," Andre said with a dry mouth. He feared Kolya had reported the full extent of Andre's treachery. He should have finished him off.

Kolya had set the fire, Andre was sure. He had probably succeeded in killing Kate. "Let me inside. I need to sleep."

After a searching look, his friend produced a key and unlocked the padlock. "Leave before dawn," he warned.

Andre grabbed the man's arm. "I will be in the front lobby. Be sure to wake me." He turned on his penlight, found his way to a padded chair. He slumped into it. The smoke stung his eyes. He pulled the videotapes from his overcoat pocket, shining his light on them. The jackets were identical, showing the smiling blonde girl from the movie. She looked happy, without a care. He slid the tapes out. American format. No tricks this time.

Should he offer them to the Captain? Blame everything on Kolya? Ask that Kolya be arrested to protect himself and his sister Tanya? He must find Tanya. He hoped the raging bull Kolya hadn't hunted her down. Maybe she was out all night working. He hoped.

The Captain was unforgiving. If he believed Kolya's story . . . If he believed Andre had interfered as Kolya tried to cut Kate's throat . . . His heart raced. He had to stay out of sight. He needed money. He could sell the tapes to Gregor. Where was Gregor now?

Andre stood up suddenly. He shined his beam along the floor, cupping his hand so the light could not be seen outside. He found the front desk with the registration sign-in book lying open to today's date. He flipped through it to the page he wanted, and tore it out. He opened drawers. He stooped to look below the counter. Unbelievable luck. The safe door had been left ajar in the panic to escape the fire. He scooped its contents onto the floor, finding cash in many foreign denominations, and documents, which he sorted through. "Jackpot," he said, folding xeroxed sheets. He stuffed the money and the papers into his pockets.

He moved on to the bar. A half bottle of cognac sat on a table. He took several gulps. It warmed his brain. His mind was speeding now. In the cash register, he found hard currency,

German marks, American dollars. The harsh air made his eyes water. He held a napkin to his nose. He walked up the stairs to the second floor. He tried the doors of several rooms, finding two unlocked, men's clothing in each and he was able to piece together a civilian outfit. He also found a stack of twenty dollar bills American.

The next morning at five o'clock he left the hotel, wearing black trousers, a heavy sweater, and a dark blue jacket under his uniform. He hid a pair of dress shoes in his bulky military overcoat.

He hurried to Irina's flat and woke her, asking her to hide him. He told her about the hotel fire, his bloody fight with Kolya, and asked her to find and warn his sister, Tanya. "Kolya will take his anger out on her."

"He has already," Irina answered. "She told him she was leaving him for the American film director, Steve. She is staying with me. But she went out last night and did not return. When I heard your knock, I hoped it was Tanya."

Chapter Seventeen

8:00 AM, Thursday, January 31

The next morning Kate's spirits soared to see the lovely Olga behind the front desk of the Olgino, her blonde braids piled neatly on her head. Beside her, her father conversed with a guest who was handing him her passport. "*Prevyet.*" Kate waved. Olga looked up, her eyes round with shock. "Kate!" Olga's father did a double take, his long bushy mustache fluttering.

Olga smoothly slid over to where Kate stood, carefully placing a newspaper on the counter. A stunned Kate could only stare. On the front page, next to a photo of the burning hotel, was a picture of her.

"The paper said you were dead," Olga whispered. With a furtive look, she beckoned Kate to step behind the counter. Kate waved a shaky hand toward Dom. "My boss." Olga nodded slowly. The newspaper folded under her arm, Olga led the two through a door into a small entryway, and then through another doorway hung with multi-colored beads. Kate was once more in Olga's room, with its travel posters on the wall, facing the Statue of Liberty, a dizzyingly comforting sight. She sank into a chair. If only she could be magically transported back home now.

"Kate," Olga said, "the morning paper—look." She pointed to the page one headline and said in English. "American Filmmakers Die in Hotel Fire." As Olga read on, Kate stared at the thin red and orange curtains at her window. They shimmered like flames. "Two badly charred bodies, believed to be those of Americans Steve Valvano and Kate Hennessey—" Olga sucked in her breath "—festival guests, were found in Valvano's room. These are the only casualties."

Who took that photo of her? The surroundings looked familiar. Of course. A photographer had snapped the picture at the Leningrad Religious Academy, during a Russian Orthodox Service held last Sunday morning. It appeared in a festival press release the next day, along with a description of the cultural excursion. In this newspaper version, those church-goers near her had been cut out. Only Kate remained, coat open, standing in a halo of light, a rapt expression on her face.

"You look like an angel," Dom said grimly.

Olga took a shy step forward and bent down to hug the still seated Kate. "I was very sad. Now I am happy to know you are alive."

Dom introduced himself to Olga, offering his hand, which Olga shook. He explained, "They have one part right, we're afraid. Our colleague Steve—it appears he's one of the bodies."

"I am sorry," Olga said.

"Last night as we watched the firefighters battle the blaze, we heard a rumor that Kate's was the other body," Dom went on. "Kate showed her ID to a festival official who promised she'd clear that up, but—" He threw up his hands.

Poor Dom, Kate thought. He looked as haggard and hopeless as she felt. She could hardly think. Had the article in the paper been written in expectation of her death? She blurted out, "People are after me, Olga. Besides the fat man, Kolya, who left Sveta and me in the cemetery to die, there's a red-haired soldier and an officer with a badly scarred face . . ." She told Olga about the attempts on her life after that night she burst into the Olgino, half-frozen.

"What must you think of us?" Olga cried, her round cheeks flushing. "I see now," she added, examining Kate's face. "You have the cut on your lip, bruises on your face, and bandages on your hand. I noticed you were limping when you walked into the room."

"After the fire—" Kate stopped. She must keep her voice low. "Americans were instructed to take the bus to the Hotel Pulkovskaya. Dom and I came here. We signed in last night as . . ." Kate held up the Kempsons' business card. "We don't want you to get into trouble. What do we do about registering our passports—against these names?"

Olga looked uncertain, then seemed to make a decision. "I will rewrite the register pages," she whispered. "Our records will show the two never arrived here. Nor do we have any Americans at this time."

"Volunteers on the transport buses took down names. Someone has written down these names as being on the Olgino bus."

"Late at night, in all the confusion, perhaps the person on the bus made a mistake. I must let my father know—" Olga took the business card still in Kate's hand, and left the room.

Dom murmured, "Masha will see the newspaper. We have to tell her you're okay."

"She'll be so worried." Kate sighed. "What if Andre's watched my video interview of Masha and Nadya? What if their phones are tapped?" She yearned for certainty. The hotel fire was certainty. Kolya's knife at her throat . . . She didn't want that kind of certainty. Just clear answers to what those in pursuit planned next.

"How resourceful can Andre be?" Dom asked softly. "The video he stole contains only faces and first names."

Very resourceful, Kate thought with a shiver, if he—or whoever has the tape now—watches it and connects Masha, Nadya and me to Anya, their new friend at the Café Soul who gave them the nitty gritty about Leningrad's gay world. Anya had Nadya's contact information and knew Masha was a festival translator. Kate didn't think Anya or any of the other women at the Café Soul would turn them in. The manager/proprietor had been hostile but Kate felt his warning to her was to protect the women who met at his café. She hoped he wasn't a KGB informer. Don't take anything for granted here, she warned herself.

Kate spoke in hushed tones. "A few days ago Masha wrote my name in Cyrillic, saying I would be called Ekaterina in Russian, and, based on my father's first name, my second name would be Danilovna. I said jokingly—'I can use that as a code if I get in trouble.'" Kate told Dom her plan, took a few index cards from her vest pocket, and wrote.

When Olga returned, Kate, who'd noticed a wind up record player on a corner table, said, "Music would be nice." Olga looked baffled. Kate showed her an index card with the question, WILL YOU CALL OUR DEAR FRIEND MASHA TO LET HER KNOW I AM ALIVE? Olga nodded slowly, comprehension dawning. She put a record on the player. A rousing Russian song with crashing cymbals filled the room. Olga turned up the volume.

Kate, her mouth close to Olga's ear, murmured. "Give only your first name. I hope Masha will remember the story of my panicked arrival at the Olgino and your life-saving kindnesses to me." She wrote down Masha's phone number and what Olga was to say, in English. "Don't say you're calling from the Olgino, in case someone is listening who shouldn't be."

Olga dialed the phone, reaching Masha on the first try.

Some good luck for a change, Kate thought, standing beside Olga, near the receiver.

"*Zdrasvuitya,* Masha. This is Olga—remember me?" She frowned, shook her head, and continued, "I'm a friend of—" she referred to the paper Kate had given her "—Ekaterina Danilovna." Olga waited. *Katherine, daughter of Daniel.* Kate closed her eyes, trying to send a silent message to Masha.

At last Olga smiled, nodding her head excitedly. She spoke animatedly into the phone, "Ekaterina Danilovna is in excellent health. Do not believe the rumors. Please come this morning—do you remember where we are? Near the Gulf of Finland. The snow is beautiful. We will take a sleigh ride. See the dancing bears." Olga hung up the phone, hissing into Kate's ear, "She said she knew the way and would come immediately."

Kate gave Olga a hug, elated that Masha had been able to decipher the message.

With a flurry of clanging cymbals and rolling drums, the song finished. The room was spookily silent. Olga moved the needle to the beginning. The music started again.

"May I keep this?" Kate picked up the newspaper from the coffee table.

"Yes," Olga said.

"Does it say how the fire started?" Dom asked.

Olga pursed her lips. "The official story is that a television set was left on all day in the room. It exploded and caused the fire."

Dom gave a cynical laugh.

"Well, they don't make things here as well as they do in your country." Olga added, "Perhaps the KGB wanted to kill someone and make it look like an accident."

Kill Steve and the woman he was with last night? Kate wondered. She took a second glance at the newspaper. "Who is this?" she pointed to the picture of a man connected to a story beneath the one about the Leningrad Hotel fire.

Olga replied, "An important officer in the KGB."

Kate threw a queasy look at Dom. She whispered, her lips

close to his ear. "He looks a little like the civilian talking in the bar with the scar-faced officer." If only she had her videotape, she could compare the images side by side. Both men had the same soft, broad face. Banal-looking even. As she recalled, the man in the gray suit had more hair than this man pictured here, who also wore a suit—a dark one—and a tie. The man in the newspaper photo wore glasses. Maybe her videotaped KGB civilian disguised himself when out in public, by wearing a hairpiece and removing his glasses. Hard to believe, she thought, that someone high up in the KGB would be after me.

The man in the gray suit had given her a brief look before he scooped something off the table and walked away from the officer. What had he picked up? Orders connected to the rumored coup? How imminent was the coup? "Can you tell me more about this man?" She tapped his photo.

"He rose through the ranks as Yuri Andropov's right hand."

Andropov, when Chairman of the KGB, Kate remembered, created the psychiatric hospitals to protect the Soviet government from protesters.

"What does the article say?" Dom asked.

Olga quickly skimmed it. "This man claims destructive elements funded from abroad are trying to destroy Soviet society through economic sabotage. KGB has duty to fight this. His comments are meant to give someone to blame for the bare shelves in the stores."

"There are lines for bread and no matches or salt in stores," Olga continued. "For many, *perestroika* has meant only new burdens and deprivations." She read aloud softly, as Dom and Kate huddled close to hear her. "'The KGB has discovered freight cars filled with onions, matches hidden in warehouses, Russian treasures are being auctioned off.'" She made a face, as she explained to Kate and Dom. "This man knows how to make people angry so they will say, 'Hands off KGB. It is our last line of defense.'"

With public opinion behind them, Kate thought, the KGB would be in power once again.

Olga's eyes once again dropped to the article. "'All divisions are ready for the war on crime,'" she continued. "'If decisive measures are not taken today to impose order then we must concede that blood will be shed.'"

Olga's lips were a straight line. "He calls on all honest citizens to report to KGB any attempts to undermine the socialist state and social order."

Everyone will be watching even more closely and informing. *How will you know who your friend is?* Kate wondered. Even Olga and her father . . . Masha . . . She trusted them absolutely. She had to trust them.

For her video project, she would read from a translation of this article and show the Andropov *matryoshka* doll, the gloomy face dominated by round, tinted eyeglasses and shaggy brows over eyes bleached of all expression.

Olga's father stepped into the room, speaking to his daughter. Olga explained, "The bus will soon be here to take all people to the Hotel Leningrad to search for personal items undamaged by the fire. You must show your key and you will be escorted to your room."

"You stay out of sight." Dom took Kate's hands. "I'll see if anything is worth salvaging."

"The *Revolution* print, I hope," Kate said.

"Kate, do not move from this room," Olga ordered. "When Masha arrives, I will lead her to you."

"On your way out, Dom," Kate asked, "will you bring me the video camera?"

"Ah, Kate." He chuckled tiredly and ruffled her hair. "Of course."

CAPTAIN VICTOR IURKOV TOOK several puffs from his Sobranie Black Russian, mulling over the phone message he had just received—that a clandestine power structure had been set up. The *suzhonnye zasedaniya* (closed sessions) would coordinate the work of local military boards, the KGB, and legal affairs departments—all in strict secret. Already police and army were on the streets of Soviet cities, groundwork for KGB control over businesses and factories. Soon men with machine guns would be stationed at printing presses. He could be called to Moscow as part of a special group to take command of *Byely Dom* (the Russian White House).

The phone rang a second time. "Captain Iurkov," said a familiar voice, with a mixture of unctuousness and disdain, "I have tried several times to reach you by phone."

"Gregor." Anger boiled up in his chest and scalded his throat. The Captain glanced down at the morning paper lying on his desk. A photo of the fire was plastered over the front page, along with a picture of an angelic-looking Kate. If she had followed orders and gone to the Hotel Pulskovskaya, the story of her death would be true. He wadded up the newspaper and threw it on the floor.

"I have something unfortunate to report," Gregor continued.

"The hotel fire?" the Captain snapped, suspicious that Gregor had set the fire and was the man in the black balaclava who went from floor to floor warning others.

Gregor ignored his question. "Your soldier Andre is a traitor. The girl is still alive."

"Not for long," Captain Iurkov muttered through clenched teeth. "I have a plan in motion." He had asked for the lists the bus drivers had collected last night. He would find the American woman's name on one and would surprise her in her hiding place, swooping down like a wolf on a helpless lamb. As a backup, he had given a copy of Kate's photo to the soldiers guarding the abandoned Hotel Leningrad, in case she arrived to search the ruins for her belongings.

Silence on the other end. Finally, Gregor spoke, his voice hesitant, "Kolya . . ."

"Ah, Kolya." *He is fishing,* the Captain thought, *to see if I know Kolya is dead, shot through the head.*

"I gave him money to see what he could do." Gregor raised his voice belligerently. "Since all else failed."

The Captain grunted. *He is rubbing it in.*

"Kolya came to me directly," Gregor said.

"When was this?"

"I have a sad story to tell you." Gregor then repeated everything Kolya had told him about Andre. "Your soldier has betrayed us. Andre beat up Kolya to protect the girl and now has the video, which he plans to use as blackmail."

By the end of the sentence he was whining. The Captain was fed up dancing to his tune. "Where were you last night?" he asked roughly.

"On my way to Siberia. Niznevartovsk."

"When did you last see Kolya," the Captain asked, adding pointedly, "your source of unlimited information about Andre's deceit?"

A pause. "Early afternoon, perhaps."

The Captain smiled. *I have got you.* "The *dejurnaya* just left my office. She reported she saw you last night, about ten-thirty, take charge of a large man, beaten and blood-soaked, who was making drunken noises in your corridor. She saw you bring him into your room. Several minutes later, she said, you claimed to be expecting an important call from Moscow and ordered her to leave her post to buy food and drink for you. Under questioning, she admitted you had given her a large tip to do so. She claims the fire started between eleven and eleven-thirty, during the thirty minutes she was gone."

"She is lying. Are you accusing me? Do you know who you are talking to? Better watch your manners." The Captain heard Gregor make a weak attempt at a laugh before he added meekly, "I guess I left the hotel in time. I hope no one was hurt."

"Four firemen are in the hospital. One critical. You can read about it in the Leningrad morning paper," the Captain said curtly. "Also two were found dead in a room on the fourth floor, incorrectly identified as Steve Valvano and Kate Hennessey," as a result of his disinformation to the reporter. "A retraction will appear this afternoon." A tiny paragraph on a back page, apologizing for the error and giving the correct names of the dead. "Officially, the fire was started by a faulty TV set that exploded."

Gregor chuckled.

"The two who died unfortunately were not hotel guests. A prostitute and her husband, a low-level informer, who happened to be helping my soldier Andre with the job you wanted done. Kolya and his wife, Tanya." He waited.

"How unfortunate," Gregor murmured. "Kolya did not seem stable when we spoke. Perhaps he shot her and then himself," he continued lamely, "after setting the fire?"

"Kolya carried a knife," the Captain said. Only the killer would know they were shot. "Hundreds of people—Westerners and other festival guests—could have died. On my watch!" Amateurs, he hated dealing with amateurs. "The entire hotel had to be evacuated."

"I am sorry for the inconvenience, Captain," Gregor said smoothly. "Perhaps you should question the *dejurnaya* again. At ten-thirty last night I was boarding my plane to Siberia. I could not delay my trip any longer, although," he bit off each word, "the jobs I requested of you—and paid for—have not been completed."

Best he treat Gregor cautiously, thought the Captain. He was—for the moment—a star in the KGB firmament. "I will put out an alert for Andre. We will find him! We will collect the tape. I will write up an order asking for an official certification of Andre's mental instability. For insubordination, he will be placed in a psychiatric ward. As far as the American woman . . ." What had she done to make Gregor so angry? "I will charge her with Anti-Soviet agitation and propaganda. Before she goes to trial, she will 'disappear' as she is being transferred in chains from one place to another. Her body will be found on a deserted road. By then the murderer—a prisoner with nothing to lose—will be back in his cell. We will launch an investigation, but the killer will never be found."

"She leaves the country tomorrow morning," Gregor said angrily. "I am many miles away. It is on your head to finish this undertaking. A great deal of money is at stake. I wonder what your superiors will say."

"Are you threatening me?" The Captain felt his face grow hot. He clamped his lips tightly together so he would not say aloud what he was thinking. *Idi na khui* (go fuck yourself). *What are your motives, mudak? The videotape is incriminating. But why are you after this woman?*

"My dear Captain, you have been under stress. You could die of a heart attack."

The Captain heard the phone on the other end slam down. He finished his cigarette in two puffs, pulled another from the pack and lit it. Gregor was a wealthy foreigner, a prospector looking for black gold. The Captain guessed that KGB officials were interested in Gregor's money-laundering potential. Who would the KGB be more loyal to? The Captain, who had risked his life for his country in Afghanistan? Or a foreigner who dealt in hard currency, plenty of it? The Captain knew the answer.

KATE SLOWLY PANNED THE video camera over Olga's spare but charming little room: her beaded entryway, the old-fashioned record player in the corner, the breakfast tray festively decorated with a red paper rose and a white and blue napkin. Kate lingered on the travel posters—Olga's dreams—that lined her wall. Would authorities ever grant her permission to travel outside the Soviet Union?

Kate turned off the camera, sinking into the overstuffed chair, eyeing her breakfast on the coffee table. She wasn't hungry but she must keep up her strength for whatever happened next. She ate two hard boiled eggs, hot kasha, three yummy rolls filled with strawberry jam, some cold sardines, pickled beets and carrots. After she finished her coffee, she longed for a refill. In the past three nights, she'd had a total of eight hours sleep. She closed her eyes, and was awakened by a soft tinkle. Her eyes flipped open. She jumped up, ready to run, her heart thudding. She sighed with relief, seeing Olga lead Masha through the swinging colored beads.

Masha hurried over. "I read the newspapers . . ." She squeezed Kate tightly. When she pulled away, her tear-filled eyes darted around the room. "Dom will be back soon," Kate said. "He's at the hotel to collect what belongings survived the fire."

Olga stepped forward shyly. "Miss Masha, I promised you a sleigh ride. We can enjoy the beautiful scenery." She glanced from Masha to Kate, mouthing, "And talk."

Several minutes later the three women, bundled in coats and scarves, left through a back door that led into a courtyard, which Kate thought was a *cul-de-sac* until she spotted a wooden gate at the far edge beyond the snow-filled swimming pool. Olga opened the padlocked gate with a key from a large ring she took from her coat pocket. Soon the three were behind the hotel tramping along a snowy path that wound through the trees.

Not long after, Kate spied the stable and, outside it, a beautiful white horse. Wreathed around his neck was a yoke of stained glass, enclosed in a narrow black frame. Silver bells on long chains hung from both sides of the yoke. It was a striking piece of artisanship. The horse was hitched to a bright red sleigh, edged in white. The landscape was white, and more snow was softly falling. The bare trees were silver, their branches blurred with snow. *This is enchanting,* Kate thought, *like something from a medieval fairy tale.* She lifted her camera to her shoulder.

Olga waved at the sleigh. "We use it for the Merry Russian Winter Festival, celebrated December 25 to January 5. I am sorry you missed it, Kate. Grandfather Frost arrives in the sleigh wearing a red robe, trimmed with white fur. He has a long beard . . ."

"Like Santa Claus," Kate said with a wan smile, homesick once again. She directed her camera from the horse and sleigh to Olga, whose eyes were shining, whose cheeks were bright pink in the bracing air.

"He carries a staff of ice with a sparkling star on its top and a huge red sack with presents," Olga smiled, looking like a little girl. "With his fairy granddaughter *Snegurochka* (Snow Maiden), he sings and dances with the children around the fir tree, and gives them presents."

Olga was trying to relax them, Kate realized, with her fairy tales. Masha's face was tense, her beautiful green eyes weary.

"Grandfather Frost—we sometimes call him Father Frost—is both kind and evil, two characters in one." Olga went on solemnly, "He is kind toward virtuous, hard-working people, and with the mean and lazy he is severe." Olga patted the horse, who nickered, steam blowing through his nostrils. "We call him *Ded Moroz*. In Russian mythology there was another *Moroz*, a creature with a long gray beard who ran around fields and caused biting frosts. His cruelty made tree trunks crack and his blows caused log huts to crumble. He liked to freeze people just to entertain himself." Olga's youthful face became hard. Was she thinking of the vicious and greedy crooks causing such devastation to her country? Kate felt chilled. Her coat, its zipper broken from her encounter with Kolya, could be closed only with snaps. Moroz's icy fingers seemed to be poking at her through the gaps between the snaps.

Olga hopped into the sleigh and held the reins. Masha scrambled in beside her. Kate shut off the camera and sat next to Masha. "We must bundle up," Olga said. "Take the animal skins from the back seat." Masha and Kate lifted up the heavy furs. Soon the skins were arranged over the laps of the three women. *Just like Anna Karenina,* Kate thought, protecting her video camera from the cold by holding it under the furry blanket.

The sleigh skimmed over the snow, bells tinkling. Flakes melted on Kate's face. She told Masha about her and Dom disobeying orders and sneaking into the Olgino. "Very wise, Kate. Anything can be bought in Leningrad at this terrible time."

Masha added, "I have news. After I spoke with Olga on the phone, I called a festival official who told me the burned bodies in your wing of the hotel were identified as Kolya and Tanya Terpsukova. Man and wife."

Kolya and Tanya, not Steve and Tanya. Kate felt a complexity of emotions. She'd hoped to find Kolya and question him. On the other hand, one fewer goon was after her. She felt sorry his wife had also died. "So Steve is alive." Kate made an effort to smile. "Good." She must ask him how he was acquainted with Tanya and Kolya.

Masha nodded. "I am told Steve is staying at the Pulkovskaya."

Kate rubbed her pounding temples. The bodies were found in Steve's room. She found it hard to believe he'd killed the couple. "That leaves Andre, the soldier," Kate murmured. And the scar-faced officer. And the civilian in the gray business suit. What to make of Steve? For that matter, what to make of Andre? Did he save her life? Or had he planned to kill her until the Kempsons came along?

"I am afraid festival officials have not reported to the police, Kate, the attacks on you and the theft of your videotapes," Masha apologized.

"I'm relieved," Kate sighed, as Masha went on, her hands fidgeting in her lap, "Everything is such a confusion—arranging for guests to pick up belongings from the hotel. Organizing a closing ceremony at the Hotel Pulkovskaya for tonight. Finding the award money—in all the economic mess—so festival officials can give prizes to winning films."

Kate peered into Masha's face. "Is anyone after you?"

"I doubt they will spend precious time searching for me—or Nadya." She put on a smile. "I have warned Nadya about the soldier's theft of the video that contains your interview of her and me. And that it now may be in anyone's hands."

Soon Olga halted the horse, who snorted and stamped his feet. "As you can see, we have many acres. In addition to the rooms in the hotel, we have a camping site with summer cottages for motor tourists." She proudly pointed out the rows of wooden triangular structures nested in snow banks and surrounded by silver birches.

She shook the reins. The horse trotted on, turning onto a path that twisted behind the cottages and opened into a large snow-covered field, filled with a smiling throng of people who wore thick coats and fur hats. "It is only here at the Olgino," Olga smiled, "that guests can watch bear games and take a photo in a 'bear hug' all year long." She guided the sleigh into a spot near the bears and to the side of the cheerful crowd. "Staff who work outside drink vodka along with guests. Everyone is happy and laughing."

Kate brought out her camera from under the blanket and turned it on. The black bears wore gold kerchiefs and danced in time to a drumbeat. The onlookers, captivated, clapped their hands. The bears looked as if they enjoyed showing off. The whole effect was peaceful and dream-like, as opposed to the ugly, nightmarish Russia she'd been living through.

Another thought intruded, *It's unnatural for bears to stand upright and dance. Are they tortured to perform this way?*

"We have four bears and two trainers, Tamara and her husband," Olga said. "They have brought up a little cub, who is gentle and nice, like their own child. You see, he is playing the drums. The couple has no children. Their life is with bears."

Kate told herself she'd become jaundiced. These trainers loved the bears as if they were their family. She put away her camera. The snow was falling faster. Olga jiggled the reins. The white horse, his head held high, trotted into a maze of birches, as if he absolutely knew where he was going. A few minutes later, through the trees, Kate recognized the parking lot where the bus had dropped them off last night. "We are approaching the main building," Olga sang out. She suddenly tensed, pulling sharply on the reins. The horse stopped near the edge of the woods.

Olga's father, outside the hotel entrance, was talking with a man in a long coat, dark-gray. He wore a fur hat with ear-flaps, also dark gray. An official-looking car was parked nearby. "*Militsia*. Police," Olga said in a strained voice. Kate's heart gave a loud thump. The policeman angled his head their way. Could he see the bright red sleigh lurking within the bare trees? The policeman turned once more toward Olga's father. "Hide in the seat behind," Masha hissed to Kate.

Kate tumbled into the back, onto the floor. Masha handed her the camera and then covered her with two fur skins. "Don't move," she said softly.

The sleigh stood still. Within the animal skins, all was silent and dark, like a womb. Kate very gingerly lifted a corner of the fur. The policeman was leaving Olga's father and ambling their way. Kate had a very bad feeling he was looking for her. She made herself as small as possible, scarcely breathing. She heard the policeman greet Olga and Masha, his voice loud as if he were standing beside her. She prayed he wouldn't lift off the animal skins.

For what seemed a very long time, he spoke with Olga, Masha chiming in occasionally. How Kate wished she knew Russian. She heard *Americanski* and knew she was doomed. She also heard Masha say, *Hotel Pulkovskaya.*

The reins jingled. Kate felt the sleigh turn around. Was the policeman leading them away to question them further? Her heart pounded furiously. Her knee was bent at an odd angle, the pain almost too much to bear. She was sweating, wringing wet under the hot furs. She was breathing shallowly. Soon she'd be out of air, would shudder and gulp in deep breaths, and the furs would shake. They were already shaking. She was trembling all over. She wanted to scream, long and loud, and jump up, shrieking, "I can't stand it." She held herself together until, several minutes later, the sleigh came to a stop and the furs were flung off. She almost cried with relief to see Masha's face peering down.

But what was this? Tears streamed down Masha's cheeks. She could hardly speak. "Sveta," she sobbed. "They have found her body. It took all my effort not to cry in front of the policeman. I had to behave as if I did not know her."

"Could things be any worse?" Olga cried out.

Kate's ears were ringing. Her head felt like a balloon, floating above the two women, looking down.

"Sveta's body has been found in the cemetery, near the pond," Masha said, grabbing Kate's arms and shaking her.

Kate slumped, as if she'd been hit in the stomach. So fat Kolya had gotten to Sveta, thinking she was Kate. That damn white scarf! Sveta, dear Sveta, whom she'd promised to help. If only, if only, she'd doubled back that night in the cemetery. Two against one—they'd have defeated that drunk.

"They want to talk to you, Kate. 'The American woman who was with her the night she disappeared,' the policeman said, 'we want to take her to the station and question her.' I was frozen with fear." Masha put her hands to her face. "Finally, Olga had the sense to say, 'There are no American film festival people here.' I added, 'They were sent to the Hotel Pulkovskaya.'"

"Why did he come here looking for me?" Kate asked, shaken.

"It is my fault," Olga cried in frustration. "Because I called the police from here, from the Olgino. I called twice. First to report Sveta's disappearance. You heard me, Kate. After you left that night, I called a second time. I asked them to disregard my first call—that someone at Sveta's residence had reported she was safely home. But they had already written a protocol. Now that her body is found here at the Olgino, it is natural the police come to talk to me." Olga's lower lip trembled. "They also want to speak with those who saw her last. They know from my report that was you. I am so sorry," Olga groaned, tears in her eyes. "For once, the police have been efficient."

She was in the spotlight of the local police, as well as on the radar of the military and the KGB. Kate closed her eyes. She wanted to go to bed, pull the covers over her head and sleep for a week. "Nadya will fall apart. I can't leave without seeing her, telling her I'm heartbroken about Sveta. Begging her to be careful."

"I will talk with Nadya. You must disappear, Kate," Masha ordered. "Sveta's brother reported her and Nadya to the local police—" she threw a sidelong glance at Olga "—as hooligans. Now the police say you were the last to see her alive." She shook her head somberly. "You do not want to be taken to the police station."

Olga jiggled the reins and once again the sleigh glided over the snow. Soon Kate saw the long row of small pyramids, the wooden windowless summer cabins. The sleigh stopped in front of the last bungalow. "We must hide you until you leave tomorrow for the airport." Olga jumped out of the sleigh and opened the door with a key. Kate, clutching her video camera, walked up a narrow snow-encrusted ramp and into the murky cabin, no more than a triangular box, equipped with a small wooden table and two stark wooden chairs. Olga and Masha followed. Olga rummaged in the cupboard. She found a candle in a holder and matches. She struck and struck until the match flared. She lit the candle. A pale light bathed the interior. It was just after 11:00 AM but seemed like dusk. When night fell, would wolves come out? Or bears?

"We will bring you food and beverages," Olga said. "More candles, a mattress, and blankets. The cabin is not heated and has no running water." She pointed to a porcelain bowl in a corner. "If you must use the bathroom . . ."

"We will return soon," Masha said. "My dear Kate, I would like to stay the night with you, but I must be present for festival closing ceremonies at the Hotel Pulkovskaya."

Olga and Masha left, locking the door. Kate paced the floor of the tiny cabin. She thought of poor Sveta, dark, beautiful and scared, sitting beside blonde, impish Nadya in Masha's living room. Nadya, meaning hope; Sveta, meaning light. Kate's eyes filled. She couldn't hold it in. She cried long and hard, her body shaking.

How did Sveta die? Was she stabbed? Shot? Strangled? Wounded and left to freeze? Kate pictured her stiff and silent. An ice maiden. A blanket of snow covering her, only her white face exposed, her dark hair feathered around it and spreading into her white scarf. How much had she suffered? Kate couldn't budge her mind from her pit of sorrow.

She hoped Nadya would find a loyal friend in Anya, that the women at the Café Soul would rally around her. That no one would persecute her, like the pitiless Captain that Anya feared, to whom the gay women reported, who sent them to the psychiatric institute for the Cure.

Kate wondered if Sveta died in the psychiatric clinic—from electroshock therapy or too many mind-bending drugs—and they dumped her here near the Olgino to implicate Kate in her death. Oh god, she was now fully Russianized. Ready to crack from it.

She hoped there would be an autopsy. But no, authorities wouldn't release results that made the psychiatric clinic look bad.

Another suspect was Nadya's mother, who'd threatened to kill Sveta, if their relationship continued. Sveta's brother, wild and unpredictable, was surely the man who spoke with Olga when she called Sveta's home. He'd said something weird, like "She's taken care of." A bad translation on Olga's part? It sounded very ominous now.

Would she ever know the truth? She prayed the bureaucrats—the police, the military, the KGB—were too corrupt and lazy to exchange information and put all the pieces together: Nadya and Sveta, lovers, reported as hooligans to the local police by Sveta's brother; Nadya, with Kate and Masha, searching for answers about Sveta's disappearance at the Café Soul; Kate's video interview, now in Andre's—or his superior's—hands, with Nadya describing her rape by the local police. That policeman just here, she wondered, had he been the one who raped and beat her?

Chapter Eighteen

11:30 AM, Thursday, January 31

Captain Victor Iurkov hurried through the lobby of the Hotel Pulkovskaya, Steve's signed contract in his briefcase. The Captain had noticed his clenched jaw when, hesitating, he studied the papers, but he signed. Steve was a pragmatist. The Captain would see to it that their new company controlled the porn market in the Soviet Union and the Eastern bloc. Steve would bring in his group of connoisseurs from America. Any dishonesty on his part the Captain would deal with swiftly. Steve could disappear at any time, as he traveled back and forth between Leningrad and New York City. The Captain smiled, contented. He could get to him even in America. He had contacts who had contacts in Brighton Beach.

"Excuse me, Comrade."

The Captain looked up to see a youthful-looking policeman in front of him, his blue-gray cap in hand. His face was bony, his hair blond, his pale blue eyes flat as stones. "Yes?"

"I am told this is the hotel for Americans evacuated from the Hotel Leningrad," the policeman said.

"Is there a problem?"

"I am looking for an American woman, Kate Hennessey, in connection with a murder."

"Kate Hennessey? A murder?" The Captain was astounded.

The young man's face showed impatience, which he quickly stifled. "A woman's body was found in the cemetery near the Olgino Motel. She was reported missing several days ago. Kate Hennessey was the last to see her alive, we understand."

Well, well. He could hardly believe his luck. He introduced himself. "Captain Victor Iurkov. Special unit. *Spetsnaz.*" Smiling now, the policeman gave his name. The two shook hands. "How did she die?" the Captain asked.

"We do not know for sure. We have asked for an autopsy. Tourists from Finland found her during a morning walk, her body half in and half out of the pond."

The Captain made a sympathetic sound.

"I was told Americans with the film festival were bussed here."

"Kate Hennessey is not at the Pulkovskaya. I think I know where she is hiding." The Captain was twitching with excitement. If murder were added to his list of charges against her, no one would dare dispute his motives in picking her up. "I also want to question her." From his briefcase he drew out the bus lists of evacuees. He had not found Kate's name on any list, nor had he found the name of her friend, Dominick Block. Deborah and Peter Kempson had appeared on two lists, for the Hotel Moskva and the Olgino. "Her colleague is an older man with a gray pointed beard," the Captain explained, stuffing the papers back in his case. "They will be found together as Mr. and Mrs. Kempson, I am sure." He would also charge Kate's friend—for conspiracy to deceive by using a false name. "First we stop by the Hotel Moskva, just a few blocks away. Follow me in your car."

The two men approached the Moskva registration desk, asked for the Kempsons, and were directed to their room. The Captain knocked loudly. He hoped when the door opened he would see the terrified faces of his prey.

The face, though terrified, was not familiar. "Hello. *Zsdravuiyta*," a tall man said, his eyes darting back and forth between the Captain and the policeman.

"We wish to speak to Peter and Deborah Kempson," the Captain said.

"I'm Peter. Deborah? Can you come here?" the man called.

She sidled in beside her husband, her eyes fastening on the Captain's face.

He clicked his heels together, giving her his most charming smile, which he knew deepened the grooves of his scars, making his face a sinister mask. He had practiced in the mirror many times. He was pleased to hear her sharp intake of breath. "I am Captain Iurkov. This is my colleague from the local police."

She blinked. "You're here about the robbery?"

Her husband added, "We witnessed the attack on the American woman."

"Kate Hennessey." The Captain paused, waiting for one or the other to say they saw her photo in the paper and heard she died in the fire. If so, he would smooth it over, blaming the carelessness of the reporter who wrote the story. The couple seemed to be waiting for him to continue, so he did. "Has she been in touch with you?" he asked politely.

"No, I assumed she reported the crime to police, saying we were witnesses. We exchanged business cards with her."

"Of course," the Captain muttered.

"You must be on the lookout for a soldier with red hair," his wife said.

The Captain nodded. He was definitely looking for him.

The young policeman was silent, shifting in irritation from side to side. The Captain struggled to keep a pleasant look on his face.

"And a fat man—he tried to cut her throat." The woman's voice rose. "He was lying on the ground, hurt. While I helped Kate gather up her belongings, he walked away."

Unfortunately, he would walk no more. He was dead. The Captain turned as if to leave.

"It was horrible. Kate, poor thing, was covered in blood. Luckily, she was not hurt badly. Her coat had been torn off." The woman paused and her husband took up the story, describing with gusto his chase after the soldier.

The Captain cut him off, saluting smartly, saying, "We will put out word about these two men—criminals who attacked a poor woman with a knife and stole from her."

"We're leaving for London tomorrow." The man held out his business card. The Captain took it, saying, "We will be in touch if we need a written report."

We have wasted thirty minutes, the Captain fumed. When the Kempsons' door closed, he muttered to the policeman, "Come with me."

Outside the Moskva, the two men climbed into their separate cars. As the Captain drove, he thought, we can call it some kind of sick, perverted murder committed by a Westerner, a *rozovaya*. We will force others at the Café Soul to speak against Kate Hennessey. Publish a sordid story in the newspaper. People will be angry, shocked by the scandal. "Serves her right," they will say when Kate's body is discovered on a deserted road. He was getting ahead of himself. An autopsy of the woman found in the pond had been ordered—he hoped the results would fit in with his scheme. Also he should be present when the Finns who found the body were questioned. He must proceed with caution.

The Captain stepped on the gas. Several minutes later, tires squealing, he swung his car into the parking lot of the Olgino, the policeman right behind him.

The two men entered the hotel, striding to the front desk behind which stood a middle-aged man with a long bushy mustache.

The young policeman glowered, muttering suspiciously, "I was here earlier. He said no Americans were registered." The man behind the counter did not flinch but answered, "We know of no Americans here."

"We are looking for a man and a woman who call themselves Deborah and Peter Kempson," the Captain snapped. The man, his face bored-looking, opened the hotel register, leafing through the pages. "No such names," he said politely.

The Captain thumbed through the register once and then again. He wanted to tear out the pages and stuff them down this man's throat. He closed the book and slammed it on the counter. "They must be here. We will search the place. Every room."

He glanced up to see a young woman with blonde braids coming their way. She curtsied, head bowed, speaking urgently to the mustached man, "We have an emergency, father, in the kitchen. We have many new arrivals because of the hotel fire. Do you need me?"

"Go ahead, my dear. I can assist these gentlemen."

The Captain asked to use the telephone. The mustached man offered the one that sat on the front desk. The Captain dialed, and barked into the phone: "This is Captain Victor Iurkov."

❖❖❖

IN THE TINY, WINDOWLESS cabin, Kate worried that something terrible had happened. An hour had passed since Masha and Olga left. She ordered herself to be calm and sensible. No doubt they were busy collecting the many items needed to make her sleepover here in the woods as comfortable as possible.

It would be a long, lonely night. Tomorrow she would slink out of Leningrad, her tail between her legs. She wanted to see Nadya before she left and reassure her. She couldn't risk it.

Was there a link between Nadya and Sveta and the scar-faced Captain talking with the man in the gray business suit? The inadvertent taping of the two men happened Friday, the night she arrived. She didn't meet Nadya and Sveta until Sunday, two days later, at Masha's flat,

Kate felt fear for Masha's safety. She was afraid for Olga and her father. Authorities could send Nadya away for the Cure; accuse Masha and Olga of helping an American fugitive.

What was happening to Steve? she wondered. He'd brought illegal porn into the country. Kolya and Tanya were found dead in his hotel room. If officials charged Steve and her, Dom too could be called an accomplice. She'd joked about it earlier, but they all could be sent to Siberia.

The lock clicked. Kate's heart gave a lurch and banged in her chest.

The cabin door flew open. Dom burst through, Masha and Olga close behind. "Oh, my dear Katie," he wrapped his arms around her, rocking her from side to side. "I heard it all. Poor Sveta."

"It's awful." Kate's eyes took in the three grim faces in front of her. More bad news? She babbled on. "You're back from the Hotel Leningrad? Did anything of ours survive the fire?"

Dom, his face drawn, answered brusquely, "Everything survived—including the print."

Why wasn't he happier? Kate wondered.

"We must hurry," Masha broke in. "We must leave for the airport immediately."

"The policeman returned—just fifteen minutes ago." Olga shook her head in disbelief.

"Luckily, Dom had made it back to the Olgino. We were in his room when they arrived," Masha said.

"They?" Kate asked, trying to absorb this change in plans. She wasn't staying in the cabin overnight. Instead she—Dom too?—must be on the run again.

"He was with your Captain," Dom said meaningfully.

"I saw him in the flesh," Olga said, "his scarred face, his partly shaved head. Evil creeping out of his pores. He looked crueler than *Moroz*. Ice in his heart. He would be happy to kill you."

"My Captain," Kate said slowly. Dom nodded. "The man in your video, his name is Captain Victor Iurkov."

"Olga saw them when they first arrived and managed to slip away and warn us," Masha said. "We hurriedly gathered up clothes, suitcases, the print, cleaned out the room. Olga led us out the back way to the stable."

Olga said softly, "I left my father to handle them. I made the excuse of an emergency in the kitchen. I hope he will be okay. Captain Iurkov asked to interview the Kempsons. My father assured him and the policeman we had no Kempsons and showed them the hotel register. I am so happy I re-wrote those pages. What if I had not?" She shuddered. "'Do you have Americans then?' the Captain asked. 'No, no Americans,' my father said. 'We told the policeman this earlier today.'" Olga looked agonized and even more so when she turned to see the cabin door wide open. No one had thought to close it. Outside the white horse patiently waited, hitched to the red sleigh.

Kate, in slow motion, moved to the door, pushing it shut. Not that the horse and sleigh wouldn't give them away if someone came snooping. This was confirmation—this whole terrible time had been set in motion when she videotaped that Captain with the scarred face, talking with the man in civilian clothes. Captain? The same Captain who bullied the women at the Cafe Soul? But why would he want her dead? There had to be more to it than that videotape. The chain of events seemed as intricate and sinister as the nested Gorby dolls.

"They meant business," Olga said, her eyes filled with contempt as well as fear. "If they could not find Kate, I was sure they would take Dom in for questioning. I overheard them say they will search the hotel, over three hundred rooms. They called for help to do this. I know they will come here to the summer cabins. While Dom and Masha were clearing out the room, I listened from the hallway and heard them say on the phone that they had found the real Kempsons at the Hotel Moskva and had questioned them."

"The Kempsons must be terrified," Kate said. "Sorry they ever got tangled up with me last night." Only last night? Her seven days in Leningrad seemed more like seven years.

"Come," Masha urged. "We must leave quickly. If we get to the airport by 2:00 PM, you will make the 2:30 PM flight and be in Helsinki in an hour."

"My suitcase of clothes? My Gorbies, my gifts?" Kate's eyes sought Dom.

"In the sleigh. They smell of smoke but the fire didn't reach them," Dom said. "Thank god, you moved into my room. The whole wing was spared. Only the three front rooms on our floor were destroyed, I was told."

Hers, Steve's—nearest the *dejurnaya*'s desk . . Who was in the third room, on her far side? Someone connected with the festival? "Can we spare five minutes to stash my Gorbies in my suitcase?"

Dom glanced at his watch and at Masha, who nodded. Dom brought in Kate's suitcase and duffel. Kate cushioned her *matryoshka dolls* among her clothes. She padded her audiotape recorder securely and rolled up her beautiful Russian calendar and poster of the burning ruble, tucking them in along the back. What remained in the duffel? A video in a plain wrapper. Yes! Steve's tape, still in the camera when Dom jerked it out of his hands. She wanted this one, for sure.

"If we make it to Helsinki—" Dom began.

"You will," Masha interrupted, steely-eyed, "if we go now—"

Dom rubbed his face nervously. "*When* we make it to Helsinki, we'll sleep in the airport overnight. Tomorrow we'll be on our way home."

And I'll kiss the ground, Kate thought. She tried to shut her suitcase. Too full. She removed a sweater and was able to close the lid. She grabbed her camera and, hands shaking, ejected the video that held footage of the documentary panel and the Olgino. She took the Laboratory of Experimental Modeling tape out of her vest pocket. She stacked the tapes on the table on top of Steve's. "I have to secure these three videos to my body. I don't want any of them seized at the airport."

"Do it in the sleigh," Dom said.

Kate donned the extra sweater taken from her suitcase, slipped on her vest, and returned the videotapes to her pockets. She hurried into her coat.

Kate's suitcase in his hand, Dom cautiously opened the cabin door. "All clear," he whispered. Quickly, he leaped outside, stashing Kate's suitcase in the back of the sleigh alongside his and the two cans of film. He climbed in beside them as Olga scrambled up into the front seat and took the reins. She held them stiffly, on hyper alert. Masha slid in next to Olga. Kate handed the video camera to Masha and was about to jump in when Olga exclaimed, "The candle! We must leave no trace."

Olga gave Kate the key. She returned to the cabin, plucked up the candle and the book of matches from the table. She rushed out, locking the door, her ears straining for sounds of pursuit.

Dom said suddenly, "They'll see footprints." Kate tossed the candle up to Masha and stuffed the matches in her pocket. With her scarf she brushed away footprints leading from the cabin. "Hurry," Masha urged. Walking backwards, Kate obliterated the tracks around the sleigh and then hopped in next to Masha. Olga jingled the reins, turning the horse and sleigh in a circle, leaving the path in front of the cabin messy but destroying shoe prints.

The sleigh rattled along through the trees, swerving to avoid fallen branches and ruts on the path; passengers ducked to avoid low hanging, snow-covered limbs. *What a picture we must make*, Kate thought, *covered in furs, breath blowing white, belongings piled high.* She threw a quick look back at Dom. His neatly trimmed beard was totally white now with snow. Grandfather Frost and his entourage. Kate wished she could videotape this journey. "Dom, can you get the masking tape out of your suitcase?"

After some tugging and lifting and use of expletives, he did, passing it up to Kate who slipped off her coat and vest. "Masha?" Kate handed her the videos from her vest pockets and lifted up her sweaters.

"Oh, Kate," Masha exclaimed. "The cold."

"I don't feel it." Her adrenalin was pumping hard; she was perspiring. "My Pavlovsk video and two audiotapes are fastened to my stomach. Secure these videos to my back. Tape firmly. I don't want them dropping out at the airport." As Masha worked, the sleigh bounced along, swaying from side to side. Kate called out, "Dom, did Masha tell you? Steve's alive—at the Hotel Pulkovskaya. Kolya died in the fire, along with Tanya."

"Yeah," Dom sighed.

"Finished," Masha said. Kate pulled down her sweaters. Masha patted her back. "You're very lumpy."

"My layers will hide my bumps," Kate said, scrambling into her vest and coat. "I hope."

Moments later, Olga halted the horse at a fork in the path. "What time is it?"

"Almost 1:00 PM," Kate said.

"It would be faster to go by metro." Olga conferred briefly with Masha, then leaned in so all could hear. "*Chyornaya Rechka* is the closest metro station but you would have a long walk in the open, no longer hidden by trees, to reach it. On your way you would meet the traffic police who may stop you if they are suspicious or bored."

"Best we travel by *electrichka* to Finland Station," Masha said, "and take the metro from there to Moscow Prospect, where we will catch the bus to the airport. A taxi is too risky."

Olga shook the reins, the horse turned left. Minutes later, the trees thinned out. "I must turn back now so as not to attract attention." Olga brought the journey to its end while the sleigh was still hidden. "The *electrichka* stops there, at the Olgino Railway Station." She pointed through the trees. Kate saw the back of a squat wooden building situated on a low embankment. "This is where you brought me, Olga, to take me back to the hotel the night I met you, cold and scared." Olga nodded. 'The platform is in front, as you may remember. You must let me know you arrive safely in Helsinki."

"We'll call Masha and use our code, my Russian name, Ekaterina Danilovna," Kate said. "And you, Olga, when it's safe tonight, must let Masha know all is well with you, that no one is suspicious that you helped us escape. Tell Masha, as a signal—" Kate thought quickly "—you're sorry she missed Grandfather Frost's—meaning *Moroz,* the evil one's—arrival. Masha will inform us."

"I am sorry you missed Grandfather Frost's arrival," Olga repeated.

Kate, Masha and Dom climbed out of the sleigh and unpacked their belongings, each quickly reaching up to squeeze Olga's hand. "How can we ever thank you, dear, brave Olga?" Kate said. "Be very careful," Dom added.

Olga, pale and serious, sat up straight. "I will stop by the bear games and find those who want a sleigh ride. I will show them the cabins and we will have a reason for the sleigh tracks. Also I will have an excuse for being outside. I hope to resume my place at the front desk, beside my father. We will offer the Captain and his men coffee and vodka."

"Don't forget about the problems in the kitchen you left to solve," Kate said.

"You can be sure the kitchen will be properly hectic if the soldiers stop by." Olga waved. The sleigh turned around and started up with a jerk, disappearing quickly within the trees.

The trio, loaded down with baggage, trudged through the snow and up the steps to the railway station. Dom and Kate shivered on the platform while Masha disappeared inside to buy their tickets.

Chapter Nineteen

1:10 PM, Thursday, January 31

Masha, Dom and Kate struggled onto the *electrichka* with suitcases, film cans, and the video camera. When they were seated, Masha whispered, "We have an hour to reach the airport, change your tickets to today, and get you through customs."

In hushed tones, Dom and Kate—with Masha's help—prepared their documents. "It can take hours," Kate fretted, "examining our declaration slips, inquiring about our money spending and changing, rummaging in our suitcases." She had bought political *matryoshkas,* a military watch—would both be declared unlawful purchases?—and pins, at Pushkin Square in "illegal" currency.

If they searched her thoroughly, they would find her videotapes, like weird growths, hanging around her middle. The tape of LEM, the satirical fashion show, might be considered a Russian work of art or "too decadent" to leave the country. Steve's video was porn, she was sure, and made with Russian citizens in leading roles. The tape of Olga standing by the Father Christmas Sleigh—proof she had hidden Kate from the authorities!

"If you miss the plane," Masha said, "another flight to Helsinki leaves at 4:30 PM—"

Kate tried to keep her voice steady. "We must make a plan B. In case Captain Victor Iurkov shows up at the airport."

"We could take the train to Finland," Dom said.

Masha shook her head vehemently. "The train takes six hours to reach Helsinki—only one hour by plane. And you will be searched twice, by Russian border guards and then by Finnish ones. If KGB become suspicious, they will bring out Klieg lights, stop the train every few miles, and each time swarm on board to hunt for you."

Worriedly, Dom asked, "American Embassy?"

Kate still carried their address in her bra.

"They cannot help if Kate is charged with a crime—even falsely charged—or taken in by police for questioning," Masha said.

The trio disembarked the *electrichka* at Finland Station, loaded down like mules on their way to base camp. Kate and Dom trudged behind Masha, Kate's heart beating like a tom tom. Masha paid their fares and they took the long escalator ride to the metro below. Fifteen minutes later they arrived at Moscow Prospect, where they caught the bus to Pulkovo Airport. At every stage of the journey, Kate waited for a hand to grip her shoulder and a voice to snarl, "You are under arrest."

As the three passed through the airport doors, Kate feared she might be sick. Not much to lose since she hadn't eaten since breakfast. They were now subject to the whims of airport flunkies, who, if suspicious, could whisk them into an office, where passports would be checked and someone notified. Dom's face was yellowish-green. Masha's eyes held a frantic gleam. "Keep cool," Dom murmured.

A huge crowd milled around, waiting to be processed for flights. Kate scoured the area with her eyes. No uniforms. Once the Captain and the policeman finished the search of the Olgino and the summer cabins, the posse could arrive.

"There." Masha pointed beyond the moving mass of travelers. She led the two to a long line. "This is Aeroflot." The line scarcely moved. Masha tried in vain to make some headway with a passing airport official. Her pleas, "*Pahzalsta, Americanski*—they must leave at two-thirty for Helsinki—family emergency," were ignored. It was 2:16 PM. "We'll never make it." Kate moaned.

"Wait here," Masha ordered and left. She returned minutes later with hope in her eyes. "I found the man we need. You will have to try *blat,* a bribe." She allowed herself a nervous grin. "The two-thirty plane is delayed by bad weather in Moscow."

Kate and Dom each put a twenty dollar bill inside their passports, along with their declaration slips and Visas. Masha took everything and strode to the front of the line, as Kate and Dom trailed behind, watching from the side. "*Pahzalsta,* excuse," Masha presented the passports to the Aeroflot clerk. He looked sullen and bored, until he lifted the dark blue covers. His eyes glinted. His nostrils flared. Those forty dollars American were worth over a thousand rubles on the black market—four or five months' salary.

As Masha answered the man's questions, Kate's eyes searched the terminal. She found no soldiers. So many had roamed the airport on their arrival. Her eyes returned to the man at the counter. He caught her look and stared back intently before he slowly turned to Masha, nodding, shoving papers her way.

Her face exhausted but triumphant, Masha signaled Kate and Dom to join her. She gave them their tickets for today's two-thirty flight, boarding passes, and luggage tags. Dom tagged their suitcases and handed them to the stone-faced man, who hoisted them onto the conveyor belt. Dom wasn't going to let the film out of his sight, opting to carry the two heavy cans, five reels, onto the plane. Kate decided to do the same with her video camera.

"I turned in your declaration forms without a problem," Masha whispered, as they left the check-in counter.

Unbelievable, Kate thought. They were getting through without a search.

"The plane was full," a dazed-looking Masha said. "Thirty-three Russian college students boarded in Moscow. I told the clerk, *Emergency back home.* Two passengers were changed to the later flight."

Dom, a wide grin on his face, managed to murmur, "You're amazing."

All it took was a little grease—and Masha's charm. "You're incredible," Kate said, hugging her, feeling as if she might collapse to the floor in relief—if she could only bend with all the tapes fastened to her body. She heard Dom say softly into Masha's ear, "What would we have done without you?" He gave her a lingering kiss. Kate smiled, turning away discreetly.

Masha, blushing, stammered, "I must hurry to the Hotel Pulkovskaya for the festival's closing ceremonies. Please call me tonight—after 11:00 PM, if you can find a pay phone at Helsinki Airport. Use your Russian name, Kate, as we agreed, Ekaterina Danilovna. I'll know that means you made it safely to Finland."

At their Aeroflot gate, Kate and Dom fumed and sweated. When the plane from Moscow arrived thirty minutes later, Dom squeezed Kate's hand and mouthed, *almost there.*

Kate said a silent prayer of thanks as Dom and she entered the airplane's cabin. The air smelled foul, as if the plumbing had stopped up. The tomato red rug wasn't fixed firmly to the floor—an accident waiting to happen—and bunched under her feet as she made her way down the aisle to her seat. She plopped down beside two young men, and placed her video camera on the floor between her feet. The young men smiled at her with shining faces. She guessed they were part of the Russian college student group.

The tray table hung down over the seat in front of her. She tried to close it, but it was broken. Her seatbelt wouldn't tighten properly. What about the engines, the structure of the aircraft? Kate worried. Look, just so the plane took off—and stayed in the sky for the hour flight. The videotapes were gouging into her flesh, beginning to feel like a steel corset. Kate sat up straighter, reminding herself not to appear too stiff and unnatural, or too lumpy.

The plane took off smoothly. She loosened her grip on the arms of her seat. The two young men next to her introduced themselves as Valeriy and Alexandre. They spoke halting English. Since she and Dom were separated, she chatted with them to distract herself from thinking about the consequences that might be facing Masha and Olga. Nadya too.

The boys, who were studying radio physics, were on their way to New York City, for a ten-day vacation. They were dewy-eyed, excited at seeing America for the first time. All expenses had been paid, they said, as a prize for writing the best essay in

English. Evidently the thirty-one other students on board going to New York City had written winning essays too.

"Who is your benefactor?" Kate asked.

"Mr. Moon." Valeriy said. "Mr. Moon is paying for everything."

It took a few seconds to sink in. "Mr. Moon" was the Rev. Sun Myung Moon, the Korean religious leader, founder of the Unification Church. No wonder he could claim millions of worldwide followers.

Kate handed the two her business card, telling them to call her if they needed help while in New York City. Valeriy shyly asked if he could write to her when he returned home. She said yes. He gave her a metal pin, "Gorky" printed on it, the city where the two boys lived.

***

SIPPING HIS COGNAC, CAPTAIN Iurkov leaned against the bar watching the young, pretty blonde woman with braids—Olga—as she served coffee and vodka to his men who were seated in a far corner of the dimly lit, red-paneled room. The search of the Olgino and the summer cabins had proved fruitless. Hotel guests had been questioned. No one had seen Americans. The staff on duty last night had not asked for passports. Each evacuee had written down a name in the registration book. The names Kate Hennessey and Dominick Block had not appeared in the register. Nor had the names Deborah and Peter Kempson.

The night staff, looking terrified, claimed they remembered no one by those names. "We were awakened. It was chaos, over thirty new guests, many rooms to prepare. Everything is a blur."

The Captain finished his cognac and set his glass on the counter. One of his soldiers had seen the blonde Olga near the summer cabins carrying people in a sleigh. The officer had flagged them down, asking for ID. Her passengers were French tourists.

Perhaps Kate and her friend had registered as the Kempsons with the Olgino bus as a trick and fled the city last night. He went to the front desk and used the phone.

The line at first was busy, busy. Then it rang and no one picked up. He was about to jump in his car and make the twenty-six-mile trip. Through the window, he saw the snow was falling harder. It could take an hour or more to reach Pulkovo Airport. He snapped his fingers at the mustached man behind the counter. "Another cognac."

Finally, his phone call was answered. After ten minutes he heard the news. Someone had found the Visas, Kate's and her friend's, in a stack of today's departures. He looked at his watch. At this moment, the two fugitives were landing in Helsinki.

He checked with the liaison staff at the Hotel Leningrad and was informed Kate's friend had picked up his and her belongings this morning. That traitor Andre not only saved Kate's life but had also warned her to flee the country. The Captain clenched and unclenched his fists. He gave a baleful look at the mustached man behind the counter, who said politely as he served him, "Our best cognac, sir, just for you."

Gregor would soon be in touch, demanding his report. The Captain would have to admit he failed. If Gregor complained to his pals in Moscow, a telephone call could summon him, not to *Byely Dom* (the Russian White House) but to *The Lubyanka* (KGB Headquarters). Or he could receive a visit from a shadow man. He must watch his back. He did not want to end up dead on a back road, or die in agony of some mysterious stomach ailment.

He decided to return to the Hotel Pulkovskaya to pressure Steve to hand over U.S. dollars before he left the country, saying a bribe was required to pacify investigators who wanted to question him about the hotel fire. He would mention his contacts in Brighton Beach, extracting Steve's pledge to return to Leningrad soon, his pockets filled with hard currency for their joint enterprise. Many people would have their hands out. When the time was right, when the Captain learned all the tricks of the movie business, he would get rid of Steve.

He gulped down his cognac in one long swallow. On his way to the Pulkovskaya, he must put out word offering a reward for anyone who found the turncoat Andre. *By the time I am through with him,* he thought, *he will beg me to kill him.*

❦

KATE BREATHED A LONG sigh as the plane landed safely through the fog. It had taken just an hour to cross the border into Finland, into freedom. Gripping the camera, she stepped inside the terminal and felt light as air, reborn. Dom was waiting, the film cans at his feet. She threw her arms around his neck. He hugged her tightly. They were safe. The tapes were safe. The two broke apart, holding hands, grinning through their tears.

Forty-five minutes later, Kate was in a rest room stall, gingerly unfastening the videos from her flesh, bringing more tears to her eyes. She was a wreck. The skin on her stomach and back was raw. She was getting steady twinges from her twisted knee. She stowed her tapes, four videos and two audios, in various pockets of her vest. They'd continue their ride to New York City not glued to her skin but close enough to feel with her elbows.

Her thin face, eyes huge and staring, gaped back at her from the rest room mirror. It would take days to shake off that hunted look. Her split lip was puffy still, the snow burn on her cheek almost gone. Before she washed her hands, she looked under the band-aids on her palm. The long knife cut was not oozing. She hoped to be mostly healed by the time she saw Gilly. But still hurt enough to receive sympathetic hugs as a prelude to a wild and rapturous night.

Kate left the rest room smiling, met Dom and they searched out digestive mints. He too soon had a smile on his face. They found a sit-down restaurant where they gobbled down some decent, very expensive food. Next they located the Finn Air gate they'd leave from the next morning, sank into padded leather chairs and crashed, surrounded by their luggage. When Kate woke up, two new arrivals were seated in the area. She poked Dom, who stirred and opened his eyes.

The blond man said, "I'm Mike, a filmmaker from Texas. This is Stan, my producer. You're from the festival, right? Are you sleeping at the airport too?"

Kate nodded.

Stan, the producer, grinned. "We're out of money." Mike added, "My pocket was picked at Pushkin Square. We were overcharged $150 on our roundtrip train tickets between Helsinki and Leningrad. I was practically strip searched at the Finnish border."

Kate shot a meaningful glance at Dom. Good thing she and Dom hadn't taken the train.

"The KGB officer went through my pockets, read every piece of paper I had," Mike said with a wince. "He searched my suitcases and discovered the Soviet Captain's uniform, military watch, and medals. He was a comedian. He held everything up, piece by piece, and sang, 'Contraband, contraband . . . ' We—and our black market goods—made it through with bribes, the last of our U.S. dollars." He held up his hands helplessly.

"Do you know why you were targeted?" Dom asked.

"I'm guessing they thought I was CIA. My passport was stamped with a lot of comings and goings to Vietnam. Because of the film we shot there."

The film about the underground tunnels dug during the Vietnam War—a film Kate had wanted to see.

"The final irony," Stan added, "it was never shown at the festival. The print was lost. Never made it to Sergei's, the programmer's room, they said."

"But it did," Kate said, "I saw a film can, TUNNELS printed on it, half hidden under Sergei's trousers. I took a shot of it with my camera."

Stan rolled his eyes. Mike said, "Well, we had fun partying. What about you? Any troubles?"

Kate shrugged, not about to go into it.

"Any sales?" Stan asked.

"Couple possibilities," Dom said.

"No one I talked to made a sale," Stan sighed. "I was told the festival was meant as a cultural exchange and to interest other countries in buying Russian films."

The four sank into glassy-eyed silence, staring at the floor. Kate closed her eyes.

The next thing she knew Dom was shaking her shoulder. "It's after ten, an hour later in Leningrad. We must find a pay phone and call Masha."

After thirty minutes of busy signals, Dom reached Masha at ten-thirty, Helsinki time. He asked for Ekaterina Danilovna, the agreed-on code. Dom grinned and gave Kate a thumb's up, repeating in a whisper, "Ekaterina's with her friend who just phoned to tell Masha that she's sorry Masha missed Grandfather Frost's arrival."

When Dom reluctantly hung up, Kate said, "I guess that means Masha's line was busy because she was talking with Olga, and Olga gave her the code that all was okay—no one found out she helped us get away?"

Dom nodded uncertainly. Kate had wanted to grab the receiver, ask Masha in plain English: What about Nadya? Does she know Sveta's body was found? Is she in any trouble? But she didn't, fearing Masha's phone line might be tapped.

Back at the Finn-Air gate, seated next to Dom, a tense Kate linked her arm through his before she closed her eyes, worried the sinister Captain Iurkov would fly to Helsinki, find them, and kill them as they slept. She wrapped her legs around her video camera and her hand touched her suitcase. Dom's feet rested on the film cans. Kate dozed, jerking awake every fifteen minutes it seemed. A huge clatter and clanging of metal shot through her body like a bolt of lightning. She sat up straight as a rod, heart thudding. The cleaning lady was emptying ashtrays. Kate looked at her watch. 6:30 AM.

Dom left the gate to find breakfast, returning with coffee

and rolls. The two ate in silence, edgily waiting for the arrival of the American group—and Steve. If he didn't show up, that could mean he was arrested. If none of the American group arrived? That could mean the coup had happened, Pulkovo Airport was closed.

Four long hours later, Steve, in the middle of a clump of people, headed toward them. Kate had to admit she was relieved. She was also angry. Surely it was no coincidence that Steve's date the night of the fire was Tanya, the woman who stepped out of Kolya's illegal cab.

Steve waved and approached with a hand-caught-in-the cookie-jar grin.

Kate stared at him coolly. He looked seedy, his lank, greasy-looking hair under his impresario's hat pulled back in a pony tail. *First on my agenda, my friend,* Kate decided, *is to find out how you were acquainted with Kolya, the man who tried to kill me.*

"My god," Steve gushed, "am I glad to see you guys. Where were you?"

"Here," Dom said, his arms crossed over his chest.

Kate noticed streaks of gray in Steve's hair. Not only had his curling iron been reduced to ashes by the hotel fire, but also his hair dye, which she never knew until now he used. He wore the costume he'd been dressed in for the documentary panel two nights ago, his white jacket streaked with grime, his black shirt wrinkled, his pink and gold ascot untied and hanging limply around his neck. He carried a plastic bag.

"I checked with the Pulkovskaya registration desk," Steve said in a rush. "They didn't have you listed. I asked festival officials. No one—not even Masha at the closing ceremonies last night—knew anything. Have you been here all this time?"

No way will I tell you, Kate said to herself, that we were hiding at the Olgino from the police, from Red Hair, and the evil Captain Victor Iurkov. She looked at Dom, glaring, who evidently felt the same.

Steve gave a broken laugh. "Hey, I talked festival management into showing *Revolution* after the closing ceremonies at the Pulkovskaya. But you guys had the print."

"Since you asked," Dom said dryly, "yes, the print—and Kate and I—survived the fire."

"I'm glad to be out of that place. A hellhole." Steve shuddered and looked like he meant it. "I don't have any clothes." He held up the plastic bag. "They burned up."

Dom rose from his chair and motioned Steve and Kate to follow him to a row of empty seats in the back of the waiting area. "We understand bodies were found in your room," he said in a low voice, his eyes icy.

A subdued and guilty-looking Steve sank into a chair next to Dom. Kate sat beside Steve. *You're cornered,* Kate thought, determined to get the truth about his connection to Kolya and Tanya.

After a long silence, Steve said hoarsely, "The woman who died—Tanya—was my date. I picked her up in the hotel bar and," he stumbled, "went out with her a few times. You saw me with her in the Dom Kino bar."

"You met Kolya through Tanya?" Kate asked, seeing recognition in his eyes at the name Kolya.

"What's this? The third degree?" Steve, even more guilty-looking, burst out, "All I know is, Tanya was scared of her husband. I didn't know she was married until she told me that night." Steve then described what happened: he'd left Tanya in his room to get a bottle of vodka, returned to find the barrel-shaped man, looking as if he'd been in a fight, banging on his door. "Tanya let the man in. I didn't want to get in the middle. A fireman woke me up in the bar, yelling, there's a fire. Lucky I had my hat and coat. It was bitter outside."

Kate exchanged a glance with Dom.

Dom stood in front of Steve. "So you never saw Kolya before that night he was knocking on your hotel door?"

"No. What's going on?" Steve asked belligerently. Then he sagged, rubbing his jaw. "I saw the newspaper story—about two bodies, Kate and me, they said at first." He gave a false laugh. "When I heard they were Tanya and her husband, I was shocked. He must have killed her, set the fire and killed himself. She told me he carried a knife."

Dom flicked his eyes toward Kate, as if asking, *What do you think?*

Kate gave a little shrug. Steve looked truly upset. She almost felt sorry for him.

"I could have been a third body." Steve muttered ruefully, "Who knew my hard currency hooker would bring me all those problem*s*?"

"Bring *you* all these problems?" Kate cried out. "What about her? She's dead." *You picked her up and slept with her, scumbag,* she added silently. *Show some compassion.*

"The Soviet police grilled me." He wiped his face with a well-used handkerchief. "The fire started in my room. Bodies in my room. I thought they were going to railroad me into jail. Thank God for *blat.* Hey, Dom," he said flashing a weak grin, "I'm out of dough. How about some lunch?"

Kate sighed. Vintage Steve, who never thought of anyone but himself, was back.

The three hauled the luggage over to a bar not far from the gate, Steve insisting on carrying the heavy print himself, a sign of a guilty conscience, Kate was sure.

They ordered sandwiches, chips and beer, sat around a small table and ate hungrily. "Real food, at last," Steve said, his mouth full. "Too bad you guys missed the closing ceremony."

As if we had a choice, Kate thought. It would have been infinitely preferable to sleeping in the airport, praying someone wouldn't sneak up and clobber us over the head.

Steve gulped down his beer. "A Dixieland band played 'When the Saints Go Marchin' In' and the judges actually marched onstage to award the prizes: gold, silver and bronze centaurs and checks. The top two winners were Russian filmmakers. Not surprising. At the end, the man at the piano sang a Louis Armstrong song. In Russian. It brought down the house."

"They gave prizes?" Kate was surprised. "I heard they lost

most of their budget when the government withdrew fifty and one hundred ruble notes."

Steve frowned. "A famous Russian ballerina contributed the prize money. Someone else was able to convert it from rubles to dollars."

"Did you touch base last night with any of our potential investors—the Dutch, the West Germans, Japanese?" Dom asked.

Steve shook his head. "I heard people flew out early. Because of the fire . . . the rumored military take-over." He grinned. "On the way to the airport this morning, we saw just three civilians on horseback, out for a morning ride. No tanks or soldiers with guns."

"That's a relief," Dom said. He scratched his jaw, frowning. "We need to follow up with the money people ASAP. We're running on empty."

Steve, almost his old cocky self, said, "Leave it to me."

Dom, eyes brooding, smiled politely. Kate could almost guess what he was thinking. Steve was a partner who'd invested $80,000 in Titan Films. They couldn't get rid of him unless they paid him off, with interest. Their small company didn't have that kind of money.

Steve dipped into his plastic bag. "Oh, yeah, the catalogues listing all the invited films finally arrived last night from Finland, in time for the closing ceremony." He gave one to each.

On the flight back to New York City, Kate read through the glossy pages of the Catalogue of the Second Leningrad International Film Festival, "Message to Man." The chairman of the film selection committee wrote: "We were delighted by the American program, consisting of almost fifty films which give a many sided picture of a large country's life."

She read on, discovering that two weeks before the festival, Aeroflot hadn't yet come through with transport for the Judges of the Main Competition. Just as the festival committee was about to cancel everything, Lufthansa donated the travel dollars.

The festival had limped gamely to the end despite the

money disaster, the changing political climate, the chaos and confusion.

The greeting from Mayor Sobchak, meant to open the festival, had closed it. "A message addressed to a man only makes sense when it passes from heart to heart . . . Today Leningrad, which only recently turned to all mankind and asked for help, receives you, envoys, from around the world as our guests . . ." With her video project, she would let the world know what was happening in Leningrad. She'd bring messages of courage and hope from her new Russian friends, from their hearts to mankind.

Chapter Twenty

10:30 AM, Friday, February 1

Gregor, his gray suit neatly pressed, his white shirt starched, walked down the long, polished corridor beside Colonel Alekseev, noticing on this, his second visit to Moscow's KGB Headquarters in Lubyanka Square, that the walls were bare, no pictures or signs to help him remember his way out. He stifled an urge to turn and run. Within this compound was the infamous Lubyanka Prison where scores of prisoners were tortured and murdered.

Gregor climbed a staircase covered with netting. "To prevent arrestees from jumping over the rail to avoid interrogation," Colonel Alekseev had told him eight days earlier when Gregor met with him, and the plan to kill Kate was set in motion. The Colonel then had praised Captain Victor Iurkov as ruthless and thorough, the right man to organize the mission. The Colonel had gone on to say with a wolfish grin, "Death is cheap. A hired killer in our country costs just twenty-five dollars—half a month's pay. A hired killer for New York City is twenty-five dollars, and airfare, plus one night's hotel."

The extra he had paid in bribes to Kolya and the extra days he had paid for his room at the Leningrad Hotel had cost him much more than twenty-five dollars, Gregor thought sourly. But if Captain Iurkov kept his word and Kate's lifeless body was rotting on a deserted road outside of Leningrad, it would be worth much more than he had spent.

The two men arrived at a massive wooden door, no name, just a number on it, and entered a large room with a gleaming desk and a thick carpet. Colonel Alekseev, a tall, powerful-looking man with small eyes and thick brows, briskly strode behind the desk and eased himself into the chair, motioning for Gregor to sit.

Gregor opened his briefcase with a nonchalance he did not feel and handed the Colonel a sheaf of papers, signed contracts that showed their company's commitment to invest much-needed hard currency into the shaky economy of the Soviet Union. The investment would provide endless opportunities for officials like Colonel Alekseev to line their pockets. The Colonel leafed through the pages, frowning.

Gregor waited, sweat trickling down his back into his underwear.

When the Colonel finished, he nodded with a quick smile. He offered Gregor a cigar, selected one for himself and lit them both.

Gregor allowed himself to savor the rich, nutty flavor of the cigar. He accepted the glass of cognac the Colonel poured. Soon the office was filled with thick clouds of expensive white smoke.

As promised, Colonel Alekseev made a phone call to Captain Iurkov and demanded a report on Kate. The Colonel listened, his eyes growing smaller, as a great deal of unintelligible noise erupted from the receiver. It had a sweet music to it, Gregor thought, surprise and fear. He pictured the Captain's face, the terrible scar bunching into a knot of panic.

"She is alive," the Colonel frowned, his black eyebrows meeting in the middle of his forehead. His hand covered the mouthpiece of the phone. "On her way to America."

"Those stupid blunderers tipped her off." Gregor felt dizzy with anger and disappointment. Iurkov had sworn to make her disappear forever.

Colonel Alekseev was looking at him as if he expected an answer. "I said, what do you want me to do?"

"Ask Captain Iurkov if he has found his soldier Andre," Gregor said, biting off his words. "He saved the *suka*'s life. Ask Iurkov if he has seized the videotape that shows him and me in conversation. Andre stole it, intending to blackmail me."

Colonel Alexseev spoke into the mouthpiece. "The soldier Andre? Is he in custody?" Again, more static at the other end. The Colonel scowled. "Andre has disappeared. Iurkov has an order out for his arrest."

"I know how that goes."

The Colonel said quietly, "Can you come into my office for a talk, Captain Iurkov? I will expect you Monday." He hung up, his eyes contrite. "My deepest apologies for the failure of this operation. We are military men. An order is an order."

"Both men deserve to die," Gregor said. Andre for his betrayal; the Captain, for his carelessness and his arrogance. "At the least to be sent to a labor camp." Gregor was nervous that the suspicious Captain Iurkov might decide to charge him with setting the hotel fire. One never knew in the Soviet Union these days. The tables could quickly turn.

The Colonel didn't answer, but stood abruptly, saying with a smile. "Are you hungry?"

The Colonel and two of his colleagues took him to the fourth floor to the special dining room, where they sat in high-backed chairs at an enormous oval table. Gregor was wined and dined with delicacies flown in from all over the world. "You speak good Russian," the Colonel said, clapping a hand on Gregor's shoulder. "But with an accent." "My mother was Russian. My father, German," Gregor answered. The Colonel's driver took him to the airport.

As Gregor stood in line for his plane ticket, he wiped his face with his handkerchief, relieved to be out of that place.

In his pocket he carried the newspaper clipping of Kate's death and her blue earrings with the two white doves. *Terrible accident,* he'd planned to say, showing the clipping to his boss, implying she died in the hotel fire. See if his boss was suspicious that Gregor had a hand in it. He hadn't said for him to go this far. If he seemed pleased, Gregor would tell him about his elaborate scheme to get rid of Kate on foreign soil: how it spiraled out of control, forcing him to kill that *mudak* Kolya and his *blyad.* He would explain that the newspaper report of Kate's death in the fire was in error. But she *is* dead, he would assure his boss. Arrested by the Captain. Her body found on a deserted road. A perfect crime. No links to me or you.

Except Captain Iurkov had fucked it up. And Kate was back in America.

Another fly in the ointment was the missing videotape that showed him and Captain Iurkov talking in the hotel bar. Hold on, he told himself. If the Colonel ordered Andre and the Captain put to death or sentenced to hard labor, who would take the trouble to transfer an American-formatted tape into Russian SECAM for viewing? The incriminating tape would disappear in the chaotic whirlwind of events in Leningrad.

Gregor looked at his watch. 3:30 PM, eight hours earlier in New York City. His boss was always on the job by 7:30 AM. He placed a call. He pictured the man at the other end, a man with military bearing sitting in front of flickering lights from many television screens, looking out the window at the Twin Towers. He got through to him on the third try. "It's Gregor." Silence at the other end. "It's me." He had grown used to *Gregor,* but it was not the name he went by in the States. "I'm at Moscow airport. The contracts are signed and filed. Let's meet for dinner tomorrow night." Time for him to take charge, all the while persuading—in honeyed tones—his boss, who was a wuss, of next steps.

He would need Rohypnol, a stun gun, perhaps Thorazine. He would dump her body where it would never be found. Once she was taken care of, he would see that he gained control of everything.

PART II
New York City

*PM Friday, February 1, 1991 through
Monday, February 11, 1991*

Chapter One

5:00 PM, Friday, February 1

Kate and Dom trudged into their mutual apartment building, weighted down by luggage, nodding at Juan, the doorman. Home at last. Kate would do cartwheels all over the lobby—if she weren't so exhausted and her knee didn't hurt. She and Dom grabbed their mail and rode up in the elevator together. Kate's thoughts were on Steve. He'd been squeezed between Dom and her in the back seat of the cab on their way home from JFK Airport when he'd asked her for his videotape. Smiling weirdly, he explained to Dom that it contained auditions for *Flying Eagles*.

She started to say, "It burned up at the Hotel Leningrad," but Dom interrupted. "Good thing Kate moved everything, including your videotape, into my room before the fire."

"Well, well." Steve gave her a smirk, as if he thought she and Dom were having a fling. She could have kicked him in the shins. Dom too, for sabotaging her plan to have a look at that "audition" tape.

When the cab stopped in front of Steve's apartment building on West 86th, he held out his hand.

Dom nudged her. "Give it to him, Kate."

She did unwillingly, sliding it out of her vest pocket.

"I'll give you a shout, Dom," Steve babbled, as he exited the cab, "if I spot promising talent. We might show it to potential backers. If they think they'll meet pretty actresses who are stacked, they'll shell out the bucks."

Meet pretty actresses, a euphemism for *sleep with.* "*Flying Eagles* is about American paratroopers, the German occupation of Holland, and the Dutch Underground," Kate muttered as the cab nosed out into traffic and continued down Broadway. "The women in it are not bimbos."

As the elevator stopped at Kate's floor, the seventh, she turned to Dom. "Get some sleep," she said before she stepped out. She walked down the hall to her apartment. Inside, in the large entry, she put down her suitcase and camera, almost floating into the living area, comforted by the familiar sights: the second hand drapes hanging lopsidedly in the corner windows behind the enormous wooden desk that took up most of the room; the red beanbag chair—Gilly's chair. The coffee table, its black *faux* marble top only slightly chipped, added a touch of class. She'd found it abandoned on the street.

Kate walked over to the desk and pushed Play on the answering machine. Three messages, two from Aunt Maureen inviting her to dinner on Sunday, one a hang-up. None from Gilly. It was early. Only five o'clock.

Her eyes drifted to the green couch, her sofa bed, bought brand new when Gilly started staying over. Above it hung the charcoal portrait Gilly had drawn. She'd sat on the couch leaning forward, her blonde hair tucked behind her ears, eyes serious behind her wire rimmed glasses. "I'd love to have a picture of you as you look now," Kate said, mesmerized by her fierce concentration, the movement of her hand lightly holding the charcoal, graceful and skilled. A dazzling sight. It almost hurt Kate to look. The charcoal scratched and whispered against the paper. The moment was perfect, intimate. As if Gilly could read her mind, she lifted her eyes and held Kate in her gaze for several seconds before she looked down at the sketchpad. When the portrait was finished, Kate said, "It's me. It's magic." She thought Gilly wanted it for her apartment, to show it alongside her other art pieces, but she didn't take it when she left. Kate was hurt. "I want a sketch of *you* on my wall not *me*." "I'll do one of me," Gilly promised. "We'll hang together," she laughed. That was just before the Gay Pride March last June.

Kate slid her tapes from her vest pockets and stacked them—three videos, two audios—on the coffee table. It took all her self control not to play the videos through her TV screen, but that would degrade the color and the sound. She couldn't wait to see the Palace at Pavlovsk in full frame, the snow covered grounds and tall birch trees, to revisit the quaint Olgino. Out of nowhere unsettling thoughts came rushing in: the wild ride in the Father Christmas sleigh to escape KGB Captain Victor Iurkov; the soldiers roaming the palace grounds, bored and arrogant, the convoy truck that nearly ran her down.

Keep busy, don't dwell on darkness. She lifted the phone, dialed Downtown TV, and booked an editing room to transfer her tapes to a master. First available opening, Tuesday. Damn! Four days until she could see her footage on a big screen.

More dark thoughts came rushing up. Nadya rotting in a psychiatric clinic, Masha and Olga in jail. Gilly breaking up with her.

She had the bends. Too quick an entry into New York City from Leningrad. She ran hot water in the tub, threw off her filthy clothes, and climbed in.

Only one reason she could think of why Gilly didn't want the sketch of Kate at her apartment. She was ashamed, having second thoughts. When they'd first met—hard to believe, it was over a year ago—Gilly wanted to go to bed right away. Kate didn't. She was afraid Gilly was experimenting and would break her heart. Kate wanted a friend—then a lover. "It's easy to fall in love for a night, a week," Kate told her. "Hard to have a friend." Gilly agreed. Two weeks later Kate brought her here to her apartment.

After they'd been lovers for a month, Gilly told her shyly, "You're the first—my first woman."

Kate had hugged her, laughing. "Were you afraid?"

"Very."

"You didn't show it."

"What about you?"

"You're my second," Kate said. "My first was in college." Gilly begged and Kate told her about the disaster, about being so humiliated that she dropped out of school and lived at home with Aunt Maureen and Uncle Burt, commuting to a nearby college to finish her degree.

Gilly kissed away her tears and said, "I'm happy Amy threw you over. You're free to be with me."

Gilly, sly and funny, could break Kate up in the most serious moments. Other times she'd be down in the dumps so far Kate didn't know how to reach her.

Gilly was her age, but she seemed older, more sophisticated. Definitely more secretive. It took her months to ask Kate to her apartment. Only then did Kate discover Gilly was an artist. Her walls were covered with sketches and paintings—thrilling, powerful, so different from her quick, sharp humor. It took Gilly a long time too to tell Kate her full name, Angelica McGillicuddy, and that she worked part-time in a downtown art gallery.

After so much secrecy, Kate was surprised when Gilly gave her a key to her apartment.

Kate stepped out of the tub, wrapped a towel around her, and hurried into the living room to see if, while the water was running, she might have missed THE CALL. No blinking red light. They'd agreed the eight days Kate was gone would give them each time to think. Kate knew what *she* wanted. Gilly still must be thinking.

Kate smoothed A&D ointment on her masking tape burns on her stomach, and dressed in loose clothes. Palms sweating, she picked up the phone and dialed. After seven rings Gilly's machine clicked on. Kate put the phone back in its cradle.

She'd been so eager to get home, so grateful to step inside her apartment. Now the walls were closing in on her. She went around the corner for a slice of pizza.

▼▲▼

ANDRE OPENED HIS EYES. He shined a flashlight on his watch. 4:00 AM. Time to leave. He wondered if he would survive. He had been wild with grief since Thursday night when his sister's friend, Irina, crying, read him the retraction in the evening paper: a tiny paragraph on a back page reporting that Tanya and Kolya—not the Americans Kate and Steve—were the charred bodies found in the fourth floor room at the Leningrad Hotel. "How your sister must have suffered," Irina screamed, "burned alive. Kolya—that *sovok*. It is all his fault."

Andre had groaned and sobbed and beat his fists against his head, ready to storm the festival closing ceremonies at the Hotel Pulkovskaya, find Steve and break his neck. "He did it. The bodies were in his room."

Irina sat him down hard. "Don't be stupid. The Captain has put out word to find you, you told me yourself." Then she added, "Stay hidden. Let me sniff around." And she did, the next day.

Andre rose from his bed of blankets on the floor. Shivering, he dressed in the dark in the clothes he'd seized from the abandoned Hotel Leningrad: black trousers, heavy gray sweater, dark blue wool jacket. He squeezed his feet into the black dress shoes—too tight. He softly closed the bedroom door behind him—he didn't want to wake Irina—and tiptoed down the hall to the bathroom, located in the part of the *kommunalka* that belonged to the other flat mates. They were getting curious about him, this cousin of Irina's from Gorky, especially one old lady who had lived here the longest and seemed to be in charge.

He closed the bathroom door, turned on the light, a dim bulb, and scrutinized himself in the mirror. He saw patches he missed when he had hurriedly applied a paste of black boot dye to his red hair. He slid the flat can of dye from his pants pocket, and did a touch up. When he finished, his hair stood up in dark, greasy clumps. He smoothed it away from his face, which was milky white. His eyes were red and puffy. He looked like an albino weasel.

He scrubbed the black off his hands and returned the polish to his pocket.

If he had not listened to Irina, if he had stormed out of the flat seeking to avenge his sister's death, he would be in jail or dead. During her poking about, Irina heard many interesting things from her friend Helena, who was the *dejurnaya* on the fourth floor of the Hotel Leningrad. Helena had seen Tanya and the film director Steve go into his room. But Steve soon left. Shortly after, a fat man, bandaged and drunk—Kolya—was banging on Steve's door. In the same hallway, a third man, with a broad, soft face and hard eyes, who spoke Russian with an accent, escorted Kolya into his room.

Andre knew at once this man was Gregor. Slimy Gregor who, the *dejurnaya* said, had bribed her to leave her post. She said she was sure from the way she was questioned by Captain Iurkov that Gregor—not Steve—had set the fire and run down the stairs, yelling "*Pozhar*" ("Fire") at every floor, a black balaclava covering his face. Gregor had killed Tanya and Kolya. Andre hoped Tanya did not burn alive. He felt a tear slide down his cheek. Why Tanya? He saw her again as the nimble ballerina, dancing on her toes, leaping with exquisite grace. She had been used and misused by Kolya. Now she was dead before she was thirty. He swore to himself he would find Gregor, and kill him slowly and painfully.

When Andre returned to the bedroom, the light was on. Irina was sitting up in bed. He hugged her. He looked through the pockets of his army uniform one last time, found a couple of folded bills which he added to his inside jacket pocket, alongside his false papers with his new name, Dimitri, his airline ticket, and the copied pages he had found in the open safe at the Hotel Leningrad.

He asked Irina to burn his uniform. His only luggage was a small valise. In it was a bread and apple jelly sandwich Irina had made.

He walked out the front door of the *kommunalka* without hat or coat. The thick sweater and the wool jacket were no protection against the sharp winds of February. He ran all the way to the Metro. His anger kept him warm.

※※※

KATE RETURNED TO HER apartment from the pizza place at 8:30 PM. It was eight hours later in Leningrad—4:30 AM. She should be tired, but she was as wired as if she'd drunk twelve cups of coffee. She called Dom, who answered on the first ring. "I'm not sleepy," she announced in a combative voice as if he were her dad trying to put her to bed.

"Me either," he said. "Come on up." She took the elevator to the fourteenth floor, a penthouse apartment, the main Titan Films office. She rang Dom's bell. "Unlocked," he called.

That was part of his "open" lifestyle—a transformation, he said, that happened after he had analysis with LSD in the sixties. She'd have thought that now, after Russia, he might decide to lock his door.

She entered and walked down the narrow hall, its walls covered with mementos from Dom's past: a still photo of Antonioni that Dom took when he worked as photographer on one of the Italian director's films; framed awards from Dom's days as an ad man on Mad Ave. Above the bright orange sofa in the living room hung a huge psychedelic poster, a remnant from *Revolution*'s first incarnation as *Summer of Love*. It advertised a rock group, The Doors, at San Francisco's Fillmore Auditorium. Next to it was a framed picture of silent film comedian Harold Lloyd, looking panicked, as he hung from a clock outside a skyscraper. Kate figured that Dom, fifty-three, fearful that time was running out, used it to prod himself forward.

The apartment was stifling. The terrace door was open to let out some of the heat. Dom had turned on the outside lights, illuminating his terrace, covered in green Astroturf, dotted with remnants of the set of Dom's first fiction film, the black and white he made in Chelsea and the Village, shot on the cheap in 16mm and blown up to 35mm for the commercial movie houses. Heavy stone gargoyles and goddesses and large stone pots in which flowers bloomed in the summer lined the perimeter of Dom's half of the space. Who would have thought Dom had a green thumb? At the western edge of the terrace between the terrace door and the Indian goddess was a small patch of the Hudson River. A weathered picket fence—a dart board in its center—enclosed a private area so the neighbors couldn't see Dom sunbathing nude in the hammock. Suburbia in New York City. In the summer, money-raising parties were held there.

Mickey, the fluffy white Persian owned by the couple who shared the outdoor terrace, hopped into the living room through the open door. He headed toward Dom, who sat at his desk, mail piled high, the company checkbook open. Purring, Mickey rubbed against Dom's legs. "He's missed you," Kate laughed.

Dom absent-mindedly scratched Mickey's head,

"I've been obsessing about Nadya," Kate blurted out. "How she's surviving. Does she know Sveta's dead?" Kate shuddered. "I wonder if anyone knows how she died. What if my name was printed in the newspaper as a person of interest to the police? How awful for Nadya to read that."

"Dear Kate," Dom sighed abstractedly, patting her shoulder. "Don't carry the weight of the world on your back."

Dom looked beat, his shoulders slumped, his face pasty. She hated to keep pushing but she must. Soon they would be on the money-raising treadmill again, so consuming it allowed discussion of nothing else. "Steve told you he had something in his back pocket to bring in money for *Flying Eagles*. If it's porn, do you want our next film made with profits from skin flics?"

Dom sat there blinking for a few moments. "We have no proof."

"That's why I wanted to keep his videotape, to check it out," Kate exploded. Dom threw up his hands. That made Kate angrier. "You saw him in the LEM dressing room handing out his business cards to the bare-chested man, to the beautiful dark-haired woman, claiming he was a movie producer looking for talent, asking them to audition—"

Dom broke in, "Kate, you'll learn if you stay in this business—it's so damn hard to raise money." He lifted his eyes, apologetic and cynical. "You don't ask many questions where it comes from."

He scratched his beard. "Look, we both know that most of the bucks Steve's invested to finish *Revolution* were made by inserting porn footage in bankrupt films and selling them to the hotel XXX pay-per-view circuit. We didn't complain then."

"This is different. He's exploiting Russian friends who are desperate for dollars. It makes me want to puke." Dom was desperate too. If they raised the money for *Flying Eagles* by next year, it could be a second year—even a third—before the film was shot, edited, and shown in a movie house in time to be eligible for an Academy Award.

Dom stared at the open checkbook on his desk. "Foreign royalties are drying up. If we make the Japanese and West German sales of *Revolution,* it won't be much. My two credit cards are maxed out. My dear Kate, I'm sorry . . ." Dom took her hand. "I hate to ask—can you go back to office temps until we start rolling again?"

Kate half expected it. Still, it was a blow. She made herself smile. "Sure." Dom had dropped her once before, just after the San Francisco shoot. She'd only been working for him for three months. He flew to Italy, hiring a prominent lawyer to gouge royalties out of European distributors guilty of creative accounting. In four weeks he was back with $30,000 in cash hidden throughout his pockets. Kate returned to work that very day.

"I'll pay the rent on your apartment, but after next week, I can't afford your salary for awhile. I must say—you're taking it better than I am. I feel like I've let you down, Kate."

She shrugged. "I'll get by." Instead of office temps, she'd go to Aunt Maureen and Uncle Burt for an advance from her trust fund.

Dom pushed his lips into a smile. "On the good side, a message from the Dutch was waiting on my machine. They've lined up potential investors. I'm off to Holland Sunday. I'll need you to work with me all day tomorrow to get everything ready, okay? I know it's a Saturday and you probably have plans."

"No problem." It would take her mind off Gilly. And Nadya. And Steve.

"While I'm away, pay only essential bills. I'll leave signed checks." He gave her a sheepish look. "As soon as Steve gets the go ahead from me, he'll be heading out to the Channel Islands to raise our half of the seed money."

"When did this happen?" So he'd scratched out travel money for Steve, despite misgivings about his ethics.

"We just got off the phone."

"When were you going to tell me?"

"Just now." Dom grinned and ruffled her hair, as if she were a child. He stretched and yawned. "We'd better hit the sack. See you tomorrow at nine?"

"Sure." As Kate rode the elevator down to her apartment, she tried not to feel betrayed. She and Dom had known each other for almost two years. Steve joined the company less than a year ago. She'd stood by Dom through his divorce. He'd cheered and clapped at last June's Gay Pride Parade giving her and Gilly the courage to march hand in hand behind Mayor Dinkins and the Lavender Janes, past people chanting, "Perverts on parade, someday you'll get AIDS." Next, she and Gilly joined a "kiss-in" in front of St. Pat's to make a statement about the church's anti-gay policies. They kissed for the first time in public. Her stomach grew tight now just thinking about it.

Back in her apartment, Kate threw a glance at her answering machine, expecting to be disappointed. And she was.

Behind the desk, in the windowsill were the broken pieces of the red clay flower pot.

Gilly had thrown it—and its African violets—on the floor the night before Kate's flight to Leningrad. Gilly had brought champagne to toast Kate's trip. In the glow of the thrilling celebration, Kate asked her to move in. She hesitated. "I'm not sure, my darling Kate. I don't know if I can live the way you want, in the open for everyone to see. It's an outlaw life: people laughing at us, calling us hateful names."

"So what if people say terrible things. There's a backlash now. Because of AIDS. Whatever they call us, we must say, "Yes, and our names are still Kate Hennesey and Angelica McGillicuddy. We refuse to be afraid. Nobody should have a say in who we are."

Gilly gathered her things and dressed. "I feel like I'm in a pressure cooker, ready to explode." Her eyes, filled with tears, begged Kate to understand. "I thought I could do what was expected of me, get married, have a family. You've turned my life upside down. It's making me crazy."

"You're a coward," Kate said shakily. *Just like Amy, in college.*

Gilly slammed the flowerpot to the floor. Kate burst out, "Go back to your boring, safe life on Long Island." Gilly ran out the door.

The next day before the airport limo picked her up, Kate, subdued, called Gilly to apologize. That's when they agreed Kate's trip to Leningrad would give them each time to think. "I'll wait for you to call," Kate said. "Yes," Gilly answered.

Could she bear it if Gilly told her it was too difficult to continue? Kate thought about Nadya and the women at the Café Soul—the horrors they went through, the obstacles they overcame to stay together.

She remembered the Russian word she'd learned from Masha, *priterpylost,* silence in the face of violence. She was just as cowardly as Gilly. She hadn't yet told Aunt Maureen and Uncle Burt about Gilly. She still kept up a pretense with them that she was dating men.

If we don't speak up and speak out about injustice and violence, Kate thought, *people everywhere—straight and gay, here, Russia, all over the world—will be treated as throwaway people, to whom anything can be done. Even murder.* Why hadn't she said this to Gilly instead of lashing out?

As Kate undressed for bed, she heard a paper crackle in her vest pocket. She pulled out the newspaper story about her death by fire in the Leningrad Hotel. Her eyes fastened on her picture and above it in Cyrillic—she sounded it out—*mertvyi,* the Russian word for *dead.* She found it hard to breathe. She told herself, *It's over. Get your mind back to NOW.*

Chapter Two

7:30 PM, Saturday, February 2

Damn this New York City sleet, Gregor thought as he stepped out of the cab. He covered his head with his briefcase, and hurried into the restaurant. "Is he here?" he asked the maitre d'.

"The usual table. Your coat, sir." The maitre d' whisked it from him and hung it on the rack.

Gregor signaled. Unsmiling, his boss—everyone called him the General—nodded. Dressed in his office attire, an expensive dark suit, he sipped a drink. His face was flushed, his graying hair pomaded into waves.

The place was packed, filled with the din of many conversations, rattling dishes, clinking glasses. Gregor sat down in front of a martini in a blue glass, his usual—very dry, straight up. He was briefly flattered that the General had ordered it for him in advance.

"You're late," the General said sharply. "I expected you three days ago."

"Red tape." And murder. Wouldn't his boss be surprised to know since he last saw him he'd killed two people. He must remember to sort through his travel expenses before he turned them in for reimbursement. He mustn't leave a clue that he'd been in Leningrad.

The General snapped his fingers and the waiter appeared. "Two Delmonico steaks with Asparagus Oscar," he said.

Gregor lifted his drink in a silent toast before he took a swallow. *He's the General. I follow orders. Or pretend to. The General used to be brilliant,* he thought. When everyone else was saying the economy was going to get better, he came up with a strategy that no one else was following at the time—long on bonds, short on stocks. That year was their biggest—everyone received huge bonuses, even the secretaries.

His boss, after two more martinis and dessert, was in a better mood. Gregor took the contracts from his briefcase. "If there's a return to a dictatorship, I don't think we need to worry."

The General gave a barracuda smile. "The Soviets will bend to the inevitability of progress, free markets, and the force of our will." He spread the papers across the table, shuffling through them, nodding.

Gregor continued, "We supply drilling equipment for oil. They'll pay us a percent for laundering money through our companies. The terms are very much in our favor. Still, these cunning Russians are learning what capitalism is all about. We must keep a sharp eye on their tricks."

"About the other matter we discussed," his boss began.

Gregor's pulse quickened. His boss had told him he was thinking about making him a partner. Had he brought the agreement for him to sign, his reward for clinching the deal with the Russians, worth millions to the firm? Months ago Gregor had sensed he was tiring of the rat race, that he wanted to groom someone else to take over, someone who'd match his skill and not let the firms' investors down.

"I'd like it seen to as soon as possible." The General raised his cup to his lips. "We're already three days behind."

"It?" Gregor asked, momentarily confused, his mind stuck on partnership.

"What we spoke of before you left," the General said impatiently.

Gregor, flustered, flushing, sprang to attention. "I'm ready to move on it tomorrow." After current problems were dealt with to his boss's satisfaction, Gregor planned to re-open the partnership conversation. He must teach this self-important prick he was someone to be reckoned with. He fixed his boss firmly in his gaze, his voice brusque, authoritative. "First, you need to make a couple of phone calls."

His boss whispered nervously, "I don't want this botched up. I'm thinking of running for Congress." He took a sheet of paper from his briefcase. When he finished writing, he folded the paper and handed it to Gregor. "Use any means you need to make it happen."

"Trust me." This time he would do everything himself.

The next morning he tapped at her door, then let himself in. She was still asleep. He stood there, watching her. When she opened her eyes, he held out the blue earrings with the two white doves.

Chapter Three

2:30 PM, Sunday, February 3

Kate left the Lincoln Tunnel, maneuvering Dom's car out from behind a huge truck, grateful that traffic was not too bad this Sunday afternoon. Going home would be a pain, with weekenders streaming back into the City. She exited at Passaic Avenue, familiar territory, so familiar her stomach already was in knots. Kingsland Park passed by in a blur and here she was at the old homestead. She parked the car curbside and killed the motor, glancing at her watch. The trip had taken thirty-four minutes.

Under the overcast New Jersey sky the yellow house where she grew up was dingy and washed out. An American flag drooped at the side.

Her eyes were pulled to her former bedroom, an attic really, boiling hot in the summer, uncomfortably cold in the winter. Her life had stretched before her from that third-floor window where all she saw were rows of boxy little homes in postage stamp yards.

She felt suffocated, as if dirt were being shoveled onto her coffin. Cripes. She hadn't had this feeling in years, not since before she left home right after college. Kate took several deep breaths. She gathered up her bag of gifts from Russia for Aunt Maureen and Uncle Burt and slid out of the car.

Except for a few patches of hard, white ice, the sidewalks had been cleared. A thick coating of snow, rimmed with gray slush, covered the yard. The outdoor evergreen crouched bare and forlorn beside the front window. Every Christmas Aunt Maureen decorated it with lights. Kate walked up the stone steps and rang the bell.

The front door opened. Aunt Maureen smiled, her eyes warm and bright. Her face was powdered and rouged. Her dark hair, threaded with streaks of gray, was pulled into a bun. Loose strands wispily framed her face. A starched white apron covered her going-to-church dress, a high-necked navy blue wool with long sleeves.

Kate, mustering a wide grin, opened the storm door. "Hi. Aunt Maureen." She wished she felt closer to her. After all, Maureen hadn't asked for a child. She took Kate in after her parents died because she was the best friend of Kate's mom. Good thing. Or Kate might have grown up in an orphanage. Living here—even after Burt came into the picture—was better than living in an orphanage.

Aunt Maureen gave her a hug and a kiss. "Hi, sweetheart. How was the film festival?"

I was almost killed. "Unbelievable." Kate remembered the day she first stepped inside this house. Aunt Maureen was married then to Uncle Dave. They'd welcomed her with open arms. Aunt Maureen had laughed a lot more with Uncle Dave than she did now with Burt.

"You look exhausted. Your eyes have circles under them."

"Jetlag," Kate said.

Aunt Maureen looked over Kate's shoulder and spotted the light brown sedan. "Your boss on the road again?"

Kate nodded. "I took him to JFK this morning. Where's Uncle Burt?"

"Working," Aunt Maureen sighed.

Good. He was out of the house. "Today? Sunday?"

"What's new? He should be home in time for dinner. Can you stay?"

No way. "I have to be somewhere later." Right. Home alone to brood.

"I made pie—butterscotch—your favorite." Aunt Maureen wiped her hands on her apron.

That was the one thing Kate learned to cook. When she moved out, she took Maureen's butterscotch pie recipe with her.

Kate put her gifts down on an end table. She slipped out of her coat and flung it on the couch, felt a stab of guilt, hung it in the front closet. She followed Aunt Maureen into the dining room. She'd once been so slim. She'd put on weight in the last couple years, making it difficult for her to walk. "What can I do?" Kate asked cheerily.

"Not a thing."

"Aunt Maureen, you wouldn't believe the great people I met in Leningrad, the beautiful places. I'll show you some videos . . ."

"I'd love to see them, dear." Aunt Maureen rummaged in the corner cabinet. She took out the good china cups and dessert plates. "Your mom's. She had such wonderful taste." She lifted out the silverware box and opened it on the table. "The silver too." Rituals performed each time Kate came for a meal or a snack.

"I think about her often." A tear rolled down Aunt Maureen's cheek.

"Me too," Kate said awkwardly, her eyes darting to the back wall, where a photo of her parents hung. Kate had an identical picture in her apartment. She felt guilty because her emotions weren't as raw as Aunt Maureen's. She was five when they died—over twenty years ago. "Bad weather and high winds," Aunt Maureen told her every time she asked when she was little. "The plane—a Piper Comanche—went down in a forest in Tennessee, ninety miles from their destination. I cried for days."

Maureen smiled through her tears. "You look so much like your mom, the same dark hair, the same expression in your eyes—curious, impatient. Wanting to swallow all the world has to offer in one big gulp."

Kate sometimes stared at the photo in her apartment, trying to feel a connection. "I'm glad I have you." She awkwardly kissed Aunt Maureen on the cheek. "Hey, I brought you something from Russia." She plucked the sack of gifts off the end table, handing Maureen the tissue-wrapped pin of colorful flowers. "Hand painted."

Aunt Maureen parted the tissue, and ooed and aahed as she pinned it to the lapel of her dress. "It's beautiful. Thank you, honey."

Kate held up the military watch. "For Uncle Burt."

"It's perfect. He'll love it." Aunt Maureen placed the watch at Burt's place, the head of the dining room table where he always sat.

"For you both, a political *matryoshka,* a Gorby doll." Kate said. "Bought at Pushkin Square." She took it apart, while Aunt Maureen watched.

"A grim crowd," Maureen said.

Kate laughed. "Masha, our translator at the film festival, told me a joke. The only change among them is a *bald* leader, then a *hairy* one . . . See, Gorbachev is bald, Brezhnev hairy, Kruschev bald. Stalin hairy, Lenin bald, Peter the Great hairy."

Maureen gave a startled smile. "The Russian authorities allow these dolls?"

"This week it's legal. Next week it might be a crime." She showed her the bottom of Gorbachev doll. "You'll notice it hasn't been signed." Kate started to put the *matryoshka* dolls back together.

"Leave them lined up in the center of the table for Burt."

Aunt Maureen carried in the butterscotch pie from the kitchen, cut it into quarters, and lifted out a slab for each. Kate's mouth watered. She poured the coffee, then sat across the table from Aunt Maureen, took a bite and sighed, "Scrumptious, as usual." Her heart gave a twinge. Aunt Maureen had worry lines in her face, wore an apologetic air as if Burt had drained the spunk out of her. She'd seemed glamorous when Kate was a child. She'd done modeling before she settled down to be a housewife with Uncle Dave. When Kate came along, they were a perfect family. They went to church every Sunday. Aunt Maureen had a blueprint for Kate's life, expecting her to marry someone in banking, have children that she could baby sit and spoil a little.

Kate searched for things to talk about. "I see you have more snow than we do in Manhattan."

"We have to find someone new to shovel. It's hard to please Burt."

Kate surely knew that. He always picked at Aunt Maureen. Not a good enough cook; didn't clean the house well. He'd been critical too of Kate—from the time he'd moved in when Kate was sixteen until she moved out seven years later, right after college. Her grades were never good enough. The way she dressed—unladylike. Her friends—unacceptable.

"Are you seeing anyone special?" Aunt Maureen asked. "You're so pretty. So full of life. You could get any man you wanted. I miss having you around here, honey."

"I miss you too." Kate gave her a quick hug, surprised to find she really meant it. Now was the time, with Burt out of the house, to tell her about Gilly. How wonderful she was. How lucky for Kate that she'd met her. She chickened out, shaking her head. "No one special." She and Gilly once had a plan. *We'll go together, tell both sets—yours and mine.* Meeting Gilly's parents was such a disaster they'd scrapped the idea of Gilly meeting Maureen and Burt. "Uh—besides bringing your gifts—I need money from my trust to hold me until my boss returns."

"He's having money problems?"

"Not really." White lie. "He's talking to potential partners in Holland. We may be shooting a multi-million dollar film there next year." Kate made herself sound cheerier than she felt about Dom's Dutch prospects. She'd noticed he'd packed other scripts in his suitcase as well as *Flying Eagles*, scripts cheaper and easier to shoot.

"The checkbook is locked in the desk," Aunt Maureen said.

"Burt has the key. I'll have him drop off a check to you. He's in the City every day."

Oh, no. She didn't want him to drop in unannounced, nosing around her apartment.

Whenever the two came to visit, Kate hid the sketch Gilly did of her. It looked too much like a lover's sketch.

The front door opened. Uncle Burt stamped in, wiping his feet on the entryway mat. "Well, well, look who's here!"

Maureen popped up from her chair and stood, almost at attention.

"Hi, Uncle Burt." What did he do to his hair? He'd arranged it in waves, using some kind of jell. That and his red face made him look like a used car dealer. Kate's stomach tensed. He always gave her a hard time, asking her about her love life with a leer. When she'd mentioned names of boyfriends in the past, he'd smiled as if he knew she was pretending. "Concern I have about homosexuals is a concern I have with all addictions," he'd told her pompously after being called down to college with Aunt Maureen. Today, he nodded pleasantly and hung his coat in the front closet. He walked into the dining room, glancing down at the remaining bites of pie on the plate in front of Maureen. "I don't think you need those extra calories," he chided.

Maureen blushed and pushed the plate away. She held up the military watch. "For you from Kate."

He examined the watch and flashed Kate a quick smile. "Thanks." He picked up the Stalin doll, examined it, then glanced at Kate, an eyebrow raised.

"Can you believe the Russian authorities allow this?" Maureen said, eager to start a conversation.

Burt put the nesting doll back together, one leader inside the other.

Why won't he ask me about my trip? Kate wondered. *Acknowledge I have a life?*

"Isn't someone from your firm going to Leningrad, Burt? Or someplace in Russia?" Maureen persisted. "Or maybe he's gone already?"

Burt frowned and shook his head.

"I thought I heard you talking on the phone . . ."

Burt stared at her, mouth tight. Abruptly he turned to Kate. "Staying for dinner?"

"I'm just popping in—"

"She needs money," Maureen broke in.

Burt's eyebrows shot up. "Lose your job?"

"Unpaid vacation. Dom's on a money-raising expedition to finance our new film." She smiled brightly. "A year from now I may be living in Amsterdam."

"A free and easy city." He made a face. Aunt Maureen frowned. With Burt, Maureen had turned into a different woman.

"If you need a job, honey, Burt has contacts. He's on the boards of three investment firms, a bank. You could get her something in the Wall Street area, couldn't you? Such an interesting part of the City."

Burt nodded slowly. "She'd have to wear a skirt." He looked her over. "Most companies have a dress code."

He was talking about her in the third person, like she wasn't there. "I need a check," Kate said, her mouth tight, hoping her face wasn't growing red from rage. "To see me through the month." Money for food, for Taekwondo lessons, for her guerrilla video class at Downtown TV. Extra to rent the editing room.

"There's always the temps," Burt said.

She didn't want to do the temps. With less work for Dom she could concentrate on her video project.

Burt made a ceremony of searching his pockets, drawing out a batch of keys, and selecting one. Kate followed him into the living room, watching as he unlocked the desk, an old-fashioned roll-top. He brought out the checkbook. "What do you need?"

Kate doubled the figure she was thinking of because she didn't want to have to come begging again next month if Dom was still beating the bushes for investors.

She tried to look over Burt's shoulder to see a balance. He

quickly tore out a check, closed up the checkbook, signed with a flourish, and handed the check to her, asking her to keep a record of her expenses—as if the money were his not hers. She struggled to be pleasant, "How are my investments doing?" She hadn't had an accounting in over a year. She'd been so caught up with Gilly. It always involved a face-to-face with Burt and he always put off the meeting—like he was guarding the U.S. Treasury.

Burt ignored her question.

Kate persisted. "Can you give me an idea how much is in my trust?"

He frowned, indicating his briefcase lying on the couch. "I'm getting ready for a business trip out of town."

"So?" She couldn't wait until she was in charge of her money—October, only nine months away! Just thinking about it gave her a wild sense of freedom. She might invest in *Flying Eagles,* if the Dutch got on board. And there was her video project to put together and polish.

"The financial files are in my office. I'll give you a print-out next month."

She took a deep breath, wanting to insist, How about tomorrow? The words stuck in her throat. She must get it together as part of her new resolve to be daring, and ask Burt for extra, more than the monthly nut. Tell him she wanted it for a trip to Leningrad for the International Gay Rights Conference.

The phone rang. Maureen hurried into the living room to answer it. "For you, Burt. Your partner."

"Not my partner yet. I'm testing him."

Don't hold your breath, Kate would like to warn his semi-partner who probably spent every working moment, unctuously scrambling to curry favor.

"I'll take the call upstairs." Burt marched into the dining room and up the stairs.

Maureen called after him, "I'll start dinner." She gave Kate a quick hug. "Don't mind him, honey. He's been working too hard." She left for the kitchen.

The desk was still open. Kate flipped through the checkbook, hoping to find a balance. There was none, although each check written to her had been meticulously recorded. On top a pile of mail, she saw an envelope addressed to her in care of Burt. It had been opened, but was empty. The return address was a Los Angeles religious right wing organization. Why would this outfit be writing to her?

Kate continued to paw through the desk, found a newsletter and a flyer from the same right wing organization. She folded up the two sheets and slipped them into her jeans pocket. Underneath another stack of papers was what looked to be an insurance policy—with her name on it.

Maureen emerged from the kitchen. "Are you sure you can't stay for dinner?"

Kate shook her head. "What's this?" She held up the policy.

"A small burial policy. Your mom and dad took it out when you were born. You were pretty sickly your first six months. After they died, we kept it up, Dave and I."

Footsteps at the top of the stairway. Uncle Burt was coming. Kate showed Aunt Maureen the empty envelope from the right wing group. "And this?"

"Probably a fundraiser," she said apologetically. "Oh, it's addressed to you." She nervously glanced toward the dining room. Uncle Burt was heading toward them, a gloomy smile on his face. Maureen fled to the kitchen.

"Why is my name on this envelope?" Kate asked. She'd moved out of this house over three years ago.

Burt gave her a fierce grin. "We still get a few pieces of your mail." He whisked the envelope out of her hand, threw it in the desk, quickly closing and locking it.

"I'm not a member of that organization." They didn't respect women's rights or gay rights. But that was an incendiary subject around here. *Come on, Kate,* she chided herself, *where's that courage you were talking about?* It was easy to come down on Gilly for not having it. What about herself? It was time for her to step up to the plate. "I'd like to read the letter sent to me in that envelope. Those people are against everything I'm for, women's rights, gay rights."

"Come off your high horse," he sneered. "You think you're such an artist. An intellectual. Too good for the rest of us—"

"And you're cold, smug and pious, pretending to be so upright, treating everyone else with contempt." Did she really say that? When she was younger, she never had an answer.

Burt nodded several times, his face growing redder. "Living your life of perversity— You haven't been able to fool me. Or God."

Maureen came in from the kitchen, wringing her hands.

"Who made you the God police?" Kate was boiling inside.

"You can't misinterpret the Bible," Burt said solemnly. "It says 'Destructive behavior can't bring happiness.' "

"You call everything you don't understand perverse, destructive. And yes, you're right. I've never changed. I've had a gay lover for over a year. Gilly. She's wonderful. She's exciting and beautiful. We talk to each other. We plan our future together. No one orders the other about. It's a healthier relationship than you and Maureen have. I'm sorry, Aunt Maureen." Tears were running down Maureen's face. Kate gave her a hug. "You don't deserve this—"

Kate grabbed her coat from the closet. Before she went out the door, she said, "Aunt Maureen, will you make sure I get an accounting before the end of the month?"

Maureen stood up straight and nodded slowly without once looking at Burt.

A few blocks later, in front of the park, Kate stopped the car, trying to calm down. She was shaking. The fight had been just as hot as the fights she and Burt used to have when she was a teenager. What she said about Gilly being her lover might not be true now. But she'd stood up to Burt.

She was sorry she'd left Maureen alone with him, to deal with his anger. Why did Maureen marry Burt? He was a friend Dave knew from the bank, had been comforting to her during Dave's grueling illness. She was low then, needed someone and he made himself available. If only she'd been more mature, she could have said, "Wait, Aunt Maureen."

Kate put the papers she'd pinched from Burt's desk on the seat beside her. The letter from the right wing religious group, a thank you "for your generous donation," was a form letter, not addressed to anyone. She skimmed the page: "Your gift will help pay for TV ads and production of action kits and videos for legislators." This group was slickly professional."Send for our training tape on how to fight those forces pursuing an 'agenda of chaos.'" *Training tape? Oh, my god.*

Further down were more bulleted instructions: "Stop taxpayer funded abortions. Oppose the gay rights initiative. Stand up for traditional marriage."

On the flyer was a paragraph so ugly she had to stop reading or be sick. *This is the kind of oppression that makes people kill themselves,* she thought.

She started the car and pulled out into traffic. A few blocks later she merged into Route 3-E toward the New Jersey Turnpike. She'd always dismissed hate groups like this. Now she had a disturbing insight into their strategy. They used inflammatory words—"gay agenda,""not entitled to special treatment under the law,""evil nature of their acts"—that produced fanatics, giving them permission to kill. Hitler must have used this tactic to excuse the destruction of the Jews.

She looked at the gauge and realized she was speeding.

The domestic partnership bill in New York was having a hard time getting through the legislature. Burt's generous donation no doubt helped lobby against it.

Had the thank you letter or the flyer been in the empty envelope addressed to her? How did she get on this mailing list? Burt's sick joke?

What else was he up to? Uncle Dave, who'd worked for the trust department of a bank, had invested her money conservatively, and gave her a regular accounting every year starting when she was too young even to understand.

She was on Rt. 495-East on her way to the Lincoln Tunnel.

She couldn't wait to get back in the City and take a shower, wash off this sickening, sticky web that always trapped her when she went back "home."

She knew the rules of the trust. Burt must account to the court with regular expenditures; must invest all money not needed by the trustee in conservative investments: treasury bonds, and Certificates of Deposit. When Burt married Maureen, he took over management of the fund. She'd left it exactly as Dave wished. Burt said he could get better returns in the stock and bond markets.

Were 1989 and 1990 good investment years? She hadn't paid attention. Maybe Burt had lost money with his aggressive approach. Maybe that's why he'd been so cagey when she'd asked him, *How much?* She'd make sure the up-to-date financial report was delivered to her within the next two weeks.

She groaned aloud. Ahead of her was a traffic pile-up near the entrance to the Lincoln Tunnel.

GREGOR SQUINTED THROUGH THE windshield. It was growing dark. Damn her! He was fed up with being a servant boy. She'd been a handful. He'd like to teach her some respect. His boss would frown on that.

He dodged in and out of lanes, traveling as fast as the traffic on I-495 would allow. He didn't want to get stopped by the police. Something vital was left behind, according to her. If she hadn't shut up . . . Finally he'd given her a glass of wine, with a roofie. At last, she was silent. She'd looked like an angel, her blonde hair in ringlets around her face.

He braked, tires squealing as he narrowly missed another car. He'd been in too much of a rush. Now he was approaching the Queens Midtown Tunnel, in the crush of cars returning to the city. He must get back to her before she woke up and realized where she was—not in her bedroom but in the cellar panic room.

Start and stop, start and stop. Fifteen minutes later, adrenalin pumping, he exited the Tunnel, turned onto East Thirty-Seventh and headed south. On Thirteenth Street he turned the corner. He was in luck. A parking spot. The trip had taken over an hour.

🚕🚕🚕

AT LAST, KATE THOUGHT, ready to scream, she was out of the Lincoln Tunnel, driving down Ninth. She turned left onto her street, then right, heading down the ramp that led to the underground parking garage of her building, about to reach under the mat for the key to unlock it. The door yawned open as if someone had driven in just before her.

She coasted inside. No one was parking. No car still had its headlights on. Whoever left the door open could have driven in hours—or minutes ago. Just too lazy to get out and push the button to close it.

She put the automobile in *Park*, hopped out, and pressed the button on the right wall. The door rumbled down. She climbed back in and drove down the incline, her headlights cutting through the shadows.

The projects were just a few blocks away. Kids breezed in through doors left open, chose a car for a joyride, and hotwired it. They took Dom's once. It was found abandoned, fender dented and battery missing, on Twelfth Avenue by the Hudson River.

She nosed the car into Dom's personal parking space. She hated to drive in after dark. When headlights were snapped off, the place was spooky. Anyone could be hiding behind a vehicle, even inside one, ready to spring out—especially when the garage door had been left standing open. She climbed out of the car and locked it.

She hurried past the silent row of parked vehicles and through the unlocked exit into the basement of her building. She passed the laundry room. Vacant. She relaxed only when she was in the elevator, rising to the seventh floor,

Chapter Four

6:30 PM, Sunday, February 3

Kate dialed and let the phone ring fifteen times. Gilly's machine didn't pick up. She dialed again and let it ring, this time twenty times. This morning when she'd called—yes, she'd given in, even though it had been decided Gilly would call her when she was ready. This morning she'd heard a click as if someone picked up, then disconnected. The dial tone had droned, flat and hostile. Now no machine. Had Gilly turned it off and unplugged her phone?

Kate, a bad feeling in the pit of her stomach, lifted out Gilly's apartment keys from the ashtray on her desk, flung on her coat and ran out the door. Dom's car would be too difficult to maneuver in the one-way streets of the Village. As soon as the elevator stopped at the ground floor, she was out of it, flying by the doorman, arriving outside in time to flag down a cab.

GREGOR TOOK THE STAIRS two at a time up to the third floor. Breathing heavily, he unlocked both locks of Gilly's apartment and stepped inside, securing the apartment door behind him. He did an arc of the living room, searching surfaces and drawers. As he was about to check the bedroom, he heard footsteps pounding up the stairs, stopping outside the door. He switched off the overhead lights.

KATE CAUGHT HER BREATH on the third floor landing, winded by the five-block run from the gridlocked cab and, after that, the stairs. "Gilly, are you there?" Kate knocked. She fumbled with the key, had trouble pushing it in. "Gilly!" The key froze in the bottom lock. She jiggled it, managing to release the lock. Still the door wouldn't budge. Finally, she understood. She rammed the key in the top lock, flipped the bolt, and pushed open the door.

The place was dark and very cold. Was someone inside, waiting? She felt light-headed.

What if Gilly were on the floor, dead? What was wrong with her? She was going crazy. She brushed her hand along the wall, felt the switch and flipped on the ceiling light.

It was a shocking sight. The walls were bare, Gilly's beautiful paintings and sketches gone. No books were in the bookcase. Gilly's television set was missing. The couch, lamps, chairs and tables remained, mute and grim. Cold air poured in from the living room window, wide open.

To her right, the bedroom door was closed. Eyes shut, holding her breath, she pushed open the door and snapped on the overhead light. She opened her eyes in slow motion. If there was an awful sight, she'd see it through a veil of lashes. No body.

The bed was stripped. Steeling herself, she opened the closet. Gilly's lifeless form wasn't sprawled inside. The closet was bare, containing only bent wire hangers strung haphazardly across the bar. No shoes. Gilly had tons of shoes. No sign of a suitcase. The bedside phone was on the nightstand, unplugged. No answering machine.

She pulled out the dresser drawers. Empty. Gilly had disappeared, taking with her all that mattered. She must have been in quite a rush. Tomorrow a moving van would pick up the furniture.

Kate searched through the nightstand drawer and cabinet beside the bed. She found a wine-red sweater in the cabinet. She pressed it against her face and smelled Gilly's perfume. Behind the sweater, in the corner, was her contact lens case marked GILLY. She opened it. The contacts were inside. Something bad's happened, Kate thought. She's an artist. No way she'd leave her contacts behind. Right? But she did have a back-up pair of glasses.

Kate let the lens case fall back beside the sweater, remembering a scene from last summer that she'd tried to forget. She'd slept in this bed, next to Gilly, and woke up to find she was nowhere in the small apartment. Out the front window, she saw her under a streetlight, standing beside a long dark car, talking with someone inside. "Someone I used to date," she explained, when she returned. "He tapped at the door. I didn't want any trouble. I didn't want him to find you here." "To know you were sleeping with a woman?" Kate asked, hurt. Gilly protested, looking embarrassed, and climbed into bed, turning away. The next morning they both pretended it never happened.

Another thought returned, unbidden, that Gilly had been playing a game the whole time they'd been together.

GREGOR SHIVERED ON THE fire escape, then peeked into the living room. Jesus! Unbelievable. She was here. He flattened himself against the outside wall, then cautiously looked in once again. She'd disappeared. He stuck his head through the window and heard crying from the bedroom. Slowly he eased himself over the sill and into the room, nerves screaming. He tried to form a plan. In his coat pocket was the stun gun, still there from this morning's job. He tiptoed to the front door, closed it and gently flipped the locks in place.

When she called from the bedroom, "Gilly?" he stuffed himself into the front closet and pulled the door shut. He must be careful not to start something he couldn't finish.

"ARE YOU BACK?" KATE called, hopeful, returning to the living room, but there was no Gilly standing there, grinning, saying, "Hi, Saucy Wench. My stuff is packed. I'm moving in with you. Hope you didn't change your mind."

Kate searched the kitchen, almost as small as a closet. A few plates, cups, and glasses were in the cupboard, and an open box of cereal. The fridge held a lonely wedge of blue cheese.

Scattered, aimless, she examined the empty shelves of the bookcase, hoping to find a clue. *Help Me,* written in the dust? She rummaged through the desk. In a drawer, she found a fragment of a love note she'd mailed Gilly just before Christmas. So she'd kept it, but left it behind like trash. As Kate pocketed the scrap of paper, she felt a sudden sharp, stinging pain and grabbed at the back of her neck, her knees buckling.

GREGOR, FROZEN FOR A moment in disbelief, watched Kate crumple to the floor. He told himself to get a move on, now was no time to pat himself on the back. He rushed into the bedroom, searched until he found what he was looking for, and hurried back to Kate. She wasn't moving. He dragged her toward the open window, panting like a mad dog, his heart thudding.

The bottom lock on the door clicked, a key slid into the top lock. Someone else coming. Who in the hell . . . No time to heft her body up and over the sill. He ducked through the window and onto the fire escape. He pressed himself against the building and peered into the room. A portly man in coveralls—he wore no coat—stood over Kate's body.

KATE OPENED AN EYE to discover that she was lying on the floor, her cheek resting against the rug. She lifted her head—it hurt something fierce. Something blue came into focus under the bookcase. In slow motion, she reached for it, and held it close to her face. It was an earring, blue with two white doves, one of the pair that the fat drunk stole from her the night he left her in the cemetery to die. She rolled over on her back, nauseous. examining the earring once again to make sure it was for real, then pushed it into her jeans pocket. How did it get from Leningrad to Gilly's?

A movement to her right caused her to turn her head. Her eyes lit on a pair of shoes, traveled up trousered legs attached to an overhanging belly. A man bent down and placed an icy, wet cloth over her face. A handkerchief. Soaked with what? She pulled it off.

"You were out cold." His eyes were suspicious. She took his held-out hand, struggling to her feet as pain sliced through her head. "Who are you?" she asked, realizing he wore a one-piece work suit, a kind of uniform.

"The super. I came up just now to check the premises and found you on the floor."

Kate saw that the front door of the apartment was open. "I must have passed out. Jet lag." The last thing she remembered was that pain, like an electric shock, at the back of her neck.

"Are you the new tenant?" the man asked.

"I came to visit . . . my friend." Gilly was her friend still, wasn't she?

"Ms. McGillicuddy? The blonde?"

"Yes." He knew her, she wasn't a ghost, a figment of Kate's imagination. "I didn't know she was moving out. When did she leave? Where did she go?"

"She's not on the lease," he growled. "Someone new is coming."

"Not on the lease?" Temporary tenant, transitory lover—easy for Gilly to vanish any time she pleased.

He shrugged. "The company keeps this place for visitors and friends. How did you get in?" He looked toward the open window. "It's cold as hell in here." He walked over and closed it, snapping the latch. He shot her an appraising look.

Did he think she came up the fire escape and in through the window?

"Looks like she left and forgot to tell you," he grunted with a sour smile. Watching her carefully, he moved over to stand by the open door.

"Just a minute." Kate walked unsteadily into the bedroom. She looked in the cabinet of the nightstand. Both the sweater and the contact lens case were gone. "Did you take them?" she called.

"Take what?" he asked belligerently.

She returned to the living room. With each step, pains shot up her neck into her head. "Who rents this apartment? Who's the company named on the lease?"

He didn't answer. His eyes were flat and cold.

Was he really the super? What was on that wet handkerchief he put over her face? She walked through the open door onto the landing, sensing his eyes drilling into her back. She heard him call, "Hey, you got the keys? Give me back the apartment keys." She heard his footsteps behind her as she ran down the stairs, holding onto the banister for balance. She pushed through the front door, jogged around the corner, and waited in front of a lighted shop to be sure he wasn't following her.

She shuddered in the frigid air, her thoughts a mish mash, roiling in her brain. The earrings had been a special birthday gift from Gilly, designed by Gilly, inspired by lines from an Amy Lowell poem. The same lines Kate had sent Gilly in her Christmas note, left behind in Gilly's desk.

With trembling fingers, she pulled the earring from her pocket, an azure blue rectangle, with two white doves, wings spread, soaring upwards it seemed to her to the top of the sky. She slipped the earring back in her pocket and pulled out the scrap of paper from Gilly's desk, re-reading Amy Lowell's lines.

My special gift to you, my darling Kate, Gilly had said. *That's us. Two white birds, soaring above the waves, screaming for joy. You can wear the earrings in public, but it will be our delicious secret.* How could Gilly say that and be part of a plot to kill her? Kate hurried along the street, trying to arrange her thoughts in a straight line. Money was one motive for wanting someone dead. Kate had gone to a lawyer and made her will two weeks before she left for Leningrad, in case their airplane was shot out of the sky because of the Gulf War and the hatred against Americans. She'd left everything to Gilly—including her soon-to-be-released trust fund. Gilly wouldn't need it. In fact, she'd told Kate, her eyes filling, "I don't want it to come to me because you died. Leave it to charity—if you don't want your Uncle Burt to have it."

Gilly's parents were rich. Kate had visited their mansion on Long Island last fall.

Uncle Burt wasn't rich, but not poor either. He and Maureen didn't know she'd made a will. Without it, everything would go to them, her guardians, if she died. Aunt Maureen had been a true friend of her mom. Aunt Maureen had made a home for Kate. Uncle Burt—well, he was definitely not a nurturing type.

Here she was, Kate realized, already at Eighth Avenue, on the way uptown.

GREGOR WATCHED HER FROM his car as she turned west at Fourteenth. He drove up several blocks, turned left and left again, heading down Ninth. He saw her figure in the distance, moving toward him. It was a cold, dismal Sunday night in February. Not a soul in sight. He parked by a construction site, reached in the glove compartment for the black balaclava and slipped it over his head. He would take her to the marina, carry her in the dinghy to the middle of the Hudson River and dump the body. If she was found, it would not be until Spring. By then, the flesh would be eaten off her bones. He caught a glimpse of himself in the rear view mirror. Only his eyes showed. He narrowed them to slits, pleased with the effect. He popped the trunk lid, then hurried into the street behind the car, pretending to search inside the trunk. As she walked by, he ambushed her, grabbing her from behind with one arm in a chokehold. At the same time he raised the stun gun.

WHEN KATE FELT THE arm clamp against her windpipe, her knees started to jump. She told herself not to panic, to take it step by step, the way she learned in class. She turned her head, to maneuver her throat into the crook of his elbow, so if he tightened his hold, she could breathe. At the same time, she flung an arm up behind her, clawing at his face. It was covered by a mask. She felt for the eyes. With the other hand she grabbed the arm coiled around her neck. She turned toward him, leaning down to loosen his grip. As she jerked her head free, something clattered to the ground. She jumped away, facing him, fists ready. His body was bulky. He wore no overcoat, just a sweater and pants. Only his eyes, wide with astonishment, showed in the mask.

She snapped her foot out, thrusting her hip into the kick, giving a yell, "Hye," as the ball of her foot landed in his middle. When he bent down, groaning, she caught him in the face with another kick. She whirled around and ran, screaming, "Help, help!" at the top of her lungs.

Four blocks later, she zoomed into her apartment building, passing the doorman, who did a double take. She rocketed up the seven flights of stairs to her apartment. Shaking all over, she unlocked the door, slamming it shut, double locking it and fastening the chain. To the right of the narrow mirror glued to the back of the door, she put a tray table, loaded with silverware, and a folding chair, piled with heavy books.

She poured herself a glass of wine, gulping it down while standing in the kitchen. She needed someone to talk to. Dom was unreachable. Masha. It was 6:30 AM in Leningrad. She'd wait. Thank god, her hurt leg was back to full strength. Thank god, for yesterday's make up Taekwondo class. She'd finally perfected the roundhouse kick.

She turned on the ceiling light and moved her practice bag, her sparring partner, out of the front closet. It was heavy, free standing, on a pole, the base filled with sand to keep it from tipping over. After warm-ups, she practiced kicks and hand and elbow jabs, watching her form in the mirror, yelling "Hye" from her abdomen where the *chi* was—not too loud. She didn't want to disturb her neighbors. An hour later she was wringing wet.

She took a shower, then grabbed a soda from the fridge, a yellow tablet, and a pen from her desk. She collapsed in the beanbag chair and wrote non-stop, pressing the pen so hard against the paper that the point sometimes tore through. The writing was jagged, furious, like the scorching energy she felt inside. Finally, she had a list, a Sequence of Events, starting with her abduction to the cemetery in Leningrad last Sunday, eight days ago.

Someone—who?—was still after her. Did he want to hurt Gilly too? Or was Gilly part of the plan . . . She couldn't finish the thought. It tore her apart.

▼₼▼

GREGOR SWERVED OFF THE Interstate, speeding along the county road until he reached the house. He turned into a driveway, tires screeching, and lurched to a stop. His balls still throbbed from the kick that *suka* had landed. He hoped no one had seen the fight, and taken his license plate number. He glanced in the rear-view mirror. A tiny scratch seeped near his right eye. Under his nose was a gob of dried blood. He spit on his handkerchief and cleaned his wounds. He exited the car and unlocked the front door of the house. Silence inside. He picked the flashlight off the table, snapped it on, unlatched the cellar door, and trudged downstairs. He pulled a chain. A lone bulb lit. She was just as he had left her, serene-looking as a baby, not a blonde hair out of place. He lifted her from the couch and carried her upstairs, placing her carefully on the bed. He ran his hands over her body. He'd like to fuck her. His boss wouldn't know. Neither would she. His balls ached; he hurt all over. He took two aspirin with a glass of vodka. Tomorrow would be a long day. He lay down in the twin bed opposite.

He woke up two hours later, panicked, sweating. He'd battled the traffic, driven back into the City to collect what had been left behind in the rush to move out her belongings. A big mistake. Now he'd tipped his hand and that bitch would have her guard up. He'd have to rethink everything.

•.•.•

ANDRE LEFT THE MARIANNA Restaurant, crossing the wide, dark street behind his new friend, Boris. The thundering metro overhead hurt his ears. The clatter followed as he and Boris turned into a roadway that led to a grid of narrow footpaths. He was in America, in Little Odessa by the Sea, with the help of Boris and many others. He should be jumping for joy, but he was exhausted and his feet were full of blisters.

They passed bungalows half-hidden by tall shrubs or fences. Dogs barked. Boris approached a fence with a BEWARE OF DOG sign on it, opened a padlock, and pushed through a door into a narrow yard. In front of them were cement steps into a cottage. Lights burned inside. Boris unlocked the door of an attached building to the right. A garage? No, it was a small room, without windows, neatly furnished with a couch, a wardrobe, two chairs, a table, and a narrow bench that held a hotplate, a bowl, two glasses, and a bottle of vodka. Boris pulled a chamber pot from under the table, then led Andre outside, showing him a path to the outhouse.

Andre had spent much of the money he had stolen from the burned-out hotel. Air fare, false papers, bribes, three months' rent to Boris, this friend of a friend of a friend of the *dejurnaya* at the Hotel Leningrad, for this room behind a high fence in a place where everyone valued privacy. Where his neighbors would keep to themselves, answering, if questioned. *"Ya nechevo ne znayu"* ("I don't know anything").

Each step of the way he had been sure he would be caught and punished. "What is the name of my job?" he asked Boris when they were inside once again. "You're a bus boy and dishwasher," Boris answered. "You start tomorrow at 5:00 PM."

Boris had introduced him to the restaurant manager, who hired foreigners like himself.

"I see a telephone. Is it mine?"

Boris nodded. "It is in the name of the man who occupies the main house."

"I am looking for this person." He showed Boris a paper. "Can you find?" Boris looked through a phone book, and wrote down a number.

Luck was following him. "I will give you a bonus," Andre said, "if you can get me a used television and two vcr's. Also black hair dye." He wiped two fingers over his greasy hair and showed him. "Boot polish. I could use a warm winter coat. Used is okay."

Boris smiled and nodded. He poured them each a glass of vodka from the bottle on the bench. The two men toasted. Boris instructed him how to use the phone. Then he gave Andre the keys to his new barracks.

After Boris left, Andre took off his shoes and socks. He'd been on the run for forty-eight hours, his feet crammed into shoes that did not fit. In Leningrad, he had paid for phony papers with his new name Dimitri, and flushed them down the toilet on the plane. He had arrived at Kennedy with no documents and asked for political asylum. The authorities had been obliged by law to give him a work permit. An appointment for a hearing was made for June, four months from now. He could disappear in plain sight with the help of the unofficial "mayor" of this neighborhood.

He dialed the number on the paper, taking pleasure in an old Russian proverb. "Revenge is the sweetest form of passion." The phone rang for a long time with no answer.

He emptied his pockets, putting everything on the table. How long would his money last?

He straightened out the bills. A small square of cardboard fell out. He stared at it, glassy-eyed. He picked up the phone and dialed again.

KATE WOKE UP—THE PHONE was ringing, the pad and pen still in her hands. She staggered out of the beanbag chair stunned she'd been able to sleep after being almost stuffed into the trunk of a car. "Hello." She waited, nerves on fire, hoping it was Gilly. "Who's there?" She heard breathing at the other end before the line disconnected. She added a second folding chair filled with books to the barricade at her apartment door.

What did it mean, one blue earring under the bookcase at Gilly's place? A struggle?

On the yellow pad she added under *Gilly's Disappearance,* Found at her apartment: one earring, fragment of note I sent her with two lines of an Amy Lowell poem. Found, but later appropriated: her red sweater, her contact lenses. Gilly would never, never leave her contacts behind, Kate decided. She wore them when she wanted to be glamorous. She didn't like to wear her glasses, a conclusive argument that Gilly had been taken by surprise, against her will.

Masha was wise, could be objective. She might have an insight into why the plot against Kate had leaped across an ocean. Even if Masha had no clue, Kate wanted to hear her friend's voice, know how she and her son were doing, how Nadya was bearing up, how Olga and her father were. She wanted to be sure that no one in Leningrad had been arrested because of her.

It was now one in the morning, 9:00 AM in Leningrad, Kate dialed Masha, but there was no answer. Kate couldn't turn off her mind. Maybe Gilly had made an identical pair of blue earrings to match Kate's, for herself. Who was the new tenant in Gilly's apartment—the scar-faced Captain Iurkov, the soldier Andre? Had one or both followed her from Leningrad and targeted Gilly too?

Chapter Five

10:00 AM, Monday, February 4

Kate felt afraid, as if she were the last person on earth. Or was she on the moon? The light was pale and cold. It was coming through the window, she realized, into her living room. The sun had risen and was peeking through the drapes, making patterns on the floor, the wall, her bed. She sat up, her heart hammering, and hurried to the front door. Her barricade of silverware and books remained.

She must contact Gilly's parents, but every molecule of her body resisted. She'd met them for the first, and last, time in September at a back yard barbecue in their Long Island home. Gilly wanted everything to be just right. She'd bought Kate a pair of silver pumps and a black designer dress with a deep V neckline, patch pockets and epaulettes. "Hot lady filmmaker," Gilly said when she saw her in it. Gilly was beautiful in her white blouse and sleek plaid skirt, her blonde hair hanging to her shoulders. "Sultry Eastern preppie," Kate teased. They looked good together, like they fit, both on a high from marching in the Gay Pride Parade. Gilly planned to introduce Kate to her parents as her lover, but as the day wore on, Kate could see Gilly had lost her nerve. It was easier to march in the Pride Parade than to come out to family.

Kate opened the Manhattan phone book. Gilly's parents owned a second home in the city, on the Upper West Side, but she found no listing. She did find an office downtown, McGillicuddy & Partners. She called, saying she was a family friend, and was told by the secretary, "Mr. McGillicuddy is out of town." Kate asked, "Do you have a number for his wife or daughter?"

"His wife is away too, in Paris; I believe her daughter is to join her there."

Kate hung up the phone, a lead weight on her chest. Gilly was going to Paris. She hadn't been dragged, kicking and screaming, from her apartment. She'd talked many times about visiting the galleries, studying art in Paris.

In her tortured brain, Kate saw scenes clearly, as if she'd filmed them. Every look from Gilly had a hidden motive, every remark a double meaning. Their first meeting at the comedy club—women's night—a set-up. Gilly marching beside Kate in the Gay Pride Parade, a charade. Introducing Kate to her parents—designed to be a humiliating flop.

As she took her shower, she realized she was seeing conspiracies everywhere, thanks to her week in Russia. Stay logical, she told herself.

Not long after the awful barbecue at Gilly's parents . . . that was when Gilly started to seem preoccupied, and by January had dismissed Kate flatly when she asked her to move in. If Gilly planned to disappear, a convenient time would be while Kate was overseas. No messy break-up scenes that way.

She had to admit she half-expected Gilly to split because she'd decided their life together was too difficult a life to lead.

Kate stepped out of the shower, dried off, and dressed. The best thing that ever happened to her was meeting Gilly. If Gilly were in trouble . . . From her desk, Kate picked up and read the Sequence of Events she'd scribbled last night. It sounded off the wall. The cops were not going to believe her.

She made a copy at the drugstore up the street. Back at her apartment, she sorted through her clothes, changing into her black dress with the V neckline. It wouldn't hurt to show a little flesh. She chose her silver shoes, not exactly suitable but the only heels she owned.

Kate walked the six blocks from her apartment, arriving at the Tenth Precinct in twelve minutes. "I'd like to speak to a detective," Kate said to a woman in a white shirt, blonde and plump, seated behind a desk that blocked access to the interior. The woman nodded, her eyes neutral. How many nutcases walk in here weekly? Kate wondered. "Someone tried to force me into his car last night on Ninth between Eighteenth and Nineteenth."

The woman winced in sympathy and dialed the phone.

"Someone here to report attempted assault." She gave Kate a brief smile. "Detective Benitez. Left, up the stairs, turn right."

Kate squeezed through the narrow space between the table and the wall and climbed the stairs, passing through a cramped entry area with worn chairs on either side. She stopped outside an open door. A latched low wooden gate barred her entrance. Within the room were several desks, all but two empty. "Detective Benitez?" she called. Neither man responded for a few seconds, then the one seated nearest, rose. He was tall and slim and wore a white shirt and dark blue vest. He unfastened the wooden gate and opened it, his eyes dropping to her silver shoes. He smiled to himself as if the shoes had caught his fancy.

"I'm Kate Hennessey. I live in this precinct." She followed him, sitting where he indicated, in front of his desk in a straight-backed wooden chair. He was young, with a chiseled face. Light coffee-colored skin stretched over high cheekbones. His blue-gray eyes flashed like gems. Even standing still, his thin hips seemed to swagger.

He quirked an eyebrow.

She'd memorized her opening lines so she wouldn't babble. "Someone is after me. It started in Leningrad nine days ago—"

He broke in, his voice brisk, with a hint of skepticism. "Leningrad? In Russia?"

She nodded. "We were invited to a documentary film festival. What happened there has followed me back to New York City. Last night I couldn't reach my girlfriend Gilly on the phone—"

"Girlfriend?" His eyes looked right through her.

"Yes." Should she tell him that Gilly's her lover? Better be careful. That information could be used against her. "She's an artist friend who does set dressing and designs ads for our film company occasionally." True enough—they'd often discussed collaborating. "I went down to her apartment in the Village." She told him about finding Gilly's art work stripped from the walls, her belongings missing. "Only the furniture was left—"

"The Village." His voice was bored, impatient. "That would be the Sixth Precinct."

He was going to slough her off. She sat up straighter. "I'm filing a report with you because when I walked home from her place, at Ninth and Eighteenth—your jurisdiction—a masked man tried to force me into the trunk of his car." His brows raised. She had his attention.

He flipped open a narrow notebook and raised his pen over it. "You didn't by any chance get a license plate?"

She shook her head, deflated. "I was too busy fighting for my life."

"Could you ID the car?"

"Black, maybe dark blue." She sighed a dismal sigh. "I don't know cars—" If Gilly were here, she could probably rattle off the make and model.

"The man—was he white, black?"

"He wore gloves, a mask." She realized now she had seen flesh around his eyes through the eyeholes. "White, I'm almost sure."

"Height, weight?"

"Taller than me. Bulky build."

He made some marks in his notebook.

"It started in Leningrad with an attempted abduction. Now—last night—somebody tried to abduct me here. I wrote down a Sequence of Events." She held her copy toward him. "If you'd like to look." Her voice trailed off. A muscle twitched on his cheek as he reached for the pages in her hand.

He read, looking up at her from time to time, his face inscrutable.

She went through the list in her mind.

1. Sunday, outside Masha's flat on the edge of Leningrad: After leaving an illegal meeting, my new friend Sveta told me she feared for her life. We were picked up by the cab driver Kolya and abducted to the cemetery. I escaped to the Olgino Motel. Sveta was later found dead in the cemetery pond.

2. Tuesday, the Palace of Pavlovsk–A convoy truck filled with soldiers tried to run me down.

3. Every day, at the Hotel Leningrad–Andre, a red-haired soldier tailed me and even broke into my hotel room as I slept—to steal my videotape. Only later did I figure out why. I'd caught two people at a table in the bar who shouldn't have been seen together: scar-faced KGB Captain Victor Iurkov, and a man in civilian clothes, possibly KGB.

4. Wednesday, after leaving Pushkin Square–I was ambushed by Kolya, the cab driver, who tried to cut my throat, but Andre, the soldier, intervened.

The detective rose, the pages in his hand, and walked over to a four-drawer file. Supporting his elbow on it, he looked down at her in her chair. "So this," his eyes returned to the Sequence of Events, "soldier who was following you saved your life?"

"I'm not sure. Maybe he wanted to kill me himself. A British couple came along. Before the soldier ran away, he stole two videotapes from me."

"And that same night," he frowned and scratched his head, "your room at the Hotel Leningrad was destroyed by fire?"

"Yes. My boss Dom and I had to move into the Olgino. Captain Iurkov found us. We had to escape . . ." She gave a short laugh. ". . . would you believe it, in a Father Christmas sleigh?"

"I'm not sure." He sat again behind his desk, leaning forward in his chair.

"The sleigh took us to the train which got us to the metro. We made it to the airport, but had to bribe our way out of the country." What was he writing in his narrow notebook? Words or doodles?

"Did you report any of this to Soviet police?"

She wouldn't mention that the police wanted to question her about Sveta's murder. Detective Benitez might call them. Could she be extradited back to Leningrad? Sweat broke out on her upper lip.

"Did you file charges in Leningrad?" the detective asked sternly, his hand under his chin, waiting for her to answer

She hoped he didn't take this personally. "We were advised not to. The police there were—are—corrupt."

He rolled his eyes, then glanced down again at the paper in front of him, appearing to re-read it.

Why didn't he say anything? "I know it sounds crazy. I have proof." When he looked up, she explained, "The abduction, referred to in Point Number One—I taped it on my recorder."

His mouth opened in surprise.

"I can bring the tape in. You'll hear Sveta's voice. She told me she was afraid she would be killed. And she was."

He frowned as he looked over the written chronicle and finally handed the pages back to Kate, chewing on his lower lip.

"The Leningrad newspaper—" she held up the clipping. "The story of my death in the hotel fire." He took it. "My picture. And under it *mertvyi*. Dead."

He glanced from the clipping to Kate and back, before returning it. He thrummed his pen against his desk. "Is your girlfriend Russian?"

Kate shook her head.

"Have you talked with her about this?"

"I haven't been able to reach her." A tear rolled down her cheek. She brushed it off. Before she looked away, she saw a shard of kindness in his eyes. She wouldn't tell him about finding the one blue earring under Gilly's bookcase. If he knew it was stolen from her in Leningrad, he'd ask how it ended up in New York City in Gilly's apartment. And Kate didn't know the answer. She didn't want to get Gilly in trouble, even if she had betrayed her. "Her dad's secretary says she's in Paris. Or soon will be." Kate blurted out, "She never would have left her contact lenses behind. I saw them in her nightstand; then I passed out or something; it felt like a bee sting. When I woke up, someone, the super maybe, was standing over me. Her contacts were missing."

He sat up straighter. "Bee sting?"

"On the back of my neck."

In an instant he was beside her. "Can I take a look?"

She nodded.

He pushed aside her hair. "Two red marks. Stun gun."

Oh god.

He returned to his chair. He gave her a funny look, as if he thought she and Gilly might have been playing around. "Want to file a complaint? Assault in girlfriend's apartment?"

"Against the super? He tried to revive me, I think. Or maybe he wasn't the super. Maybe he'd been hiding in the apartment all along. He could have been the man in the black mask who mugged me on the street."

He wrote in his notebook. "Did you get his name—this super?"

She shook her head.

"Did he witness anything?"

"I didn't ask. I just wanted to get out of there."

"Do you think there's a connection between the attempt on Ninth Avenue and whoever used the stun gun on you in the apartment?"

"Yes."

He nodded slowly. "I know someone in the Village precinct, the Sixth. We work the same chart. I'll see what he can find out."

Kate jotted down Gilly's name and address on an index card and handed it to the detective. "It's a company apartment. Gilly wasn't on the lease."

Detective Benitez leaned back in his chair. He was about to hand her the Sequence of Events, then asked, "Okay for me to keep?"

She felt weak with relief. "Yes. My boss is out of town. I have no family in the City. I wanted to leave a record in case," she drew in a long breath, "you know, something happens to me."

He nodded gravely. "Write down your name, address and phone number." After she'd done it, he smiled. His teeth were white, like in a toothpaste ad. He gave her his business card. "If you think of something more, anything, even if you doubt it's important, call. I'll ask my boss if I can work with you."

"Thank you." She impulsively grabbed his hand and squeezed, then stumbled out of the room, trying not to limp. Her feet were killing her.

GILLY OPENED HER EYES. The room was filled with shadows and dappled light filtered through the skeletal trees outside the window. She had a sensation similar to being under water or in a forest. Comforting.

It took her a few moments to realize where she was. In her own room, in her own bed, sunlight collecting on her blanket in a tantalizing design. She traced it with her fingers. She played with the sunlight and the blanket, arranging the folds into new shapes.

The last she remembered was accepting a glass of wine before dinner, and now it was daylight. Why was she still in her clothes?

The twin bed opposite hers was a rumpled mess. He'd been sleeping beside her, perhaps watching her as she slept. She didn't like that one bit. She rose from the bed, tiptoed toward the door, slowly turned the knob and pulled. The door squeaked open. His bulky form suddenly appeared. "Time to get ready," he said.

KATE HOBBLED WEST TOWARD her apartment complex. With each step, new blisters erupted on her feet. As she passed the driveway to the building's underground garage, a fluffy white Persian cat strolled through the open garage door. "Mickey, how did you get here? It's dangerous." She scooped him up and carried him, squirming, into the building and up the elevator to the fourteenth floor.

She rang the bell of Dom's neighbor Sheila, and when the door opened, handed over the fat cat. "Mickey was in the garage."

Sheila's round face showed horror. "He was on the terrace. I never had my apartment door open today." She glanced toward Dom's place, thinking, Kate was sure, that Mickey had sauntered into Dom's living room from the terrace, out his open front door into the hall, onto the elevator and into the basement. "Dom's away," Kate said.

Sheila scratched the cat's ears. "Mickey, you're a magician." He leaped from her arms and disappeared. "Thanks, Kate. I shudder to think what could have happened. You look terrific. All dressed up," Sheila smiled before she closed her door.

Kate, suspicious, twisted Dom's doorknob. As she guessed, unlocked. He'd locked it Sunday when the two of them left for the airport. She hadn't been back since.

She opened the door softly, stuck her head in and heard noises from the living room. Was Dom back from Holland? She took off her heels—exquisite relief—and walked quietly down the hall. To her left, the terrace door was open. To her right, Steve, his curls bouncing, was scrabbling through one of Dom's desk drawers.

"Steve?"

He looked up guiltily. "I stopped by to pick up more Titan Films brochures. Hey, you look hot!"

Kate let her heels fall to the floor. "Brochures are in a box in his bedroom closet."

"Thanks. I'm on my way tomorrow to the Channel Islands."

He was wearing tight jeans—she'd never seen him wear jeans—and a form-fitting gold shirt that showed love handles. He disappeared into the bedroom.

"So you heard from Dom?" She needed to know how to reach Dom.

He grunted something that sounded like no.

"I thought Dom asked you to wait on the trip to the Channel Islands until he gave you the go ahead—until he was sure the partnership was jelling with the Dutch." No answer. Typical Steve. "I'm picking up his phone messages," she called.

On the way to the answering machine on the desk, Kate spied Steve's briefcase, unlatched, leaning against the bookcase opposite. She heard him go into the bathroom and close the door. She pushed Play on Dom's machine. A male voice blared out, receding into background noise as she knelt and opened the briefcase. Inside were two thick brown envelopes. She pulled a videotape from one. On the jacket were still pictures. The young man who played the swan in the satirical fashion show at Leningrad's House of Cinema, naked except for his swan tail, leaned over a dark-haired beautiful woman lying on a bed. She'd played Beriya, Stalin's right hand man. Kate was surprised by how quickly Steve had packaged a slick-looking videotape from the raw footage he shot in Leningrad.

In the upper left corner were Tanya and Irina, nude from the waist up, in a clinch. He was using poor, dead Tanya in this way! It took all her control not to walk into the bathroom and confront him. At the bottom of the jacket was printed *Neva Black Silk Productions. Was it a DBA,* she wondered, *or had he incorporated to sell these sleazy tapes?*

She dropped the video back into the envelope and hurriedly opened the second one. It was stuffed with a fat stack of bills. Thousands of dollars in one hundred dollar bills. Across the envelope was scrawled, Captain Victor Iurkov. My god, how did Steve know that creep? And why was he giving him money—lots of it? No address on the envelope. Again, she wondered if Captain Iurkov were in Leningrad or New York City?

The toilet flushed. She jumped. She slid the envelope of money into the case and was about to close the flap when she spotted what looked like an airline ticket and pulled it out: JFK, first class, no less, to Leningrad. Well, well. Was Steve hand delivering the cash and the porn to Captain Iurkov? From Leningrad he was booked on a flight to the Channel Islands. What was this? Way down at the bottom of the briefcase? A bottle of Head and Shoulders Shampoo.

The bathroom door opened. The machine had finished playing messages minutes ago. She let the ticket and shampoo fall back into the case and closed the flap. It made a noise. She quickly moved to the desk. Steve entered the living room. She grabbed up one of Dom's yellow sheets of paper with his notes to himself, pretending to look it over.

Steve glanced from her to the briefcase. His eyes narrowed.

His face flushed. If looks could kill, she thought. "Can I get you anything?" she asked, hoping her face didn't show her anger at how he was deceiving Dom—and her. Steve snatched up his case and carried it into the bedroom. She heard him rooting through Dom's closet.

She pushed Play again on the answering machine and this time wrote down the messages. First was a writer asking how to submit a film script. Next was the bank reporting Titan Films was in the red to the tune of $500. She'd transfer from Dom's personal account—she hoped he had money in it—to cover the overdraft. The School of Visual Arts left an invitation for Dom to do a guest lecture for a cinema class. He'd like that. Last was a goodie from a former backer. "Hey, Dom, I received the treatment and budget for *City Women*. Send me the screenplay." Interesting. The script was in Dom's pile of assets, gathering dust with the others. Was Dom offering it to former investors as a back-up if the World War II film fell through? It sure would be a lot less money to shoot.

When Steve came out of the bedroom, he carried a fistful of brochures and his briefcase. Kate felt him staring a hole in her, but ignored him. She lifted two checkbooks out of the desk drawer he'd been searching through when she'd burst into the apartment. She sat at Dom's desk, making sure that the checks he'd signed in advance were still there. They were—not that she dare write any, except to clear up the overdraft. She looked over the stubs, relieved to find Dom had paid the rent on his and her apartments.

Kate waited until Steve left. She locked Dom's apartment behind her and went down the back stairs to her place—still in her stocking feet, changed out of her dress clothes into a warm-up suit and running shoes. She returned to Dom's and walked out onto the terrace. A wind was kicking up off the Hudson. The sunset was beautiful. She did warm-ups and practiced Taekwondo moves, letting her yells rise up like thunder from her diaphragm where the *chi* was.

Kate knew Dom didn't care about Steve's porn, but the

money earmarked for Captain Iurkov could just as well be coming to Titan Films as an investment in whatever their next film would be. She assumed Titan was paying for Steve's first class plane ticket to the Channel Islands, with a stopover in Leningrad. At a time when the bank account was overdrawn and Dom couldn't afford her weekly salary.

When Steve first invested with them, she wondered if he'd signed partnership papers and had been given shares in Titan Films. A corporation could hold shares of another company. Would that make Dom liable for what Steve did in the name of Neva Black Silk Productions?

An hour later, Kate was back on the streets in comfortable clothes. It was almost 8:00 PM. She took the subway, aware at all times of the people around her, arriving at the Soho gallery on Broadway where Gilly worked part-time. Lights burned inside. She'd never been here. When she tried the door, it opened. She entered the large space, white, with high ceilings. In the main room stood a rough-hewn wooden pillar, connecting above to a thick wooden beam that split the ceiling. Like a cathedral. Colorful, imaginative artistic works in a variety of styles hung on the walls at intervals.

Wouldn't it be wonderful to see Gilly's paintings here one day?

To her left, a sleek young woman, her hair immaculately groomed, exited a small open office and headed her way.

Kate smiled. Her upper lip stuck to her teeth. Nerves. "I'm looking for Gilly? Angelica McGillicuddy?" She prayed this woman knew something useful and would share.

"Angelica's not in. May I help you?"

Kate hesitated. Everything—the woman, the surroundings—seemed so perfect and controlled. She didn't want to jeopardize Gilly's job by saying, "She's missing." That might seem irresponsible of Gilly. Or that she was Gilly's lover, and worried. More than the woman would want to know.

"Are you here about a piece of art you're interested in? She'll be away a couple of weeks, at least, I understand."

What a relief! Kate thought. *She's okay.* But still, away two weeks—at least. No good-bye? And why did she move everything out of her apartment? "Right, right." Kate managed a smile. "She told me she was going to Paris. I didn't realize she'd left."

The woman warmed up. "Out of the blue, she said, came a chance to tour Paris galleries with her mother. She sounded so excited."

Excited, not under duress. Kate struggled to be pleasant. "A lucky break." The woman seemed friendly. How much more could she ask? The question was out of her mouth before she could stop herself. "Did she leave you a forwarding address or phone? I just found out she's moved."

The woman shook her head, frowning, her eyes growing troubled.

One too many questions. "Thanks, anyway. I'll check with her dad." Fat chance. Kate gave her a half wave and went out the door.

A dead-end, except—Kate's shoulders slumped—the Paris trip had been confirmed as real, by Gilly herself. After she returned, she'd be living someplace else, someplace where Kate wouldn't be able to find her.

It was still early. Restaurants and stores were open, the sidewalks filled with people. Kate walked up Broadway to Houston, turned left onto Bleecker, and left again, watchful, checking for cars that might be following. Finally, she stood in front of Gilly's former apartment building. She raised her eyes to the third floor. No lights glowed in the front windows. The new tenant, if there was one, wasn't home. She watched the building for several minutes. No one entered. She tried Gilly's key in the front door. Eureka! It worked. She hurried up the stairs and listened outside Gilly's apartment. No sounds from within. She knocked loudly, then tried her key in the lower lock. *Please, please let this work.* She wanted to see if someone else's clothes were hanging in Gilly's closet. The key wouldn't turn. She tried the top lock. No luck. The locks had been changed. *I'll be back again,* she vowed. As soon as a light burned in the window, she'd be on the third floor landing knocking at the door.

Kate was hungry and tired. She ducked into a hole-in-the-wall, and ordered a hot dog and drink. She'd call Detective Benitez tomorrow and tell him about the pile of cash in Steve's briefcase in an envelope marked for Captain Iurkov, the very man who'd turned the Olgino upside down searching for her and Dom. She hadn't even mentioned Steve to Benitez. That would be a long, convoluted story. She'd also tell the detective that Gilly had notified her art gallery job she'd be vacationing in Paris.

She sent a silent message, *Gilly, send me a post card so I'll know you're okay.*

When Kate returned to her apartment, she tried to read, but found herself staring at the page, then at the wall. Finally, moving like robot, she opened the sofa bed, changed to her sleeping clothes and lay down, drained, feeling as if she had no bones, no blood, was paper thin and might just float away with the slightest breeze.

GILLY RIPPED THE PAPER to bits and threw the pieces in his face. Clutching her purse, she scrambled out of the car and ran. "Get back here," he shouted. She stumbled down one row of vehicles and up another. It was confusing, like being in a maze. Her high heels made it hard to run on the concrete. She mustn't twist an ankle or she'd be done for.

Just when she thought she'd lost him, headlights loomed up behind her. She slipped into the middle of a line of autos, darted into the next row and the next. She must search for the fence, circle the lot, find the exit. She turned left, breathing hard, running out of steam. She slowed her pace, felt for doors that opened. Several cars later, she stopped, backtracked, tried once more the handle on a van. She couldn't believe her luck, unlocked.

She jumped inside, crouching on the floor, her eyes riveted to the windows above and the darkness outside. A few moments later, lights appeared, growing brighter until they flooded the car. He'd seen her get in. She took off a shoe, the heel like a spike. The vehicle passed—in slow motion, it seemed—beams dimming, then disappearing. It could be another driver, looking for a parking space. She'd wait and see. Every ten minutes headlights seemed to swoop around, washing over the ceiling of the car. *Him,* she decided. *He's relentless.*

Chapter Six

12:15 AM, Tuesday, February 5

Kate stirred. Was that a click, the lock on the front door turning? She sat up in her sofa bed, heard a banging like many cymbals being slammed together. The tray of silverware had crashed to the floor. She leaped out of bed. She saw a wedge of light from the hall, with someone standing in it. Oh my god, the door was open.

They had a key. They'd come for her. The chain was holding fast, thank god! "I'm calling the cops," she yelled. She'd have to protect herself until the police arrived. She must keep cool, marshal her energy. *Remember,* she said to herself, *the leg is the longest weapon you have.*

"Kate!" a ragged voice croaked. "I'm sorry."

Was she dreaming? "Gilly, is that you?" Her voice was barely recognizable, as if she'd been through a terrible ordeal.

Kate ran to the door. Through the crack, Gilly's blonde hair gleamed in the dim hall light, a beautiful vision, but it was real. She unlatched the chain.

Gilly stumbled inside. "I didn't know where else to go." She was in high heels as if she'd been to a party. Under her black coat, she wore a white turtleneck and burnt orange skirt. Over the sweater was a belted cinnamon-colored vest. She looked sleek and chic—except for her hair. Usually pulled back, with stray blonde curls popping out, it now hung tangled to her shoulders.

Kate's eyes locked into hers. She felt the same thrill as that night they'd first met at the Comedy Club. She studied Gilly's face. No marks.

"I know you don't want to see me."

"What do you mean?" Kate wailed. "I've been looking all over for you."

Gilly shook her purse. "I have no money, no plastic. A taxi is waiting downstairs." Her face screwed up. "Oh, Kate." Tears rolled down her cheeks. Her mascara was running.

"Are you hurt?"

Gilly shook her head. "I have to pay the driver."

Kate grabbed a tissue from the bathroom, handing it to Gilly, who took off her glasses and wiped her eyes. She was in her glamorous attire but wearing her glasses, not contacts.

Gilly, trembling, held Kate's arm as they descended in the elevator. "I escaped at JFK," she said. "Otherwise, I'd be in Utah now."

"Escaped? Utah?" What happened to Paris? Kate was about to ask, but they had reached the ground floor and were on their way to the entrance. The night doorman, concern on his face, opened the door. Kate had a sudden panic attack. What if this was a ruse? She asked, "George, can you step outside and keep an eye on us?"

As Kate and Gilly hurried down the walkway, Kate's eyes searched nearby shrubs to see if anyone lurked. The cab was across the street to her right, headlights burning. Someone might be hiding in it. She didn't want to believe it of Gilly. She had to take a chance. When she reached the driver, she held up some bills and signaled him to roll down his window. She looked inside. No one crouched on the floor.

Kate handed the cabbie the fare plus a twenty dollar tip. His face lit up. "Thank you. Good luck, young lovers," he said before he drove off. "How did he know?" Kate asked.

"I told him my money's gone." Gilly turned to Kate, a question in her eyes. "I have to get to my lover." Kate took her hand and squeezed it, sure of only one thing. It felt so right to have Gilly here beside her.

•••

GREGOR GRIMLY WATCHED INSIDE his car beyond the cab as the two women, deep in conversation, leaned into each other. His balls were still tender from the kick that bitch had landed last night. He was drenched in sweat, tired of pussyfooting to keep in his boss's good graces. He opened the glove compartment, reaching for the black mask. He'd like nothing more than to swoop down on the pair, and take them both. He had the stun gun, the thorazine.

Steady, he told himself. He was so close but so far. The doorman—that *dolboeb*—was outside the building, watching.

Hand-in-hand, the two crossed the street. They disappeared inside the apartment building.

He was about to pull away from the curb when a passing car slowed and turned right a few yards away, coasting down a ramp, its headlights burning against a white façade.

A parking garage was attached to the apartment building. That information hadn't been in the report. He inched closer, saw a man push his hand through his open car window and insert a key into an outside lock. The garage door opened; the man drove in.

The door didn't close. Gregor quickly reversed into the space left by the cab, hurried out of his car and across the street. He ducked under the open garage door, expecting it at any moment to come crashing down. Made it inside!!

He hid behind the nearest parked car. Where the devil did that driver go? In a space to Gregor's right, the man's headlights were burning but he didn't seem to be inside his vehicle. Suddenly his head popped up. He must have been searching for something on the floor of the car. The headlights snapped off. The man climbed out of his auto, a shopping bag in hand. He walked to the entrance and pushed a button on the right wall; the garage door rumbled down.

Gregor watched him walk toward the back of the enclosure and disappear through an exit. He waited ten minutes, then followed. Would he need a key? He turned the knob. Open Sesame! He walked through the door into the basement of the apartment building. How easy was that! The laundry room to his right was vacant. It was after midnight. Further down the hall were two elevators and behind them, a service elevator, which he took it to seven, stepping out in front of the trash disposal chute. He made a left through the entrance to the hallway, where he drifted, door to door, until he found the apartment. Both were now in the same place. That would make things easier. And harder. Next time, he'd not be so nice to either one.

He left the building the way he entered, through the basement, pushing the button to raise the garage door. He was eager for a night's sleep in his own bed.

※※※

KATE POURED WINE, HANDING a glass to Gilly, who stood frozen by the entrance to the kitchen. "Thanks." Gilly gave a tentative smile. She stepped out of her high heels, took a deep swallow of her drink, staring into space.

"Gilly, talk to me," Kate said.

Her eyes were anxious and confused.

Kate told herself to stay strong, not let emotions rule. She needed the full story and nothing but the truth.

Gilly twisted strands of her hair around her fingers.

"I thought you were going to Paris."

She gave a worn out sigh. "He told me at the airport."

"Who?" Kate broke in.

"Randall."

Randall? She'd never heard of him. "Who's he?"

"He works at my dad's company." She sighed again.

Kate added water to the coffeemaker and spooned coffee into the basket, telling herself not to be misled by soft looks and sighs

"Randall pretended I was going to meet my mom in Paris for a tour of museums," Gilly said haltingly, her voice bitter. "After he parked in the airport lot, I had bad vibes. I asked him what was going on. He looked funny. He handed me a letter from my dad, who said he was sorry, but he had to save me from my immoral and unstructured life." Gilly glared, her face a mixture of hurt and anger. "I was to go—not to Paris—but to a clinic in Utah, a psychiatric place where they convert you . . ." Her voice was thick with emotion.

"Convert you?"

"You know, from gay to straight. Randall was going with me," her eyes grew steely, "to make sure I arrived."

Kate was stunned. Psychiatric clinic for the Cure. Just like in Leningrad. "How could they do that?" she asked. "You're over eighteen."

"My dad wanted me to check myself in voluntarily. I can't understand—how did he guess?" Gilly asked.

"Maybe when we were at the house for the barbecue," Kate mumbled, leading the way into the living room, knowing full well how he knew. She should have told Gilly at the time.

The open sofa bed took up half the room. She put her wine on the coffee table, then she closed up the bed, and put the pillows on the couch. Gilly looked so desolate, Kate wanted to hug her. "I know how close you are to your dad. To have him trick you this way, it's hard to wrap my mind around it. I didn't know such places existed in the U.S."

"Me either." Gilly's face was worried, so earnest. "Randall showed up early Sunday—yesterday—saying I needed to vacate my apartment right away. I thought it was strange, but Dad telephoned. He was leaving for overseas. An important client was coming to town, he said, and they needed my place." She took a gulp of wine. "All very rush, rush. Randall helped me pack my belongings. The furniture stayed. It belongs to the company."

"So Randall is your dad's flunky?" Kate burst out.

"Maybe," Gilly said slowly, "you could say that."

"Your dad's company has the lease?"

Gilly nodded. "They keep a few places around the city. Dad was the one who suggested, 'Go to Paris. Have a nice trip with your mom until a new apartment opens up.'" Tears welled in her eyes.

"Bait and switch." Kate could believe Gilly's father was that sneaky. "Terrible things ran through my mind," she said. "Your art, your clothes, everything of yours was gone."

"You came down to find me," Gilly murmured. "Thanks."

"When your answering machine didn't pick up—" *I was scared to death,* she almost said. She sat down on the sofa, pulling the coffee table closer. Gilly sank down beside her. Kate was very aware of Gilly's shoulder touching hers. She was also aware of the one blue earring with the white doves sitting in an ashtray on the coffee table. She'd wait for Gilly to see it, and let her explain how it arrived in New York from Leningrad.

Gilly took a swallow of wine, and then another. "In the letter, my dad wrote, 'I've always given you everything you want. Now I want you to do something for me. Go to the clinic, get help, and return to the daughter we've always known and loved. Give us news we can share with friends. I want only the best for you.'" Her voice broke and her eyes overflowed with tears. "He said I was being influenced by outside sources, and if I didn't try to fit in, he'd cut me out of his life."

Kate wanted to take her in her arms. "Oh, Gilly, I'm sorry." She patted her shoulder instead.

Gilly cried a little bit more, then wiped away the tears with her hand. "I asked Randall, 'My mother, does she approve?' 'She's in France. She'll be as pleased as your father. And as I will,' he said, smiling, as if he'd caught a rare butterfly." She turned to Kate with stricken eyes. "I went out with him a few times, mostly before I met you."

So Randall was more than a flunky. "You're undecided between Randall and me?" Kate asked with a sinking heart.

Gilly grimaced. "I've known him since I was little. He used to haul me around in the company car before I had my own. He'd take me out on the boat sometimes. Dating-wise, we didn't click. He's older—"

"He came by last summer. I saw you through the window standing by his car."

She removed her glasses and ran a hand through her hair. "Oh, Kate, it's been awful—worse the last few months, with my father pressuring me to get married and have a family. He's thinking of making Randall a partner. He got it in his head we two would be a perfect fit. Randall's tapioca, but there's something creepy under his blandness." She put her face in her hands. "My life was all mapped out. I didn't intend to fall in love with you."

Kate left for the kitchen. She wanted to lie down with Gilly, hold her tight, and tell her all the awful thoughts she'd had—at the empty apartment, the precinct, the art gallery. Worrying that Gilly was in danger, that Gilly had left her, even that Gilly had been part of the plot to murder her. Kate brought in the coffee carafe and two cups and put them on the coffee table. She poured them each a cup. She sat across from Gilly in a straight-backed chair. "So Randall and you were at the airport, he gave you your dad's letter . . ."

"I felt ambushed, hurt, angry. I jumped out of his car and ran. I found an unlocked van and hid on the floor. I could see headlights on the ceiling as he drove through the lot looking for me. Every time I thought he'd given up, the headlights came around again. It was a nightmare. I took my shoe off, ready to slug him if he tried to drag me out. When I was sure he'd gone, I left the van. My wallet was missing from my purse. No money or charge cards. I searched for a cab that would bring me to you. I didn't know where else to go." She rubbed her forehead.

"You were going to Paris—or so you thought," Kate said

softly, "and you didn't say good-bye."

"You made it clear everything was over." Gilly's eyes blazed. "You called me a coward. You told me to go back to my boring, safe life on Long Island." Her mouth shook. "You returned my gift, the blue earrings with the white doves."

Kate felt very still. "What do you mean? The earrings were stolen from me in Leningrad. I need to know how they ended up with you."

Gilly appeared surprised, shaken. "Randall, when he came by Sunday morning, handed me an envelope. The earrings were inside. No note. Randall said he found them lying outside my apartment door. The earrings were us," she said intensely. "Two white birds. I thought it was a rotten way for you to break off with me."

If the earrings meant so much, Kate wondered, why did Gilly leave one behind? Kate stood and picked it out of the ashtray on the coffee table. "I found this under your bookcase."

Relief filled Gilly's face. "Everything was such a rush. I didn't know it was missing until we arrived at my parents' home." She opened her purse and offered Kate the other earring.. "Now you have the pair."

Their fingers brushed. An electric charge shot up Kate's arm. She placed both earrings in the ashtray. "You believed Randall, that I'd really say good-bye in such a spineless way?"

Gilly threw up her hands. "I thought you'd given up on me. I thought, what the hell! I'll go to Paris. If Kate doesn't want me, I'll get over her. I'll come back to the City and look for a full-time job in an art gallery. And take my time to decide how I want my life to be." She finished her wine, took a drink of coffee. She asked, her eyes troubled, "The earrings—you say they were stolen?"

Kate hesitated just a moment, then threw caution to the winds. "By a fat drunk who took me to a cemetery and left me there to die." She walked back and forth, pouring out everything that happened to her in Leningrad, ending with the masked man assaulting her four blocks from her apartment. "I made a record of the attacks. I gave a copy to Detective Benitez. I have his business card." She took her original Sequence of Events from her desk and handed it to Gilly, who removed her glasses, reading, frowning, murmuring, "Oh, Kate, my dear Kate. How awful."

After she finished, she came to Kate. The two stood inches apart. Her arms reached out, then fell to her side. "I almost lost you. I was too damn stubborn to phone, so hurt by what you said. And—" Gilly sucked in her breath and held Kate with her eyes.

Green near the pupil, rimmed by a circle of blue. Sexy eyes, Kate thought. *Nearsighted eyes.*

"—I wasn't sure I could take the stress. My father is pushing me to marry and have a family. Instead, I'm living a secret life. Not able to talk about the one I love at work, at home. Or share my joy, always censoring." Gilly waved her hands in a helpless gesture. "You must feel it too."

"I do." Kate touched her cheek, then broke away, and refilled their cups.

"That nightmare in Leningrad? Why—?" Gilly asked.

Kate drank most of her coffee before she spoke. "The country is falling apart. I thought at first the kidnapping to the cemetery might have been a random crime because I'm a woman, a 'rich' American, freer than Russian women." She enumerated on her fingers. "Then too I attended an illegal meeting at Masha's. I'd taped the wrong footage—an officer in uniform—with my video camera. I thought the bad things would stop after Andre stole my tapes. But it became worse: the hotel fire; the newspaper report that I died in the fire." Kate showed Gilly the clipping from the Leningrad newspaper. "*Mertvyi* means dead."

"How did they get that photo of you?"

"During a Russian Orthodox service, one of the festival's cultural programs." Kate felt jagged from the coffee. Her brain was spinning, the synapses crackling. "Nadya asked me how it is to be gay in America. My hotel room could have been bugged. On the videotape, after Nadya did her interview, I talked about that awful time in college. It was one of the tapes Andre stole from me. Maybe he handed it over to authorities. I talked with the gay women at the Café Soul and heard their stories."

Gilly, looking confused, glanced down at the list.

"Sveta told me she was *rozovaya,* pink, in love with Nadya. She was afraid for her life. I let her down. I didn't go back into the trees and look for her." Kate realized she was jabbering, but couldn't stop. "Kolya must have killed her. We both wore white scarves. He thought she was me. I should be dead, not Sveta."

Gilly seemed dazed, overwhelmed by the detail. Still Kate babbled on. "Now—a masked man has tried to grab me off the streets of New York City. Did everything begin here, follow me to Leningrad, return here with me and now is waiting . . . Tell me more about your dad's flunky, Randall."

Gilly sank down on the couch, lowering the Sequence of Events to the coffee table. "He's more than that. He's important in my dad's company. He speaks many languages, helpful in contract negotiations. After he and I cleared out my apartment, he took me to the house on Long Island. My dad called again, out there, in case I was growing skeptical, I suppose. Mom was already in Paris. It was just Randall and me. I was upset—all the rush, confusion, the earrings that I'd given you suddenly back at my door, with no note from you . . . He was consoling. He gave me a couple of drinks to calm me down. I was out like a light, woke up the next morning in my bed, in my clothes. I realized he'd been sleeping in the twin bed opposite—in case I tried to run away, I suppose." Gilly shuddered, shook her head.

"Did he make a move on you?"

"He wouldn't dare. My dad—" She stopped. "Before tonight I'd have said, my dad wouldn't stand for that."

"Was Randall in Leningrad last week?"

She said uncertainly, "He travels for the company."

"Did you see him while I was gone?"

Gilly frowned. "No. You think it's all tied together? That Randall pretended to find the earrings outside my door? That he's . . ." She shook her head slowly. "I can't believe it."

"He wore a mask, the man who tried to force me into his

car. I may have scratched him around the eyes. I kicked him in the groin. Was Randall the worse for wear this morning?"

"I didn't notice scratches. He was quieter than usual. Maybe because of a guilty conscience at what he was about to do, ship me off to Utah."

"There's also the so-called super." Kate told her about his appearance, not being sure if he played a role. "I found your contacts in your nightstand. I was afraid you'd been taken by force. I passed out while I was searching the living room for clues. When I woke up, this man in coveralls was putting a wet cloth on my face."

"Chloroform?"

Kate shrugged. "When I checked the nightstand again, the contacts were gone. Someone took them while I was unconscious. Detective Benitez told me I was hit by a stun gun." She lifted up her hair to show Gilly the marks on her neck.

Gilly stood. "Does it hurt?" She lightly brushed the spot.

Her touch was like fire and ice. "It felt like a bee sting." She mustn't dissolve. "Did you ask Randall to come back to the apartment for the contacts? Did he give them to you?" That would mean Randall was in the apartment at the same time she was.

Gilly shook her head. "He told me he didn't have time. I thought, dammit, I'll be in Paris, of all places. I'll have to be blind if I want to look glamorous."

"You're so vain," Kate said, her mouth quivering toward a smile.

Gilly burst out laughing. Kate joined in. Gilly reached out. Kate fell into her arms. "You feel so good. I thought I'd lost you."

"Me too, my darling Kate," Gilly said in a muffled voice.

"Hey, I have something." Kate broke away. From her dresser drawer she lifted out the lacquered pin she'd bought at Pushkin Square. "It's hand painted. On black papier mache."

"What exquisite detail." She held it tenderly. "The artist must have used a miniature brush and a magnifier."

It seemed even more beautiful, admiring it with Gilly. The white-bearded man standing in the sleigh, surrounded by clouds of snow, drove the hurtling horses, brown and white. Seated beside him was a wide-eyed young woman. "Grandfather Frost carrying the Snow Maiden," Kate said, "away from the bright rays of the sun which would melt her."

"Dear Kate, I promise not to melt." Gilly fastened the pin to her cinnamon-colored vest.

"And this." Kate handed her the khaki tassled cap. "When I saw it in Gostiny Dvor, I thought of you."

"It's a fez!" Gilly put it on her head and ran into the bathroom to look in the mirror. She came out smiling.

"You look like the mischievous genie summoned from Aladdin's Lamp." Kate took her hand and bowed. "I must set you free."

Gilly gave her a twisted smile, then sighed. It turned into a yawn. She clapped a hand over her mouth. "Sorry."

"We should get some sleep." Kate re-opened the sofa bed. She gave Gilly an extra toothbrush and a T-shirt to sleep in. After Gilly lay down, her eyes remained wide open, staring into space. Kate sat beside her, reading aloud from Perelman's collection, the piece they both loved about the restaurant in lawless Macao, where every dish served was a form of tapioca. Breast of tapioca. Tapioca under glass. Tapioca Randall? At last, Gilly's eyes were closed, her breathing regular, and she had a smile on her face.

Feeling like a traitor, Kate searched Gilly's purse. No contacts case with GILLY written on it. The super must have collected it while she was on the floor, out cold. If Randall had taken it, he surely would have given it to Gilly.

Maybe tapioca Randall did find the earrings outside Gilly's door. If so, who left them there? And why? Was it a warning? The cab driver Kolya had first taken her earrings at the cemetery. Who did he give them to? The soldier Andre? The scar-faced Captain Iurkov?

GREGOR JERKED AWAKE, UNCERTAIN for a moment where he was.

On Long Island? No, in his own bed in his apartment. The phone was ringing. After 2:00 AM. Who was calling at this hour?

A man's voice at the other end growled, "*Zdrasvuitya*, Gregor."

He sat up in bed, his heart thumping. He sometimes had nightmares of a gun between his shoulder blades; the grotesque, grinning face of Captain Victor Iurkov behind him.

The man continued in Russian. "I have something you want."

"Who are you?"

"I have videotape—"

"Tape?" Gregor asked.

"—that makes you a criminal, that shows you talking with the Captain."

Gregor sucked in his breath. "Where are you calling from?"

The man laughed softly. "America, the land of plenty. New York City."

"Who sent you?"

"Andre. I am Andre."

So the *mudak* slipped through the fingers of the KGB. "You're a fugitive."

"How bad you want video? I'm asking $20,000."

"$20,000?" Gregor struggled to collect his thoughts.

The two bargained for several minutes. When an amount was agreed on, Gregor said suddenly, "I can meet you in two hours." *4:30 AM*, he thought, *still dark*. "How about the marina?" He gave him the address on Manhattan's West Side. "We can have a private meeting—" It would be a very private, final meeting! "—on my cruiser." Not his, the company's. "If we finish our business to our mutual satisfaction, I have another job for you."

"You think I'm brainless?" Andre asked harshly. "Meet me at the Deli Marketplace, Brighton Beach Avenue. Second Floor. Tomorrow noon." Andre gave him a street number. "I will bring tape. You bring money in paper bag."

Gregor tasted bile. Who did this *svoloch* think he was, threatening him, a respectable, productive member of the community? It would be his word against that criminal's. "How will I recognize you?"

"I recognize you." Andre hung up the phone.

Gregor slowly lowered the receiver to its cradle. Brighton Beach, he knew it well, the Russian enclave in the southern part of Brooklyn. He made himself a drink, scotch in milk. He took several sips. The incriminating tape would mean nothing to U.S. authorities. It would not connect him to the botched attempt to force that dark-haired *suka* into his car on Ninth Avenue. On the other hand, if—no, when—he truly made her disappear, Andre and the video could be thorns in his side.

If his boss somehow got hold of the tape and realized Gregor had hired killers to get rid of that *suka* overseas . . . disaster.

Gregor decided to show up at the Deli tomorrow with a bag of money, less than they had agreed on. He would size him up. Once he had the tape, he would get rid of that gnat. He was an illegal. No one would care if he disappeared.

▼▲▼

ANDRE SLID OUT THE videotape from its jacket, taking a long look at the happy young woman pictured there. He inserted it into the VCR and pushed Play. He smiled when Kate appeared with a beautiful blonde—they were kissing. They must be sisters, he thought. He fast forwarded to Competition Hall at the Hotel Leningrad. The red curtains rose. A choir sang the Soviet National Anthem, "Nation of the working class, and my beautiful motherland." A tear came to his eye. He missed his country. He watched newsreel footage of Stalin, scenes from World War II. He listened to the president of the film festival press-centre speak about the recent Soviet troops in Lithuania, the shooting of the cameramen in Riga. The man continued, "People appreciate brave reporting from dangerous places, once again, artists take risks and once again everyone has to rethink what it means to create." Andre felt moved.

Next on the tape, beyond the man with the monkey, was

Captain Iurkov at a table in the bar talking with a man in a gray business suit, limp hair falling over his broad forehead.

I must not forget why I am here, Andre thought. *To avenge my beautiful sister, Tanya.*

Tomorrow he would catch the slimy rat Gregor in his snare. The *mudak* would soon know what hell was.

⁂

KATE OPENED HER EYES. It was still dark. Gilly was on her elbow, looking down at her. "What's happening to us, Kate?"

"Let's call Detective Benitez. Press charges of attempted kidnapping."

"Randall did it at my dad's request. I can't press charges against my dad."

"Your dad—" Kate debated whether to continue.

"What?" she asked, on the offensive

No one could speak against her father but Gilly. "At the barbecue, at your parents' place last September," Kate said haltingly, "you were so eager to introduce me. You bought me the designer dress so I'd make a good impression. Your dad was drinking. He took me into his study and asked me how much money I'd take to break off with you. A business pal of his had snapped a picture of us kissing in the Gay Pride Parade. Your dad showed me the photo, informed me he'd hired a private detective. Your dad knew about us before he met me."

Gilly buried her face in the pillow.

"I should have told you. I'm sorry." Kate added softly, "Do you think he or Randall will follow you here?"

"My dad is overseas. Randall—I can't believe he'd come to your apartment without my dad's say-so."

Kate rose up as if electrified and jumped off the bed. She'd become too relaxed since Gilly arrived. She once more barricaded the front door. When she returned to the living room, Gilly was sitting up. The light by the bed was on.

"Why now, Kate? Both of us under attack? It's weird. Like

we're both being stalked."

"We know who's after you. Your dad and Randall, because they want to make you into something you're not. I'm not sure who's after me, except it's someone who knows me and hates me. Or wants the money from my trust." Kate frowned. "Uncle Burt has no idea I made a will leaving everything to you. He behaves as if my trust fund is his when I ask for cash." She dropped into the bean bag chair.

Gilly left the bed, grabbing up a blanket, flopping down next to Kate, and spreading the coverlet over them. "You think he's skimming?"

"I asked him for an accounting—demanded it, in fact. I also found a life insurance policy on me in his desk. That he keeps locked."

"For how much?" Gilly asked, wide-eyed

"Aunt Maureen said it was a small burial policy my parents took out when I was born. For all I know, Burt could have rolled it over into something bigger, with him as beneficiary, worth lots of money if I died." She bit her lip. "Burt and I got in a terrible argument before I could ask. I slammed out the door." Kate jumped up from the chair and returned with a yellow pad and a pen. She sank down beside Gilly and headed the page List of Suspects. "Burt had propaganda from a religious right wing group that hates gays. It was addressed to me in care of him." She wrote on the pad. "Herbert Hensley, Uncle Burt," she said aloud. "And there's the new member of our Titan Films team, Steve." She told Gilly about finding the package of money, thousands, in Steve's briefcase addressed to scar-faced Captain Iurkov.

"Was it a payoff?" Gilly asked, her voice shaky. "To Iurkov for trying to kill you?"

"I'm not sure what Steve's motive would be." Kate shook her head uncertainly. "But he's flying to Leningrad in secret. He has a slickly packaged tape of porn with him. More likely he's going into business with the Captain. A joint enterprise. Masha explained it to me. It's part of Gorbachev's economic restructuring, to allow foreign investment." Still, Kate wondered, how did Steve and Iurkov ever find each other? And was Steve's Neva Black Silk Productions tied in some sly way to Dom's Titan Films? She wrote down Steve's name. "What do you know about the super in your building?"

"I've never seen him."

Kate's pen scratched against the paper. "Also we should find out who the new tenant is." Below Super, she jotted down New Tenant (Russian link?).

"If the new tenant is linked to Russia," Gilly said in a low voice, "that may implicate Randall and my dad, since the company has the lease."

Kate knew Gilly didn't want to hear it, but she had a sick feeling they could be involved.

Gilly pressed her lips together, her eyes blazing. "I'll find out from Dad's secretary where he is and call him."

With an apologetic look at Gilly, Kate added Randall and Gilly's father to the list of suspects. Gilly looked so hurt, Kate rushed to ease her pain. "We have to think outside the box," she urged, "consider anything and everything. This is a wild idea too. What if my parents' plane crash wasn't an accident? What if someone killed them and now wants to murder me?"

"But, Kate, your parents died when you were five—over twenty years ago," Gilly said uncertainly. "Did your Uncle Burt know your parents? Does he have business interests in Russia?"

"I know for sure he didn't have business interests in Russia twenty years ago," Kate said. "Neither did Uncle Dave or Aunt Maureen." Why had she said that about someone killing her parents? It was stupid. She knew why—to make Gilly feel better about her dad and Randall being on the Suspect List.

Kate suddenly sat up straight. "I brought Aunt Maureen and Uncle Burt a Gorby doll as a gift and that started a conversation about Russia. Aunt Maureen said she'd overheard Burt on the phone say someone from his office had gone to Leningrad or was going there. But Burt denied it." Burt was shorter, wirier than the man in the black mask who'd tried to pull her into his car. Burt's wanna-be partner—Kate wondered what he looked like. Did he have a big stomach like the "super" in Gilly's building? She wrote Burt's Partner? on the pad.

Gilly took Kate's hands. "Oh, Kate, it's overwhelming. It's coming to a terrible climax soon. I feel it. We mustn't let each other out of sight."

Chapter Seven

11:00 AM, Tuesday, February 5

Kate opened her eyes, a feeling of peace descending as she saw Gilly asleep beside her, her blonde hair a circle of light around her face. Kate eased out of bed. She took a shower, dressed, and made coffee. When she returned to the living room, the sofa bed was closed and Gilly, fuming, was behind the desk hanging up the phone. "His secretary says he's in Alaska."

"Your dad?"

Gilly nodded grimly. "I'm calling his hotel. Okay?"

"Sure." Kate, uneasy, handed coffee to Gilly, who took a gulp.

"I'll ask him why he didn't talk to me. I'll tell him," she gathered courage, "I may file charges." Gilly clenched her jaw and dialed. Her voice was shaking when she asked for her dad. Her face fell. "It's urgent. Ask him to call his daughter." She gave Kate a panicked look. Her eyes grew determined. "Tell him I'm at Kate's." After she hung up, she said, "I want him to know the mission failed."

Good, she was fighting back. Kate hoped Gilly would make an official complaint against her dad and Randall. The whole disgusting motive would come out, attempted kidnapping to Utah for conversion from gay to straight. Gilly's dad would justify it, saying he'd done it out of love, to rescue his only daughter from Kate, a dangerous influence. Was she dangerous enough for Gilly's dad to kill? "I booked an editing room at Downtown TV for today at one o'clock, to copy my Russian tapes to a master." Gilly looked tired, tense and worried. "Maybe I should cancel? I could play them for you on the VCR through the TV, but that would cause some dropout in the color."

"We're not going to stay inside and hide." Gilly bit her lip. "We're a team. You can punch and kick. I can yell." Her face lit up. "Oh, Kate, I can't wait to see your tapes."

Kate gave her a lingering hug, then pulled away. "We'd better hurry." She handed Gilly jeans, a belt and a sweater. "If you don't want to wear your dress-up clothes . . ."

Gilly headed for the bathroom. When Kate heard the shower turn on, she dialed the precinct. "Benitez's day off," a male voice said. "He'll be here tomorrow at 8:00 AM."

She left her name and number. She wanted to update him—so he'd have the picture as it was evolving. Gilly was safe, and had disturbing information. Steve, with his incriminating plane ticket to Leningrad and cash for Captain Iurkov, should be added to the Sequence of Events. Uncle Burt should be added too—the life insurance policy on her, his shiftiness about giving her a report on her trust, and—Had Burt's wannabe partner been in Leningrad the same time she was? All of what she had was scatter shot. She needed hard proof.

She collected her tapes, a legal pad and a pen and dumped everything into her duffel. "You're beautiful," she said when Gilly returned to the living room, her face scrubbed and glowing. The dark green sweater was perfect with Gilly's blonde hair and blue-green eyes. She'd rolled up the too-long borrowed jeans. Kate handed her socks and a pair of old running shoes.

Gilly stepped into them, tied the laces, and did a fashion model twirl showing off her makeshift outfit. "Perfect."

Kate lifted the earrings with the white doves from the ashtray and fastened them in her ears, where they belonged. With a wry smile, Gilly attached Kate's gift, the lacquered pin, to her sweater. "The ice maiden ventures forth."

The two hurried into their coats and out the door, which Kate double locked. With a look as if they were going into battle, Gilly grabbed Kate's hand. "I kept the key to my apartment; maybe on our way back home—"

Music to Kate's ears. Gilly thought of Kate's apartment as home.

"—we can sneak in. Try to find out who that new tenant is."

"The locks were changed. I tried last night before you arrived."

As they rode the bus downtown, Gilly, her glasses perched on her nose, sat up straight as a wire and Kate's eyes scoured the faces of passengers and new fares as they entered.

***

GREGOR CARRIED A PAPER bag with two packs of money: newspaper strips, cut to currency size, sandwiched between one hundred dollar bills. The day was sunny, more like spring than winter, Gregor thought, walking past a grinning old man who played the accordion outside the Deli Marketplace. Gregor opened the door and walked inside, thirty minutes early. In his coat pocket were his gun and silencer.

The market was packed, so noisy he doubted a gunshot could be heard. A good place for a kill. He played the images in his mind: Ram the gun in Andre's belly, grab the videotape, pull the trigger and flee.

Gregor made a sweep of the ground floor, passing counter after counter of dried whole fishes, smoked fish, meats, caviar, searching for a rear or side exit. He passed deli salads, potato pancakes, borscht and sour cabbage soup. He missed his mother's Russian cooking. A portly lady behind a counter asked if he would like to purchase puffs of fried dough, "filled with meat, egg, cherries, or cabbage." Gregor shook his head, his mouth watering.

He finished his exploration. No way out except the way he had entered. He climbed the stairs to the second floor. Wall-to-wall people browsed among the many tables filled with breads and desserts, among them his favorite jam-filled cookies. To his right, in front of the steam table, was a line of hungry customers passing by containers of pickled herring and onions, buckwheat kasha, pelmeni dumplings, and blintzes.

Something hard jammed against his spine. A voice said in Russian, "I have gun. Look straight ahead. Give me money."

▼▲▼

ANDRE KEPT A STEADY pressure on the folded razor pushed into Gregor's back. With his other hand, he snatched the brown paper sack that Gregor held. Andre smiled. Bargain hunters surrounded him. No one could see what he was doing. If he slit this murderer's throat, the mass of people would hold his bleeding body upright while Andre made his escape.

Andre shook open the paper bag and saw two thick packs of money. With only one hand free, he could not count the bills. If this tricky *dolboeb* had swindled him . . . Andre stuffed the bag into his coat pocket, resisting an urge to flip open his razor, slash through Gregor's clothes, and carve Tanya's initials into his flesh, leaving him with cuts that would bleed, break open and ooze, reminding him of Andre each time he moved. Too bad Gregor's screams might attract attention.

"Where's the tape?" Gregor hissed, twisting his head around.

"Eyes straight ahead," Andre grunted, shoving the handle of the razor hard into Gregor's spine. "Be nice. You get tape." Gregor stood still. Andre quickly reached around him and threw the tape in front of him. As it clattered to the floor, Andre stepped backwards and was swallowed up. Like quicksand, he thought, turning and shoving through the swirling mass of bodies toward the stairs.

GREGOR SCRAMBLED TO REACH the tape, now kicked along by many feet. His eyes glued to the floor, he bounced from person to person like a football linebacker; then he fell to his knees. He spotted the tape an arm's length away and snatched it. He stood, his eyes raking over the faces around him, flicking to the center of the milling throng, hoping to spot a desperate figure pushing through the bodies. He wanted to see what the two-timing, double-crossing, blackmailing *derrmo* looked like. Gregor threaded himself through the crowd and arrived at the stairway, peering over the handrail for someone in flight who might be Andre. He found no one but everyone. He then pressed on through the mob on the stairs to the ground floor and dashed outside, looking to his left, his right, and across the street. "Dammit, dammit." He paced in a circle, spitting out curses. Passers-by stared. He ducked his head, and took long strides until he reached the elevated train.

ANDRE SLID OUT FROM the shadows of a nearby store. He followed Gregor down the street and up the stairs to the metro. He waited near the tracks several feet away, his back to Gregor, counting the money inside the paper bag. The packs contained mostly paper. The cheating weasel had given him only $2,000 of the $5,000 agreed on. He would make him pay.

The oncoming train screeched to a stop. Andre entered behind Gregor and rode in the same car, using all his effort to stare ahead into nothing and keep his face a mask. The slimy *sovok* didn't recognize him. He exited forty-five minutes later with his quarry. Above ground, Andre asked a passer-by in English, pointing to the street sign, "Where?" "Wall Street," he was told. The heart and soul of America.

As Gregor entered a tall building, Andre was right behind, stepping into the elevator with him, smiling at his own cunning. The elevator stopped at the eleventh floor. Andre exited with Gregor, turning the opposite way. He pretended to read a sign, watching from the corner of his eye. Gregor pressed a buzzer beside a door. An answering buzz admitted him.

Andre waited a few seconds before he pressed the same bell and entered a reception area, ready to appear lost. The woman at the front desk was busy with someone else. Andre slipped by her in time to see Gregor turn down a corridor. He followed. He could kill him here.

Except he wanted to play with Gregor a while longer. He hoped to force more money out of him. The man was not to be trusted. *Maybe I will never have a chance like this again,* he thought, as Gregor disappeared into a room and closed the door.

GREGOR TURNED ON THE TV monitor inside the vacant board room. He wanted to make sure he'd received what he paid for. He pulled the tape from its envelope, ready to insert it into the video player. A note fell out, written in Russian: This is a copy. I have original. Meet me tomorrow same time and place with another $5,000. "So that's your game, you filthy snitch," Gregor grunted.

A noise behind him made him turn. Standing less than three feet away was a man with greasy black hair, piercing blue eyes—the whites bloodshot. He wore an overlarge topcoat. "Yes?" Gregor snapped. His eyes lit on the edges of a brown paper bag peeking from his coat pocket, opposite the pocket his hand was hidden in. He realized the man was Andre! Jesus! Was he going to shoot him?

The man's eyes smoldered. "You killed my sister Tanya, left her to burn to ashes."

Gregor edged toward his pistol in his coat, at the end of the table. The door behind Andre flew open. Sylvia, a thick-set woman in a light blue suit, stood in the doorway. "Mr. Bonham, the boss is on the line." She indicated the wall phone with its blinking button.

Andre, cursing, glared from her to him, as if deciding whether he could take them both. He spun around, slamming into Sylvia. She yelped. Gregor heard him running in the hall. "I'll see you're deported, you *dolboeb*," he shouted. "You'll be put to death. You won't escape."

Avoiding Sylvia's astonished eyes, Gregor lifted the receiver with dread and related his bad news: Gilly never made it to Utah.

His boss, the General, went into a harangue, "Fucking moron! You should have escorted her into the airport, given her the letter there, not in the parking lot. First you should have calmed her down with a drink, drugging her just enough so she'd be woozy but could still walk onto the plane. Better. Wait to give her the letter after the plane landed and she was on her way to the clinic." Five minutes later, Gregor, feeling like a punching bag, the dial tone buzzing in his ear, lowered the receiver.

"Self-important prick," Gregor muttered. "She would have understood very quickly she was going to Utah, not to France. The airport police would have been all over me." He kicked the wastebasket across the room. "Our names in the papers, how would you like that, *mudak*?" he yelled. Jesus he was losing it. The doorknob was turning. Sylvia was back in the room. "Everything okay?"

Gregor, with an effort, controlled himself. "You know how he is."

KATE, WITH GILLY BESIDE her, sat in the editing suite at Downtown TV. In front of them were two broadcast SVHS decks, each with a monitor. As the tape copied to the master, Kate logged in the start and stop times of each scene, thrilled to be taking this first full-size screen look at her guerrilla footage with Gilly by her side. "There were rumors of a military coup." Kate paused the tape. Alexei's sad smile filled up the frame.

"Our gallant, fearless tour guide." She pressed Start. Alexei intoned softly, "Nostradamus predicted a great upheaval for the USSR—to take place this year, in six months and twenty-four days." Gilly counted on her fingers, murmured, "August 1991?" She turned to Kate gravely. "He should be the opening shot for your video!"

"Yes," Kate said, with an enthusiastic grin. Next were the sellers hawking their political *matryoshkas* at Pushkin Square, pleading, "Please you, look you here, a real photo-realism." Kate pointed out the dealers in black market currency skulking nearby and the KGB cars enclosing the square. "Predators." Gilly shivered. "Vultures and hyenas waiting to gobble up everything in sight." She took off her glasses and rubbed her eyes, more green than blue now, red-rimmed with dark smudges underneath.

"How are you doing?" Kate asked. "Trying not to think too much." Gilly's fingers brushed Kate's cheek. "I like being here with you, getting my tour of Leningrad."

"Now we're at the glorious Palace of Pavlovsk of Catherine the Great," Kate said. Gilly murmured, "The white expanse . . . tall trees with snow-covered boughs . . . It's gorgeous, uplifting."

With bonus footage! Kate was ecstatic. In her zoom into the back of the convoy truck she'd caught Captain Iurkov, his scarred face, like a devil mask, in the midst of the drunken soldiers. She'd been right. It had been no accident, that truck almost running her down. Kate paused the tape. "That's him, Gilly, one of the bad guys who's after me." Now Benitez could take a look at Captain Victor Iurkov. Damn that Andre had stolen the videotape with the clearest view of him in the bar talking with the KGB man in the gray business suit. Forget it, Kate. Benitez would not be interested in the Russian bad guys, presumably still in Russia, unless they could be linked to someone in New York City.

"He's grotesque," Gilly shuddered.

"He can be my shock cut," Kate mused.

Gilly gave her a questioning look.

"A jarring, unexpected cut." Kate pulled the tapes, original and master, from the deck and inserted her second videotape, selecting another master from the nearby shelf. She wrote on her yellow pad, Documentary Panel of Filmmakers. The Soviet audience speaking about their hopes for the future would give Gilly a glimpse of the decent people of Leningrad, the intellectuals who believed their country would succeed in its journey toward democracy.

Kate stole peripheral glances at Gilly, who seemed transfixed, and gave a drawn-out sigh when the scene concluded. "After the panel ends, Kate—there's your shock cut to the scar-faced Captain."

"Brilliant," Kate said. The next segment was The Fire. The editing room fell away as firemen fought the blaze at the Hotel Leningrad, while evacuees milled about the parking lot. "See those fourth floor windows, with the glass popped out, rimmed in soot," Kate said, feeling as panicked as she had been then. "My room and Steve's." She felt Gilly touch her shoulder, and wanted to turn into her, hold her and be held. But she kept the tape moving, her eye on the monitor. A few moments later, Steve appeared plainly. She paused the tape and inched it forward. He wore his director's hat—arrogant and vain, in the gritty context of the fire. He stood at the far edge of the hotel lot beside a KGB car like those surrounding Pushkin Square. A man in uniform was beside him, his officer's hat tilted up at an angle . . .

"Oh, Gilly, this is proof for Benitez, the two of them together—Captain Victor Iurkov, palsy walsy with Steve. It won't be just my say-so about the money I found in Steve's briefcase addressed to Iurkov." She'd make a copy of this section for Detective B. How did Steve meet Iurkov? Of course. "The missing porn tapes. Andre must have stolen them from Steve's room when he was searching for my tape of the KGB man and Captain Iurkov in the bar. When Andre realized the tape he wanted wasn't in that batch, he passed the pornography on to the Captain, who then paid a visit to Steve." Kate grinned.

"Steve must have been terrified." Now his panic at Helsinki airport made sense. "I'm sure the money in Steve's briefcase is a payoff to Captain Iurkov to smooth the way for the 'business' to continue." Kate realized she was muttering out loud. Gilly was looking at her, dazed, quite pale.

They'd had nothing to eat all day—only coffee. Kate brought back sodas and peanut butter crackers from the lobby vending machines, which the two polished off in record time. "Shall we stop and come back another time?" Kate asked.

"Oh, no, your scenes—your *Messages from Leningrad*—are wonderful. Overwhelming. Charming. I want to absorb it all. It will give me a lens, I hope," Gilly added gravely, "to understand what's happening to us now."

"We're ending upbeat," Kate said softly, pushing Play. Olga's room appeared, with its beaded entryway. "You'll meet the women who saved our lives, mine and Dom's. Olga is in the blonde braids. Masha has the beautiful green eyes." The two stood beside the white horse, with its yoke of stained glass and dangling silver bells, hitched to a bright red sleigh. "Used by Grandfather Frost and the Snow Maiden during the Merry Russian Winter Festival."

Kate listened, enchanted once again by Olga, cheeks pink with cold, looking like a little girl as she related the fairy tale. "Grandfather Frost and his fairy granddaughter *Snegurochka* (Snow Maiden)—sing and dance with the children around the fir tree, and give them presents." Olga went on solemnly, "Grandfather Frost—we sometimes call him Father Frost—is both kind and evil, two characters in one." Olga patted the horse. "We call him *Ded Moroz*. In Russian mythology there was another *Moroz*, a creature with a long gray beard who ran around fields and caused biting frosts. He liked to freeze people just to entertain himself."

Kate glanced Gilly's way. She was thoughtful, touching the lacquered pin on her sweater with its miniature painting of Father Frost and the Snow Maiden. Was she thinking of her own father? Kate wondered. To Kate, he seemed two characters in one—a man who gave gifts and froze people just to entertain himself. But she didn't know him like Gilly did.

The tape finished with the dancing black bears, surrounded by the rapt and smiling vodka-drinking crowd. "Soon after," Kate said to Gilly, "I learned of poor Sveta's frozen body found in the cemetery pond."

Chapter Eight

6:30 PM, Tuesday, February 5

Gregor, from his car parked across the street, watched the two women enter the apartment building. First the damn bitches got away, now the blackmailing Russki *mudak* knew where he worked and lived, and his boss, that *khui*, had chewed him out. The dark-haired *suka* must disappear before his boss returned. Tonight, he told himself. He'd cleared out the tools from the trunk of his car. He carried a large suitcase on wheels in the back seat. This morning early he had gone to the marina, prepared the boat, alerted security not to be concerned if he arrived there in the middle of the night. Out of town visitors were expected early the following morning, he'd told them. Since the day was forecast to be sunny, he planned to give his guests a run down the Hudson if the water was not too choppy.

Andre would be next, dirty blackmailer. Colonel Alekseev at Moscow's KGB Headquarters had given him empty promises. Andre had not been killed, nor had Captain Iurkov, he suspected. Andre was here for more than money. He wanted revenge for Tanya's death.

Tomorrow, Gregor decided, he would meet Andre to pay his next installment. He would arrive very early, catch him on the street and kill him before he entered the Deli Marketplace. Just another mob hit in Brighton Beach.

After this work was done, he could return to himself. No, to a better self. *Gregor* was a persona who'd emerged in Leningrad. Who'd orchestrated a murder plot with KGB Colonel Alekseev. Who'd killed two people, set a hotel fire, and got away with it. If his boss only knew, Gregor's chest swelled with pride, that under his Wall Street suit and tie, he had become just the right partner, merciless, ready to take control of the firm.

❖❖❖

KATE WAVED AT THE doorman behind the front desk. "Something for you," he said, and handed her a package from under the counter. It contained no postage, no address, just a name—hers. She peeked inside the wrapping. It was a videotape in a *Revolution* box, with a black dot on the spine. "I don't believe it," she said in hushed tones. Elated but scared, she showed Gilly. "It's my tape, one of the stolen ones." She glanced at John. "Did you sign for it?"

John shook his head no.

So no messenger service brought it. "The man who delivered this—was his hair red?"

John shook his head. "Black, greasy."

Captain Victor Iurkov? A shiver slid down Kate's spine. "Scarred face?"

"White and smooth."

The two boys beside her on the Aeroflot plane—the moonies. She'd given them her business card. Did one have black hair, a white face? She couldn't remember.

Upstairs in the apartment, Kate pulled the video out of the jacket. A paper fell out, folded in triplicate. It seemed to be a catering menu of a restaurant, the Marianna. A printed note was attached, in English: "I have information to save your life," she read aloud to Gilly. "Come tonight after 5:00 PM. Marianna, Brighton Beach. I helped you in Leningrad. I am sorry I stole your videos. You are brave artist. Signed, A friend."

"Come tonight to Brighton Beach?" Gilly said. "He must be

joking."

Kate pushed the tape into her VCR. She took a deep breath. Playing it might degrade the color but she had to know if the tape was hers—and if so, which one it was of the two that were stolen. When the first shot appeared, the Hermitage across the Neva from the Leningrad Hotel, she shrieked, "My interview of Nadya. I thought it was lost forever, in someone's filthy hands, someone who'd hurt her. You have to see this now, Gilly." Kate fast forwarded through Sergei the festival scheduler's messy room, filled with papers and film cans; the dining room, with its vast array of food; the Molnia Cinema's crowded auditorium, the enthusiastic audience asking questions of Dom about *Revolution*.

She pressed the Pause button. "Here we are—in my hotel room, with Nadya and Masha. When Nadya told the police of Sveta's disappearance, she was taken to a back room and raped. Sveta's brother had already reported the two women as gay."

"Oh, Kate, how awful." Gilly sat abruptly on the couch.

Kate, too wired to sit, pushed Play. The cut on Nadya's cheek oozed blood and her eye was black. She sat up proudly, the red carnation that Kate had given her pulled through the buttonhole of her blouse. She introduced herself in English. "I am Nadya, I am seventeen." Her chin jutted out, her voice wavered. then became stronger and stronger. Masha translated gravely. "In Soviet Union, they call us hooligans or pinks. We are raped and beaten or sent away if we are pink, *rozavaya*, and do not follow orders. I have good friend, Sveta. It was miracle. She has made my life so happy. Sveta's parents have a man chosen for her to marry. We love each other. We do not want to be with anyone else."

The scene continued, through Nadya's fears of what might have happened to Sveta. As Kate listened, she glanced back at Gilly, saw the shock on her face, felt the same horror herself as when she'd first heard what gay women endured in the Soviet Union—the drugs, the electro-convulsive therapy in a psychiatric clinic, bullying by the KGB, and some women—unless they entered a traditional marriage—persuaded to take the change, with surgery and hormones, to become a man.

Gilly's eyes were filled with outrage and sorrow. Above her head, on the wall, was the sketch she'd made of Kate. *The two of us in one frame,* Kate thought with a rush. She could intercut Nadya's interview with footage of Gilly sitting under Kate's portrait.

The scene drew to its end with Nadya sobbing, "I am afraid Sveta may be dead. Her brother is very wild." She wiped her eyes. "Also my mother said . . ." She gave a shuddering sigh ". . . if I did not stop she would find a way to end it. Meaning, she would kill Sveta. Or send me to a mental institution."

Kate paused the tape. Gilly's eyes were riveted on the closeup of Nadya, her face filling the television screen.

"Oh, Kate, what a nightmare. How will she survive?" Gilly, pierced to the heart, rose from the couch on shaky legs. So much had happened in the past twenty-four hours—so much information for her bursting brain to process. She disappeared into the kitchen. "I'll make us tea." She filled the pot with water and turned on the burner.

"I only hope Nadya's not in a psychiatric clinic," she heard Kate say. Then Kate was beside her, sliding an arm around her waist. "Gilly, I wonder if your dad checked out what treatment you'd receive at the Utah clinic?"

Gilly struggled to keep her voice even. "In business matters, he's ruthless. The end justifies the means." He'd tried to pay Kate to leave her. He'd hired a private detective who'd spied on her and Kate, who'd most likely crept into her apartment, rummaged through her desk and dresser drawers. Had he found the love letters she'd hidden on the top shelf of her closet? Funny, crazy little secret messages, warm and sexy.

Oh, my god, where were they? "Kate, I just realized, your letters were missing from my closet. I packed in such a hurry—I was so flustered. I woke up to see Randall, telling me I had to move out that very day."

"He had a key?"

"Yes, I was surprised. Then not, since it's the company apartment."

"So he or the private detective could go in and snoop any time."

"It makes me sick, Randall spying, more than the private eye. Both of them reading our private stuff and passing it on to my dad."

The kettle whistled. Gilly made cups of jasmine tea. The fragrance rose up around her, catching her by surprise, making her think of a summer evening. Kate grabbed a box of chocolate chip cookies. The two returned to the living room sofa.

"I hope Nadya finds someone now that Sveta . . ." Gilly's eyes stung with tears. "What would I do, Kate, without you?"

Gilly finished her tea before she noticed the blinking light on the answering machine.

"My dad," Her heart squeezed. Would he apologize for treating her so callously? Be outraged and sympathetic when he heard of the attacks on Kate? He wasn't a murderer. He did betray her, but only because he loved her. He'd always told her that she was the best thing that ever happened to him.

Kate pushed Play. Dom's voice, hoarse with fatigue, rumbled, "Making progress. See you soon." He left the phone number of his Amsterdam hotel.

The second message was from Masha. "Ekaterina, I do not want to leave this news on machine. But I just got through to your line after trying two hours. Sveta's killer has been found. According to paper, her brother did it. The authorities say they found blood evidence in Sveta's home. Nadya is a wreck but she will bend and not break. I will send you letter." Masha continued, "No one reads letters going out but packages and letters coming in are carefully opened, especially from U.S., hoping to find money or chocolate. Be strong, my friend."

Kate put her face in her hands. Too much, seeing Nadya's interview again. Hearing now how Sveta died. Stricken, she turned to Gilly. "Sveta must have been dead when Olga spoke with the man—her brother—on the phone." She remembered Olga telling her his cryptic sentence, "She has been taken care of."

"Her brother was very wild, Nadya said." Kate's mouth twisted. "Oh, Gilly, I went through agony, blaming myself for not going back into the trees to look for Sveta. I just kept running until I reached the Olgino."

"If you hadn't, Kolya would have got you. Or you would have frozen to death."

"Sveta said to me, 'So sorry I think is my fault.' She screamed to Kolya, 'Don't hurt her. Let her go. This is a mistake.'" Kate handed Gilly Masha's translation of the audiotape of the abduction. "She must have thought her brother paid Kolya to kill her. She was apologizing for putting me in danger. When she arrived home, maybe she accused her brother of arranging a murder for hire. Anyway, they fought, he killed her, took her body to the cemetery pond near the Olgino because he found out—with Olga's telephone call—she'd been there with me, the American." Kate moaned. "I feel rotten."

"We'll never know exactly how it happened," Gilly murmured, her breath against Kate's cheek, making Kate feel that together they could do anything.

After a second cup of tea and several cookies, Kate re-read the printed note attached to the Marianna Restaurant flyer.

Gilly frowned. "Maybe we should call that detective."

"He won't be in until eight o'clock tomorrow morning. What if this 'friend' in Brighton Beach really does have information to save my life? He—or she—gave me back my missing video. That's a plus."

"Or is using it as bait."

"True. I don't know if Andre kept the videos he stole or passed them on." To the masked man? The moonies? "Oh, Gilly, don't you see? We might get conclusive proof for Detective Benitez. That footage of Steve with Captain Iurkov—that's not about me but about Dom and our company, Titan Films." Kate paced over to the window behind the desk, returned to Gilly. "I'm tired of waiting for the bad guys—whoever they are—to make the next move. We're in America, not Russia."

"Brighton Beach is a haven for illegals from Russia," Gilly said, frowning.

"The meeting place is a restaurant—most likely filled with people," Kate said slowly. Gilly burst out, "We should take Dom's car—it's safer—not the subway. We can get away fast. Do you have a map? I'll drive."

Kate handed her the Atlas from her bookcase. Gilly opened it across the desk and traced her finger over Brooklyn. "When I had my car," she said lightly, "I did some sketching in Brighton Beach—the shops, the people. The faces were wonderful." Her anxious eyes met Kate's.

Gilly was scared, as she was, that it might be a trap. Scared what she might find out. Plenty to be scared about. Kate stuffed the Marianna restaurant flyer into her jeans pocket.

▼▲▼

GREGOR JERKED TO ATTENTION as a light brown, two-door sedan nosed out of the apartment building garage. An arm shot out the open window and keyed the garage door shut. The car coasted up the ramp to the street. Kate was in the passenger seat. Gilly was behind the steering wheel. The birds were leaving the nest. The hawk would follow. He started his car, then turned off the engine. Better to be here when they returned.

Thirty minutes later an automobile entered the garage and the door remained raised. Gregor waited ten more minutes before he drove in through the open door. The garage was empty of people. Most of the spaces were filled. He didn't want to take anyone's permanent slot.

A couple of vehicles had parked horizontally end-to-end along the back wall. Just as he'd remembered, to his left just a few feet from the entrance, the garage curved leaving a pouch in the wall, out of the way of the path of the incoming cars. He was able to maneuver his car into that alcove, facing the street.

He transferred the black mask from the glove compartment to the the seat beside him. He must remain flexible, consider various scenarios. He could wait outside the service elevator on the seventh floor. Wait for Kate to empty the trash or go up to the fourteenth floor, the film company office. If the two were together, he'd take Gilly first. She'd never know what hit her. When she woke up, the dark-haired bitch would be gone. Best to strike here in the garage when the two returned—if conditions allowed.

▼▪▪▼

GILLY GUIDED THE CAR onto the Brooklyn Bridge from the FDR Drive. The East River shimmered with colors, reflections from the bridge and nearby buildings. The dark velvet sky, deceptively beautiful, was filled with glittering stars. She mustn't be lulled.

What happened in Leningrad had been orchestrated from here, she was almost certain. By someone who knew Kate was there. Kate's Uncle Burt. Or Kate's slippery colleague, Steve, who *was* there.

Or, Gilly suddenly recalled, with an icy feeling down her backbone, her dad! Kate had announced the festival invitation at the September barbecue, laughing about taking a film called *Revolution* to Leningrad. Her dad's eyes had gleamed with pleasure at Kate's good fortune, Gilly thought at the time. He'd asked Kate for the specific dates she'd be gone.

Gilly exited onto the Brooklyn-Queens Expressway, then merged into Route 27, which turned into Ocean Parkway. A few miles later, she turned left onto Brighton Beach Avenue—with its hodgepodge of shops, delis, cafes and bistros, and signs in Cyrillic. Tonight traffic was light. They'd made the trip in forty minutes. It was after 8:00 PM. "Can you see an address?"

"There it is," Kate pointed.

In the next block, Gilly slid the car into a parking spot, grateful she'd found one within dashing distance of the restaurant. After the two women stepped out, Gilly made sure the doors were locked.

The elevated train roared overhead. Gilly held her ears as she followed Kate across the street. She'd been willing herself not to be afraid, but her body was betraying her, her knees jumping so crazily she could scarcely walk. She was relieved to see pedestrians ambling along the sidewalks despite the chilly winter night, and lights burning in shop windows. When they arrived at the restaurant, they paused outside, straining to see within. Impossible.

Gilly's hand trembled as she opened the restaurant door which led into a vestibule. A menu was posted on a wall, alongside a flyer advertising the night's entertainment, ANNA AT THE MARIANNA. At the right a stairway, decorated with tiny Christmas lights, led downstairs to—where? Rest rooms? A dining area? A soundproof room where people disappeared forever?

Gilly peered into the restaurant proper through the glass of the vestibule door. Many diners sat at tables filled with platters of food and bottles. The walls were dark red, lit with soft lamps. Chandeliers hung overhead. A staff of waiters in tight, dark red uniforms stood at attention at the edges of the room or served food and drink.

Suddenly, the vestibule door opened. Gilly jumped. A man wearing a white T-shirt and black pants signaled Kate, smiling as if he knew her. His dark hair was slicked down. Blue eyes glittered in his pale face. Gilly wondered if he was the man who'd dropped off the videotape with Kate's doorman. Or the masked thug who'd tried to drag Kate into his car. He motioned them inside, pointing to a red-cloth-covered table in the middle of the room. Gilly's eyes searched the premises, squinting into the shadows, dreading that she would see the familiar face of her dad, or Randall.

He's so polite, Gilly thought, as the man pulled out chairs, side by side, for her and Kate. He made a sign as if to say, wait here, and hurried away. "You know him?" Gilly asked in a shaky voice. Kate, her mouth a straight line, eyes like lasers, twisted in her chair, looking at faces, most likely searching for Burt or

Steve. Or the scar-faced Captain. Gilly waited for a signal from Kate to sprint away, every muscle in her body on high alert.

The man with the slicked down hair returned with a buxom woman, her blonde tresses piled high. She wore false eyelashes. The woman smiled, nodded, and sat down across from them, speaking with an accent, "I am Grusha. I know English." The man stood beside her, erect, with military bearing.

Gilly noticed threads of red glinting within the greasy black stuff covering his hair. Shoe polish? This was getting weirder and weirder. She examined his pale face, with almost colorless freckles sprinkled across his nose, dark smudges under his eyes.

"Andre," Kate whispered.

He brushed his finger over his lips. "Dimitri now."

So this was the red-haired soldier, now black-haired. Andre, now Dimitri, who'd stalked Kate all over Leningrad. Why was he in America? Gilly felt light-headed.

"How did you know where I live?" Kate asked.

Andre listened to the blonde woman, then reached in his pants pocket and put a business card on the table. He spoke in Russian, laughed harshly and spoke again. The woman raised her eyebrows and said, with a neutral look at Kate, "He took it from your hotel room in Leningrad. He says you tricked him. He stole the wrong videotape from your jacket. It made trouble for him with the Captain. He says he surprised you too, by coming to your flat in New York City."

His eyes were smoldering, Gilly thought. Was he angry about the trouble Kate caused him?

Kate burst out, "You saved my life in Leningrad, I think."

Grusha, with an appraising glance at Andre, translated. Andre blushed. "*Da.*" He straightened up proudly, jabbing his thumbs into his chest. "Bus boy and dishwasher. I learn English." A slow grin spread across his pasty face.

Gilly turned to Kate, who was smiling, but her eyes were thoughtful.

He pointed to Grusha. "My friend. Safe to talk."

Kate introduced Gilly. "Nize meet you," he said in English,

then spoke in Russian.

Grusha said, "He wants to know if you are sisters." Gilly shook her head. Kate nodded yes. His eyes flicked from one to the other. He smiled uncertainly.

"Close friends," Kate said. "We watch each other's backs." The interpreter seemed at a loss.

"Protect each other," Gilly glared, sending the message (she hoped) that she and Kate were forces to be reckoned with.

The woman murmured to Andre, now Dimitri, who nodded grimly. He jabbed the air with one hand as he conversed with Grusha.

Grusha's face was neutral. "He say, 'Very busy tonight. I wish you come sooner. I have important papers for you to see. My shift ends midnight. Have dinner. See the show.'"

Gilly's stomach growled. She'd had nothing to eat all day but junk.

"You will be glad," Grusha smiled, and raised her eyebrows as Andre spoke again. "He says he has information to keep you alive. Facts he can prove."

Gilly threw a burning look at Kate. If they stayed for dinner and a show, they'd be leaving the Marianna very late. The streets would be deserted.

Andre hurried away toward the back of the room, where a fat man in a suit, arms folded across his chest, glowered. Andre spoke to him before he disappeared through a heavy curtain. Grusha followed. *What's going on in that back room?* Gilly wondered.

THE AIR WAS FILLED with guttural, rolled "r"s, the murmur of Russian conversation. Kate looked around the dining room. "Everyone is dressed up. We're wearing jeans and sneakers."

"The better to run with," Gilly said. "Do you trust him?"

"Information he could prove, he said, maybe who hired him to come after me and why. Something to show Detective

Benitez."

Gilly nodded with worried eyes.

"He didn't hurt me when he sneaked into my hotel room while I was asleep. He stopped Kolya from cutting my throat." Kate eyed the many diners, laughing, eating, drinking. It all seemed ordinary. "He looks beaten down, as if he's really on the run."

The two women were greeted in Russian by a waiter and the menu was in Russian. After a moment's panic, Kate found an English translation on the back.

The two smiled at the waiter, who smiled in return. Kate said, "*Prevyet,*" and whispered into Gilly's ear. Gilly said, "*Spaceba.*" The man, very handsome and svelte in his tight dark red uniform, grinned broadly and answered, "No prrraaablem."

Another couple joined them at their table for six. They spoke Russian, but changed to English when they discovered Kate and Gilly were Americans, not Soviet immigrants.

Quickly the table was filled with platters. In thick accented English, the woman pointed out blintzes, Russian-style gefilte fish, roast beef, cabbage and grape leaves stuffed with lamb, and Russian patties and pelmeni dumplings. "I can never decide what to eat," she smiled at Kate. "When I was growing up in Leningrad, we didn't have much to choose from. It's amazing." She waved a hand over the table. "Many of these dishes have not been available to the average Russian for many years."

The waiter added plates of chicken kiev and bowls of black caviar to the table, then stood just feet away. Another waiter's sole job was to refill vodka and wine glasses. The couple at their table made toast after toast and drank each time, signaling Kate and Gilly to join them. Kate noticed Gilly was bringing her wine glass to her lips, pretending to sip, and signaling Kate with her eyes to do the same. Kate nodded. The wine might be drugged, a special concoction for her and Gilly.

"I feel like we're on a cruise," Gilly said, faking a festive smile, as the grilled sturgeon steak and lamb shish kebab platters landed before them.

The husband smacked his lips. "For me, the eighty-proof vodka is the best part." And by the time the entertainment started, he and his wife had finished over half the bottle, as well as much of the food. His wife apologized. "Most Russian immigrants have led hard lives, full of fear. Public events were staged. The Marianna and other places like it in Brighton Beach, with good food, kind service, singing and dancing, are for us the realization of a dream."

Her husband winked. "There is still some mystery as to how some locals own million-dollar waterfront condominiums here yet have no visible means of financial support." He whispered, "A recent report in the daily paper listed members of a Brighton Beach gang accused of racketeering, narcotics trafficking, extortion, illegal gambling, and loan-sharking."

"Like Al Capone's Chicago," Kate said. Where one could wind up with a bullet in the head at a moment's notice.

The entertainment started after the dessert, fruit strudel. A female singer, Anna at the Marianna, belted out Russian and American songs. She was blonde, overweight; her hair fluffed out in puffs around her face like Marilyn Monroe. She wore tons of make-up, a white fur over one shoulder, a metallic blue tight-fitting dress that showed bulges and curves. The audience loved her, occasionally singing along with her.

During Anna's breaks, the piano player sang in Russian and English. The crowd danced, fast and slow. "Look," Gilly said, pointing to a woman on the dance floor. "She's in jeans, like us." The woman wore a zebra-print top, tight black jeans with zippers, and golden snakeskin pointy-toed heels.

❦

"DASVIDANIYA," KATE CALLED OUT when the Russian couple, weaving and waving, left the table. The Marianna was clearing out. It was almost 1:00 AM. At 1:30, Kate became uneasy. "Where's Andre—Dimitri?" To her, he was Andre.

"We should leave," Gilly whispered.

Just as the two women were about to sneak toward the door, Andre burst through the back curtain, an overcoat folded over his arm. He held up a large brown envelope and waved it in the air. Grusha, the blonde translator, followed closely behind him.

They sat across from Kate and Gilly.

Andre put the envelope on the table between them. He nodded soberly. Glaring into space, he talked in fits and starts, as Grusha translated. "I was recruited by my superior, Captain Iurkov, who was hired by a man who spoke Russian with a foreign accent, who paid in hard currency, U.S. dollars. Our job was to kill you and make it seem like a random crime or accident."

Kate's heart sank. A man who spoke Russian hired Captain Iurkov to pay Andre to kill her. She was no closer to the truth than before.

"And I was to seize this tape from you." Andre pulled the video from the envelope. "I am sorry for your trouble, Kate. I did not want to kill you. I wanted to know you better. I had to follow orders."

Kate saw the *Revolution* jacket, the black dot on the spine. "My other missing video."

Andre, nodding, motioned for her to take it. Grusha spoke. "He says he has duplicates; you take original."

Why had he kept copies for himself? "*Spaceba*," Kate said.

The conversation continued with Grusha explaining so smoothly Kate almost forgot the woman was there. Andre's eyes filled as he told Kate about his beautiful sister Tanya. "She was married to the greedy fat pig Kolya, who sent her out as a hard currency hooker. I made terrible mistake paying Kolya to help me. Because of him, Tanya was murdered." He rubbed his face, looked at Kate bleakly with bloodshot eyes. He glanced over his shoulder before he began whispering in Russian. Grusha seemed just as frightened as she translated in hushed tones. "The Captain is looking for me. Many things happen here. Gangs in Moscow and Leningrad are friendly with gangs in Brighton Beach, with money coming back and forth."

"How did you escape Russia?" Gilly asked.

"I hid in the burned out Leningrad Hotel night of fire. I found money—enough to buy my freedom. I stayed with Irina, who helped me."

"Irina?" Kate asked. The woman who made sure when she left Masha's illegal meeting she got into Kolya's taxi. Who did porn with Steve. "She was a friend of Tanya?"

He nodded sadly. "Both in same business. Irina put you into cab. She and my sister were told it was for robbery, not murder. I am sorry, Kate." He looked contrite.

Anything to survive. "Is Irina in America?"

He shook his head emphatically, his eyes angry. "I am here because my sister's killer is here. His name is Gregor. The same Gregor who paid the Captain to have you killed. You know him? He has office in Wall Street."

Kate's heart thudded. "My Uncle Burt's office is there." She turned to Gilly.

"So is my dad's," Gilly said shakily.

"I found this at the registration desk in the burned out hotel." Andre handed Kate folded papers, which she opened with trepidation. The first page was a Xerox copy of a passport photo. The face was familiar, the broad-faced man who looked like the civilian in her videotape talking in the bar with the scar-faced Captain. He also resembled the KGB official pictured in the Leningrad newspaper.

Below the photo, Kate read: Passport Agency: NE Center New York. The man was not Russian. Not KGB. An American. The name beside the photo was Bonham, Gregor Randall. The second page was a copy of his Visa—in Russian—with the same photo, the round face and sneering eyes. A faint grin.

Kate was surprised how calm she felt as she showed the papers to Gilly.

"Randall," Gilly cried out, as if she'd been hit in the stomach. "He's worked for my dad for years."

A smoldering anger grew in Kate as she pointed out to Gilly the cities, typed in Cyrillic, he was allowed to visit. "Moscow and Leningrad. The third city I can't decipher."

Andre said, "Nizhnevartovsk."

"The dates of his stay, 240191 to 010291, coincide with mine."

Gilly's eyes were filled with horror and disgust. "He wants to be a partner in the firm. My father wants me to marry him. I can't bear it, Kate." Her voice shook. "Everything that happened to you is because of me."

Kate held Gilly close, dimly aware of Grusha and Andre talking softly in the background.

Gilly raised her head from Kate's shoulder. "It's Randall. Only Randall. He's power hungry. A megalomaniac. My father is not involved, he's not a killer."

You said yourself, Kate thought, *for him, the end justifies the means.* "He did try to pay me to stop seeing you," Kate murmured, but was sorry when Gilly moaned, putting her head in her hands.

Andre rocked back and forth, a brutal look on his face, and exploded in a torrent of Russian. Grusha nodded, said urgently, "He says, be careful. Gregor is evil man."

Andre took Kate's hand, then Gilly's. Grusha's eyes were shooting sparks as she repeated Andre's words in English. "I meet this Gregor Randall at the market deli tomorrow noon. He knows I have video he wants." Andre mockingly tapped the tape on the table. "A copy of it. He knows he needs to come to me with money. I make sure he does not bother you again." He reached in his pocket, held out his fist, and opened it. In his palm was a folded razor.

Grusha grinned fiercely. "It will cut a hair in half."

"*Spaceba,*" Kate said. Nothing she'd like better. She wanted vengeance for all he'd put her and Gilly through. "But in America we do not take the law in our own hands."

Lights flickered. A white-aproned boy—he didn't seem to be more than sixteen—began to mop the floor. Kate looked at her watch. Almost 2:30 AM. She threw a quick look at Gilly before she took Detective Benitez's card from her pocket and put it on the table. "This man can help us," she explained to Grusha. "You and Andre, come back with us to Manhattan." Grusha's eyes grew wide. Gilly looked at Kate if she'd gone crazy.

With rising excitement, Kate continued, "Early tomorrow the four of us will go to the precinct. Benitez can take a statement from you, Andre. We'll show him the copy of Gregor Randall Bonham's passport photo and his Visa, give him the videotape of Gregor Randall talking with Captain Iurkov. When Andre meets this creep at the deli market, Benitez can be there too."

Grusha murmured Kate's proposal to Andre, who listened with narrowed eyes, looking troubled when she finished. "Is it safe for Andre to talk to police?" Kate asked. Grusha hesitated, then answered, "He has new papers; he has job. Remember to call him Dimitri."

Kate stood. "Can I borrow the phone? I'll call the precinct and leave a message for Benitez that we'll see him tomorrow at 8:00 AM with proof that Gregor Randall, a U.S. citizen, conspired to have me killed in Leningrad and is still in pursuit of me here in New York City."

Chapter Nine

3:20 AM, Wednesday, February 6

Snug as a bug, Gregor thought, in his car nestled against the wall in the alcove. He was almost dozing when the garage door opened yet again and once more headlights flashed in his eyes. He ducked down below the dashboard, inching up to steal a peek. The light brown sedan eased in. Gilly was behind the wheel, Kate beside her. Two baby chicks, ready for the plucking. My God, nearly 3:30. Where were they all this time? He felt uneasy.

Probably to a dyke bar in the Village. He'd visited once.

Women everywhere, dancing with each other and kissing. It disgusted him and turned him on.

This time of night the garage was deserted. He slid the black balaclava over his face. With his left hand, he pulled the release latch under the dashboard. His trunk lid popped open. He must be prepared for anything.

The sedan stopped on the ramp, parallel with his car. Had he been spotted? The dark-haired bitch Kate was getting out and coming his way. He put his hand on the ignition key, ready to burn rubber.

Good, she was heading over to the wall switch to close the garage door. Not even looking his way.

He watched Gilly continue to drive down the incline, turning right, toward a parking space several feet away. Her back was to him. Could it be any more perfect? He wouldn't have to touch Gilly.

Kate was in front of him, a few feet beyond his right fender. Gregor eased his car door open and slid out. Before she could press the switch, he was behind her, the stun gun raised.

Suddenly, she turned. She looked into his eyes, stepped back, raised her fists. Oh, no, you don't. He zapped her on the bare hand with the stun gun. She whimpered as if the breath had been knocked out of her. He yanked her to him and pushed the gun into her neck, firing again. She collapsed. He threw a glance over his shoulder—Gilly was still traveling forward toward the parking spot, oblivious. He dragged Kate's limp body to the rear of his car.

ANDRE HAD BEEN SLUMPED in the back seat, nearly asleep, his head resting on the arm of the door when he felt the vehicle stop and go into reverse. He opened his eyes to see Gilly backing up the car. Where was Kate? He twisted to look out the rear window. The garage door was open. Had she stepped outside? He noticed the automobile parked in the alcove near the entrance, a shadowy figure moving behind it. Whoever it was slammed down the trunk lid, darted into the driver's seat, and gunned the motor. Just before the car roared away, Andre caught a glimpse of the driver's face covered by a black balaclava. "Gregor!" he yelled. Grusha woke up with a start. Cursing, Andre scrambled over the seat into the front. "She is in the trunk of his car!" Grusha was shouting in Russian and English. "She is in his trunk. Go! Go!" Gilly stepped on the gas. The sedan jerked out of the parking space, turned right, squealed left, and up the ramp.

GREGOR SWITCHED ON HIS headlights, swerving onto the one-way street the wrong way, nearly ramming an oncoming car. He wrenched the wheel sharply and clipped the fender of an auto parked curbside. Gilly hadn't seen him take the *suka* down, he was sure. She would look for her girlfriend and find she had vanished into thin air. If she had seen his car, no matter—he had removed the back license plate and covered the plate in front with mud. He was untraceable. He felt euphoric. Powerful.

GILLY DIDN'T UNDERSTAND A word that Andre was yelling. Grusha screamed in English, "He knows it's Gregor. He wears a black mask as he did when he set fire to the hotel in Leningrad." Gilly's hands on the steering wheel were slick with perspiration. The car bounced out of the garage. She hit the brakes. She couldn't see to her left, beyond the bushes at the end of the drive. She honked her horn to warn pedestrians, then hit the gas, lurching forward across the sidewalk, about to turn right. Andre bellowed in Russian. Grusha shrieked, "Go left. He turned left." Gilly prayed she wouldn't collide with another vehicle turning into the one-way street off Ninth. Luck was with her.

As she passed Kate's apartment building, she rolled down her window and yelled, "Police, police!" hoping the doorman would run outside to check. Andre, beside her, yelled, "*Militsia.*" Grusha screamed, "Help, help," from the back seat. No one stirred. The street remained deserted. No apartment lights in nearby buildings snapped on.

Gilly felt like she was under a giant waterfall, the water roaring and crashing down around her. She gave a quick look up Ninth, no cars. This time of night the avenue could be a raceway. She floored the gas pedal, rocketing across Ninth, following the taillights of the speeding car as it crossed Tenth, then Eleventh. All the while, Andre was sputtering, Grusha repeating in English. "No license plate. If we lose him, he will be easier to find without a license plate."

Gilly was right behind him as his car turned north onto the West Side Highway.

"Where are we?" Grusha asked Gilly.

"Near the Hudson River." Gilly hunched her shoulders, tensed her body. She had to win this race. By the time she reached Thirty-Sixth Street, several automobiles had pulled in front of her. "Damn, damn, damn, I've lost him. Did he turn?"

"I didn't see," Grusha moaned. Andre cursed.

It's my fault, Gilly thought. *Kate's going to die because of me. My cowardice. My stupidity.* She was ready to crumble. He couldn't be far. If she only knew which way to turn. He'd been heading north on the West Side Highway. "He lives on West End," she muttered. "He may take her there." *That would be convenient*, another voice in her head said. *He might take her across the George Washington Bridge.*

She turned east on Fortieth Street and headed up Tenth to Fifty-Seventh, then zigzagged west and up West End Avenue, slowing down at his apartment building. "Look for cars parking—or parked—without a license plate." Should she try to find a precinct? Let Andre out of the vehicle—or Grusha—to search for a policeman? Or look for a phone to call 911? Grusha spoke English, but she wouldn't know what to say. If she let

Andre and Grusha out together, she'd be facing Gregor Randall alone.

※※※

KATE OPENED HER EYES. She had a terrible headache. She was being thrown side to side, bouncing up and down like a basketball. She held her hand close to her face. Absolutely black as pitch. Where was she? She smelled oil and rubber. The trunk of a car.

She remembered facing the masked man in the apartment garage. He'd zapped her with—of course, a stun gun. After that, she recalled nothing.

Where was Gilly? Did he have her too?

Andre and Grusha had been asleep in the back seat of the car. Did they wake up in time to see what happened?

She couldn't die here. How could she save Gilly, if she couldn't save herself? Breathing heavily, sweating and shaking, her next thought was to bang her fist on the trunk lid and scream. She mustn't panic. She must find her center. If the car had folding rear seats, she could kick and push them forward, out of the way, and scramble into the cabin of the car. No. The sounds would alert him she'd revived. When/if he opened the trunk, she'd have an advantage by pretending to be unconscious.

Kate moved her hands over the floor and found the spare tire. She pushed her fingers into the well the tire rested in. Rags. Anything else? A toolbox? Something sharp to help her pry open the lid? Or a jack. She could force open the trunk lid with a tire jack. Nothing.

She peeled away the carpet and underlay, then removed the panel covering the taillight closest to her upper body. She rotated her body to a kicking position, and kicked and kicked trying to dislodge the tail light so she could stick her arm through the hole and wave it about, catch someone's attention. Too difficult. She was exhausting herself and her oxygen. One good thing—getting rid of the panel covering the light allowed some dim illumination in the trunk.

She fiddled with wires and knobs in the trunk's locking mechanism. The trunk light flickered on and off, providing a small but significant source of hope. She continued to play with the lock. If only she had a tool to work with. Again, she searched every inch of the floor, hoping to find a screwdriver left behind. He'd cleared out everything. Her heart was beating really fast. She closed her eyes and tried to collect her thoughts. But all she could think was, *This bastard is going to kill me or I'm going to die in this trunk.*

※

ANDRE TURNED TO GRUSHA, who was moaning "He will kill her!" from the back seat, and motioned for her to be quiet. Beside him, Gilly sighed in despair as she leaned her head against the steering wheel. The rat had disappeared.

Suddenly, an idea came into Andre's head. Grusha had told him—as if she were a tour guide—when they were on the highway, "There, to the left, is the Hudson River."

"Grusha," Andre said breathlessly, and twisting around, took her hand. "Tell Gilly there is a place he asked me to meet him. Very private, he said. A boat. On the Hudson River." Grusha passed on the information.

Gilly cried, "The Marina. Oh, my god." She rolled down her window, shouting "Police, police!" The car jerked forward, turning left a few blocks later. Andre moved his razor from his pants pocket to his coat.

※

GREGOR SPED OVER THE rise in the highway, taking a sharp right onto the exit ramp. He tapped his brakes at the stop sign, listening. No sounds from the trunk. He'd given her a good dose. He'd slap her awake after they were on the boat, so she'd know exactly what was going to happen. He drove under the parkway overpass and halfway around the traffic circle, exiting on the ramp closest to the river.

Ignoring the No Thru Traffic signs, he entered the underground garage, inserting his card key in the slot. The gate opened. No garage security on duty this time of night. He turned left and continued around the underground circle.

He'd find a parking spot in the permit only section close to the door, stuff her in the suitcase, haul her out of the garage, and up to the wrought iron gate. Unlock it and enter the docking area, pulling her to the cruiser moored at the end of the pier. Almost 4:30 AM; sunrise was at 7:00. He would have to work fast. Only one security person would be stationed in the bungalow. He'd rely on the stun gun, using his semi-automatic only if absolutely necessary. If Kate's bloated body rose to the surface, he didn't want bullet holes in it.

▼▲▼

KATE WAS NAUSEOUS, HER temples throbbing. The car was spinning as if on a giant turntable. She yanked up carpet from the floor of the trunk and found cables and wires underneath. She pulled on them, not sure what would happen, hoping to rip out the electrics so he'd be without brake lights or taillights or turn lights. Maybe a cop would stop him—if any were out cruising this late.

She heard a pop. She felt a puff of air. The trunk lid started to rise. She could hardly believe that she'd managed to unlock it. This was her chance. The car was slowing down. He must be approaching a stop light. The trunk lid rose higher. She prayed she wouldn't land in front of oncoming traffic. She tucked her head into her chest, rolled out, and thudded onto the ground, landing on her hip and shoulder. The breath was knocked out of her, but she managed to rise up on all fours, then scramble to her feet.

Where was she? Not outside. Some place dank and dark,

like a dungeon. Lit by only a few weak bulbs. Behind her was a loading platform and closed metal doors. No exit, it seemed, except up the ramp. The car had seemed to twist and turn forever as it made its way down to the bottom of what appeared to be a *cul-de-sac*.

His car screeched to a stop several feet ahead, the trunk lid bobbling. Beyond it were a few parked vehicles. His door opened, the car interior lit up. She didn't see Gilly inside. He was running toward her, yelling, "*Blyad! Shalava!* Dirty slut!" He carried something in his hand.

"Where's Gilly?" Kate shouted. "What have you done with her, you cowardly fuck?"

"She's safe. She'll never know what happened to you."

Her shoulder hurt, her hip was throbbing. "I know who you are. You don't need to hide behind that mask."

"And I know you. Dirty, filthy, lesbo dyke." He tore off his mask and grinned.

He was less than three feet away. He looked ordinary, like an accountant perhaps, with his baby face. He wore no coat, just a dark sweater and dark pants. Lank hair drooped over his forehead. His light blue eyes were hard as marbles.

"Poor Kate," he mimicked, making his voice high. "Why has Kate disappeared from my life? Maybe this time my father offered her enough money to make it worth her while."

"Do you know what Gilly calls you?"

"I'm her savior. She thinks of me as family." He gave her a chilling smile.

"She calls you a creep. Tapioca Randall," Kate taunted. "Too scared to do your own dirty work. You paid KGB Captain Iurkov to do it."

His face flushed. Blood vessels popped out on his forehead. "You'll see. You'll be begging me for mercy." He lunged toward her and grabbed her wrist. "Now the fun starts," he said harshly.

Fear gave her an adrenalin surge. She straightened her other arm, twisting her upper body suddenly to the left, jerking her wrist from his hand, hearing in her head her master teacher's voice: *The elbow is the strongest point of your body.*

She rammed her elbow into his face, felt it crunch his nose and glance off into his eye. He grunted in pain. She fumbled for the back of his neck, thrust her leg behind his and shoved him to the ground. A dark oblong object lay beside him. She kicked it away from his body before she picked it up. The end with the two prongs was obviously the business end.

He was sitting up, holding his face. Then suddenly, he attacked, grabbing her around the legs. She flopped to the ground, and he fell on top of her. She managed to wrap her legs around his torso before he could pin them down. At the same time, she pressed the stun gun into his cheek next to his ear and fired twice. His body jerked, and slumped over. She used her knees and feet to kick him off her.

Dazed, she struggled upright. The garage was spinning. She took several deep breaths, then sprinted up the ramp and around the underground circle, stun gun in hand, her run sputtering out in a halting shuffle. She prayed she could reach the entrance before he roused and followed. She was hurting—hip, shoulder and elbow. She looked behind her. He was still lying on the ground. "Help," she shrieked to no one. "Police." Her voice echoed in the cavernous enclosure.

Chapter Ten

5:00 AM, Wednesday, February 6

Gilly realized that she'd never have found the entrance to the marina's underground garage if she hadn't been here many times before. For an instant, she was frozen. A special card key was required to open the automatic gate. No one was in the booth. She didn't know for sure that Kate was here. Nerves on fire, her heart about to jump out of her chest, she yelled, "Fasten your seat belts," and pushed down the gas pedal. The car—poor Dom's car—crashed through the closed gate. She took a left at the stop sign. Alternately revving the motor and tapping the brakes, she drove as fast as she could down the winding incline that ended in the bowels of the garage.

A few moments later, she heard what sounded like animal cries. She rolled down the window.

"Calls for help," Grusha said. "Female." Andre's eyes were closed as if he were praying.

"Hold on, dear Kate," Gilly murmured.

GREGOR FELT AS IF he'd been thrown against a wall. He eased himself to a sitting position. His nose was bleeding and throbbing. She'd pay for this big time. He'd seen her limping up the ramp. He could catch her easily before she reached the exit. He carefully raised himself off the ground. Halfway to his car to get his Sig-Sauer and silencer, he realized he'd left behind a clue, the black balaclava. He went back for it, stuffing it in his pants pocket, and returned to his car. He sank into the front seat with a groan. His head ached. He could hardly think. A heavy gloom fell over him. Gilly had made fun of him behind his back. He brooded for a few moments before he came back to himself, his despair turning to anger.

AT THE NEXT CURVE, Gilly spotted Kate, hobbling toward their car, a sight so sweet her heart twisted. She was hurt, but she was alive! If he'd hurt her bad, she would tear him apart. Tears clouded Gilly's eyes. At the same time, Andre exclaimed, "Kate!"

Kate gave a half wave, and pointed behind her. Soon she was leaning in the open car window, trying unsuccessfully to smile. Her mouth was jerking, tears filled her eyes. "You found me."

"Thanks to Andre!" Gilly searched for words. "It was a wild card." She took Kate's face in her hands. "I was so scared." Still babbling, she pressed her lips against Kate's.

"Hurry," Grusha ordered. "Inside."

As Kate limped to the far side of the car, Andre tumbled over the seat into the back.

Kate climbed in beside Gilly, who gave her a hug, then pulled away to ask, "Is anything broken?"

"Just bruises. I smashed his nose. He's down there, unconscious." Kate weakly waved the stun gun. "Let's get out of here and go for help."

In the back seat Andre and Grusha argued in explosive bursts. Gilly turned to see Andre open the back door closest to the wall. "We go, find police," Grusha pleaded, holding his arm. "Gilly, Kate—" she said helplessly as Andre shrugged her off and slid out. "He says he will stay in the dark along the wall and sneak up behind. We must drive into the bottom of garage and block this murderer's car." She moaned. "Andre is a hot head. I am very worried."

"We can't leave Andre," Kate said. She added thoughtfully, "I'm praying this creep thinks it's just the two of us, Gilly. That he didn't see Andre and Grusha when we drove into the garage."

Gilly let the car coast down the incline. Randall's vehicle came into view. It faced the far wall, the trunk wide open, front door ajar, headlights burning. Her eyes searched the ground for his body. She saw nothing.

ANDRE, IN THE SHADOWS, moved quickly down the ramp. When he reached the loading dock, he saw the car, interior lit, Gregor inside, his back to him. Andre dropped to his knees and crawled beneath the loading dock. When he reached the near wall, he stood, creeping along it for several feet. He felt a puff of cold air, saw a thread of light. A door in the wall. Another way out of this dark, unfriendly place.

He continued along the perimeter of the garage until he was hidden within the small group of vehicles parked below Gregor's car. The slimy rat had stripped off his mask, and was opening the glove compartment. Andre took his razor from his coat pocket, smiling to himself. *What a shock that sovok will have when he sees me!*

⁘

GREGOR JERKED HIS HEAD around as headlights blazed through his rear window. The brown sedan was coming up behind him.

Beside Gilly was Kate. What in the hell—? Someone was in the back seat. Plans were changing. He took his semi-automatic pistol from the glove compartment, inserted the magazine with nine shots, and fastened on the silencer. Gilly, Kate and friend would be victims of a deadly carjacking.

⁘

GILLY STOPPED THE CAR at the bottom of the ramp about thirty feet from Randall's. She put the gear in neutral and pulled the emergency brake. "Where's Andre?" she whispered.

"I can't see him," Kate said.

"Over to my left," Gilly said. "See the small crack of light. That's a door in the wall that leads into the park and the marina, where there's a security shed and residents who live in their boats year-round. Run outside and scream for help. I'll keep him talking."

"I'm not leaving," Kate replied.

"I stay too," Grusha said.

Gilly yelled through the open window. "Randall. This is crazy."

Gregor Randall climbed out of his car, shoulders drooping, arms limp at his sides. "I'm sorry, Gilly." He was breathing through his mouth. His nose was crooked. He looked abject, like such a loser.

"Did my dad tell you Kate would be in Leningrad?"

He tried to smile, then winced. "We made a plan, he and I—"

"So my dad—" She felt sick, everything she'd eaten at the Marianna rising up. "He asked you to follow Kate to Leningrad, and hire someone to kill her."

Randall laughed softly. "When it comes to that, he's spineless. It was my idea and brilliant, to make her death seem like an accident in a corrupt and lawless country. I was there on business, closing a deal that will make your dad and me lots of money." He paused, expectant, as if waiting for applause. "Too bad I hired incompetents. They delayed me getting back. To do what the boss—your lily-livered dad—wanted, haul you off to Utah while your girlfriend was out of the country," he said roughly. His eyes were distant and cold. She was looking at a stranger. "Too bad for you, Gilly, that you tailed me here." He raised his arm.

"Grusha! Duck," Kate cried, yanking Gilly down below the dashboard with her.

Gilly heard a muffled bang, a chink and a thud as she crouched next to Kate. She reached for Kate's hand. "Are you okay?" Kate nodded. "You?" Gilly touched her face, her chest, her arms. "Yes," she croaked. "Grusha?" A tiny voice from the back seat answered, "I'm okay."

Gilly kept her head well below the dashboard, as she raised her eyes. A bullet had gone through the windshield. A bullet hole was in the seat back where she'd been sitting. "What's happened to Andre?"

"I'll put the car in drive," Kate said raggedly. "You release the emergency brake and press down the gas pedal with your hand. I'll steer. We'll keep our heads down. We'll ram him."

※※※

ANDRE CREPT UP BEHIND Gregor, softly as a cat, pouncing before he could shoot again, jerking his head back by his hair, about to slice his throat. "This is for my sister Tanya, you *dolboeb.*" Gregor wrenched away, but not before Andre's razor tore through his cheek from his jawbone to his eye. That same eye was wide with shock as he hissed, "Where did you come from, you goddamned *musor?*"

Andre gave chase as Gregor ran toward the sliver of light in the wall, turning back once to shoot—missing by a mile—then firing at the light brown car that was bearing down on him. Andre heard the crack of glass shattering. A headlight was dark. That was all he hit, a headlight.

He saw Gregor fling open the door in the wall and dash outside. He was right behind, stopping at the opening to peer out around the edges. A panorama opened up: a path covered in a sprinkling of snow, a wrought iron fence, behind which was a lighted harbor, with boats of all sizes tied up at a network of docks.

Where was Gregor? There, fumbling at the tall metal gate that secured the dock area.

GREGOR'S FACE DRIPPED BLOOD. How the fuck did Andre get here? The bastard had cut through his cheek. He could feel the flesh flapping, air coming through the wound into his mouth. He spat out blood. How in the hell had Andre found the two women? And who was the fourth person?

His key turned, he pushed open the wrought-iron gate, and entered the main dock. He swerved left onto a walkway, leaping over the handrail to the dock below. He would get to the cruiser. He could get away. Tie the boat at a marina in Jersey, across the river. Get to the airport. Leave the country.

GILLY CLIMBED OUT OF the car. She could see through the open door in the wall that the wrought iron gate was open. "He's heading for the cruiser." Why didn't he go through the park? she wondered. To find him in the dark, in the trees, in the miles and miles of park, would be impossible. Cautiously, she stepped outside, followed by Kate, stun gun in hand, and Grusha. To Gilly's right was a thicket of foliage. "Stay behind the bushes until we know what's going on. The lighted bungalow to the right, beyond the gate? That's security."

"Should we call for help?" Grusha asked in a hushed voice.

"If the guard has a gun, he might hit Andre not Gregor." Gilly's eyes scanned the grid of docks, looking for a shadow chasing a shadow, listening for feet slamming against the wooden boards. Could it be? Both had ended up in the frigid waters of the Hudson? "I see someone going through the iron gate. It's Andre." Where was Gregor? "Let's make a run for security."

▼.▲.▼

IN A FLASH ANDRE was inside the marina, his feet pounding on the boardwalk, his head swiveling as he tried to spot Gregor within the maze of boats and walkways. There he was, on the lower dock! Andre sprinted left onto a catwalk, and jumped over the rail to the wharf below. He steadied himself on the icy, rocking walkway, trying not to fall, thankful for the squat lamps edging the pier, spilling their glow into the lapping waves on either side. He hurried after Gregor, who stumbled toward the large vessel moored at the end. He planned a getaway by water.

Gregor turned, lifted his pistol and fired. Andre felt the breeze as the bullet whizzed by his right shoulder. Close call. He continued his pursuit. "You missed, you *mudak*!"

Just before Gregor reached the boat, he shot again, squeezing and squeezing the trigger. Nothing happened. The gun had jammed. Suddenly, Gregor's feet went out from under him and, with flapping arms, he fell. The gun flew out of his hand. Andre roared like a wild animal and leaped, going for Gregor's throat with his razor.

Gregor put his hands up for protection. Andre grunted,

"For Tanya. Kate. Gilly. Grusha," slashing, left and right, across Gregor's palms.

Andre grabbed a fistful of sweater, pulling Gregor close, moving in for the kill, Gregor flailed, his bloodied fingers curled like claws. Andre's head snapped, as he felt Gregor's fist connect first with his jaw, then his eyes.

The razor was slapped from his hand. "Slimy weasel!" Andre grunted, prepared to choke him.

Gregor squirmed out of his grip and grabbed the guardrail, hoisting himself to his feet.

Andre lunged, but missed. He rubbed his eyes, still stinging and watering from the punches. When his vision cleared, he saw Gregor, now at the end of the dock, vault over the railing.

Andre hurried to the pier's edge, expecting to see Gregor thrashing in the icy river. Moored in front of the large cruiser were inflated rubber dinghies. A motor sputtered to life. Gregor was in a dinghy, heading out into the choppy black water.

"*Dolboeb, mudak,*" Andre yelled. "*Oomritye!* Die." Among the inflatables was a second rubber raft with a motor. He would follow. As he started for the railing, he realized something was wrong with his eyes, and his legs were so heavy he could barely move. Gregor had gotten in a few good punches. Do not be *dooroc,* he told himself. Gregor was cut bad, his cheek flapping open from his jawbone to his eye. His hands were slashed to ribbons. He would not be able to control the raft. Andre watched the small craft bounce and swirl in the strong river current before it disappeared in blackness.

❖❖❖

Kate, her legs like Jello, crept toward the large shape at the end of pier. She held tightly to the stun gun, prepared to use it. As she grew closer, the bulky figure turned into Andre in his overlarge coat. Thank god, he was alive. "Andre," she whispered, touching his shoulder. He jumped and turned. His face was bloody, his eyes swelling. "You're hurt." She brushed his cheek with her fingers and showed him the blood. He shook his head. With a happy cry, he scooped up something from the deck, held it out. "Gregor. I got him," he said, holding up his razor.

"Where is he?" she asked.

Andre pointed to the rubber rafts moored in front of the cruiser. In the split second of silence before Andre, cursing, flung out an arm toward the river, she heard a put-put-put from that same direction.

"Stop him!" Kate cried. "He's a killer. Police! Somebody call the police!!"

Frantic voices broke through the din. Kate looked up. On the walkway above were Gilly, Grusha, and a tall man in a winter jacket, shining a flashlight their way. "Kate, Andre. Are you OK?"

"Yes," Kate answered. "He's in the water. In an inflatable."

"Police are coming," the man shouted. He swept his beam out into the river. The light reached the middle. Nothing to be seen but the lapping water.

Andre, his shoulders slumped, touched Kate's arm. "Sorr-ry." She hugged him. "Oh, Andre, what would we have done without you? *Spaceba*. Many times." As she rocked with Andre in her arms, she heard Gilly call, "Wait for us," and Grusha say, "We're here," as they pushed into the clinch, all of them holding on for dear life.

When they broke apart, Kate's eyes met Gilly's. "He'll never make it. Andre got him with his razor. I broke his nose. The river's choppy. It's cold and black as ink. He has no coat."

Chapter Eleven

7:00 AM, Wednesday, February 6

Gilly huddled next to Kate inside the marina's tiny security shack. She'd burnt out all her fuses. The wires in her brain were sizzling; her body was a hollow shell. She watched the people mill around and come and go: a terrified group of year-round residents in bathrobes and coats; blue-uniformed police from harbor patrol.

Across from her, poor Andre, eyes swollen, was slumped on a wooden bench, arms folded over his chest like a fighter who'd gone twenty rounds with a maniac. His coat, torn and dirty, was buttoned up to the neck.

Beside him, Grusha was scarcely recognizable without her false lashes, her eyes two dark currants in a white pudding. Her blonde hair, once upswept, was in tufts and snarls, sticking out all over her head, drooping down around her face. Thank God, Grusha had agreed to come along. If she and Andre had been alone in the car, neither would have understood a word the other said. Or if she'd been alone . . .

The door to the security shack opened. Gilly half expected to see a moon or stars of blood. But there was the early morning sunlight, streaming in. "No sign of him," the policeman said, stepping in and closing the door. "Strong currents. He might show up in spring at a full moon and low tide. With the other floaters." The man barked out a laugh.

By 8:00 AM, NYPD officers from the Twentieth Precinct had arrived and were asking questions. Gilly went first, to explain why everything ended in this marina. "My dad's cruiser is docked here." She heard herself speaking in a monotone. She couldn't seem to stop clasping and unclasping her hands. "It sleeps six, but it's mostly used to entertain my dad's clients, on day trips." A couple of years ago—before Kate came into her life—she, with her dad and mom, had cruised the Hudson in that boat. Randall was at the controls. He understood the currents and the tide.

Sergeant Murphy, an officer with close-cropped hair, was waiting for her to continue, but her mind wanted to hang on to that day that seemed so perfect at the time.

"It's called the *Angelica,* after me." Lunch was champagne, caviar and paté ordered from Zabar's. They'd journeyed past the Statue of Liberty, docked in New Jersey for dinner at a waterfront café, admired the sunset over the New York skyline. "It's so beautiful on a summer evening," her dad had said as they returned to the marina. "The lights come on, the water calms down. You think you're in the Mediterranean." His face was relaxed, his eyes shining, a soft smile on his lips. She'd almost forgotten he could look that way. The next day she'd sketched that memory of his face.

The sergeant, his pen poised over a notebook, prodded kindly, "Ma'am?"

"The boat is named after me. Randall—Gregor, as he called himself—was going to kill Kate there. I never thought any of us would get out alive." Gilly stood up suddenly, overturning the metal folding chair she sat on as she rushed for the door. She made it outside and miraculously Kate was holding onto her, sliding her eyeglasses off her face so they wouldn't fall, as she threw up in the water.

"Thanks," Gilly managed as Kate dabbed at her mouth with a tissue and steered her back into the squat wooden building. Someone handed her a paper cup of ginger ale, which she pretended to sip. The thought of anything in her stomach made her shudder.

The next few hours passed in a haze for Gilly, like she was watching a movie. By 9:00 AM, everyone had made a statement. Grusha translated for Andre, whose face looked deathly pale. Beads of perspiration dotted his forehead. Grusha called him Dimitri, acting as if she were his wife. Kate handed Sergeant Murphy a business card, saying, "Detective Benitez is working the case. It began in Leningrad, ten days ago." Kate said excitedly, "I left him a message we'd be at the precinct at eight this morning. Can you please call and explain why we're delayed?" The sergeant picked up the phone and dialed.

A few minutes later, Grusha cried, "He's shot." Andre's coat was open and his sleeve pulled off one shoulder. His white t-shirt was torn and bloody. Andre looked surprised as if he'd only just realized it himself. "Oh, Andre," Kate said, leaning over him, touching his face "you've been hurt all this time." The others circled around him as an NYPD officer eased off Andre's coat, examining his upper body. "Give him air," he growled as the sergeant called an ambulance.

Grusha climbed into the back to ride with Andre. Kate called, "Where are you taking him?" "Roosevelt," the EMT said. "Grusha, wait there," Kate said. "We'll find you."

By some miracle, Gilly, Kate beside her, was able to make it from the security shack into the underground garage to Dom's battered car, its windshield shattered by a bullet, a headlight missing, the front grill smashed. "Can you get us home?" Kate was asking her, her eyes large and bruised looking. Gilly swallowed hard and nodded.

She slid behind the steering wheel. On the car floor was the videotape in the *Revolution* jacket, along with the papers that showed Gregor Randall was in Leningrad the same dates as Kate. Andre's proof—all important, forgotten briefly in the mayhem—had survived. Kate, with a cry, scooped it up and put it in her coat pocket.

Gilly's leg was quivering as she stepped on the gas. She maneuvered the vehicle up the winding ramp and out the exit, navigating through mid-morning traffic. Twenty minutes later, light-headed with relief, she nosed Dom's car into its narrow parking space inside his apartment building.

Outside, on Ninth, she and Kate flagged down a cab to take them to Roosevelt Hospital. They found Andre in a cubicle in Emergency, sitting on a cot, his chest bare, a thick bandage over his shoulder. He was sitting up. A good sign, Gilly thought. On a chair beside him, Grusha said, "Flesh wound. He had antibiotic."

Kate gave a cry of joy, then spoke in a rush, "I hate to ask—but can you come with us to give a statement to Detective Benitez?" Andre listened gravely as Grusha translated. A shadow of a grin flickered on his beat-up face. He gave a thumb's up.

Grusha helped him on with his bloodied t-shirt, the sleeve cut to accommodate the dressing. She draped his bulky overcoat over his shoulders.

The four then took a taxi to the precinct where Detective Benitez was waiting. Grusha translated Andre's story. Kate handed the detective the copy of Gregor Randall's passport and Visa and the incriminating video of him deep in conversation with Captain Victor Iurkov. After Benitez heard everyone's account, he nodded slowly. "It started as a hate crime, spun out of control."

Grusha asked, pointing at Andre, "He wants to know, Kate, why did Gregor Randall want you dead?"

Gilly saw the hesitation in Kate's eyes, before she mumured, "*Rozovaya,* lovers," pointing at herself and Gilly. Gilly tensed. Will Andre and Grusha judge us? Think we're perverted or sick or evil?

A variety of expressions—surprise, disappointment, distress—passed over Andre's face. Kate grabbed his hand. "You're my friend. You saved my life." He managed a smile. "Okay, Kate."

"This man Gregor—he loved you?" Grusha was asking, her voice hard, her face sympathetic. Gilly shook her head. "He loved money, power. He wanted control of my dad's company." She turned to Detective Benitez, wanting him to understand the complexity, the reality. "My dad knew him all these years. He never saw how ruthless, greedy, self serving he really was. My dad was too busy making money."

The detective's blue-green eyes bored into her.

Gilly burst out, "My dad wasn't in on the plan to kill Kate. Gregor Randall told me—Kate heard him."

"But he *was* in on the plan to ambush you to the Utah psychiatric clinic," Benitez said softly.

Gilly nodded, her chest heavy. "A business colleague gave him a photo he'd taken of Kate and me at the Gay Pride Parade. My dad hired a private detective." Her lips felt numb. "He knew the dates Kate would be in Leningrad. He passed the information on to Randall; the plan was to move me out of the apartment while Kate was overseas. Make me disappear, no forwarding address." She felt Kate touch her arm. "Typical," Gilly flared. "A quick fix. A few weeks of drugs and therapy, maybe shock treatments . . . And I would marry Randall or someone like him. My dad had—has—political ambitions. He wants me to be someone he can brag about, not an outsider."

"We'll be questioning your dad," Benitez said roughly. "You understand?"

Tears filled her eyes. He'd lost Gregor Randall. He'd lost her. If this story made the newspapers— She hoped he wouldn't have a heart attack. "He wants me to be different than I am. But he loves me."

Benitez looked down at his notes, then up at her, his face like carved stone, his eyes blazing. "Gregor Randall was your Dad's right hand man, making deals for the McGillicuddy Company in the Soviet Union." He continued, steel in his voice, "Sergeant Murphy of the Twentieth called me. In a briefcase in Gregor Randall's car, they found papers setting up shell companies to transfer payments to offshore banks. The Department of Justice, the IRS, the SEC will be looking into this. They'll be checking McGillicuddy's annual revenues to see if the company has any income from illicit trade: oil, arms, human trafficking."

"Human trafficking," Gilly moaned. "He couldn't be involved in that."

Benitez raised his brows.

She put her face in her hands, felt Kate's arms around her, heard her murmuring, "It's okay, okay." She struggled to collect herself. The detective handed her a box of tissues, his eyes warm and sad. "I'll keep in touch," he said.

No one spoke in the cab on the way home. The four took the elevator to Dom's apartment—which, Kate said, was big enough for all to crash in.

Inside, Andre murmured something to Grusha. "*Golodnyĭ.* Hungry," Grusha said. Kate found eleven eggs in Dom's refrigerator and half a package of bologna. Grusha scrambled the eggs, Kate fried the bologna. The bread was stale but it didn't matter when toasted and covered with heaps of strawberry jam.

They ate in silence. Finally, Andre, his eyes half closed, hands over his belly, smiled.

Kate pulled open the couch; Andre and Grusha fell onto it. Gilly covered them with a blanket. She and Kate crawled into Dom's bed and held on to each other, cradled together.

Chapter Twelve

10:30 AM, Monday, February 11

Gilly fought back tears as she pulled an armload of clothes from her closet and threw them across the bed. Quickly, she folded slacks, skirts and blouses, and put them into her suitcase. A husky voice behind her said, "Angelica." She steeled herself, then turned around. He looked so old. He was in the doorway, in his pajamas, his hair scruffy, his eyes tired and red. He smelled of alcohol. "Dad. I thought you'd be at the office. I didn't see your car," she said.

"It's in the shop." He tried to smile. "I heard noises. I was lying down, feeling sorry for myself." He stepped into the room, steadied himself on the doorjamb, then took a deep breath, throwing his shoulders back. "Well, you've got me in quite a mess."

He's blaming me, she thought. *Stand up to him.* "You've talked to Detective Benitez?"

He nodded. "Yeah, on Friday." His eyes grew hard. "I *should* say, your girlfriend has got us both in a mess. Are you here to help me out of it?"

"I came to get my things. I'm moving in with Kate," she said. She folded her remaining clothes into the suitcase and closed it with a snap. "Why did you sneak around behind my back? Why didn't you talk to me? Always too busy, both you and mom."

"Angelica, my own little girl . . ." He held out his arms.

"Dad, you got yourself in this mess! Your arrogance, your need to control, letting Randall run wild." She was shaking.

"I told Benitez I was shocked. I had nothing to do with Randall's crimes."

"Do you know he tried to kill Kate? Even me, he tried to kill me." She felt tears running down her cheeks. "Is that what you wanted, to kill us both?" She held his eyes with hers, hoping with her intensity to pull out an answer. She wanted him to say he was so very sorry, to beg their forgiveness, hers and Kate's, to tell her he had no idea what Gregor Randall was up to.

His eyes slid away from hers. "Oh, god, after all these years." He wiped a hand over his face. "Who would have thought? I told Randall nothing shady. Just get Angelica back to thinking right, I said. I love you, baby." His speech was a little slurred, his skin baggy from the alcohol. "I want to save you from a rotten life. My darling girl."

Gilly saw Kate, who'd been outside loading the car, standing beyond him in the hall. How long had she been there? Gilly wondered. She shook her head, motioning for Kate to leave. Things could get out of hand.

"The police came by Friday," he said. "The office is buzzing with rumors. The Department of Justice will be looking at our books. I've hired lawyers, the best. I may be able to get out of this without going to jail. But the newspapers, the stories will ruin me."

Kate must have made a little sound. He turned around.

"So you had nothing to do with trying to get me killed?" Kate asked, red-faced, glaring.

He sucked in his breath. "I wish I'd thought of it. You make me sick. Get the hell out of my house."

Gilly yanked the suitcase off the bed. As she brushed by him, he clutched her arm. She shook him off. She and Kate hurried through the living room, her dad in pursuit, his words hitting her in rapid fire. "All the time, money and love we put into you, never trying to put too much pressure on you, asking for very little in return and you spring this shit on us. Don't expect anything more from either of us."

Gilly opened the front door, then turned to face him. "Even if you never speak to me again, I don't care."

In an instant, he'd raised his hand and slapped her across the face. He took her by the shoulders, pushing her outside and marching her down to Dom's car parked in the driveway. The whole time Kate followed, clawing at his pajama shirt, trying to keep him from hurting Gilly further.

"Stay away from me," Gilly screamed as he marched back into the house. "If you bother us, we'll move somewhere we won't be found." She felt Kate's arms go around her. She heard her heart pounding like a jack hammer. Or was it Kate's she heard?

※※※

WE'RE ALL RAW, KATE thought, as she parked Dom's automobile in his spot in the garage. Thank goodness, they'd stowed most of Gilly's stuff in the car before the fight.

Silently, she and Gilly each took a box up to Kate's apartment. The two of them made room in the front closet so Gilly's clothes would fit. They hung Kate's coats in the closet by the bathroom and half-rolled, half-dragged Kate's kick bag with its heavy sand-filled base to the back wall.

Half an hour later, the car was unpacked. "Last load," Kate called to Gilly, putting the filled-to-bursting shopping bag on the floor. Suitcases and boxes were scattered from the front alcove through the living room. Kate watched as Gilly at the far wall arranged a painting, one of her best, on her easel. It was an oil of a saxophone player, wearing a rumpled blue shirt and black pants, hunched on a box while he played golden notes outside a Times Square theater.

Gilly came toward her, so graceful and beautiful. Kate's heart filled with joy. "How are you doing, sweetie?"

Gilly put on a chipper smile. "Better."

"I'll make some tea." Kate ducked into the kitchen and put on the kettle.

"Bring some cookies too," Gilly said, unpacking shoes from the shopping bag, pushing her hair away from her face. She had that determined set to her jaw, that fanatical look in her eyes she always got when she began a project, determined not to stop until it was finished.

The bell rang. The doorman hadn't buzzed up. Kate sped to the door, peering through the eyehole. She saw no one. No more surprises, please. Like the scar-faced Captain. Or a smirking Gregor Randall, dripping wet. C'mon, Kate, get real. He just now crawled out of the Hudson? Still alive after six days? "Who is it?" she asked.

A figure moved in front of the peephole, a small voice said, "It's me."

Kate opened the door. "Aunt Maureen." She drew her inside and hugged her. Her hair had been cut and styled, softly framing her face, so much more flattering than the bun she'd worn for years. She looked slimmer too, as if she'd been dieting. "You look wonderful—so rested."

Aunt Maureen's eyes crinkled, then she was looking past her, a question in her eyes. Kate said, "Gilly's moving in. My friend I spoke to you about." *Spoke* was a little tame, Kate thought. During her fight with Burt last Sunday, she'd *yelled*—comparing her loving relationship with Gilly to Maureen's dismal marriage with Burt. Kate blushed, remembering. "I was going to call and apologize."

Maureen blinked. Her whole face lit up, dropped years. "No need." She took Gilly's hand. "I'm glad to meet you, my dear, at last. I'm delighted Kate has found you."

"Come in and sit down," Gilly said shyly.

Kate took Maureen's coat. "Is that a new dress?"

Maureen shook her head. "It was in the back of my closet."

Kate remembered now. The dress had been a favorite of Uncle Dave, Aunt Maureen's first husband, who'd been so dear to Kate, like a father.

Maureen picked her way into the living room, dodging cartons, waiting as Gilly whisked a pile of scarves and underwear from the sofa to make a place to sit. "That's gorgeous," Maureen said, staring at the oil canvas propped on the back of the couch, leaning against the wall.

"It's Gilly's, called 'Lake of Fire.'" Kate said proudly. The kettle whistled. As she made tea in the kitchen, she heard Gilly say, "Kate and I found this secluded inlet at the far end of Long Island. I slaved for hours trying to get the painting right." The day was one Kate would never forget. She loved watching Gilly work. She was focused, driven. When the light changed—the sun was going down—Gilly had started over with a new canvas.

Kate came in with the tray of tea and cookies, admiring the painting as if seeing it for the first time. Gilly had captured the feeling of that day in early summer, the two of them crazy in love. The mood was dramatic, urgent: the brilliant setting sun, glowing golden on the water, the clouds drenched in colors.

"We have to find just the right frame," Gilly murmured.

The sun would never leave, Kate thought, would stay forever in its feverish blaze. Like Keats wrote in his poem.

"And the sketch near it, on the wall, why it's you, Kate."

Kate nodded, setting the tray on the coffee table.

Maureen sank into the couch. She ate a cookie, took a sip of tea, heaved a sigh. "I needed that." She reached into her purse and handed Kate a thick paper folded in triplicate.

Kate recognized the insurance policy she'd spotted in Burt's desk.

Maureen said, "The burial policy your parents took it out when you were born. You should have it now." She made a face. "Not worth much. About $2,000." Kate threw a look at Gilly, remembering their late night conversation when they made a list of suspects. Kate had speculated it might be a multi-million dollar policy with Burt the beneficiary, that he just might be the person who was trying to kill her.

Next Maureen gave Kate a large brown envelope. "When I

went by Burt's office I wasn't sure I'd get this. So I didn't call to tell you I'd be stopping by."

Kate fumbled the envelope open and drew out a slim booklet. The cover page was titled, Financial Statement for Katherine Hennessey, today's date, February 11, 1991. "You're a miracle worker."

Maureen looked pleased with herself. "He was afraid I'd make a scene."

"Good for you!"

"I asked him and he told me," her face turned pink, "he's taken some of your money. He wouldn't say how much," she burst out.

Was his law office in the red? Did he have a mistress? Kate wondered. She squeezed Maureen's hand. "Don't worry. You gave me a family. You and Dave. And then Burt came along. I miss Uncle Dave."

"So do I," Maureen said.

Kate felt butterflies. How much did she have? She hadn't kept track. She'd been careless. Her fault—no one else's. As she flipped through the pages of the financial report, the numbers all swam together.

She took a file from her desk drawer, comparing the pages in the current report with the last one she'd received—impossible—two years ago. She had chills. She felt as if her head were about to explode. "This is mine?" Net assets were up twenty-five per cent from the report she'd received at the end of 1988.

"The market dipped with the fear about the Iraq War, Burt said, but now that the war's begun and it looks good for our troops, the market's climbing again. Still it's no excuse for him taking any of what belongs to you."

Did it matter? He'd made a small fortune for her with his aggressive investments.

Maureen's eyes were bleak. "I'll see he pays you back. Every cent."

"Aunt Maureen, it's okay." She'd thought he might be trying to kill her, but he was just a thief. "I plan to make him sweat. Make him think he might be facing a law suit."

Gilly, in the beanbag chair, nodded emphatically.

"I'll ask for a financial printout every week until the money transfers to me on my birthday in October." Next time she wouldn't be so forgiving. "And," Kate took a deep breath, "I'll need an advance to hold us, Gilly and me." Gilly's generous allowance from her parents was history. If Dom returned empty-handed from Holland, she might not have a job herself.

She mustn't be negative, Kate thought. If they couldn't make *Flying Eagles,* they could film that script Dom's former investor phoned to say he was interested in, *City Women.* They could shoot most of it in Dom's apartment and on the huge terrace. She'd be on the set every day learning directing, camera angles, lenses.

If Dom did seal the deal with the Dutch, she could invest in the movie in exchange for points. She could pay off Steve's contract with Dom, get rid of him and his porno company. She found a yellow pad on her desk and jotted down some numbers. She felt dizzy with possibilities. "Aunt Maureen, thank you. It's been a long, hard day for you."

"I'll let Burt know you're coming to his office." Maureen, smiling gamely, stood as if to leave.

"If you decide . . ." to get rid of that hypocritical cold fish, she finished in her mind. "If you want to be on your own," Kate hoped she would, "we could find you an apartment here."

"That would be fun," she laughed, "to be neighbors." She kissed Kate and Gilly good-bye. Kate watched her walk down the hall and turn the corner to the elevators. Her step had a tiny spring.

After Kate closed the door, Gilly smiled, "She's lovely."

"Much too good for Burt," Kate muttered. She lifted the Financial Report off the desk, flipping the pages to Assets, showing Gilly. "Just so you know."

Gilly shook her head in wonder. "It's like a dream."

"This is what I'm asking Uncle Burt for. Now." She handed

the yellow pad to Gilly. "I can't wait to see his face when he sees these numbers. He'll pass out."

"You're becoming a capitalist," Gilly said with a sly grin.

Kate grinned back. "You're right." Inside she was cheering. Gilly was coming to life again. She leaned over Gilly's shoulder and jotted another figure on the pad. "The International Gay Rights Conference is planned for Leningrad for this July. If it happens, it'll be a big step for the Soviets. We have to go. It could be their Stonewall."

"You aren't afraid?"

Kate took a deep breath. "The police have arrested Sveta's brother so I'm no longer a person of interest." Scar-faced Captain Iurkov was another matter. She'd still have to watch her back. "I think often of Sveta and how she died so young. I wonder how Nadya is surviving without her. You'll meet her, Olga too, and dear Masha. You'll love them. Oh god, I haven't called the Soviet Embassy to ask for the papers to invite Masha to the U.S. Dom will have a fit."

Gilly gave a short laugh. "I think he'll understand—you've been a bit preoccupied."

The two continued to unpack and put away. Kate said, "We can take a high eight camera, a tripod, and tapes to Leningrad and pick up a small crew over there. We'll make it a separate piece from what I have now, my *Messages from Leningrad*. We'll ask gay Russian men and women, the pinks and the blues, for interviews on camera, and we'll add their stories to Nadya's. It will be a kind of courage project. We'll show *our* faces on camera and link *our* stories with theirs."

Gilly's eyes turned worried. Kate grabbed her hands, hoping to make her understand the importance. "We'll compare the U.S.S.R. with the U.S., the whole ugly mess we've been through—the murder plot, Uncle Burt's right wing hate groups, your dad and the Utah psychiatric clinic. We can't stay hidden, silent any longer. We owe it to Sveta's memory, to Nadya's bravery. To the guts of the women at the Café Soul, who'll help us make discrete inquiries about who in Leningrad will show his or her face on camera. We can't stop fighting. Even here in the U.S. it can always go back to where it was before Stonewall. When the tape is finished, PBS might pick it up. It will be a history, so hopefully history won't repeat itself." She felt lighter than she had in months, her heart and mind expanding, her whole world opening up.

Gilly smiled uncertainly. From an open suitcase she pulled out a paint box and a cylinder of paper, which she unrolled. "I did this sketch of my dad one summer night before I met you." She showed it to Kate, several emotions flickering across her face. She started to tear it in two.

"Save it," Kate said. "For awhile, then decide."

"Oh, Kate." Gilly took her hand. "I feel like I'm jumping off a cliff."

"We're jumping together," Kate said.

Gilly kissed her gently, her lips brushing over Kate's, traveling down her throat. Kate ran her hands over Gilly's body, removed her blouse. In a tangle of golden arms and legs, they made love on the couch under the "Lake of Fire," where the sun would remain at the Magic Hour, forever flaming, drenched in all its colors. Orange, pink, turquoise. Purple and maroon.

As well as a successful author, Kay Williams (left) is a professional actress who has played a wide range of leading roles at theaters around the U.S. For several years, Kay worked behind-the-scenes with an independent filmmaker in New York, traveling with him to Leningrad in 1991 where she received the idea for *The Matryoshka Murders*. Anything could happen here, she thought, in this city at this desperate time.

Eileen "Jo" Wyman, Kay's writing partner (right), helped organize photos and notes collected from the trip, and together they drafted a plot and wrote this thriller that begins in Russia and jumps across an ocean to New York City.

Eileen, known to friends as Jo, an amazing, talented woman, tragically passed away on Sept. 6, 2013, just after *The Matryoshka Murders* was completed. Jo worked in radio-TV and began her writing career in comedy, crafting jokes for speech writers and comedians, humorous fillers for magazines, and captions for cartoonists. She loved humor—from punch line jokes to surreal comedy to wit and word play—filling file box after file box with her wry, pithy descriptions.

The authors' move into the crime-ridden, sleazy Hell's Kitchen of 1977 provided the catalyst for their award-winning thriller, *Butcher of Dreams*. Kay's wide ranging acting credits and theater experience gave focus to this character/plot driven mystery that centers around the struggling 42nd Street repertory theater where much of the action takes place.

Kay is also a co-author of the comic romance *One Last Dance: It's Never Too Late to Fall in Love*, started by her journalist father Mardo Williams, and finished by her and her sister Jerri Lawrence. *One Last Dance* has won several awards, including an Ohioana Award (to Jerri and Kay) for writing and editing excellence.

Coming next (dedicated to Jo)—Part One of a Series: *New York City, Collected Letters, 1956–57: Were We Ever That Young?*, the hilarious, heart-breaking and hair-raising adventures of two starry-eyed girls from the Midwest (Jo and Kay) who arrive in New York City with big dreams of success. Part Two of the Series will be *San Francisco, Collected Letters, the Sixties*.

Discussion Questions
Topics to Consider

1. Minutes after guerrilla filmmaker Kate Hennessy and her new Russian friend Sveta enter a cab on the outskirts of Leningrad, they realize that their lives are at stake. What happens? Who has arranged for the cab? Although she almost dies, Kate's training and ingenuity disrupt this attack. Explain. Consider further attacks on her life. In Leningrad: Her attack as she walks back to her hotel from Pushkin Square. In NYC: in Gilly's apartment, her assault on the street, her abduction in the underground garage.

2. After the kidnapping and Kolya, the cab driver's attack, Kate searches her mind for what provoked such violence. Is it a simple robbery gone wrong? How does the environment prove as dangerous as her attacker?

3. In Chapter Two, the reader learns more about Kate's abduction as Andre, Kolya, and Captain Iurkov enter the story. The reader realizes that political forces seem to be operating against Kate. Describe the hierarchy of power that is triggering this violence. Describe Captain Iurkov, Andre, Kolya. What are their motivations for attempting to kill Kate?

4. The need to secure what Kate considers to be an incriminating videotape puts her in more danger, and Andre's role increases as he attempts unsuccessfully to steal the videotape on several occasions. Explain how he is able to enter her room. Is the 4th floor *dejurnaya* a tool of the KGB or an indication of the general lawlessness and widespread corruption?

5. When trapped in Kate's room, what suggests that Andre is becoming sympathetic to her, possibly feeling an attraction toward her despite his assignment to kill her? He does eventually succeed in stealing the tapes. Under what circumstances? How are the tapes dangerous to Masha and Nadya if they reach the authorities?

6. In the opening scene of Chapter One, Kate seems somewhat tentative and even vulnerable as the women's meeting is drawing to a close. What thoughts suggest this? What hints do you receive about the lives that Masha, Nadya, and Sveta are forced to lead in this first chapter? Their lack of power in their own homes and in society? As the story progresses, describe the mistreatment experienced by Masha, who is divorced from her husband, by Tanya, who is married to a bully, and by the women at the Soul Café who are leading "underground" lives, whose lives are considered a crime against society.

7. How do the experiences of the "moonlight" persons compare with women living alternative lifestyles in the United States? Consider what Nadya says . . . what those at the Soul Café report. What are some of their experiences as Part I evolves? In Part II, how does Kate recognize that even in the United States, although not government sanctioned, that the "cure" is considered by some a "fix" for those who have chosen an alternative lifestyle?

8. What hardships are experienced by the common people in Leningrad in 1991? Contrast the luxury of the film festival and the hotel with the home of Masha and her mother: The food, the décor, etc. Consider the degree of poverty, the tight money, untrustworthy police, the KGB, the corruption and how it influences the behavior of characters in the book: Tanya, Nadya, Masha, Kolya, Andre, Gregor. Paranoia and fear are inbred as Masha notes: "The KGB has made us a country of snoops and informants."

9. Kate suspects that the film festival's daily bulletins, and the Laboratory of Experimental Modeling performances might be subject to political punishment. Why might authorities object? Tour guide Alexei seems unafraid to express economic and political truths as well as sharing highlights of Russian culture and history. What insights does the reader gain from Alexei?

10. Describe the chaotic conditions that exist for those showing films at the festival. Describe instances where Titan Films as well as others experience loss, possible piracy. The chaos seems to parallel that taking place in the streets. Describe the corruption that seems rampant, the need for bribery, the dishonest use of power with impunity. Consider the behaviors of Captain Iurkov, Kolya, Gregor in this light.

11. Olga reveals the old fables and traditions of the culture during the sleigh ride at the end of Part I. What do these passages add to the story? Are they important? Necessary? Why? Russian food is another cultural aspect detailed in both Part I and Part II. Think of the delicacies served at the Marianna Café.

12. Sveta's disappearance becomes an obsession with Kate. Does the phone response, "She's been taken care of," give relief to Kate? To you, the reader? What do Kate and others theorize about her fate if she survived the pursuit in the cemetery and the weather? What happens to Nadya after reporting her missing friend? In Part II, Kate's learns about Sveta's death and who is responsible. Does this ease her guilt?

13. Why are the stolen earrings an important clue? Trace their history from Leningrad to NYC.

14. Kate's impulsive decision to travel alone to Pushkin Square to secure the Matryoshka political dolls propels Part 1 to a climax, leading to disaster for Kolya and Tanya. How? What are the repercussions for Andre? For Kate?

15. Once Gregor enters the story, the political implications escalate, and the motive for Kate's abduction and attempted murder become focused.

The videotape of Gregor that Kate has filmed by chance is incriminating, but why? Who is Gregor's boss? Who is Gregor? Is Kate's danger related to the political situation in Russia? Why? Why not?

16. How does Andre's stealing Kate's business card become an important plot detail in Part II? As well as self-preservation from Iurkov's wrath, Andre had another reason for escaping to NYC. What was his mission? How was he able to afford the cost of his escape? What help does he have in his escape from Leningrad—and once he arrives in Little Odessa by the Sea? Why does he feel the need to assume a disguise? Had contacting Kate been part of his plan?

17. Captain Iurkov seeks revenge on Kate, who lives despite efforts to kill her—and on Andre—who has failed in his assignment to kill Kate. The fire offers Iurkov a chance to trap her, to make her "disappear," he thinks. What is his plan? How does Kate outsmart him?

18. Brave friends are lifelines for Kate. How does Olga help Kate when she first appears at the Olgino Hotel and then again as everything spins out of control at the climax of Part I? Masha becomes instrumental in her escape to Finland. How? What is the significance of Kate's Russian name: Ekaterina Danilovna? In Part II, unexpected persons become lifelines for Kate. Explain. Who is Grusha?

19. Steve, Dom's partner, seems a liability to Titan Films. How does he take advantage of Tanya? What illegal dealings does he arrange with Captain Iurkov? In Part II, what indicates that his dealings with Captain Iurkov are progressing? Is he in danger from Iurkov? Why is Dom reluctant to fire him?

20. Gregor's motive for wanting Kate killed is a mystery in Part I, but revealed in Part II. What is his motive? Back in NYC, why is Gregor still intent on retrieving the tape, willing to accept Andre's extortion, at least superficially? What is his plan for Andre? He tricks Andre with the payoff. How? Andre tricks Gregor with the tape. How?

21. Gregor's political influence becomes evident as Captain Iurkov and Gregor have a face-off. Gregor's role in the power hierarchy is described by the insecure Captain Iurkov who had been a hero in Afghanistan. He knows that Gregor, because of his company's commitment to invest hard currency into the shaky Russian economy (with the potential to line the pockets of powerful leaders), will be favored. Back in NYC, does Gregor continue to have such power? How has he failed?

22. Back in NYC, after Kate is attacked in Gilly's apartment and on the street, she decides to alert the authorities in case her attacker succeeds in killing her. Detective Benitez seems skeptical at first, but begins to think Kate's story has credibility. Why? Why was she hesitant to contact the authorities?

23. Personal relationships are described and suggested during Part I and

Part II. What do you know about Kate and her significant other, Gilly? Kate's history seems somewhat rocky because of her family situation. Consider her parents, her Aunt Maureen and her current uncle, Burt, who, in Kate's opinion, has failed as a replacement for Aunt Maureen's first husband, Dave. It becomes apparent in Part II that Uncle Burt has failed Kate, not just emotionally. Explain.

24. Greed is an important theme in the novel. The greed of Andre, Kolya, Captain Iurkov, Gregor, Steve, and even Tanya drives the plot. Explain the "hunger for wealth or status" each experiences. Is greed the primary "driver" for Andre? For Tanya? Is fear a factor for either? Greed also seems to be a driving force for Uncle Burt and Gilly's father, Mr. McGillicuddy. Explain.

25. The terms, *cold blooded and heartless,* might be descriptive of some of these characters. Kolya, Captain Iurkov, Gregor. Even Mr. McGillicuddy. Explain.

26. How is the title *The Matryoshka Murders* reflected in the novel? "Inside Gorbachev was Andropov, next was Brezhnev, followed by Kruschev, then Stalin, a small Lenin, the Czar Nicholas, and finally Peter the Great. The Gorby dolls seemed to say perfectly what the Russian people felt about their lives under *Glasnost,* Gorbachev: The more things change the more they stay the same." Is this true for the lives of the characters in Part I? Consider Masha, Olga, Andre, the "moonlight" people? Does the danger Kate experiences have any relationship to the political reality in Russia? Why? Why not?

27. Although a minor subplot in Part I, an attraction seems to be forming between Masha, the interpreter for the Film Festival, and Dom, Kate's boss and the President and CEO of Titan Films. His plan to have her visit him in America may or may not materialize. How difficult is travel for Russian citizens?

28. What future do you see for Kate? Gilly? Andre? Captain Iurkov? Steve? Mr. McGillicuddy? Although Aunt Maureen and Uncle Burt are minor characters, what future do you foresee for them?

29. Is Kate's hope realistic... that she return to Leningrad in the summer to film and document the flagrant human rights violations, especially toward those who are called "moonlight" persons? This becomes more realistic at the end of Part II. Why?

30. The suspense in the novel frequently is heightened by the reader knowing more than the character (dramatic irony). In Leningrad and in NYC, the reader frequently knows the danger lurking for Kate when she doesn't. In Part II consider the following: In Gilly's apartment? On the street? In Kate's underground parking garage?

CPSIA information can be obtained at www.ICGtesting.com
Printed in the USA
BVOW01s1631101114

373804BV00002B/5/P